Portraits of an Artist

A Novel about
John Singer Sargent

Mary F. Burns

Word by Word
Press

San Francisco, California

Praise for *Portraits of an Artist*

❦

"An evocative rendering of the great portraitist, John Singer Sargent, as seen through the eyes of the subjects of his most famous paintings. A *tour de force* of historical and psychological imagination."
—Paula Marantz Cohen, *What Alice Knew, Jane Austen in Scarsdale*

❦

"John Singer Sargent painted some of the most compelling and psychologically revealing portraits of his day, while remaining an enigma to those who knew him. Burns skillfully brings the subjects of his portraits to life, telling their stories in their own voices as the mystery of who Sargent really is, and the culture that both supported and constrained him, is gradually and artfully revealed."
—Laurel Corona, *Finding Emilie, Penelope's Daughter, The Four Seasons*

❦

"Set in the Europe of 1882, the writing is richly subtle and each character exquisitely drawn. One hears murmurs behind doors and the truth just beyond the corner until the hearts of two women— one very young and one very beautiful—are broken forever. In the end of this fascinating novel, however, it is the portrait of the young artist himself, still an enigma, which lingers in the reader's mind. Wonderful writing!"
—Stephanie Cowell, *Claude & Camille, Marrying Mozart, The Players: A Novel of the Young Shakespeare*

❦

ஐ

"John Singer Sargent was brilliant, glamorous, rich, famous—and very private. Mary F. Burns' sensuous, fascinating and highly original novel takes us behind the veil of that privacy by offering a provocative guided tour of some of his wealthy, polyglot portrait subjects. Many of them knew each other, and Burns deftly explores their connections with one another and their tangled relationship to the magnetic but enigmatic artist. Glittering surfaces reveal surprising secrets in bedrooms and galleries, and you couldn't ask for a better docent as you travel from Paris to Venice to Florence to Nice. You'll likely never look at Sargent's glorious portraits in the same way again because Burns has given us a new way of appreciating their genius."

—Lev Raphael, *Rosedale in Love: A Gilded Age Novel*

ஐ

"*Portraits of an Artist: A Novel About John Singer Sargent* is a work of historical fiction based on the life of a brilliant yet troubled artist of the late nineteenth century. A contemporary and associate of high celebrities such as Henry James, Oscar Wilde, Edward Burne-Jones, and Sarah Bernhardt, Sargent's meteoric rise to fame followed by his striking fall from grace, and his retreat to London, are the tragic underpinnings of his unforgettable career. The stories behind two of his finest paintings, "The Daughters of Edward Darley Boit" and "Madame X", are also explored in context. Told in first-person perspective from the points of view of numerous individuals who figured prominently in Sargent's life, "Portraits of an Artist" is an unforgettable reconstruction of a talented man's search to find meaning in life through art. Highly recommended."

—*The Fiction Shelf of The Midwest Book Review*

Portraits
of an Artist

₮

It is art that makes life, makes interest, makes importance...
and I know of no substitute whatever for the force
and beauty of its process. *Henry James*

₮

Every portrait that is painted with feeling is a portrait
of the artist, not of the sitter. *Oscar Wilde*

₮

I do not judge, I only chronicle. I follow the merely
visible elements, nothing more. *John Singer Sargent*

John Singer Sargent

Self-Portrait c. 1886

Prologue

I see them now in mirrors, on darkened windows, in waking dreams—all the faces I have painted. Children, and men, and women. Always the women, with their languid eyes, their tense, anxious lips, their serene brows and haughty noses.

John Singer Sargent, a painter of portraits, that's who I am. I chose to be a painter of portraits because I was very good at it, because I liked the acclaim, the society, the weekends at country houses outside Paris and London and Florence—and because it paid well, very well. I died a rich man. Childless, unmarried, though not unloved—no, not unloved.

The portraits of my friends are the book of my life—my paintings are the words that I can never find to explain myself, to defend myself, even to know my very self. Two portraits in particular, painted before I reached the age of thirty, haunt me even now, more than all the rest. One became a private grief, softened by time but never truly healed. The other, a public scandal that changed everything. Together they turned me from a young man, a foolish man, into a sad and sorry shadow that only I could see when I looked in a mirror. I wonder if you can guess which ones they are? As the years dragged on, I endured as the entertaining, successful, eccentric old swell who ate too much, smoked too much—and let no one come too close.

As I cannot easily speak for myself, and as I yearn to be known, at least a little, I will allow my portraits to speak for me—their stories will illuminate mine. You may say that I am still keeping myself one step removed, so that you, reader, will not come too close—well, that's as may be. It is there in those portraits you must seek me, if you would know me.

I am the painter of portraits.

❧ *May 1882* ☙
Siena

Violet Paget

I remember the day it started, the first hint of trouble, the scent—and I'm not overstating my sense of this—of tragedy, of doom. Larger than life characters inevitably stumble, with consequences far beyond what ordinary mortals encounter. And John was not only larger than life, he was filled above the brim with it, tamped down and still overflowing, as the saying goes.

I sat at my writing desk in the villa's morning room, contemplating with satisfaction a letter I had received from him the day before. It was but a note in length, a reply to my own of the previous week, and dashed off with his usual humor and barely decipherable handwriting. We frequently addressed each other as "twin"—born the same year, we had become acquainted early in childhood and became fast friends as our families met again and again in various parts of Europe and England—his family the quintessential American expatriates comfortable anywhere but America, mine the slightly down-at-the-heels Anglo-European peripatetics always on the lookout for cheaper lodgings. Our mothers directed the family's destiny, though affecting not to; our fathers were gentle ciphers, shadows in the background.

Dear twin, so looking forward to seeing you soon—shall have lots to do, the Salon and all that in full swing, much attention being paid to yours truly, I am become a great swell, etc., and have been showered with so many commissions I am able to treat my friends to dinner all the time! All my people likewise eager to see you again. Yrs, JSS

The door to the room opened with a shrill creak, and my mother's melancholy tone, languid and fretful, met my ears, setting my teeth slightly on edge.

"Ah, Violet, here you are."

I did not turn to greet her, but was perfectly able to envision her morning *déshabillé*: the thinning, fair hair blowsy and only partly brushed, and the inevitable glass of *café* she carried about like a talisman all day long. "Yes, Mama," I said, stifling a sigh, "as you see, here I indubitably am."

I felt scrutinized, as always, and wondered in what manner Matilda—in the safety of my irreverent interior monologues I always called my mother by her Christian name—would chastise my looks today. My somber dress with its high Gladstone collar and no jewelry? My long oval face with its sharp, chiseled nose—as if I could do anything about that! I felt warmth rising to my cheeks, and yet, I rebuked myself, she had barely spoken.

"Thou hast a nervous look about thyself this morning, Violet," she said as she drew near. "Dost thou plan to leave us again so soon?" I rolled my eyes. I had long abandoned commenting on her occasional Quakerish pronouns, an affected relic of some four years' residence in Philadelphia.

I put down my pen and turned to face her.

"Nothing escapes you, does it, dear Mama?"

"I know my own child, if that is what you mean." Matilda stood at my elbow, her pale blue eyes lighted with a gleam mixed of mischief and pique. "I hope you will deign to leave your books later today to receive the guests I have invited for dinner." She sipped at her *café*, which I could see was silvered over with a light scum of milk, the once hot beverage now insipidly lukewarm. Then, as I did not answer, she prodded further, "I do think thou art still too young to go travelling about as thou dost, Bags."

There it was again, that awful nickname! I pushed back my chair abruptly, nearly knocking her over as I rose and walked to the window. Matilda stepped back in dismay as her coffee sloshed over the brim of the glass.

"Mama, I am nearly twenty-six years old!" I said, trying to keep my voice even. "And please don't use that old nickname. I ... oh, never mind, this is too old a tale!"

6

A knock at the door brought us to a sudden halt.

"The morning post, *signora*," came a timid voice in the hall.

"Then come thou in and deliver it," Matilda snapped, and plumped herself down on the silk-covered sofa near the fireplace, where the ashy remains of the morning fire sent forth a reminiscence of warmth.

The servant, a girl of about fifteen, curtsied to the space midway between me and Matilda, and choosing not to ruffle either one of us, as I assumed, by delivering the mail to the other, she placed it hastily on a table and nearly ran out the door.

A little about the dreary tale that is my mother's history: she had married quite young to escape the tyranny of her disputatious, moralistic Welsh father, and had subsequently produced her first child, my brother Eugene, by her husband Captain Lee-Hamilton, who died when the boy was ten. I recall, when asked on one occasion about Matilda's first husband, I mordantly replied, "That deplorable marriage ended almost at the church door," and said nothing more about it, though in truth it had lasted some sixteen years. Four years later, Matilda married Henry Ferguson Paget, my father, a poor but charming cosmopolite of French origins and vague, aristocratic pretensions. He had been engaged as Eugene's tutor, and was a tireless inventor of much imagination and few results. By the time I was born, my grandfather had conveniently passed on, leaving Matilda with an inheritance sufficient to afford us some of the best second-rate lodgings in the lesser capitals of Europe.

Calmly settled now on the sofa, Matilda spoke again. "And where do you think of going this time?" She watched greedily as I sorted through the mail, hoping that the larger stack of envelopes was inscribed to her—Matilda cherished her correspondence, and wrote nearly as many letters as I did myself.

"You know very well, Mama, that I have planned to go to London again this summer, to look after Eugene's publishing interests." *And my own*, I thought to myself, knowing Matilda was much less interested in her daughter's writing than in her son's.

"Ah, dear Eugene," she said. "Your brother's poetry so completely reflects his sensitive nature." I could tell she was watching me closely, but she seemed satisfied as I nodded agreement; I wasn't dissembling. "It is such a tragedy his poor health keeps him from travelling to London with thee, but we have the most complete trust in thy ability to represent him to the publishers."

"Indeed, Mama," I said, "I have every hope of finding a publisher without much trouble, given the appreciative reception to his poems in London two years ago." I gazed out the glass doors open to the marble terrace—the lilting sounds of birds filtered through the trees, and the slanting sun poured itself upon the green Italian hills. *If only this enticing scene could tempt him to rise from his sick bed*—but it had been several years now, and my brother seemed no nearer health than when he first fell ill, after a harrowing flight from the Prussian attack on Paris where he had been a promising junior diplomat. Everything in our little household revolved around Eugene—where we lived, how long we stayed in any one place, what we ate for dinner—the invalid's delicate temperament ruled us all.

I stifled a sigh.

Having sorted the letters, I carried over a respectable mound of mail to Matilda, who received it with a satisfied smack of her lips.

"And before thou goest to London?"

"I shall travel through Paris, that I might see John and Emily, and dear Mrs. Sargent."

"What, are not the whole family there? What of little Violet, and dear *Mr.* Sargent?

"I believe they are all in Paris, but I speak of the ones I wish to see most."

"My dear Violet," my mother said, less attentive now as she became absorbed in her letters, "my dear Violet, you are much too … particular … oh, my, here's a letter from that interesting Mr. Whistler, the artist we met in Venice last season! How I enjoyed his conversation!"

With Matilda deep in a rapture of news and gossip, I was free to turn to my own letters. The first to catch my eye was from my friend Mary Robinson, with whom I was planning to stay—I devoutly hoped—for many weeks over the summer. We had frequently met to write in each other's company, often in a little cottage by the sea or in the Lake Country, and to share our visions and plans for a future life together. Her letter was dated the 15th of May, written from Epsom Cottage.

My cherished friend, I so long for you! And look forward ever to your coming in June. The spring is more than lovely this year, and I know we shall have the best weather when you arrive. I've arranged for lodgings in Pulborough, in Sussex, a sweet little place with a rose garden in the back going all the way down to the river. When we have thoroughly tasted the delights of London, and you have pro-cured as many publishing contracts as even you may be satisfied with, we will pack up our duds and retreat to our precious nest, there to create and write and favor each other with the brightest intelligence and sweetest delights. I have only time for this brief note, as Mabel is about to descend upon me and take me off to gather flowers for an evening party Mama has been planning most diligently. All my love and affectionate kisses, yours ever, Mary

I kissed the letter and held it close, then put it in my pocket.

Some hours later, as the sun was well past its zenith, I rose from my writing desk and stretched. It had been a good day's work, and I felt in a fair way of being mistress of the convoluted German script that closely covered the manuscript pages. I hoped to translate the children's stories in the manuscript into a satire on royalist manners—it would be my second major publication. I had published a number of essays and most recently, a study of 18th century Italian culture, un-der the pen name Vernon Lee—the stigma of being a "lady writer" being tolerated only for torrid romances and Gothic horror tales—which I forthrightly admit I read voraciously, with equal feelings of contempt and envy.

A sudden knock on the door brought me whirling round to re-ceive whatever presumptuous stranger was interrupting me. But a familiar voice and, the next moment, a smiling face changed my an-noyance to buoyant cheerfulness in an instant.

"Ralph Curtis, *buon giorno, amico mio!*" I pounced on my old friend, and we exchanged kisses happily. A sudden thought struck me.

"And are you, pray, one of the guests Mama has invited for din-ner?"

"Verily and so forth, dear Violet," replied Ralph, removing his soft hat and tossing it somewhere into the interior of the room while keeping an arm wrapped about my shoulders. He shook his head like a dog emerging from a lake, his hair a tumble of shining blond curls.

"And not only I," he continued, walking me over to the open salon doorway, and gesturing to the grounds below. "*Mater* is here as well, and some of those people she always has about her, Bohemians and so forth." He thrust his head and shoulders out the door and proceeded to give an ear-splitting whistle.

I looked out upon a small party of people just alighted from their carriage. Ralph's mother, fashionably dressed, looked up upon hearing her son's whistle. She affected to chastise him with a shake of her finger and a smiling frown, then waved enthusiastically to me. I returned the greeting with equal delight. There were two young men, raffishly elegant in slouch hats and capes, one holding a small furry creature, probably a dog, I thought, with one of those particularly piercing, yappy little barks.

"I can't tell you how glad I am to see you, Ralph," I said, smiling at him as we turned back into the room.

"You must tell me all that you've accomplished in the months since we last met," he said, then catching sight of the papers strewn across my desk, he exclaimed, "What's all this then? Ancient manuscripts, crabbed handwriting in some indecipherable language?" He picked up a page and peered at it closely. "Egyptian, methinks, or is it Chinese? Have you added archaeological linguist to your many accomplishments, dear Violet?"

"You know very well that it is German, Ralph, and in point of fact, it's only some thirty years old, not so ancient, you see. And what about you—have you painted anything new?"

He picked up another piece of paper, one written in my hand, and read it aloud, ignoring my question. "*The Prince of the Hundred Soups!* What a delightful-sounding title! It makes one want to dive right in, especially if the soup is good, ha ha. I say, Vi, you are uncommonly clever, have I ever said that before?"

"Oh, Ralph, you do me such good, just hearing your nonsense," I said, and grasping his hand, gave it a little kiss.

He dropped the paper back on the desk and wandered over to the shelves of books, where he idly ran his fingers over the titles. He paused, extracted a cigarette from a gold case in his jacket, and lit it with a match from an ebony box on a nearby table.

"I'd love to have one of those, Ralph, may I?" I reached out my hand to the gold case he held toward me. "Why, I've never seen cigarettes so perfectly rolled!" I leaned forward as he struck a match.

"Yes, indeed," he said, "new invention this, one of our chaps back in America, lad from Virginia and so forth." We puffed in silence for a moment. "Was some kind of contest, some manufacturer of the darned things offered seventy-five thousand dollars cold cash if someone could invent a machine to do it faster, and by golly, this chappie did."

"Seventy-five thousand dollars!" I gasped. "You Americans all seem to have so much money!" I knew Ralph's family was wealthy; perhaps such sums meant little to him, but I couldn't conceive of such an amount all at once. "No wonder Papa is so keen on his inventions, if that's what they can be worth!"

We smoked in contented silence.

"Violet," Ralph said after a few moments. "Have you heard lately from Scamps?"

"Why, yes, just yesterday," I said. "I wrote to him that I shall be in Paris in about a week's time, on my way to London. He has two new paintings at the Salon this year, as you must know, and already the journals are expiring with delight over *monsieur* Sargent's creations. He says he's become quite in demand, a great swell about town, it would seem." I gazed narrowly at my friend. "Why, pray, do you ask?"

I knew that Ralph and John were related—their fathers were cousins—and had become fast friends when they both enrolled as students at the *atelier* of the artist Carolus-Duran several years earlier in Paris. It seemed odd that he was asking *me* for news of his relation.

"Oh, well, if you're going there in person, you can see for yourself," he said, abruptly putting out his cigarette. Ralph had only two ways of moving: languidly or abruptly, and one never knew which was coming next.

"See *what* for myself?"

"Why, whether he's going to marry *notre chère* Louise, dear girl." He paused, arching an eyebrow. "You know he painted a truly charming portrait of her for the Salon this year."

"Louise Burckhardt? I can't imagine that he would marry *her*."

"Well, they're awfully close chums," Ralph said mildly, looking around the room and patting his pockets as if he'd misplaced something, "which is a good start, in my humble opinion. And he's got to marry someone, don't you think?"

"I absolutely do *not* think that," I said with some vehemence. "Why do people always think that being married is the only thing one must do?"

"Well, if you don't think he would marry Louise, do you think it's because of *her*, or because—" Ralph paused ever so slightly. "Because he is not interested in women?"

I held myself in silence for the space of several breaths.

"It has always been my perception," I said slowly, "that John takes great delight in both men *and* women, and that he does not treat one sex over the other with any *particularity*." I paused to think. "And I would say further, *de toute façon*, he is not interested in marriage at all." I paused again. "He is equally interested in every person he meets, but he doesn't seem to care whether people are interested in *him* or not, or perhaps, one might say, he finds no one *necessary* to him, to his happiness. That is his great strength, and will, I think, be his downfall."

Ralph looked at me curiously, and seemed on the point of asking me about my dire prediction, then changed his mind.

"And you, Violet Paget, in what, or in whom, are you interested?" Ralph asked, a teasing look on his boyish, honest face. "Shall you ever marry?"

I burst out passionately.

"Whether man or woman, heavens above!—we need to be left alone to follow our Muse and not be tied down to some everlastingly tedious family, quarreling endlessly about their own selfish wants and preferences!"

I stopped suddenly as I realized the import of what I had said, but it was no more than Ralph knew anyway. He smiled.

"Been spending a bit too much time with Matilda and Eugene, eh?" he queried with a knowing look.

"Forgive me, I shouldn't rant like that," I said, "but then, you know how it is, don't you, Ralph?"

"Indeed I do," he said, with a slight shrug. We heard footsteps along the hall announcing the approach of our mothers and Mrs. Curtis' entourage, and he gave another smile and a wistful shake of his head. "Indeed I do."

That night, lying in bed wakeful from an excess of wine and company, I thought again about John and Louise Burckhardt—I knew her slightly, another *jejune* American who wandered through Europe with an ever-watchful mother at her elbow—and wondered at the uneasy feeling it gave me. Would he marry her? *Should* he? Although I held the matrimonial state in scant regard—and certainly it was not an option for one such as I—I knew that for a man in John's position—a rising artist, a figure in *society*—that a well-bred, lovely wife with money was more than an asset, possibly a necessity. But did he love her? Could he love anyone, woman or man? If the latter, would he take that risk? I knew it was becoming quite the thing amongst a certain crowd, particularly in London, but still…. Questions buzzed around my brain like summer flies over rotting fruit, which is what my brain seemed to be at this late hour. I dismissed them all for future contemplation, first-hand, when I would see John in Paris in a week's time.

Enough, then. Good Night.

Ralph Curtis

Women see this sort of thing very differently from men, don't you think? I mean to say, Violet is probably the most intelligent woman I know, and smarter than most men I know, and yet I could tell she was running all sideways about John and what I'd said about him and Louise.

Not sure why I mentioned it, really. Just that there'd been a great deal of jawing among our crowd about the two of them—*they seem so right for each other, they make such a handsome couple,* that sort of thing. And then, lately, more serious whispers about why they *weren't* getting married, and even whether the lady was being compromised in some way—which is utter nonsense to talk in such a way in these modern times, in my opinion.

I had seen Louise, talked with her, earlier in the spring. We were walking in the Luxembourg Gardens, and though it was April, it was a very hot day. She and I are old chums, don't you know, Boston families, doomed to wander the Continent—well, I shouldn't say 'doomed'—I rather like this life, and my painting, if I would get myself to do more, blast it. If only I could get a little further from Mater. Anyway, as I say, Louise and I were walking rather aimlessly that day, and we started talking about John.

"I dined with him last evening," I said. "At *Au Petit Fer à Cheval,* in the *Marais.*" I was puffing away at a cigarette as we strolled in the still air of the park.

"The *Marais?*" Louise echoed. She shuddered slightly. "I have heard that is a very dangerous part of the city, the Fourth, isn't it so?"

"It is indeed," I conceded. "Certainly for ladies, and occasionally for gentlemen." I smiled. "But you know Scamps, he has this irresistible halo of goodness around him, like armor, and he enchants all who fall within his ken, so *les animaux du Marais* were all so many fawning beasts at his feet."

Louise paused, stared at me for a long moment, and then walked on silently.

"And were there so many of them, *les animaux* as you say, at his feet?" she said.

Blast! I felt my face getting red as I recalled the evening in greater detail; I shouldn't have even brought the subject up.

"Oh, as to that, one doesn't keep count, don't you know," I said, trying to laugh it away. But vividly before my eyes were the two young men at the table next to ours, one who evidently knew who John was, and who, introducing himself and his companion with exquisite politeness, invited us to join them at their table for an after-dinner drink. There followed a great deal of often serious but very pleasant conversation, discussions of art, music, love and philosophy, much laughing and continued drinking, until the four of us were the best of friends and swore we would never part. Even through the haze of wine and absinthe, though in general I know I am no great observer, I saw glances exchanged between John and one of the young men, Michel— glances meant to be hidden, I thought, and, well, rather intense. After a while I had to insist on leaving and return to my hotel, I was that done in. I was surprised when John put me in a cab by myself and stayed behind, but there was no chance to say anything other than good night.

I became aware that Louise was watching me closely again, and I shook myself out of my reverie. Not the time to be musing about all that.

"And, verily, I say to you, dear lady," I said, patting her arm which I held in my own, "when young men are in pursuit of high adventure, even so small and mean a place as the sodden streets of the *Marais* can afford a bit of a thrill." I dashed my cigarette onto the ground, and paused to light up another.

"How you can smoke in all this heat," Louise said.

We continued to walk in silence for a while. I spoke again.

"I've seen your beautiful portrait, you know, at John's studio. It's going to be a smash at the Salon, I just know it."

Louise smiled, yet looked more sorrowful than if she hadn't

smiled at all. I felt the greatest sort of kindness and care toward her, don't you know, like a brother.

"Do you mind, very much?" I said.

"Do I mind what, exactly?" she said, her eyes wary as she glanced at me.

"Why, all this——" I waved my hand. "This fuss with Scamps and you, don't you know."

"What an extraordinary question, Ralph," she said. She looked away to the dull splash of a small fountain, tucked in a quiet corner where no children ran or jumped. I felt I had not angered her but I saw that she seemed suddenly weary. I led her over to one of the wrought iron benches near the fountain, where we sat down. I leaned back into the bench, studying the upright form of my friend—the straight back, the poised head under a large, white, flimsy hat, her hands crossed one upon the other on top of her equally flimsy white parasol, its point securely grounded in the fine gravel of the garden path. Yes, I should like to paint her, too, I remember thinking.

"The whole *fuss*, as you call it," she said at last, "has been rather, well, bewildering." She lifted her head to watch a pigeon fly from the ground to alight upon a branch of a lemon tree. "And I had thought that, perhaps——" She paused one moment more, then said in a low voice, "I really have only myself to blame."

She turned her gaze to me and said, as if she were offering a kind of proof, "He was such fun last summer!"

"Yes," I said, still lounging back. "Beckwith told me something about it."

Louise's eyes narrowed slightly.

"Beckwith," she said, and turned again to watch the fountain.

I couldn't help myself. "Are you in love with him?"

"Another extraordinary question," Louise said. "Really, Ralph, you do press one so!" She rose gracefully from the bench, and looked down upon me. "Are *you*, pray, in love with him?"

I gazed up at this suddenly formidable, suddenly penetrating woman, and eventually located an answer.

"We are all, all of us, in love with John," I said. I continued looking up at her, finding the words to describe what I had seen and thought. "He makes us love him, he pulls us to him like some great iron magnet, and we are stuck, unable to pull ourselves away."

"And when," Louise took up the simile after a moment's thought, "also like some great, iron magnet, the pull is reversed and we fall away, slipping off the cold, hard surface, he does not notice the filings he has shed." She paused again. "He lives in his work—his life is his painting, like a lover that demands all. I don't think there's room for anyone else." She turned away and opened her parasol, then spoke once more. "My sister saw it straight off, and saw it wouldn't do, and saved herself."

I pulled myself forward and rose slowly to stand beside her. I held out my arm for her.

"Is it as bad as all that?" I said, and waited. All around us, the air shimmered with heat, and the birds were silent in the shade of the trees. I did so want to protect her, to help her, but what was I to say?

"Yes," she said finally. "It's as bad as all that."

Now you see, my idea of the thing was that Louise should just do a full-on rush at John, leave him no room but to make a declaration— he'd be overcome in a moment, and he'd do the right thing. I was sure of it, but I could see she was in a bad way, and so I just tried to be sympathetic and cheer her up when I could. Don't understand women much, never did. Beginning to think I don't understand men much either.

❧ June 1882 ☙
Paris

Edward Darley Boit

For my part, I can trace the beginning of all that happened to that day early in June at our house in Paris, Florence's fourteenth birthday; John was there to help us celebrate, but he and I had crept off to my library for a chat before luncheon. We were discussing his meteoric rise to recognition at the Salon, about which he and I disagreed.

"This will never do," John was saying, "if you count them all up, so far I've got an actor and his wife, their monstrous children, the alluring Dr. Pozzi, and the wives of three *petits* civil servants!"

My friend threw up his hands in frustration, and strode over to the cart to pour himself a whiskey. He downed it in one gulp, and turned to me, sitting patiently through his furious lament. "She keeps me out! Paris looks down her nose at me, because I am a foreigner, *un Américain!*"

"Come, come, John," I said. "This is the fourth year—in a row, mind you—that the Salon has accepted one or more of your paintings for the exhibition—and you are barely twenty-six years old." I leaned back in my leather chair, lightly caressing the cigar which, unlit, tempted me to reach for a match and set it alight. I resisted with an inward sigh, hearing my physician's admonishing voice. *No more than one a day.* I picked up my glass of sherry instead, and brought it to my lips.

"Oh yes, of course," John said, pouring himself another whiskey. "The Salon recognizes my talent, I know it well—but *those* paintings come with no money attached to them. With the exception of

Pailleron, great actor and playwright that he is, I paint no one but *petites bourgeoisies* and such friends of my own who oblige me by sitting in my cold studio and drinking up my wine!"

I looked at my young friend—he was indeed very young, to me, old and tired and worn as I felt these days. "Are you in such straits, John, that you cannot afford refreshment for your sitters? If you need something—" I broke off at the look on his face.

"How kind you are," he said, shaking his head. "I'm horrified that I've shown you what an ungrateful brute I can be." He held out his hand to me, and I took it and clasped it in my own. "I have no need of a loan, my friend," he went on. "I've just collected my fee from Madame Subercaseaux, the wife of the Chilean consul here, you know, and also Isabel Valle, that is, Mrs. George Austen now, she just married that chap in the foreign affairs office." He released my hand and sat down heavily on the leather chair next to me. As I watched his face, I could almost see the calculations as he mentally reviewed the state of his finances. I knew that most of his income went to supporting his parents and two sisters—but I thought he had been doing well enough the last two years to make that an easier burden than previously. How else could he have afforded his own studio and separate apartments in the city?

"No," he repeated, reaching for a match to light the cigarette he took from a gold case. "No, it's not money I lack at the present moment." He drew deeply of the fragrant tobacco, and looked sharply at me. "I have a reputation to build, Ned. My art, my talent shall— *must*—command not only the highest prices but also the honor due to great art." He grinned and rapped his knuckles on the wooden table near his chair. "I say this in all modesty, of course!"

He picked up his sherry glass from the table and drained the contents. "And all the beautiful *Parisiennes*," he went on, "all those ladies of ancient lineage and pedigree and delicate sensibilities—they will swoon when they see me coming, and beg me to immortalize them in oils, eh?" He laughed softly, inhaled, and leaned his head against the back of the chair, releasing a stream of smoke into the air.

I smiled at him, and shook my head. "You have every right to dream so ambitiously, my handsome friend," I said, "especially as regards the 'swooning ladies'." I leaned forward, took up the match box, and lit the cigar. I drew at it gratefully and sank back in the chair.

"My Isa informs me," I continued, "that all the ladies are gossiping about you and our inimitable Louise, the *Lady with the Rose*." I contemplated his now troubled face. "You and she were together a great deal last summer, so I understand."

"My dear Ned," he began, then stopped. His face was clouded, his eyebrows drawn into a deep, scowling V. He smoked furiously for a moment, then glared. "Well, I may as well come right out and say it, her mother's the one I fear. She's forever arranging afternoons and picnics and theatre suppers til I'm ready to run at the sight of those blasted feather headdresses of hers down the boulevard. I'm very much afraid that painting Louise's portrait was a huge mistake."

"Poor Louise," was all my reply.

"Ah," John paused to smoke, and resumed, "yes, poor Louise, to have such a mother, so bent upon ruining her life by making her marry me." Then, upon catching my raised eyebrow, he said, "Yet, in truth, I don't think she's got any expectations of me, truly I don't." He kept his voice even but with some effort, as he said this, although I could tell he hoped I would not notice.

"It would not be strange if she did," I said gently. "And I doubt she's the only one with such hopes."

"Oh, I'm not such a catch as all that, you know." John dashed another segment of ash into the tray. "For all that Louise Burckhardt is lovely and intelligent and amusing, for all that—we're like old chums, don't you know, we're very jolly together, and that's all there is."

"Not such a bad basis for marriage, that," I murmured.

We were silent a few moments, smoking, thoughtful. I watched the pale rays of the sun struggle through the low clouds of a rainy spring day, seeking the hope of reflection from the pewter ashtrays, the delicate crystal glasses half-filled with golden liqueur, and the decanter itself, the line of pure liquid much lower than it was an hour before. Outside, the street life of the city of Paris murmured three stories below my library in the elegant house at 32, Avenue de Friedland, where my family and I resided when our travels brought us to the City of Light.

"If I ever *were* to fall in love," John said, looking up at the painted ceiling, "I believe it would have to be so overwhelming a feeling as to send me almost into despair—because even so, I shall not marry. Indeed, I think I may not even fall in *love*, when it comes down to it." He looked over at me; I was shaking my head again. "It would never do, you know," he insisted, "as I *must* paint, and work, and prosper—all of which requires diligence and single-mindedness—and a wide-ranging freedom!" He crushed his cigarette into the pewter tray with emphasis. "No room for a wife in my studio."

"I understand you, I think," I said after a moment. I thought of my little family, and how long it had been since I had been free to paint, but I did not sigh over it. "I cannot feel the same, but I shall no longer dispute with you—nor tease you—on this matter." I looked up quickly, smiling, to show this was not said in anger. "But you are young, John," I said, "and, it seems to me, have not yet been in love." I raised a hand at his start of protest. "Indeed, when the arrow strikes, you'll feel very differently, I'm sure." I paused. "Family, you know, and children—"

I felt him watching me, lips pursed, and he shook his head a fraction. I was sure he had been informed, through mutual friends, that Isa and I had been blessed with two sons, in the early years of our marriage, but they had died, the last before he was a year old. Our other children—four girls—were guarded like precious objects, and so far luck or the gods seemed to be favoring them. The eldest, Florence, was fourteen today—the fact that she had lived past the age of ten was frequently dwelt upon by my wife *en famille*, which even I, though understanding her fully, found a touch morbid. I saw John shake his head again and I spoke.

"You have an extraordinary talent, John, and nothing must stand in its way. Nonetheless," I added, smiling, "you must submit to being one of the most eligible young bachelors in Paris."

The low tone of the luncheon bell sounded just then, muffled and sonorous, and we prepared to join the rest of the family in the dining room. John quickly stood up and brushed a bit of ash from his coat. I rose more slowly. Anyone looking at us might think we were brothers: both tall and well-formed, with dark hair, short-trimmed beards and mustaches, although the deeper lines about my eyes and the increasing grey at my temples clearly showed who was the elder.

I took a last, lingering pull at my cigar, and reluctantly laid it on the tray to die out in its own time.

Isa Boit

I thought the two of them had spent quite enough time off on their own in the library, smoking and drinking—without me—and leaving me with all the looking after for the birthday luncheon. Yes, I know this sounds like complaining, and after all, of what use are men when it comes to birthday arrangements? Yet I longed to be in their company, to hear and see and speak of all the luscious and exciting sensuality of the world of art in Paris. I could never get enough of it.

"I thought you'd become lost in the attic," I said when they entered the room. I tried to sound light and cheerful, but from the look on Ned's face, I didn't fool him.

"My dear, how marvelous you look," my husband murmured as he kissed my cheek. "As entrancing as the day we met." My heart was pierced immediately, and I could have wept to see his dear face looking at me with such care and love. I turned to our guest with a smile I hoped was not too tremulous.

"John, how very good it is to see you! Please, do sit right there, across from Florence." But instead of sitting down, he caught my hand, kissed it and started to sing a jolly little tune that seemed familiar to me. I looked up at him, puzzled.

"Don't tell me you don't remember that song!" he cried. "We sang it several times not two months ago, in the Pailleron's grand salon—ah, yes, I see you remember it now." We sang a few lines more, and laughed happily.

I could see that John looked with interest throughout the luncheon at our four girls, noting their dress, their expressions and mannerisms.

"How delightful to have your children at meals with you," he said. "It was always the case when I was growing up, but so many families banish their children to the nursery until they're so grown up they're ready to marry and leave the house altogether—and where's the fun in that?"

"I agree with you completely!" I said. "How else are they to learn proper manners, and social conversation, without the example of their parents before them?"

"I dare say your brothers' children are not deprived of social skills, though they dine in the nursery," my husband said, giving me, I thought, a mischievous look.

I snapped my fingers in the air to show my contempt. "My brothers, who imagine themselves so democratic in their culture and customs, would do well to see how truly democratic and egalitarian we *expatriates*, as they choose to call us, really are in our daily lives." I settled my napkin across my lap, and tried for a cooler tone; the younger girls looked a bit alarmed at my vehemence. "It is here, among the most cultivated people in the world, that *liberté, égalité, fraternité* are both truly believed and truly lived."

"I believe you are perfectly right, my dear Isa," John said. "My family have always found an atmosphere far more *simpatico* to our expressions of personality, our—how shall I say it—our need for a larger play of individuality, a greater freedom of mind and spirit—here in the capitals and ports of Europe and England, than in the prim, dry drawings rooms of Boston and Philadelphia."

I smiled at our charming young friend, and gave the servant the sign to begin serving the luncheon.

"I understand you were born in Florence, is it not so?" I said. "But surely you have been to America many times?"

"Yes to the first, and alas, no, as to the second," John said. "It must be six years now since I travelled there with my mother and my sister Emily for the very first time—but I remember it all quite distinctly, and with great fondness! The people there are all so ... enthusiastic!"

"Yes," I said, "and they have so much to be enthusiastic about." I adopted a very nasal tone, mocking my fellow Americans. "We have the tallest buildings in the world, and the largest parks, and the most…this, that and everything!" If a lady could snort, the sound I made would have fit that description. "Such tiresome boasting and such pathetic pride about mere magnitude." I waved my hand as if to dismiss everything west of London.

"But surely, my dear," interposed my husband, "don't you remember what a delightful time we had visiting Niagara when we were first married, and all the lovely summers we spent at your family home, those long, twilight evenings walking about on the lawn?"

"Dear Ned," I said, "how could I not enjoy whatever climate or company I might find myself in, as long as you were there with me?"

The servants arrived with the soup. I was glad to see that the new girl, Marie, whom I had recently engaged, was quick and adept at serving, and spilled not a single drop.

"I must say that I was impressed beyond my expectations by the ordinary man in the street, aye, and the woman in the street as well," John said. I saw him glance at Marie as she served his soup, and he seemed about to say something, then waited until she left the room.

"I particularly noticed quite a difference in the servants there, you see," he proceeded to say, in a slightly lower voice. "Here, they all glide in and out unobtrusively, so silent, so seemingly content with their place. But over there, in America—I believe they call them 'the help', don't they?—they have a decided air of being only temporarily in that position, and would, the next week or month, be opening a shop of some sort in the business district!"

"Yes, I believe I see what you mean," I said. "Frankly, I find that 'business' is pretty much on everyone's mind back there, even the wives and mothers in the great houses—very little thought given to art, or literature, or philosophy." I lifted a spoonful of soup. "Not at all like here."

"Oh, but Isa, that's all to the good, you see, at least for me," John exclaimed. "I have taken great care to submit my paintings over the last several years to all the important New York and Boston exhibitions—those very 'wives and mothers' of whom you speak are eager, hungry even, for the anointing oil of European art, music and culture. They see me both as one of *them*, and one of, well, *us*—we who are *of* Europe."

"So you do not consider yourself as first an American, *monsieur*

John?" The question came from Florence. I smiled at her approvingly; her French was perfect, spoken with a pure, delicate accent. "Are you then Italian, as you were born in Florence?"

Her question made him laugh aloud.

"Not at all, my dear *mademoiselle* Florence," he said, grinning. "I suspect I'm rather a sort of strange beast, part English beef, part American moonshine, part French escargot, and part Italian Parma!"

"And a beast who can speak all of those languages, plus German, like a native of each country," Ned said, smiling.

I saw that Florence was looking at our guest with her usual calm, grave expression, and was thinking very hard. The next course came in, and the conversation changed.

Throughout the rest of the meal, I watched as John gave more and more of his attention to Florence. I tried to look at her as if seeing her for the first time, or perhaps, seeing her as a gentleman might look at her. It struck me I would have to begin paying attention to all that in a year or two. Her face was not pretty in the common way, but distinctive, even arresting—strong and a bit angular. Her hair was thick, and hung in curls about her face and onto her shoulders, often falling across her cheeks and eyes, a curtain of dark brown. Perhaps we might start arranging it differently, now she was getting to be a young lady. And her eyes! I watched as she looked straight at John once as he was speaking to her. Her eyes had the pure dark gleam of unsullied brown in the irises, lashes dark and thick both above and below her eyes, a voluptuous oval frame. But there was no accompanying modest blush of a young lady scrutinized by the opposite sex, however gentlemanly—just a firm, steady gaze that held his own with equanimity. Her cheekbones were high, her nose a little too narrow, perhaps, and her lips, though not plump, a perfect pointed bow.

Her eyes moved away from his face, and I could tell that he, like myself, felt abruptly, oddly, released. Florence and I caught each other's gaze, and something in her face sent a chill through to my heart.

Ned was speaking, and I caught the flow of his words somewhere in the middle.

"... this afternoon, my dear Florence? What would suit you, or delight you most on this, your day of days?"

"Papa, I should so much like to go to the Salon," she replied without a moment's hesitation, "and see *m'sieur* John's paintings, especially the beautiful Spanish dancer that everyone is talking about!"

"Oh, yes, Papa, yes, do let's go!" Jane, next in age to Florence, jumped up and ran over to throw her arms around her father. "We do so much want to see them, all the paintings!"

"What a painting the two of you would make right now," John said, and I saw what he saw, through his painter's eyes—the girl and her father, the one pale with round blue eyes, her hair a fall of dark blonde curls every which way, her blue satin dress shimmering with light from the high windows; and the other, dark-bearded and dark-eyed, wearing a deep charcoal-grey woolen suit thrown into further darkness by the brilliance of his white shirt and collar. What a portrait that would be!

My two youngest daughters—Mary Louisa and Julia—were begging to be taken as well, but a look from me silenced their pleas. They were too young to be out in such a crowd as filled the Salon during the six weeks of exhibition, I said, and that was that.

"Well, then, my dear, you shall do exactly that!" Ned beamed at Florence, and turned to our friend. "John, is it possible you might be able to accompany us?"

I could see that John found it difficult to speak at that moment, confronted with the shining tableau before his eyes. I knew that words did not come easily to him at the best of times, and he often spoke as he painted—dashing at the canvas to place just the right color and texture, then retreating as suddenly to take it all in from afar. As he hesitated, all around the table turned their eyes to him.

Then Florence rose from her seat and walked round to stand at his side. I held my breath. Leaning toward him, she placed her lips on his cheek, a cool, chaste touch—did he not rather offer her that cheek? it occurred to me—and said, "*S'il vous plaît, m'sieur* John, we would be so honored to be in the company of *l'artiste lui-même!*"

"Florence!" I felt impelled to interrupt. "Pray, do not take liberties with *monsieur* John, perhaps he does not like being importuned by little girls."

A dull flush suffused her face, she looked down and took a step back from John's chair.

"Little girl, indeed, my dear Isa," Ned interposed. "Today she is embarking on womanhood, *n'est-ce pas?*"

"Not at all," said John, almost at the same moment. "No liberty

29

taken here, no unwelcome liberty." He caught Florence's right hand as she turned away, and lightly holding it between his two hands, raised it to his lips for a brief kiss. "I shall be the honored one, dear Florence, and indeed" —turning to the rest of the family—"most honored to accompany you all to the Salon this afternoon."

I was embarrassed at the awkwardness I had caused, but John's graciousness helped to shift it away as quickly as a cloud passes over the sun. But I could not help giving a look at my husband, a look I knew must give away my deep anxiety—his face, after a moment, mirrored mine—and I fear that John may have witnessed the exchange. How could we have known such sorrow and pain would flow from that whisper of a beginning?

Louise Burckhardt

I had not yet seen my portrait at the Salon—finished, framed and signed by the artist, and the day we had chosen to visit was not starting out auspiciously. My mother and I breakfasted early, she chattering away insensibly while I tortured myself. *Would he be there today? Why should he not be? What if we just miss him? What if we actually meet him?*

When we were finally dressed and ready for the carriage, I began to lose heart, and almost told my mother I wouldn't go, but it wasn't worth the fight, which I would ultimately lose, of course, as my own deepest desire was sadly, shamefully the same as my mother's for me—to be John's wife.

We entered the Salon with seemingly all of Paris intent upon suffocating together in the various rooms of the *Palais de l'Industrie.*

"Now there is true art," intoned a lady of uncertain age but definitely American origin. She leaned toward the title card affixed to the frame of a large scene of peasant life by Jules Breton. "Ah, 'Evening in the Hamlets of Finisterre', so touching, so realistic in its use of foreground and perspective!" Her companion, an older gentleman with whiskers in a style now gone by, nodded briefly. "Peasant life," added the lady approvingly before moving on, "laboring ever, snatching a moment of love or rest as the sun sets, what a moving theme! The artist has true sensibility to the human condition."

"Insufferable pretension," I muttered under my breath.

"What did you say, dear?" asked my mother, who was busy looking high and low for a sign of our quarry.

"Nothing, Mama," I said, trying very hard not to notice her anxious searchings.

"Oh, oh, there he is, there he is!" she exclaimed, and off she went, like a high trotter from the gate. I steeled myself for the encounter, and followed gamely in her wake. I could see John half a room away, head and shoulders above the crowd, and I recognized Ned Boit, equally as tall, standing near him. That would mean Isa would be there as well, no doubt, and I felt some relief at the thought. I liked Isa; she was forward, and transparent, and interesting. We drew close enough for me to see that she had seen us approaching.

Isa touched John's arm with her fan and when he looked at her, she indicated with a glance of her eyes where he should look next, a gleam of amusement in her own. They could see my mother's fantastical flounce of feathers, held aloft by her otherwise distinguished pompadour of grey hair, floating their way above the heads of the crowd. It looked to me as if John grimaced, and all but winked at Isa before composing his features in an appropriately welcoming smile; maybe it was my imagination.

"John, dear John," called my mother when she was still several yards away, but bearing down the distance quickly. I attempted to look unruffled and unconcerned, as I always try to do, by her antics and attire.

"Oh, my dear, we have found you at last!" my mother all but gasped into John's face.

"I was unaware, *chère Madame*, that you were seeking me at all," he said with a graceful nod of his head to her, and then to me. I smiled back serenely, I'm quite sure. "But here I am, you see, surrounded by friends whom you know as well, eh?" He turned to Isa and Ned as if to present them.

"Lord, of course, the lovely Boits, so good to see you again," she said, tapping Ned with her fan, and leaning forward to kiss Isa on both cheeks. "*Et les jeunes filles aussi! Charmantes, charmantes,*" she cooed, as she chucked Jane under the chin. The two girls curtsied slightly and smiled, and Florence leaned up to touch her lips to my cheek. I kissed both her and Jane, and standing close by Florence, my particular favorite, I felt her lean slightly into me, and she wound one of the ribbons of my pelisse around her finger as we stood there.

"Louise," Ned said, "we understand you are quite a sensation this year." He smiled, and amended his remark, "that is, your *image* is a sensation! If only there were some way that your lovely singing voice could be attached to the painting, your fame would spread worldwide! How shall you go on with all this adulation and renown?"

"The adulation and renown is all for the artist, *n'est-ce pas?*" I said, smiling, and then, impulsively, I leaned up to John and kissed his cheek. Why shouldn't I? I caught Isa's eyebrow lifting slightly, and I laughed nervously. "The poor model," I continued, "has had to endure the long hours of posing in the cold, damp studio, and now the acclaim is all for the brush strokes and the artful folds of fabric and the delicate blush on the flower!"

"Nonsense, Louise, how you talk!" my mother protested. "When we were in Mr. Sargent's studio"—she said it loud enough for everyone in the room, and it was a large room, to hear quite adequately—"it was never cold or damp, and he always had the most delightful spread to refresh one's spirits!"

"We were just on our way to see your gypsy dancer," I said, to fend off further gushing from my mother. I looked into John's eyes, those warm, brown, merry eyes that reflected his evident delight in being the center of attention—but there seemed to be no special light there for me. I felt my heart sinking but rallied quickly. "Perhaps you know best how we are to find her amidst this impossible exhibition?"

"Impossible to be sure," Isa interposed. "It would appear that simply *everyone's* an artist these days, and the whole world is here to see their work!" She waved her hand at the high walls crammed floor to ceiling with paintings. "The catalogue says there are more than five thousand six hundred paintings this year—nearly double over last year's exhibition!" She looked around in amazement and a touch of scorn. "For most, the frames are at least well worth looking at."

"*Maman,* how can you say so?" Florence cried. "It takes my breath away, each one of them is so beautiful!" She placed her hand on John's arm, and looked up at him. "*M'sieur* John, do help us find your Spanish lady, and *La Dame avec la rose blanche.*"

"Of course, my dears, of course, I shall lead the way," he spoke heartily to the assembled group. With Florence on his left, he offered his right arm to me—I hoped he did not see my mother's approving smile as she turned to claim Ned's arm. I desperately wanted to discern what he was thinking, but his happy face was impenetrable.

As we made our way across the now-scuffed hardwood floors and through the high doorways between the galleries, acquaintances and admirers stopped us again and again to add their praises to John's growing renown. Although comfortable enough among friends, I knew that John was able to do little more than nod and smile in a crowd, ill at ease with so many well-wishing strangers.

We halted abruptly at the edge of a crowd gathered in front of *El Jaleo*, or *The Gypsy Dancer* as it was being called in the art journals and newspapers. Someone with a loud voice seemed to be holding forth before the amassed onlookers; snatches of his utterances—it was a man's deep voice—could be heard, "… somewhat puzzles me … judging by the semblance …."

A woman standing near us recognized John and, with an amused smile and a lift of a well-shaped brow, tapped the person in front of her, indicating he should make way for *"Monsieur Sargent, l'artiste."* *"Ah, bien sûr,"* was the reply, and that gentleman in turn touched the arm of the person in front of him, until a clear though narrow path was made for John and all of us in his party to advance.

In front of the enormous painting—it was nearly eight feet high and eleven feet long—a middle-aged, somewhat portly man, with the air of a professor or a lecturer, was pointing at the canvas with no little indignation.

"Is this art?" he said. "These low types of men and women, sitting in the background against a dirty wall, their mouths open, heads flung back yowling with the degraded music that, no doubt, has sent this gypsy woman into contortions that no living woman could actually replicate! And here, a white spot for teeth, another one for eyes—in their approximate places, as you see, to make up a face, but no real face can be seen!" He paused to take a breath, and suddenly noticed that the crowd before him was very quiet, some with thin-lipped smiles, and all glancing at the tall, bearded young man who stood at the very center, Florence on one arm and me on the other. I felt indignant on John's behalf, and spoke up boldly.

"Tell me, *monsieur*, what is it you are protesting so loudly? The style of the painting, or the morality of the subject?" He seemed affronted by my question, and lowered his brows at me as if at an especially impertinent student in a lecture hall. "Or perhaps," I continued, as the smiles of the audience grew, "you have never seen such passionate dancing as this, and therefore cannot imagine that such sensuous abandonment is possible?"

"*Mademoiselle*," he said at last, drawing himself up to his greatest height, which could not have been more than five foot six, "I protest that the artist, whoever he may be, has thrust upon the spectator the necessity to work out for himself what is the reality behind these *impressions*"—he sneered as he pronounced the word—"of men and women, motion and dancing, light and dark! As if he were too lazy indeed to put into it the labor of presenting the details, the actual eyes and mouths and clothing of these unsavory persons!"

I turned to look at John, who seemed quite amused, and looked back at the lecturing man. "Here is the artist himself, *monsieur*, why do we not ask him if he was too lazy, in your estimation, to do the job properly?"

The room was completely silent with the collected breath held by the highly entertained audience. People just walking in were *shushed* by those present, and all waited to hear what John would say. He cocked his head a bit, as if considering thoughtfully, then spoke with the utmost politeness.

"I shall not defend myself or my work, my good sir. However, I will say this, if you consider the persons in the painting as so unsavory, as you say, then I wonder at your desire to have them painted in greater detail!"

A burst of applause and laughter rippled through the gathered crowd as the lecturing man, red-faced and silenced, glared at John, and then stalked from the room. As people began moving away, we gathered around John with our congratulations.

"My dear John," said Ned, clasping him on the shoulder. "I have never heard you so eloquent and ready with a sharp reply!"

"It must be the effect of the company I'm keeping," John said, smiling at me and gently patting my hand as it lay lightly on his arm. "One is made bold by the heroism of one's defenders."

"You are both heroic!" cried Florence, watching us with shining eyes. "I wish I had such courage to assert myself!"

"Ah, I'm sure you do, Florence," said John, kindly. "There will come a time when you will be tested, as we all are, and you will find your courage, never fear."

Florence's face took on a somber hue, and her eyes dimmed slightly. "*Oui, m'sieur* John, I am sure you are right. Someday."

"Now," said John, "shall I lead you to an even greater triumph, my *Lady with the White Rose*?" He patted my hand once again. "It shall be like looking into a mirror, eh?"

"Except that Louise has got a white dress on," Isa pointed out, "and isn't holding a rose just at the moment—so it will be more of a positive-negative sort of arrangement—rather philosophical in a way, I think. If only we had one of those new photographic cameras, how interesting it would be to capture Louise and her portrait side by side."

"My dear Isa," I said, disengaging my arm from John's, and taking hers in my own—I felt I needed to be a little apart from him before we saw the portrait. "You are a most original thinker! I quite envy you your active mind, ranging through art and philosophy and science as you do. Please teach me how to do this myself, I implore you."

We began to move slowly through the crowded halls, John and Ned first, with the two girls on either side of them, then Isa and I and my mother, who trailed behind us, drawn this way and that by greeting various acquaintances and taking mental note of the fashions and fabrics, about which she was intensely interested.

We came to my portrait. I realized I had been nervously engaging in conversation with Isa, putting off the moment when I would see it again, and in such a public setting. It had been several months since that last sitting in John's studio, back in December, a time I was constantly driven to remember in detail, with heightened emotions, and yet harassed myself with obsessively ruthless self-criticism.

Something about it was different, some indefinable change from the last time I had seen the portrait. Just as I stepped forward to try to see it closer, the crowd milling around in front of it seemed suddenly to disperse, and our little party were practically alone before the painting. John moved to stand at my side, and I felt as if he were holding his breath, studying my face, my real face, as intently as I studied my painted one.

I remembered what he had said to me, that last day, when my

mother was out of the room. He tended to talk in a rambling, gossipy mode as he painted, punctuated at times by enthusiastic shouts and bits of singing.

"It's a good face, even pretty, but also—I think you will like this," he said, *"—arresting."*

"Arresting, am I?" I said. *"Do I stop you in your tracks? How do I arrest you?"*

He looked at me quizzically. "My heart is your captive," he said, lightly, *gallantly, with a bow.*

I had looked at him coolly, but said nothing; and now, as I stared at my portrait, I saw there what he had most likely seen in my face that day. I shuddered.

"I rather think not," I murmured, answering him at last. I bit my lip, and took a deep breath. Musn't give myself away, I thought, and then a sound escaped my lips, half laugh, half sob, because hadn't I already, beyond recalling, given myself away?

"Louise?" John said, drawing my eyes to his. It was as if there were only we two in the whole world.

"How could you?" I said in a low voice. He looked startled, perplexed. His lips moved in a soundless question.

"How could you expose me so?" I whispered, then the next moment, aware of the others watching us, I smiled, brilliantly, and spoke louder.

"You've caught me perfectly!" I exclaimed. "I feel like a metaphor of myself, standing here looking at a more authentic me than I am in the flesh!"

How we ever escaped from that room, that building, I will never know. I am not ashamed to say that I sought the oblivion of undiluted wine after dinner, alone in my room. I'm sure he has no idea how he has tortured me with his insight, his revelation of my most intimate thoughts and feelings—not only to me, but to the entire world to see and guess at! Horrible, horrible, and yet, I cannot help but love him. Yes, I admit I want to be his wife, but failing that, I would be his mistress if only he would have me.

Florence Boit

I have found my old diary among some things my sister Jane had carted up to the attic before she passed on, and I admit my heart beat a little faster when I saw it. The first words beckoned, and I was drawn in to remember those early years, awful and sad in one way, yet surely the most intensely, deeply, intimately alive time in my life. Is that not sad, to be an old woman, well traveled and experienced in the world, and yet to indict my life with such a thought?

Here is the first entry, the day that John Sargent came to luncheon for my birthday; I wrote it that night before going to bed.

Mon cher ami,

Today is my fourteenth birthday, and Papa has given me this beautiful journal, bound in dark red Morocco leather, with a special new kind of pen that was just invented by Monsieur Cross, that one does not need to dip in an inkwell every time in order to write—c'est magnifique! Now to begin.

I am the eldest daughter of Edward Darley Boit. We had two brothers but they died, and now it is just I and my sisters, and of course Mama and Papa, and dear Henny, our nurse who is nearly one hundred years old, she says. She has been with the family since Mama was a girl. I don't really believe she is one hundred, but she does look awfully old.

I am no innocent, as the novels say, because I have lived in Italy and Germany, England and France, though Mama and Papa are Americans from Boston. They tell me I was there when I was three years old, but I do not remember it. We are always travelling. I like to travel, because one can keep to one's self and still see everything interesting, and not have to go to some old school.

Our governess, Mademoiselle Trippert, is strict but underneath très gentille. She has been with us two years now, as we have been here in Paris all that time, the longest we have ever stayed here. Before her, long ago, when we were at our villa Cernitoio, which is twenty miles from Florence near the famous forests of Vallombrosa, we had that horrible little Signora Signorini—we called her Missus Missus behind her back! She would smack our fingers if we gave the wrong answer. But she always fell asleep in the afternoons, snoring quite loudly, and then we sneaked into the garden and were free for at least an hour, and as we never told on her, she never told on us. We have all learned to keep secrets, except Papa, although he tries.

I cannot write any more just now, as it is almost time to put out the light and sleep. But I have to say just a little about The One who is most important to me, who was a splendid hero today. He is just the most handsome man I have ever seen. He looks like Papa, but younger, and he has a lovely smile. I blush when I think of it, but he kissed my hand and it made me feel all shivery. I shall write more another day. The letters look nice and black on the white paper of my book.

Au revoir! Votre amie, Florence Dumaresq Boit

The Sargents in Paris
Violet Paget

I made it to Paris with less trouble than expected, but as much as could be endured. One of the first items on my list was to visit the Sargents, who were staying with John in his apartments.

"The trip was tedious and awful, dear Mrs. Sargent," I said in response to the older woman's question. "So warm for June! And not a *limonada* to be had that was worth drinking the whole time on the train—and the food! It gets worse every year." I helped myself liberally to the pastries and coffee on the tea cart.

"I think it's marvelous how you travel about so, Violet dear," said Mrs. Sargent. "I should never be able to withstand the exertion, certainly not all on my own." John's mother was a small, plump woman whose "delicate health" had dictated her own family's constant perambulations throughout the Continent and England for the past thirty years. I recalled John remarking to me once in a rare fit of candor that the only place his mother found unhealthy to live in was America.

"Indeed," cried Emily, the elder of John's two younger sisters, "I wonder you are not frightened to death, Violet, with all the strangers you must meet and mix with, and changing trains in the middle of the night, all by yourself!" Poor Emily—the adjective seemed indissolubly affixed to her name—was an actual specimen of delicate health, having suffered a fall in her early childhood that was so badly managed by doctors and her parents, though with all the best intentions, that her subsequent "rehabilitation" had left her permanently lame, enfeebled and hunchbacked.

"Oh, as to all that," I said, waving my hand, "it's all grist for the writing mill." I bit into a cream-filled pastry and closed my eyes in delight. "My dear Mrs. Sargent, I cannot thank you enough for indulging me with these delicious morsels!"

"Indeed, Violet, I remember very well how much you liked them as a girl," Mrs. Sargent said. "And very glad we were to have you about the house in those days, scrambling about with John in the *campagna* and the ruins of Rome—you were a great friend to him, our dear John."

"Mama," said Emily, pouring herself another cup of tea, "you speak of John as if he has passed away!"

"Well," said Mrs. Sargent, "we see little enough of him, though we live in the same apartments."

"He is much in demand, Mama, as you know," Emily said. "He is making quite a name for himself," she nodded to me, shyly proud of her brother, "and he is never without an invitation to a *salon*, or a dinner, or the theatre, or a weekend at some country house."

"Ah," I said, "our dear Scamps is of course a great man, and the toast of the town. The famous American in Paris! Or rather," I amended, "as I understand from the American papers, he is there considered a 'French' painter of American origins."

"I think it's lovely that everyone thinks John is so mysterious," said Emily. "He has depths that cannot be plumbed by even the most discerning critic, although the general public, of course, sees nothing but the most shallow appearance of good looks and large paintings."

"Emily has become quite the social commentator," Mrs. Sargent said, smiling and reaching over to pat her daughter's hand. "Especially when she is defending her brother."

We sat silently for a moment, drinking our tea. I glanced at a journal that lay face-down on a little table next to me.

"Ah, I see you have the May issue of the *Contemporary*," I said, turning it over.

"Yes, indeed," said Emily, smiling slyly, "and it contains a most interesting and intelligent essay by one 'Vernon Lee' on the extraordinary subject of vivisection!"

"Vivisection," I said, assuming a professorial air, "is at once a contemporary scientific necessity and a growing moral anachronism. I speak of the experiments that are of a torturing nature, of course, not simply experiments upon living animals." I was, of course, quoting myself.

"It is quite an opinionated essay, I must say, dear Violet," said

Mrs. Sargent. "Many of our Boston friends are quite in a flurry about it, so you must watch yourself in company."

"Oh, as to that," I said, laughing. "I should tell you, the very funniest thing was heard by Mama at a dinner last week, some American of immense *étourderie* had seen the essay, and was demanding of the company, 'Who is this darned chap, this Vernon Lee? I'd like to face him down, I would, standing in the way of scientific progress!'" I laughed again. "I daresay I could charge at least several francs admission to see that bout, eh?"

"How astonished he would be," said Emily, "to know that the author is a woman!"

A trim parlor maid came into the room to replenish the pastries on the cart, and we once again helped ourselves to the delicious cakes.

"I understand," I said, "that John has painted a marvelous portrait of your friend Louise Burckhardt."

"Yes," said Emily, with a sniff. "And we hear of nothing else from Mrs. Burckhardt, horrid, detestable woman, who comes here on a daily basis to further her execrable designs on my oblivious brother."

"Why, Emily," I said, surprised. "I've never heard you speak so uncharitably before! Good for you, dear. You've chosen your object well, I must say."

"John could do worse than marry dear Louise," Mrs. Sargent said mildly. With one eyebrow raised, however, she looked thoughtfully at me. "However, I do not think that John is likely to marry her, despite all Mrs. Burckhardt's machinations."

"Hummph," said Emily. "I wonder she should keep trying, especially after her failure to foist Louise's older sister Valerie on him!"

"Really?" I said. "How extraordinary! A veritable Mrs. Bennet! Pray, what happened there?"

"Oh, nothing scandalous," said Mrs. Sargent. "Valerie has a little more sense than her younger sister, I do believe, and saw right off that John wasn't interested in her, so she found someone to marry all by herself!"

"One wonders what Louise must feel at being put up in her sister's place," I said.

"Louise seems always serene and unflappable," Mrs. Sargent said, thinking it over. "It is perhaps the more necessary for her to be so, with such a mother, but I admire her stoicism."

"And what does John think of all this?" I said, though I rather doubted they would know what he was really thinking—so few of even those closest to him ever did.

Emily and her mother exchanged quick glances, and Emily spoke first.

"It's so very odd, you know," she said, leaning forward, her voice lower. "Last summer, he and Louise spent ever so much time together, singing and playing duets and performing for all their friends at parties, and then they even spent a whole weekend at St. Pierre."

I showed my amazement with raised brows. "Surely not alone?"

"Well," Mrs. Sargent said, looking uncomfortable, and sending an admonishing glance at Emily. "I *think* Mrs. Burckhardt was there," she said, "but I *know* that John's friend Mr. Beckwith was certainly there."

"Oh my," I said, and sipped my coffee. "And then?"

"Well," said Emily, "even *we* expected some kind of announcement, especially when John came back to Paris in September and started painting her portrait, but although everything seemed to be moving along in one direction, suddenly, it was not." She shook her head. "After the portrait was done, he went to Venice, as you know— I believe he visited your family then, did he not?—and he seemed to forget her entirely. We, of course, did not question him."

Just then the drawing room door opened, and Violet Sargent ran in.

"My little twin!" I exclaimed, and opened my arms to receive the young girl who flew into them. "Dear little Vi, how have you been?"

"I've grown, haven't I?" the girl said, standing back and twirling about so that her short white dress ballooned about her.

"Oh, yes, indeed," I said, laughing. "You must be three inches taller than when last I saw you—and you are, what, sixteen at least?"

"Oh, if only I were sixteen!" said Vi, seating herself on a plump footstool near me. "Three whole years away from long dresses and putting my hair up and going to balls!" She sighed noisily as she lifted a pastry from the tray and placed it on a china plate. The contrast between her boisterous liveliness and her older sister's bent, still frame added a special poignancy to my perception of the family scene. But still, how different from my own family! *Here is true affection and attachment*, I thought, and stifled a sigh. I roused myself to respond.

"I hope you will find them more to your taste than I did myself, dear," I said. My dislike of such social customs was well enough known to the Sargents that no more needed to be said.

"And what are you working on now, Violet?" Mrs. Sargent asked, our previous subject, though intensely interesting to us all, suspended by her youngest daughter's appearance.

"Oh, what I hope will be a very interesting little parable of social commentary," I said, glancing at Emily and smiling. "You, Emily dear, will no doubt approve, especially as it will be very whimsically presented as a puppet-play."

Emily and her younger sister both clapped their hands in delight.

"It sounds perfectly charming," said Mrs. Sargent.

The drawing room door opened abruptly, and John poked his head into the room.

"Mama," he said, "I've just been sitting with my father, and I'll join you in a moment, but—" he broke off short as he saw me, and immediately came into the room.

"My dear friend, dear Violet," he exclaimed, bending to kiss me roundly on the cheek. He towered over me as I beamed up at him.

"It is so good to see you in such good health and spirits, my famous friend," I said.

"Ah, but you are the famous one, according to the latest screeds of the literary critics!" He smiled broadly. "And can you give us all your time today? Shall we take you to the Salon?" Without waiting for an answer, he turned to his mother, flourishing several tickets in his hand. "Shall we ask Violet to go with us to the *Comédie-Française* tonight? Pailleron has given us a box!"

Delighted exclamations greeted his remarks, and everyone talked at once, finding it a most agreeable prospect. Edouard Pailleron was one of the greatest comic actors of the day, and John had recently painted not only his portrait, but also his wife and his children, earning an enormous sum for the work. John turned back to me.

"May I accompany you to the Salon now, this very instant? Or are you engaged elsewhere?"

"There is nothing I would rather do," I said. "I have already descended upon the grumbling old badger of a *concierge* at my *pensione*, and have the afternoon completely at my own disposal. It remains to be seen, however," I added with a smile, "whether she will allow me back in again tonight!"

"Who could refuse you anything, famous author as you are!" returned Sargent. "And if we have time, you must come with me to Ned and Isa Boit's house and meet them and their daughters. Just give me five minutes and I'll be back here directly." He looked at me thoughtfully. "We must talk," he said in a low voice as he bent to kiss my cheek again, and quickly left the room.

"It's a matter of business, essentially," John said as he and I walked swiftly through the crowded streets toward the Salon. "I leave nothing to chance, you see."

The boulevard was bustling in the warm afternoon sun, filled with the sound of carriages and horses, newspaper hawkers and lively arguments from the sidewalk café tables. With my arm tucked firmly into John's solid grip, I felt swept along by an irresistible force.

"Do you call your art, 'business', then?" I asked, looking up at his strong profile. "Is it not your passion, your means of expressing all that you think, all that you feel, in short, all that you *are*?"

John waved his free hand in the air before us, as if parting clouds of mist. "My art—my *real* art—is in here," he said, tapping his chest to indicate his heart. "From there comes what is most true, most ardently beautiful—and the best is still to come." He paused, his lips drawn tight as he pondered. "But in the meantime, I know how to make a name for myself—and money, too!" He stopped abruptly, and looked me full in the face. "With enough money, then I can turn my hand to my real art and not care what anyone says!"

I laughed and pushed him forward to keep walking.

"I read in one of the *feuilletons*," I said, "a description of your Spanish dancer as, what was it?—'bizarre, daring, but ingenious, hellish and smart'!" I quoted. "*Hellish!* Is that how you want your painting to be known? If so, it sounds as though you already care nothing for what people say."

John laughed heartily. "One needs a thick skin in this business," he admitted. "But don't you see? That sort of thing captures everyone's attention! People are talking of nothing else this season but my 'hellish' and 'ingenious' paintings!"

"And is Louise Burckhardt's portrait 'hellish' or 'ingenious'?" I asked, the audacity of the question clear in my mind. I wondered how he would take it.

"Rather the latter than the former," John said with an air of studied indifference. He glanced at me.

"So you, too, have heard the rumors," he said, his brows knitting slightly.

"I hear what I hear," I said, with what I hoped was a pure Gallic shrug. "More to the point, is there anything to hear, as they say, from the horse's mouth?"

John threw his head back and made a loud neighing sound, causing the passersby around us to start and stare at him.

I laughed in delight. "Scamps, your reputation will soon be in shreds if that's how you present yourself in public!"

"Indeed," he said, skipping a step or two with a trotting motion, "I am more horse than man, a veritable centaur, am I not?"

"I'll rein you in," I said, pulling at his arm, still laughing. "Come now, dear man, the truth!"

"Alas, dear lady," he sighed, settling back into a slower pace, "what truth there is to tell is precious little." He nodded to a gentleman and lady who crossed our path at the corner, where we stopped for a moment to survey the stream of carriages and bicycles, and find an opportunity to launch ourselves into the street.

"The long and short of it—there is nothing between me and Louise Burckhardt, nothing, that is, but a very friendly and utterly calm relation." I wondered at his insouciance, but his face revealed nothing.

"Marriages have been contracted on far worse grounds," I said, amused to hear myself taking Ralph's side of the argument.

"I have no thought of marriage at the present time," John said decisively. It seemed the end of the subject. I pressed my friend's arm in silent sympathy, and let him see it in a bright smile and nod of my head.

"But what was it, then," I said after a moment, "that you said, there in your drawing room, that we 'must' talk about, if not Miss Burckhardt?"

John was silent for several long moments, and seeing we were drawing near the *Palais de l'Industrie*, slowed his pace. When he spoke

46

at last, I had to lean toward him to hear.

"Have you seen my cousin Ralph recently?" he said. "I understood that he was in Italy, and planning, with his formidable mother, to pay a visit to you and your family. He—ah—left Paris rather abruptly in April."

"Yes, indeed I have," I replied promptly. How curious that the two of them, related as they were, should be so carefully inquiring of me about each other! "He and dear, brutal Ariana dined with us not two weeks ago, in Siena. He said he was planning to come to Paris in July."

I hung fire a moment, then added, as casually as I could, "He asked about you—and Louise."

"Did he?" John seemed interested, but kept his face composed. "To what end, may I ask?"

I pondered my reply for several moments. John and I had generally been candid with each other, but only as far as his reserved nature allowed, and rarely on what one would call *personal* relations, but it seemed to me that he was changing—witness this very time, his speaking quite openly about Louise, and his view of the "business" of art. I took the plunge.

"He asked if you were likely to marry her," I said. "And then, when I gave my opinion—which was, I tell you freely, that I thought it unlikely—he asked me another question." I paused again, looking up at his profile as he stared steadily forwards. "He asked me if I thought you would not marry her because you didn't like *her*, or because you simply didn't care for women?"

I felt the arm entwined with mine stiffen, though John walked as steadily as ever.

"And your response to that?" he asked quietly.

"Why, I told him," I said, striving to sound matter-of-fact, "and I hope you'll understand my point of view, I told him that it seemed to me you took great delight in both men and women, and that you seemed not to treat one sex over the other with any *particularity*—I believe that was the word I used—and that—" Here I faltered, wondering whether to deliver my final pronouncement or not.

"And what, pray?" John prompted, eyeing me narrowly. "What else did you say?"

I stopped our progress at the foot of the steps to the *Palais de l'Industrie*, and faced my friend. "I told him that you in turn didn't seem to find anyone necessary to *you*, and that although it was your great strength, it would probably be your downfall."

John gazed at me with wide eyes, taking in the reverberations of such a prophecy.

"And what in the world, dear friend," he said at last, "did you mean by that?"

I smiled broadly. "I haven't the faintest idea!" I said. "One says such things, you know, for effect, and then, sometimes, they mean something later, upon reflection."

"You have not then," he said, matching my joking style, "taken it up for reflection? No insights to impart as yet?"

"Not as yet," I said, laughing and shaking my head. "But I promise you, if an epiphany breaks upon me someday, I shall surely write to you and reveal your destiny!"

"I can ask for nothing more," and John bowed his thanks. He paused a moment, consulting his watch. "If we move along smartly," he said, "we will have time to see the essentials here and still make it to the Boits' in time for tea. I've told them all about you." He looked down at me with, I noted, a little smile in his eyes that did not quite reach his lips. "I do so want you to see their splendid daughters, the eldest particularly! Children are such an immense study, don't you know, they are quite superior, independent little beings, despite all the fuss their papas and mamas make over them. I quite delight in watching and listening to them, especially the girls."

I checked my own less sympathetic view on the subject of children, and only smiled my approbation of this plan as we walked the final steps to the doors of the *Palais de l'Industrie*, blending with the crowd that slowly moved into the temple of art.

The Boits at Home

Isa

"So here you are at last, Miss Paget," I said, pumping her hand enthusiastically as I led my visitor into the sitting room. "Or should I say, 'Mister Lee'?"

"Oh, either one will do, my dear Mrs. Boit," Violet said with a brilliant smile. "I answer to both, and to a good many *sobriquets* of often questionable taste, I do assure you!"

"Indeed!" I invited Violet to be seated on a small, puffy sofa covered in flowered silk of a primarily yellow hue—I noted with dismay some wearing of the silk on the left armrest, it was barely two years old—then seated myself on a chair next to it. "Please let me help you to some tea," I said, readying a cup and saucer. "Milk? Sugar?"

"Neither," said Violet. "I prefer my tea strong and unadulterated, if you please."

"Indeed," I said, hiding a smile. John had indicated his friend was slightly eccentric, and highly opinionated.

Violet accepted the cup and after taking a sip, glanced around the room. It was furnished to a lady's taste, my taste, *one with rather bright and gaudy tastes*, I expect she thought, and it was small, almost intimate in size, and arranged for confidential female conversation. Why I should be nervous about this woman's judgement of me, I couldn't fathom, but perhaps because I'd heard such disconcerting things about her from John.

"Am I to meet the charming *jeunes filles*?" she asked. "I've heard so much about them from John. He finds them, what did he say, so very clever and so picturesque, that I was hoping to catch a glimpse of them today."

"And so you shall," I replied, gratified that John had complimented them. "I shall call them to us in a moment. But my dear Miss Paget," I continued, "I thought John was to accompany you here to-day?"

"He has, as a matter of fact," Violet said. "But just as we walked in the door, a very tall man with a beard, who looked the very picture of John in about ten years' time, came and swept him away, leaving me to meet the *redoutable* Mrs. Boit all on my own."

"My dear husband, yes," I said, nodding and rolling my eyes slightly. "I fear he has gotten some notion in his head, he told me this morning, that he has been quite taken up with, and wanted to consult John the instant he arrived." I glanced inquiringly at my guest, caught by what she had intimated. "But am I known to be so very *redoutable*, as you say? I had no idea I carried such a reputation."

"My dear madam," Violet said, "in your little *communauté des expatriés américains* you are renowned for your clever and incisive opinions, your patronage of the arts, and your critical faculty of exposing literary pretensions. I assure you, I came fully prepared to be closely examined on my recently published exposition of eighteenth century Italian *commedia dell'arte* and the birth of modern Italian drama!"

I laughed and shook my head; either she was dissembling or she knew how to flatter. "I cannot believe that you fear any such thing, Miss Paget," I said. "In fact, according to all my sources, *you* are the formidable one, and I hear such things of you that quite intimidate me." I turned away and pulled a long velvet cord that hung on the wall behind my chair. The new servant appeared moments later in the doorway.

"*Marie, s'il vous plaît, mes filles, tout de suite*," I said. The girl curtsied and left the room.

"I have been reading your book," I continued as Violet helped herself to a slice of lemon cake from the tea tray; she had a formidable appetite, at any rate. "And I found it most unusual, quite splendid actually, that your presentation of the 'aesthetic' understanding encompasses *all* arts—music, drama, literature, painting—and does not focus on only one."

"Thank you," she said. "I owe so much to Mr. Walter Pater for inspiring me, and of course that strange man, Oscar Wilde, whom I met in London last year," she said, and sipped her tea. I nodded my encouragement. "A most unaccountable person, Mr. Wilde," she continued, "an unceasing talker, he prattled on in a sort of lyrico-sarcastic maudlin *cultschah* which he kept up for half an hour together, and then, his taste in clothes! Orange and white one day, purple and green the next—I fear he is giving 'aesthetics' an undeserved reputation for self-centered indulgence masquerading as artistic sensitivity."

"I couldn't agree with you more regarding his appearance," I said, pouring myself another cup of tea. "However, I have found him so personally amiable, and so very humorous, that it is easy to forgive his sartorial whims."

"Oh, I think the creature is clever, and that a good half of his absurdities are mere laughing at people." Violet nodded knowingly. "The English don't see that, I'm convinced."

The door opened, and my four girls entered the room. The two youngest, Mary Louisa and Julia, headed straight for the tea table.

"Ah-ah-ah, *mes petites*," I interposed, a hand held up in reproof. "What kind of impression will you make on our distinguished guest with all this scrambling after tea and cakes?" I was glad to see the immediate effect of my admonition in the behavior of my little darlings, who quietly edged behind their older sisters with their hands folded primly over their pinafores.

My daughters stood before Violet and curtsied beautifully as I said their names.

"*Enchantée!*" murmured Violet, nodding in turn to each girl. She patted the space next to her on the sofa, and held her hand out to Florence.

"*Mademoiselle*, if you please, sit by me," she said. For some reason she seemed particularly interested in Florence. I glanced at my Jane, whose girlish beauty was quite breathtaking, but as I tried to watch with a stranger's eye, I could see there was a seriousness and depth in my eldest daughter's face that might prove interesting to an intellectual such as Violet.

I spoke to Florence as she seated herself next to Violet.

"And have you seen your papa?" I said, helping the other girls to cake and tea.

"*Oui, Maman*," said Florence, her voice low and pleasant, just as she had been taught. "He was in the entrance hall with *m'sieur* John just now." She turned to look at Violet, regarding her with a cool appraisal that made her seem much older than her fourteen years. "He

51

said they would come to us here very soon." She took the cup of tea I handed to her, sipped it, and turned to Violet again.

"*Mademoiselle* Paget," she said, "we have heard so much about you, from *m'sieur* John, and read about you, too, in the journals, that we have been quite wild to meet you in person. You are a great and old friend of *m'sieur* John?"

I could see that Violet tried not to smile too broadly at the emphasis Florence had placed on the word "old."

"Yes, we have been friends since childhood," Violet said. "Our families met in Florence, and often when we were in Rome, John and I would wander for hours, day after day, among the ruins and museums."

"You must tell me all about him, dear *mademoiselle* Paget," Florence said, taking Violet's hand in her own which, I always noticed with some dismay, were large for a girl her age, though slim and delicately boned. Florence's eyes caught Violet's own and held them intensely.

"Please call me Violet, dear Florence," she said, and leaning over, kissed the girl's smooth, cool cheek.

Ned

We were standing in the grand hallway of our house, on the second floor at the top of the dark, curving staircase. I looked at it as a painter might—a portrait painter, like John. Wide planks of polished oak laid down in a broad herringbone pattern were visible beyond the borders of a pleasant, well-worn Persian carpet in pale shades of blue, grey and green with subtle gold spots. I always liked that carpet. Flanking the entrance to the *premier salon* were our favorite possessions: two enormous Chinese porcelain vases, six feet tall, whose highly reflective surface and curves caught the light from the windows opposite in a most delightful way to the eye. Deep within the recesses of the room, where neither the gas light nor the window light penetrated, a mirror above the mantle gathered the gleams from the hall to itself, and threw back a silvery shimmer.

"I should like to paint them here, in this hall," John said to me, waving a hand at the doorway. "These vases are tremendous! The way they catch the light—"

"Yes, they have travelled with us many a year now," I replied, laying a hand on the cool surface of the porcelain. "We take them with us, you know, because we bought them the year Florence was born, and Isa—well, she seems to feel they brought us good luck."

John stepped nearer and placed a hand on my shoulder. "And may they continue to do so, dear Ned."

"I should so like to capture them while they are still girls, still children," I said, trying to shake off a creeping melancholy. "And as you know, I am no portrait painter, only landscapes for me, or I might attempt it myself." I sighed. "We have them only for a few years, and then they will suddenly be grown up and gone to homes of their own."

"Well, I shall do my best to arrest their childhood," John said. He stood studying the space a little longer. "This puts me in mind of some of the Venetian interiors I sketched last year—I must return there soon, I must explore that dark, shadowy realm again, to get it really just so." He mused a little in silence. "And also, the positioning, something in the style of Velasquez' little princesses, *Las Meninas*, on a very large canvas, *non?*"

"Whatever you wish to do will be fine with me," I said. "I leave it all in your hands, and trust implicitly that you will bring forth a masterpiece!"

"And so it shall be!" he said confidently. "Only," he added, "I will not be able to commence until late in the autumn, possibly not until November. But there will still be plenty of time before I have to submit for next year's Salon."

"Already thinking of next year's exhibition, with this one not yet closed, eh?" I said, laughing. "The artist as forward-thinking businessman—which is why I can tell you are truly an American, despite your foreign upbringing!"

"Indeed!" he said. "It must be in my blood, *n'est-ce pas?*"

"It must indeed," I said, then hearing the hall clock strike five, I waved my hand toward the massive staircase. "Now let us get up to tea and chat with the ladies, shall we?"

Florence

I admit I have done very little with my time lately but peruse my forgotten diaries—how strange a feeling it is to read one's own thoughts many years after they were written down, how passing strange to see one's self at such a distance of time and experience. My life now is so inexpressibly *other* than what it was in those days in Paris when I was a girl—unconscious of my fate, unaware of what was to unfold for me, for my family, not only in the next eighteen months but in all the time that was stretching out before us. Mama died while Julia was still a young girl, and Papa remarried—to Florence Little, a friend of Mary Louisa's, which was the cause of some distress and tension in the family, though sadly, not for long, as she died giving birth to her second son, not five years into their marriage. How unfathomable life is for we hapless souls who live it!

But my mind is drawn to those strangely happy days in Paris in the early eighties, and especially to try reaching an understanding about my obsession with John Singer Sargent.

5 June 1882

Mon cher ami,

Here is more about my family: Mama's name is Mary Louisa Cushing Boit but everyone calls her Isa. The Cushings are a great family that go back all the way to Eric the Red, an infamous Norseman who was very much a pirate and pillaged the coasts of England and Ireland in the very, very long ago days, so long ago it wasn't even called England, I think. My sisters are, after me, Jane Hubbard Boit, who is now twelve and is my best friend usually except yesterday she spilled hot chocolate all over my desk and ruined a poem I was writing, but she was sorry so I forgave her with great magnanimity. Mama says the first virtue of the ancient Greeks was magnanimity, which is like Christian forgiveness but without God.

After Jane is Mary Louisa. She is eight and very independent for her age. She is already a trial for our mother—I think it is because they have the same name—and the frequent contests of their stubbornness against each other are a sight to see! Then, last, notre petite ange, Julia Overing Boit, who is only four but sometimes in her eyes there is a serious sadness that bespeaks une vieille âme, says

Papa, an old soul who has lived many times and seen much of the woes and joys of the world. I think it is true.

Now that I am a young lady of fourteen, as Mama says, I must think more of my appearance, and help her with company and being in society. I am sure this is my destiny, to be a lady, a fine lady. In fact, I helped her today to entertain our eminent guest, Miss Violet Paget, who is also an author of books, and uses a different name than her own, because she is a lady. And then, of course, He was here, too, and I felt very strange in my heart when I saw how attentive He was to Miss Paget, but she is a very, very old friend of his, and I cannot imagine that he could ever be in love with her, so after a little while I felt better. He teased me about the way my hair was arranged, but He was very kind and gentle, and it did not bother me. How I love to hear his voice! And he played the piano while Jane sang a song, it was very lovely.

Au revoir!

I remember that afternoon very well, and the evening that followed it—the first intimation, even to myself, that there was some chthonic force at work, a subterranean river making its way to my smooth surface.

Just before bed, I sat at my dressing table, fixed on my image in the mirror. The room was lighted by two candles in an entwined candlestick which I had placed on the dressing table. I moved it to the left, then back again, then held it slightly in front and above my head, to get a better view of my face. The glancing shadows played tricks on my eyes, which from one angle looked expressive and dreamy, from another, blank and flat. I put the candlestick down and stared at myself. Dressed in only my nightgown, I contemplated the flatness of my chest, and lightly placed my hands where my breasts should be.

A tap at the door made me drop my hands, but it was only Jane, come as usual to spend the last sweet moments of the day with me, before sleep and dreams took us.

"Hello, Florrie," she said, coming swiftly over and throwing her arms around me. She pressed warm lips to my cold cheek. "Why, you are quite chilled through! You mustn't sit here in your nightgown any longer." Though younger, Jane was used to taking charge of me, coaxing me out of the chair and over to the bed. She threw back the coverlet and crisp linens and felt the cold sheets with a practiced hand. Even in summer the interior rooms of the stone and marble building were cool and damp at night. "Wait, wait, though, dearest, just a moment, while I get the warming pan."

Obedient to my sister's commands, I stood by the bed and turned round slightly to glimpse myself in the full-length mirror that stood in a corner nearby. I looked like a ghost even to myself—what must others think of me? What did *he* think of me?

Jane was quick with the coals in the warming pan, and in moments the sheets had lost the worst of the chill, and she bundled me into bed, snuggling under the covers with me.

"I thought *m'sieur* John was perfectly wonderful this afternoon, didn't you, Florrie?" Jane whispered, knowing in her heart what I wanted to talk about.

"Yes," was all I said at first, then, with a sigh, "but we won't see him again until November at the soonest."

"But he was so attentive to you, didn't you think? He spoke with you particularly, I noticed, as he was arranging us around the room, to decide on the best possible setting for our portrait!" Jane was always encouraging. "You'll see, when he comes back, we'll see him every day for days and days! " She kissed me, boundless in her enthusiasm.

"I don't want to wait until November," I said, complaining. But I kissed her back, and put my arm around her as we snuggled close under the covers. We were silent a moment, listening to the city's night sounds far away.

"Florrie, may I ask you something?"

I nodded my head, but Jane was silent a moment longer.

"Do you ... do you remember either of our brothers?" she said at last. It was a subject that was rarely mentioned in our family.

I almost stopped breathing, and felt a slight pressure in my chest; but even when I breathed again, the pressure continued.

"I—don't know, Jane, I—" I fought to calm the blood racing to my head; my heart was beating fast. "Why do you want to know?"

"Well, Henny says there was Neddie, and then John," Jane said slowly. "She showed me a picture of Neddie, once, when mama and papa were away." Jane eyed me with some trepidation.

"Henny should not have done that," I said, though not severely. I thought a moment. "I don't think I was old enough to remember much," I said finally. "Little John died before I was born, and Neddie...I remember some noisy games and such. I was very little when he, when Neddie … went to heaven. He was only nine then."

"But, Florrie," Jane persisted, "I remember a boy, when I was *very* little, I remember a boy playing with me on the floor in the kitchen, in Italy where we lived then, don't you remember?"

The pressure in my chest was so enormous I could scarcely breathe. I pulled my arm away from her shoulders and sat up, heaving great, shaky breaths and gasping.

"No," I said, scarcely a whisper. "No, you are wrong … a servant's child … there was no boy in our family when you were little." What was wrong? Why was I feeling so distressed?

"Florrie, what's the matter?" Jane leaped up to help me. "Shall I call Henny? Shall I call Mama?"

"No, no, I'm all right," I replied, grabbing her hand to keep her from running into the hall. "Wait with me, just wait." Jane sat with worried eyes and watched my breathing, which gradually grew more even and deep, until my color was restored and I was myself again.

I drew my sister into my arms and kissed her several times. "It's all right, Janie," I said. "Maybe I was too excited today."

Jane kissed my cheek, and helped me back under the covers.

"Shall I blow out the candles for you, Florrie?"

"Yes, *merci*, Jane," I said. "And do not worry about me, I'm fine."

Jane turned at the door and stood outlined against the light from the hallway. "Good night, my dear Florrie, sleep well."

"Sleep well, Jane."

Emily Sargent

I had importuned my brother to allow me to visit his studio while Violet Paget was still in town, and afterwards go on to lunch. Violet was leaving for London that afternoon, and had particularly asked to see the studio and his current commissions before she left town, and I so longed to be out of the house and moving about. When we reached my brother's studio, I quite felt in my heart how terrible it was for him to watch me struggle up the stairs to the top floor—I'm certain he wanted to swoop me up in his strong arms and carry me, as he used to do when we were younger, but that wouldn't at all do now. Once there, I needed to catch my breath for a while, so I sat on his old, worn velvet sofa by the fireplace, and sipped some lovely tea his housekeeper brought just for me, such a thoughtful woman.

John and Violet stood near the high, open windows not too far from me—I do believe they hadn't the faintest notion I could hear them talking, but I clearly heard every word they said. Sometimes, I've noticed, when one is an invalid or diminished in some physical way, people just assume you can neither hear nor see, in addition to being crippled or lame! A most remarkable attitude, and yet, I don't blame them for thinking that way—we poor invalids need to assert ourselves more, perhaps, but I am, sadly, one of the most compliant of a passive race.

"First impressions?" Violet was saying, in response to a question of John's about her having met the Boits the other day. "Logically, it seems one should not trust them implicitly," she said, "and yet, there is a freshness, an almost *innocence* of knowledge or sensual imprint that allows a first impression to weigh more heavily upon one's intuition, one's judgement, than perhaps it is merely rational to allow." I thought this a very astute perception.

My brother smiled indulgently. "Dear Violet, you always manage to use ten words where two would suffice!"

"Really, Scamps," she protested. "If they are all valuable words to help communicate the best information, the best of one's thoughts— why, I might as well tell you to use less paint or fewer brushstrokes in your portraits, and what would you think of that?" How ably she defended herself! I must pay attention and see how it is done.

"You are utterly correct," John said, bowing his head in submission. "I should think you the greatest bore and meddler in the world should you attempt to tell me how to paint. I apologize most humbly, my friend, and urge you to make use of all the words at your disposal—in French, Italian, German, English or Farsi, for that matter!"

The two then stood quietly for a moment, taking in the light and the sounds let in by the open windows. John glanced my way and smiled at me, and I nodded back. I turned my head as if to examine some portraits in progress near my sofa, and hoped they would continue their conversation. After a moment, Violet spoke again.

"But as you ask it of me, I am glad to tell you what I thought of them all," Violet said, turning further into the window overlooking the street. "*She* is a sharp one, no doubt—Mrs. Boit, I mean—and very emotional. Lord, rivers of emotion run through that woman, deep and broad. I fairly trembled at her intensity, especially when her daughters were present." She looked at John, who merely nodded, waiting for her to continue. I thought this was perhaps a little too dramatic, although I had met Isa Boit a number of times, and her intensity *was* a bit alarming. She made me feel fluttery, as if my heart were beating fast in anticipation of some dreadful or tragic event.

"*He*, of course, your dear Ned," Violet went on, "is charming and harmless, but he floats about like a pale ghost in that house of females—as how could he not, with so much of his life given over to navigating those currents throughout the family?" My, how she did give her opinions so very decidedly! I imagine this is what comes of being as educated and well-read as she is, although, to be fair, I have read a great deal myself, and yet, do not offer my ideas with such confidence. It must be the personality behind the ideas, I decided.

"And the daughters?" John asked.

"Oh, well, the younger ones are well-behaved, which is enough and more than enough to say about children in these liberal times!" Violet shook her head and smiled. "Heaven preserve me from such a fate."

"I thought you didn't believe in heaven," John teased, lighting a second cigarette from the first one he had just smoked. Now this was an interesting topic—I was becoming very interested in the spiritual nature of mankind, and wondered a good deal about heaven.

"And I don't, except to swear by," Violet was saying. Ah, well then, that's that, I thought.

Several moments of silence passed.

"Florence?" my brother said.

"Yes, I've saved the best for last," Violet said. "There was something about her, I don't quite know what it was, but she seemed older, older than she should be, and different, somehow, from the other girls." She mused a moment. "Am I so far from that adolescent time myself that I forget how crushing it can be? Always on the cusp and not allowed to step over? And time, you know, is eternal for one so young—so many hopes and dreams, and every day seems like a year when what one wants is always just ahead and out of reach." She held her hand out for John's cigarette and he gave it to her, waiting as she puffed delicately then handed it back, and spoke again.

I could not say I was shocked, as I have heard that some ladies actually smoke cigarettes, but it was quite startling to see Violet take one so boldly! But what was it she had said about being an adolescent? It rang true to me, that time in my life had been so very curtailed, "cabin'd, cribbed, confined", more than for most.

"So much time before her," Violet was saying urgently, in a lower voice, and I almost missed it. "And yet I had the distinct feeling she is looking straight at running out of time, of not—of not living long enough to get what she wants, or be who she wants to be."

"My dear Violet, this is strange indeed," John murmured. I echoed his feelings in my own heart.

Violet shook her shoulders a little, as if rousing herself from morbid thoughts.

"There is great intensity in that one," she said. She looked up at

John, sharply. "Beware, my friend," she said. "I think her feelings for *you* are very strong, and could affect you in some way."

"She is a child!" he protested.

"She is more than that," Violet insisted. "And if, as you intend, you will be painting their portrait, you will be much thrown together." She took the cigarette from his hand again, and waved it in the air. "I say this only to put you on your guard. I say this to you as a friend."

Their eyes caught, and held for several moments. I felt distinctly uncomfortable, and yet, I had a sense inside me that what Violet was saying was true.

"I bow, as ever," John said at last, "to your superior intelligence."

"Nonsense!" said Violet, handing back the cigarette.

I decided I had eavesdropped long enough. Both of them turned at the sound of my voice as I rose from my sofa at last.

"John," I said, "please come and tell me who all these delightful people are!"

They joined me as I went to stand before a half-finished portrait of a young man, dark and dreamy-eyed, wearing a Spanish hat at a rakish angle.

"Oh, that's Baby Milbank, don't you know," John said. "Just started at my old *atelier* this past year, jolly lad, they run him ragged, you know, being the junior." He gazed affectionately at the portrait, and touched the canvas with a brush of his fingers. "Excellent model, Milbank." He glanced sideways at me. "You might rather know him as Count Albert de Belleroche, latest scion of *la famille de Belleroche*, though Baby was born in Wales, of all places." He turned to Violet, saying, "Emily has an encyclopaedic knowledge of aristocratic family genealogies, American, British and French—she knows them all!" I smiled at the compliment, and looking at him, I could feel the tears starting in my eyes.

"You are too dear, John," I said, and taking his hand, I kissed the back of it swiftly. John kissed the top of my head with great tenderness.

Violet turned away, seemingly moved by this show of emotion. She approached another canvas, somewhat obscured by a scarf thrown at hazard across it, which she drew back. A young, mustachioed man gazed out with frank, dark eyes, his full lips sensual, the dark curls of his hair falling across his forehead from under a wide-brimmed hat. His brown coat had slipped off one shoulder slightly, revealing a strong, smooth neck and collarbone under a gauzy white collarless shirt.

"This is most intriguing," she said, peering at it closely. "Why, it looks like that gondolier we hired to pole us around, last autumn in Venice!" She turned to John, her eyes questioning.

"That's precisely who it is," he said. He walked over to stand at her side, gazing at the painting with her, as I too drew near.

After a moment, I shuddered slightly, and moved away. Something about this portrait was intensely disturbing to me. "He looks like a hungry wolf about to leap out and devour one," I said.

John pulled at the scarf Violet had drawn back, and let it fall across the painting once more. "Yes, a wolf," he said softly. I thought I saw his hand tremble slightly as he drew back, but it could have been a trick of light.

"Shall we go to lunch, then?" John asked abruptly, turning to me.

"Yes, John, I'm starving!" I declared, and taking my brother's hand, we prepared to leave the room. Violet walked behind us, glanc- ing about the studio, suddenly dim as a cloud passed over the sun. Looking back, I saw her shiver as if touched by a ghostly hand, and she moved more rapidly to follow us out of the room.

❧ *July 1882* ☙
Paris

More Visitors to the Artist's Studio

Carolus Duran

From across the narrow street, I stood gazing at the dark and ancient building that housed John Sargent's studio in the *Rue Notre Dame des Champs*. I had been here before, but not for some three years. I glanced at the top floor, and saw him in the window, pulling at some heavy draperies, changing the light perhaps. The place wasn't far from my *atelier*, the school of Charles August Émile Durand, one of the most well-known of Paris' portraitists—until recently. *Ah, Fortuna, velut luna, statu variabilis.* The student shall overtake the master. I shrugged. I'm not dead yet, I remember thinking, and laughed aloud. Let us go see what he's up to.

I crossed the street and pulled at the iron door-bell, then stepped back to look up. One of the large windows in the studio opened onto a narrow balcony overlooking the street. I saw John step out, and was gratified to see a look of surprise as he peered over the edge and hallooed down to me.

"*Bon-jour, cher ami,*" I called up to him, throwing back my head and waving my gold-topped cane. "*Est-ce que je peux monter vous faire une petite visite?*"

"*Bien sûr, maitre!*" John replied, and gestured that I should come up. "*Vous êtes le bienvenu!*"

Though many years senior to my former pupil, I climbed the steps with the vigor of a much younger man, and was barely winded when I arrived at the door of the studio. We embraced, kissing each other's cheeks.

"You are looking very well, *maître!*" John exclaimed. He moved to help me with my cloak, a dark green velvet, very closely cut down so the nap was as felt, and utterly soft; it was one of my favorites. I glanced in the large mirror by the door, and was satisfied with my appearance. I wear my beard in an older style, pointed at the chin, with the mustache twirled up at the edges; I feel it helps to counteract the always unruly, wiry curls on my head. *Grâce à bon Dieu* I have so much of it! I straightened my lapels, and lightly touched a gold and purple enamel flower stick pin my wife had given me on my last birthday, dear woman.

"I have some excellent cognac here which I am delighted to offer you, early in the day though it is," John said, inviting me toward the inlaid table and chairs near the north windows. I graciously inclined my head, and seated myself, my cane still in my hands. I gazed non-committally about the room, setting my face carefully so as not to reveal any thoughts I might have about the several paintings on display. With a start, I recognized my own portrait, the one John had painted in 1879; he won an Honorable Mention at the Salon for it that year, and was awarded the honor of exemption from jury selection from then on. Quite a coup for a man of twenty-three years.

I frowned slightly as I remembered the journals' reception of this portrait of me: there had been a cartoon mocking my appearance, though the portrait itself was widely praised. I had worn pants with wide stripes of alternating though dark colors, ruffled shirt cuffs, and a flimsy knotted scarf at my neck instead of a tie—unconventional, perhaps, even for me. I had long known that I was both adored and detested by Paris society as well as the newspapers and journals that presented the tattle of the town—thus the portrait, and the artist, were much talked about for several weeks. I tried to repress a slight wince as I recalled one critic's comment, "Mr. Sargent has the trick of making the 'human face divine' more so, infusing a soul into his model where very little exists."

John, bearing two generous portions of cognac in large snifters, presented one to me and sat down. We saluted one other, and swirling the cognac around in the glasses, gave ourselves over to inhaling the pure fragrance of the spirit. After a few moments, we tasted it.

"*Vraiment!*" I spoke first, my eyes closed. "Nectar of the gods!"

We smiled, and sipped a while in companionable silence. But I could tell John was wary—it had been a long time since I had come to his studio, although we had seen each other, talked and eaten dinner together, out in the Paris cafés and boulevards, many times over the last year. I think he divined this was no simple, spontaneous visit. He waited for me to speak first.

"Your Spanish dancer," I said at last, gazing out the window at the rooftops of the seventh *arrondissement* arrayed below. "Everyone says she is a masterpiece." I glanced sharply at John from the corner of my eyes, a flickering glance, then back to the window.

"Oh, not everyone," he replied with a laugh.

"Pah!" I waved a dismissive hand. "Everyone who counts, then." I pulled a cigarette case from my jacket and flicked it open, offering it in John's direction; he accepted and chose one for himself. We smoked for a few moments.

"It seems that the pupil has outshone the master," I said, trying to smile, and almost succeeding. I saw a pained look cross his face, and an awkward pride. His paintings were receiving a good deal of praise in the art journals, but he would not have missed the fact that my portraits at the Salon this year were being largely ignored, the first time in nearly twelve years.

"The success of the student does honor to the hand of the master," he said gently.

I watched him closely. He knew as well as I that the critics no longer referred to John Sargent as a student of Carolus-Duran's *atelier*—he needed no such pedigree anymore—and this in two short years after launching his own career.

Our eyes caught and held each other's in a stare that revealed to me many emotions on his side—pride, impatience, compassion—I hoped that mine revealed nothing. I didn't want his pity, or his understanding. I wanted to know what he was going to do next. I looked away and changed the subject.

"Your work shows that you have lately been to see Velasquez," I said, sipping at the cognac, which was truly good.

"Velasquez is God," he answered, nodding his head as if contemplating that thought very thoroughly. "His interiors..." he broke off, drew on his cigarette, then started talking in that young way I remembered well, impulsive, joyous, trusting.

"I'm going back to Venice soon," he said. "After all the blinding white light of Morocco—it rained dreadfully in Spain, the entire time, so we sought the heat further south and got it in abundance! Now I need to seek the shadows, the darkness of cool marble and water-stained wood, the elusive men and women of the alleys of Venice, do you see?" He flicked the cigarette ash toward the window. "You've been there many times, haven't you? You know what I mean."

I nodded, but kept silent.

He stood up, restless, impatient as only youth can be to live fast and hard, immediately, no waiting. I stifled a sigh. I am older than I tell myself—I no longer have that pressing weight on my heart, my mind, to seize life and shake it loose.

"I want to paint something that no one has ever painted before," he was saying. I almost laughed at that—doesn't every artist? We are all touched, however lightly, by the finger of the god, and long to be gods ourselves, bringing forth new creations, and yet, so very few achieve it. Michelangelo, Rembrandt, Titian. We stumble in their foot-steps, and wait at the closed door. I roused myself from these melancholy thoughts, and realized that John was standing before me, watching my face.

"You think I'm foolish, don't you?" he said, but it was said humbly.

"You are an artist," I said, looking up at his wide brown eyes. "To be an artist is to be a fool."

He grinned at that, and then laughed and offered me more cognac. I felt oddly ashamed, as if I was contaminating something clean and good with my cynical heart, my old man's resentment at being passed over.

"*Merci non*, my dear," I said. "It is time for me to move on."

He walked down the stairs with me, and held open the heavy street door. I thought of what he had said about Venice, and turned to offer him a bit of advice.

"In Venice," I said, "beware going too much into the shadows and alleys—they can claim the heart of an artist, so much so that he never returns to the light."

I saw he was puzzled by this, but after a moment he nodded, and we said *au revoir*.

Louise Burckhardt

It was the end of July, two days before John was to leave for Venice, and I knew I wouldn't see him for several months. I took my courage in my hands, as they say, and went to his studio.

As I turned the corner onto the *Rue Notre Dame des Champs,* I saw a man and woman departing his studio, and John at the door waving them off. I waited until they were well down the block, then, as John stepped back into the vestibule to close the door, I called his name as I crossed the street. I saw the smile freeze on his face as he recognized me, then a flash of puzzled concern at seeing I was alone, so unusual a condition, I own, that it took him a moment to register the meaning; it left him stumbling for something to say.

"Why, Louise," was all he managed as I came up to him, slightly breathless. I couldn't help but look quickly up and down the street, as if I feared to be seen.

"May I come inside?" I said quickly, taking a step nearer.

"Of course, please, come in." He opened the door, glancing up and down the street in imitation of my anxious looks. There was no one else around.

I immediately began the ascent to his studio without another word. A feeling of dread tightened my chest; perhaps he felt the same? From every rational point of view, I knew that he had made it perfectly clear that everything was at an end between us, but my heart told me not only that I could not believe that, but that he could not really mean it. He must not.

Once inside the studio, John took refuge in silence. I walked across the room and came to a stop before the open windows. I tried to keep from shaking as I recovered my breath and gathered my courage to begin. His face today—so transparent somehow! He looked as if waiting to hear his fate with great respect and a deep willingness to be humbled.

My first words startled both him and myself.

"Have you no sherry or, or something stronger, to offer me?" I placed my reticule on a small table by the window, and turned to him with a peremptory air.

Stammering excuses under his breath, John leaped to execute my wish. He poured a large glass of sherry for me, and then, after a brief hesitation, one for himself.

We drank in silence, I sipping at the glass until my breathing evened out and I seemed, at least, collected. I put the glass on the table.

"You will wonder why I am here," I said. I fought with a brave smile to compress my trembling lips. "And without Mama, for once!" I laughed, a high, bright note that echoed in the vast room.

John nodded.

I took a step toward him, and raised my eyes to his. I did not care if he saw all my feelings in my face—I wanted him to know where I stood. He opened his mouth to speak but I held up a hand, stopping him short. I kept my eyes on his.

"Last summer," I began, took a deep breath, and continued. "Last summer, when we spent so much time together, and those lovely days and evenings, in the country—" I glanced down, then folded my arms across my chest, and looked up again. "I thought you loved me." I stared at him, defiantly. "There, I've said it," I said, holding my chin a little higher. "I don't care what you may think of me, saying such things to a man—I've done worse, as you know too well—to *you* who obviously don't care—anymore—if you ever did."

I stumbled to a halt, and pressed my lips together to keep myself under control. I spoke again.

"I—didn't expect to feel as I do," I said, trying hard to explain myself. "I thought—I thought I would be more—free, or not so—" I left the thought unsaid, and started again. "You have left me alone, you want nothing from me, and I—I have so much to give you."

John opened his mouth twice to speak, and seemed to despair of knowing how to answer. We faced each other in silence.

"Louise," he said at last. "What do you want me to say?"

"Say that you loved me—at least a little—at least at one time!" I nearly panted the words, my crossed arms so tight I could see my knuckles white against the dark dress. "Do you not know how I am bound to you? You must tell me."

"Louise, why do you ask this of me?" he said. "What possible good could it do you, now?"

I swallowed hard before I answered. "I could make myself out to be not such a great fool, if—you actually had felt for me what I thought—that it was worth what I—"

He groaned softly, and turned away.

"I blame myself." He spoke in a low voice, but I heard every word. "I should not have believed your protests, that you were willing, without needing more, to give in to the passion of those summer nights." He ran his hands through his hair and pulled at it. "I should not have let the moment overcome us both!" He turned back to me and raised a hand to touch my cheek.

"You do not deserve the pain I have caused you, dearest Louise," he began.

"Don't!" I cried, breaking away from him. "Don't call me 'dearest' anything! I'm so clearly *not* your 'dearest'!"

He had no words to say to me, but hit his forehead with the heel of one hand, cursing himself under his breath.

I spoke again.

"I do not understand what I did wrong, what went wrong," I said, my arms again hugging myself as I walked on the bare floor from painting to painting, though seeing nothing. "We laughed and sang so well together, we had such lively conversations—and *more*," I said, finally stopping and turning to look at him from several feet away. "You know how much more. And I loved you—I *love* you," I said. "No woman could give you more than I gave, no one could love and support and understand you as I could do still—your art, your talent, your place in the world—no one more than I! And yet you have abandoned it all—you have abandoned me. How could you not want…us? *How could you not?*"

"Louise," he said again. He shook his head, and groaning again, sat down heavily in a chair. He put his head in his hands, gripping his hair as if to tear the thoughts from his brain.

I walked slowly, silently toward him, and then I was kneeling beside him, one hand on his arm, and I turned his face to mine.

"Please," I said. "I do not need to be your wife, if I can only be your lover."

Sargent drew a long, shuddering breath; tears sprang to his eyes.

"I cannot," he said in a whisper. "I cannot love you—as any honorable man should—" He broke off and turned his face away. He took a deep, steadying breath, and spoke again. "I cannot accept what

71

you offer, nor give you what you want, my dear Louise—and dear you must always be, a dear friend, I must say it—nor can I offer you anything you should be willing to accept. I am not who you suppose me to be. You deserve so much more than I can give!"

I bent my head down, my forehead lying on my hand against his arm, and thus we were, very still, for a few long moments. At length I lifted my head, pressed a kiss on his brow, and stood, brushing my skirts absently as I struggled to regain my poise.

"Don't you think I know what you can give, and what you cannot?" I said simply. "I may be a fool, but I've lived in Paris long enough to give over being entirely stupid."

At that moment I heard footsteps rapidly ascending the stairs, and a man's voice hallooing as he reached the landing and without ceremony opened the door to the studio. John leapt to his feet, and I turned away toward the window. It was Carroll Beckwith, Sargent's oldest friend and fellow artist, who had a half-interest in the lease of the studio, though he used it infrequently.

"What ho!" he said casually, beginning to remove his hat, then abruptly he stopped and surveyed the scene. "I say," he said, "Dreadfully sorry for bursting in, what?" He looked from John's flushed face to my stiff form. I saw him grimace apologetically at John. "Shall I go?" He didn't wait for an answer. "Yes, that's it, I'll just go as quickly as I came," and he turned to leave.

"That is not at all necessary," I said, keeping my voice even and courteous. I picked up my reticule. "I am leaving this moment, thank you, Mr. Beckwith." I smiled tremulously at John, and spoke again. "After all, this is your studio, too. You have every right to be here, and as I say, I'm just going." Stepping closer to John, I put out my hand, which he instantly took and pressed warmly. "Good day to you, John," I said. "I shall give Mama your best compliments, and please convey mine to your family when you see them next."

"I shall, Louise, indeed," he said.

Beckwith obligingly held the door open for me as I swiftly left the room. I could only imagine the conversation that would erupt after my departure. Once outside, I gave vent to my feelings in a most unlady-like expression.

"Damn that Beckwith! Damn them all!" I said, quite out loud, and felt all the better for it.

Carroll Beckwith

As soon as we heard the street door close behind Louise, I approached John with all due caution, on fire with curiosity.

"No, old man," he said, pouring himself a glass of whiskey. "Do not ask. There is nothing I will tell you."

"John, John," I said, shaking my head. "What's there to ask? It's pretty obvious what was going on." I tossed my coat and hat on a chair, and took the whiskey bottle from him, pouring myself a glass. I downed it gratefully—I'd had a long afternoon, showing visiting cousins from Philadelphia around the city. I decided to give John some time to recover.

"Thank God for this studio," I said, studiously looking away from him. "I shall hide here to avoid being with my cousins for the rest of the evening."

John had walked away from the table, and stood in the softening light at the north window. I thought it would make a good pose for a portrait, and told him so.

"What, me?" he said, and shrugged it off. He muttered something I couldn't quite hear, except for the last few words: "...so tired of painting portraits."

"Come, my boy," I said, going up to him and putting a hand on his shoulder. "Don't be discouraged. The lady's portrait is bringing you fame, even if the lady herself is—well—bringing you grief."

He looked sharply at me, but I could see he knew I sympathized. The ghosts of their passion seemed to hang in the air, settling on the furniture like slowly falling leaves. And after all, I had been there when it all happened. I saw everything, before and after. This, now, this scene I had just almost witnessed, had been inevitable.

We three had gone to St. Pierre for several days, last summer, to the house of a friend who said we could stay there, though as it turned out, he was mostly absent himself, off on some rural assignation in the next village, I supposed—and his wife was altogether gone, he didn't say where. *The servants will take care of you*, he had told us, and they did, in that odd way that French country servants have—making you feel as if you have imposed on them, but nonetheless providing prodigious amounts of ham and fowl and, as it was summer, fruit pastries and berries in cream, no doubt they made quite a feast of it below stairs— all with an air of suffering martyrdom that made us quite laugh at them—after they'd left the room.

I thought it quite daring of her, to come unescorted to a stranger's house with just the two of us, and wondered how she had pulled it off with her *mama*. No doubt she had counted on our friend's wife being present as chaperone; I do recall her blanching somewhat when it became clear she would be the only female there. But Lord, there was a houseful of servants! In and out of every room, on the grounds, popping up on the stairs and in the halls when you least ex- pected them. How anyone, even a mother, could imagine danger to the innocent and untouched in such a crowd, one has to wonder.

But I am being disingenuous. It did happen.

It was amusing to me at first to be the third wheel, I believe the term is, and play the role of invisible observer, one I'm particularly good at. It was the Saturday evening that it happened, the last night before we were to go back to Paris. We sat late at dinner, it had been warm, very warm, all day, but a cool breeze struck up after ten o'clock; rain was likely in the night. The servants had been dismissed after I had wheedled a second bottle of port from the houseman, helped by a small gold piece I found in my pocket.

Louise was flushed from drinking rather more than she was used to, I imagine. Her dark hair had come undone a bit from its pins, and the curls softened, I thought, her too rigid jawline. Leaning forward in the candlelight, she looked even younger than her nineteen years. She looked beautiful, radiant even, especially when she gazed at John. Ap- parently I didn't exist, but that was fine with me. I preferred a more sophisticated type of woman, not a blooming American girl looking for a husband.

John was at his best—joking, singing, playing the piano—and looked to be hugely enjoying himself. He was getting rather drunk, and it took a lot to bring down a man of his size, but he held it well.

He bid me go to the piano and play something, a waltz, something he and Louise could dance to. I obliged, and watched them dip and sway among the Louis Quinze chairs and ottomans with some alarm for our friend's furniture. They swept out through the open doors to the terrace, and danced away into the night.

I finished up playing all alone, and listened for some sign of them returning. After a while, I took up the bottle of port and went out onto the terrace myself to take in the night air. The stars were magnificent, the moon a sharp white scimitar in an onyx sky. I sat on a lounging chair with pillows and drank myself to sleep.

Their voices, though soft, woke me. I almost spoke, but kept silent instead, invisible in the shadow of the house, as there was only faint starlight to see by. The two of them walked slowly arm in arm up the terrace steps, and stopped before the door to the drawing room, some twenty paces from me. The soft light from the room embraced them as they stood there. I held my breath.

Louise's dress was tumbled and creased; her back was to me, and I could make out that the hooks along the spine were mostly undone. Her hair was completely fallen, dark thick locks of it on her shoulders. John caressed her hair and her arms, leaning in to kiss her passionately on the lips, then on her cheeks, as if drinking in the tears that I knew, somehow, lay upon them.

It was a touching scene. Their passion grew with more embraces, and I knew what had happened, and what was about to happen—again. He nearly swept her up in his arms as they entered the house. I stood up quietly and followed, watching from the corners as together they almost ran up the short staircase and into Sargent's room—the first at the top of the stairs.

I was motionless for some moments, then moved with a sigh to return to the drawing room. I lit a cigarette. The tobacco cleared my head somewhat. I suddenly felt very tired, and in need of sleep myself. It was a heavy burden, watching her fall in love, give herself to him, and I knowing what awful disappointment lay ahead for her. I could only hope she was strong enough to bear it. I made my way up to my room, farther down the hall from John's, and didn't even pause before his door to listen. I am, after all, a gentleman.

Some time later I was startled awake upon hearing a tap at the door, and John's voice.

"Carroll, old man, are you in there?"

I realized I had fallen asleep on my bed fully clothed, though thank God I had put out my cigarette before doing so. I struggled up and opened the door.

"What is it, my boy?" I said, yawning hugely. He looked, despite the hour and his recent vigorous activities, fresh and young and blooming. His hair looked newly washed, and he wore a collarless shirt and pants, no shoes.

"You can't imagine what's been going on," he said, and slipped by me into the room.

"Oh, can't I?" I said, and shook my head. He looked at me sharply and laughed.

"I should have known I couldn't get anything by such a one as you," he said. He clasped me by both shoulders and shook me a little. "She's such a beauty! So keen, too, she understands me, she understands my art! I…" he broke off at the look on my face, and stepped back. I couldn't help, for once, showing my—what shall I say? My concern? Disapproval? Pity?

"Why do you look like that?" he said.

"Like what?" I parried to gain time, and moved to find a cigarette and light it.

"Like you disapprove of me," he said, watching me closely. "Like you … pity me."

I drew in the cigarette smoke, and exhaled slowly. "I must be thinking what it will be like, once you're married."

John smiled triumphantly. "Marry?" he said, shaking his head. "No, you don't understand, she doesn't want to marry me."

"Doesn't she, then?" I said. "Well, there *is* something new under the sun after all, it seems."

He raised his head, defying me. "She said it herself; she doesn't want to be in my way, to hinder my art. She is content to, well, *be* there for me, as independent as I shall be." He could hardly contain his awe at the grace of such feminine largesse. "I am her first," he said, almost bashfully, half to himself, but clearly wanting me to know.

"She is not *your* first," I said mildly.

He shrugged, so like a Frenchman. "She is my first *lady*."

I gazed for a long moment at my friend. I had the advantage of him by a few years, and a much more cynical, suspicious nature—and a great deal more experience with women.

But I knew I could not convince him he was wrong.

"Well," I said at last. "If that is the case, then you have indeed found a pearl of great value, and I congratulate you." I couldn't resist. "But nonetheless, I think you will find that you have gained a wife, not a mistress—in time."

He waited a moment before answering me; I could see him wavering, and felt a pang that I had introduced the serpent of doubt into his little paradise.

"Do you think she is deliberately trying to ensnare me?" he said.

"Lord, no!" I answered him immediately. I did not believe that myself. "She is as unconscious and unscheming a soul as ever walked upon the earth, and you should not think otherwise."

He looked relieved, and then wary. "But...?" he said.

I started to speak, then thought better of it. "You do not want to hear my opinion," I said.

"Yes," he said quietly. "I do... Carroll?" I had turned away, and his saying my name turned me back again.

"For God's sake, John," I said. "She's nineteen! She's conventional—her parents are both respectable and wealthy—your people *know* her people—all of you, all of *us*—we come from the same towns, the same stock! And despite all our gallivanting about Europe and affecting a fine cosmopolitanism, we are Americans, and—damn it all, it won't do. It won't do at all, and you know it." I had surprised myself with my own vehemence—I didn't know I felt it all so keenly.

There was a long pause.

"Then I must marry her," he said.

"Or you must let her go," I said.

We simply looked at each other, the dreadful choice hanging in the air between us, then John brushed past me without another word, and left. I sat down heavily on the bed and lit another cigarette.

❧ *September 1882* ❧
Venice

At the Palazzo Barbaro

Ralph Curtis

I sat blowing smoke rings into the high ceiling of the second drawing room in the Palazzo Barbaro, watching them disappear into the twilight shadows. My parents frequently leased the three floors above street level in the expansive, ancient palazzo for our annual sojourns in Venice; I wouldn't be surprised if they ended up buying it eventually, *Mater* was so attached to the place. To me, it was in some ways a convenience, in others most decidedly not—this always living with one's parents. This autumn, however, I had luckily persuaded John to stay at the palazzo for a term, particularly as the topmost floor was available to serve as a studio—it was empty, bare down to the floor, but with magnificent tall windows at either end, north and south, that let in the most lovely light to paint by.

Thinking of him up there painting made me think of the painting I was *not* doing. At this moment, I could hear the light tread of many pairs of feet on the floor above me, women's feet, lightly shod, women John had cajoled, with his excellent Italian and ready cash, to populate the bare, cold *terrazzo* with their shawl-clad, lithesome forms. But, due respect, it's not as if they were all young and beautiful—far from it. Some were downright elderly, but even then, I have to admit, Italian women have a something in their eye, in the way they look at one, or rather, often *don't* look at one. Maddening, and yet, stirring something up.

My cigarette was down to its last ember, and I snuffed it in a small brass tray which the old servant—who came with the palazzo—had set beside me just for that purpose. I thought with idle amusement about the man, who seemed ageless in his agedness, and who silently appeared at one's elbow with just the right whatever-it-was one needed at the moment—an ash tray, a glass of whiskey, a piece of cheese with fresh bread. It was uncanny.

At this particular moment, I realized what I needed most was another cigarette, and I had none. I glanced over my shoulder to see if, by chance, the hovering servant were there, a lighted cigarette already proferred. But alas, my fanciful image of the man was dashed—I remained alone in the vast room.

I eventually became aware that the footsteps overhead had ceased, and at the same time, heard sounds of descent, like a flock of birds, wings whirring against the wind, rushing by outside the door in the dark, cool hallway. Moments later the door opened, and John came striding in, lighting a cigarette as he did so.

"My savior!" I cried, reaching up a hand to catch the packet of smokes that he unerringly and presciently was tossing my way. He walked to and fro before the empty fireplace grate, his eyes alight and his gestures animated, almost explosive.

"What an afternoon I've had of it, Ralph!" he exclaimed. He came to a stop before me, his eyes gleaming. "You must come up and see, you must!" He held out a hand to assist me to rise from the chair where I was slouched.

I felt drawn in almost without a will of my own, as I always did with John, and put out a hand which was readily clasped as my friend nearly lifted me to a standing position. "Come, come, you must see," he insisted, and we left the room and mounted the stairs to the fourth floor, the *portego*. Cool even at the height of summer, though often airless in September when the wind seemed to have deserted all of Italy, the vast space was cavernous and shadowy in the falling dusk. Near the window were paints and canvases, most of them small squares no more than eighteen inches across. They were mostly of the women in John's *coterie*, in various poses about the bare room, standing in ones or twos, doing nothing other than being beautiful in the light and shadow. One painting in particular, more vertical than the others by nearly ten inches, caught my eye.

It depicted a narrow alley with crumbling, exposed brick and plaster walls—what isn't crumbling, in Venice? I thought—the perspective sharply slanted as the two walls and the pavement raced to the very center of the far back of the painting, where a reach of hazy afternoon sunlight whitened a wall with windows and trellises over-flowing with plants. A dark doorway was set into the right half of the alley wall, and a woman in a black, fringed shawl and a full, frilly, pink-ish lavender skirt, stood nonchalant, one arm crooked with her hand on her hip, one foot resting on the doorstep, as if hesitating at the moment of entering. She gazed out obliquely, not at the viewer, nor at the man opposite her, who, in a heavy cloak with a furred collar pulled up as against the cold, and a hat pushed back on his head, gazed in-tently at her, as if waiting for a response, a reply, a *yes*? He had a slightly military air about him—a soldier on leave, perhaps. The pink of the woman's skirt gathered to it the only real color in the painting; the rest was taupe and grey, brown and black.

John was standing slightly behind me, watching and waiting for me to speak first.

"This is very good," I said after a while. I tapped the painting lightly. "Where on earth do you get your ideas, Scamps?" I said, turn-ing my head to look at him. I was surprised to see the color rise to John's face—or was it just the setting sun's last rays shifting through the window?

John shrugged, said nothing.

"I like the severe perspective, very much," I continued, turning back to the painting. "The light at the far end of the alley, too, is very good, makes it seem as if we are, for the moment, in another world, there in that alley, quite separate from the rest of everyday life that is going on under the sun."

Neither of us said anything for a moment, then I spoke again, try-ing for a lighter tone.

"The gentleman seems very much to be hanging on the *signorina's* very next breath, don't you know? As if his life depended on her an-swer, and so forth." I turned away, fighting down the bitterness of my own failure to paint. "Maybe you should call it *Flirtation Lugubre*, eh? They seem fraught enough, more as if they were about to commit murder than agree upon a romantic assignation!"

John looked at me closely, and the silence between us grew.

"Oh, dash it all!" I exclaimed, turning back and looking straight at him. "Sorry, Scamps, I'm just—it's just that I, well, damnation, I out-right envy you! There, I've said it." I tore my eyes away, and turned as if to go, but his hand on my shoulder stopped me, turned me back, caught me in a fierce embrace.

"You have no need to envy me," he said, his voice low, muffled against my hair. "You have talent, too, my dear Ralph. And your life lies easy before you, easier than mine."

We drew apart, and a long look held us for a time where we stood. I could feel the tension flow away, and I tried for a return of cheerfulness. I shook John's shoulder lightly.

"Come," I said, "let's be off to Florian's and have some wine!" We set off in better spirits, arm in arm, to bathe in the humid air of a soft Venetian twilight.

Violet Paget

It was September in Venice, the beginning of the season, and I had been invited to Palazzo Barbaro to partake of one of Ralph's mother's *evenings*. It was so amusing to see how Mrs. Curtis vied for the *crème de la crème* of Venetian expatriate society with another Boston matriarch, the redoubtable Mrs. Bronson, who this evening happened to be among the guests.

I could see Mrs. Bronson observing everything with a narrow eye, but she was not often able to find much wanting. The two ladies, indeed, patronized and resented each other in equal measure, and never missed an opportunity to "catch" one another in some social *faux-pas*.

It came to me after a time that tonight it was I who was the object of Mrs. Bronson's critical observation. I was talking about my book to a few interested persons, and I noticed that she sat half forward as if on alert to find that Mrs. Curtis had, after all, made a huge mistake in inviting this strange woman who just might turn out to be an horrific bore.

I was aware of the raised eyebrow, the amused smile half-hidden behind Mrs. Bronson's fan, and was inclined to quit the room in high indignation, or worse, to call out the lady with some devastating judgement, but happily the attentiveness of my hostess, and the encouraging smiles of Ralph and John held me to more civil account. Mrs. Curtis had recently procured a copy of my "Studies of the Eighteenth Century in Italy" and had begun the conversation by asking why I had chosen that time period to study. Fifteen minutes had already passed while I vouchsafed my answer—not so very long a time, I thought, though long enough for *society*. I could see that Mrs. Bronson was practically panting to see how Mrs. Curtis would handle the situation.

"We are at present much in the same condition as were our ancestors of the days of Montesquieu, with regard to the Middle Ages," I continued saying, assuming an air of professorial authority. "They *knew* that the Middle Ages had existed, they *knew* that certain wars, for example, had been carried on and certain laws enacted during that period, but that the Middle Ages had had any civilisation of its own, much less any art, never entered their minds!" I stopped to sip delicately at a glass of sherry, and resumed immediately.

"There is, similarly, I know, a general notion in the rest of Europe that the eighteenth century did not actually exist in Italy," I said. "In fact, I have even known some Italians who have denied its occurrence on the grounds that no one had ever found any evidence of anything whatsoever having happened during that time!" This drew an appreciative chuckle from several guests, and I held off speaking again to allow Mrs. Curtis to seize the opportunity to deftly move the evening along.

"Until *now*, my dear Miss Paget," she said. "You have given us ample evidence that a great deal of interesting art, literature, theatre and philosophy happened right here in Venice, to say nothing of Florence and Rome, of course, in that century!" She turned to a rotund Italian gentleman who was sitting next to her on the sofa, and addressed him in a manner not to be ignored.

"*Signore* Rotolini, I happen to know that you are very fond of Cimarosa's lovely songs from that time, is it not so? Perhaps you would favor us with a performance, now that Miss Paget has introduced us so charmingly to Cimarosa's time?"

"Ah, *Signora* Curtis," the man said, his voice mellifluous and low, "my poor voice would make but a humble return for the brilliance of such an evening as we are enjoying in your palazzo tonight, but if you insist." He rose from the sofa almost before he finished speaking, and walked with great dignity to the grand pianoforte across the room. Mrs. Curtis' raised eyebrow was now directed at John, who immediately understanding her communication, hastened to the piano, sat down, and readied himself to accompany the great singer. A few whispers occurred between the two as to selection, tempo and key, and the musical part of the evening was underway. I glanced toward Mrs. Bronson, who, deflated, took another glass of champagne from the servant to support her spirits during the singing.

After a few moments, Ralph sauntered over to me and folded his long frame into a fragile-looking *settocento* chair next to mine. We listened in appreciative silence to the Italian maestro, and even more to John's excellent accompaniment.

"He's so good at just this sort of thing," I whispered. "Spur of the moment entertainment, jumping into it at the slightest indication—how did he know to do it? And how *does* he do it so supremely easily, as if he were playing a child's nursery song?"

Ralph smiled and inclined his head to whisper back. "He saw my *mater* look at him," he said, "which is cause enough to make a dead man jump from his grave and dance, if she bid him to."

I suppressed a snicker, and glanced at Ariana Curtis, whose stiffened back seemed to threaten us with terrors untold if we kept up our whispering.

Ralph, who knew this only too well, motioned to me to follow him, a silencing finger to his lips, as he rose and led the way to the far end of the room, near the open windows overlooking the Grand Canal. Lighting a cigarette, he offered it to me. With a swift look back at the assembled company, I shook my head.

"So," I said in a whisper, my head a little to one side, appraising my companion. "So, all your curiosity and concern about our friend and Miss Burckhardt were for nought, eh?"

Ralph closed his eyes briefly, then opened them and blew smoke out the window in a fierce stream.

"Yes, but it has not been without its cost," he said, his mouth a grim line.

I considered this. "Do you mean, its cost to *him?*"

"No," said Ralph. "To *her.*"

"Ah," I said. I rested on this for a long moment.

"How do you know this?" I asked. Ralph looked at me then, with almost an impatient air.

"We talked about it, she and I," he said simply, and returned to looking out the window. The splash of the gondolas' oars, the calls of the gondoliers to each other across the still water of the canal rose like birdsong in the night to our perch high above.

"And then," he continued, "there was a scene, in John's studio."

I raised an eyebrow and turned to look at him.

"And how do you know *that?*"

"Beckwith walked in on them," Ralph said. "High drama and all that, he said. John looked 'beaten down', he said."

"And the lady?"

Ralph drew on his cigarette, coughed briefly, and sighed.

"Said she was 'wrought up' and swept out the door with a high hand."

I nodded, and stayed silent. I turned slightly to look at the party at the other end of the room. Signore Rotolini was just finishing, and the applause rippled toward us in diminishing waves. Someone had risen to speak to John, and appeared to be urging or persuading him to something, to which he was good-naturedly assenting. The next moment he was beginning a Chopin nocturne, and the little assembly settled down again to listen. I turned back to Ralph.

"I don't know her very well," I said, my voice low. "Will there be—that is, do you think there will be any trouble?"

Ralph tossed his cigarette out the window—it described a brief orange arc before it disappeared. "Trouble?" His voice was sad and scornful at the same time. "Not from Louise, not her, never." He paused a moment. "But I do think Scamps had better look to himself, don't you know, or there *will* be trouble."

I looked keenly at Ralph on hearing this remark.

"Do you think he's likely to be leading young ladies on in a manner that will, what—bring breach of promise lawsuits to his door?" When he didn't respond immediately, I touched his arm with a tentative hand. "Or worse?" I said, and found myself holding my breath.

"All I know is," Ralph said, rousing himself, "is what I hear, in London, of the way that Mr. Wilde and his friends are carrying on— you know they're friends, Wilde and John—there's all sorts of talk, and so forth, even in Paris—some law they passed there not long ago, I mean in London, everyone's talking about it—and if Scamps isn't careful, there'll be talk about him as well."

I took in the import of this communication with a deeply furrowed brow, and a feeling that it was not a surprise.

A rustle of silk and a breathing presence made itself felt behind us as we faced the windows, and we turned in time to see Mrs. Curtis bearing down upon us, a severe look on her face. Without a word, we submitted to the daunting authority that bore us back to the assembly near the piano.

Late in the evening, when most of the guests had already departed, I lingered in chat with Ralph and John in a secluded, more intimately grouped collection of small sofas and comfortable chairs. Servants were replacing candles burnt low, and refilling glasses equally low.

"And so, my dear twin," John was saying to me, "other than a few, hurried letters, I've heard nothing about your stay in London in the summer, and your journey back here through Germany."

I took a large sip of sherry, despite having already had more than I was accustomed to, and shook my head. "The Rhine was an awful sell, John," I said. "Dull and dirty brown, the same as the people we met along the way."

Ralph looked at me in mock dismay. "Why, Vi, that's rather harsh on your lovely Allemagne! I thought you doted on all things German."

"And so I do," I returned, with some fierceness. "But I do not let my feelings dictate my perceptions. If something is ugly, or lacking in virtue, I call it out, no matter my personal sensibilities."

"Oh, ho!" cried John. "Quite true, and just, I'm sure, Violet." He smiled at me, and raised his glass. "I salute the high ground upon which you stand!" He drank from his glass and continued. "I, on the other hand, do not judge, I only observe." He paused a long moment as we waited for him to go on. "I leave it to others to do the judging," he said at last, more solemnly than before.

"And judge they will," Ralph said darkly, with a quick glance at me.

"But surely, my twin," I said after a moment's thought, "surely you must see in your paintings how you have exposed your subjects—

I refer to your portraits of course, your sitters—in all their mental and emotional nakedness! Others see it, and many have commented," I continued, pressing him, "and I can't believe you are able to deny that you see them *as they really are*, and *that* is what you paint, despite your so-called lack of judging."

John frowned. "I paint what I see," he said abruptly. "It is the *viewer's* own perception, informed by his own emotions and experience, that interprets what he sees on the canvas, for better or for worse. I have nothing to do with *psychology*, as they're calling it nowadays. I follow the merely visible elements, nothing more."

I sniffed at that and tossed my head. "Well," I said, "say what you will, I maintain *on your behalf* the greatness of your powers of penetration and presentation, even if you insist that you do nothing more than copy the *merely visible* elements."

"I have no such powers, dear Violet," he returned, frowning again. "In fact, I am damnably thick-headed and insensitive." He drank half a glass of whiskey at one gulp. "I wouldn't be surprised if some day I'm called out for it."

I eyed him in surprise, and opened my mouth to contradict him.

Ralph interposed at this point, having a strong dislike of disputes, especially between friends. "So Germany did not suit, Vi," he said. "But what about London?"

"Oh, London!" I decided to let Ralph divert the conversation. "I met the most odd and wonderful creatures there this time—the Morrises among them, and went to balls and soirées and luncheons with all the Bohemians in Chelsea! I must tell you, I have begun writing a novel that exposes all their egotistical, decadent, self-indulgent ways—what fun that will be!"

"Now *there* is judging with a vengeance," John said. "Aren't you concerned that these *creatures*, as you say, will rise up against you when they recognize themselves in your book?"

"You sound just like Mary!" I cried, remembering my friend's disapprobation of my proposed novel. It had become a continued source of discomfort between us during my stay in England, and the memory pained me. "Must one always be so circumspect, so trammeled and bound by society's view of one's self as to defeat one's Muse? I will not submit!"

"I honor your independent spirit," John said to me. "But if one wishes to be a success in the world," he added quietly, "there must be circumspection, and prudence."

Ralph looked keenly at him. "Is this, then, *your* policy?" he asked. "You intend not to compromise yourself in any way that would endanger your success?"

Sargent had turned to meet Ralph's gaze; they sat side by side on a small sofa. His stern look softened, and he placed a hand on his cousin's shoulder and shook it a little. "That is my intention, my dear Ralph," he said. "But as you know, good intentions are the paving stones to the Gates of Hell, are they not?"

Later, in my own room where I had to face my fears and thoughts each night alone, I went over the scenes of the summer between me and Mary Robinson. There was one day in particular that was etched in my mind.

We had been sitting together in the parlor on the ground floor of the lovely small cottage near the river, just as Mary had described in her letter to me. Despite the calendar, the morning was damp and cold enough for a small fire in the grate. I was bent over papers and pen and ink at a table I had claimed as a desk, and Mary was reading quietly near the front window, a warm shawl wrapped around her shoulders. Our cook, an excellent woman from the village of Pulborough, had just taken away the remains of mid-morning tea, and the sounds of her scrubbing in the kitchen and of the maid straightening the bedrooms provided a suitably domestic background hum for the little cottage.

"Listen to this, please," I said. Mary dutifully paused in her reading, and looked up expectantly.

"A poet is a double-natured creature," I read from a page I had just been working on, "with a baser and a nobler nature, and his whole life consists merely in receiving as many and various impressions as both his natures can receive. A poet must know the stars, and know the mud beneath his feet; he must drink the milk *and* the absinthe of life—he must love purely and impurely, with his heart, with his fancy, and with his senses." I paused and looked at Mary, who was frowning slightly.

"My dear Violet," she said. "Have you forgotten that your own brother is a poet, to say nothing of *me*? Surely you do not believe this of me, or of Eugene?" Mary's frown deepened. "*Love impurely*? Whatever do you mean by that?"

"Oh, well, of course, it needn't apply to *you*," I said, and shrugged. "Nor to Eugene either, for that matter, though he is hardly in a position to act on *any* part of his nature at this point, I dare say." I could feel Mary's disapproval in her silence, but I went on talking. "I had this same discussion with my friend John Sargent, the painter, you know, and he was very much struck by the idea—said he thought he could understand such a double nature—said it put him in mind of the way Rembrandt painted portraits, with light on one half of the face and the other half in shadow, to show that Man has both a dark and an enlightened side."

Mary did not respond to these thoughts, which I know she found disturbing, and turned back to her book. After a few moments, I spoke again.

"I'm thinking of writing a novel, Mary dear, once I'm done with the *Hundred Soups*, and I'm thinking I shall style it as a kind of morality tale about the leading lights of the aesthetic movement, such as we've seen so many and terrible examples of in London the last few years!"

Mary appeared to be thinking this over. "You mean to pattern the characters on people whom we know?" she said carefully.

"Why, yes!" I cried. "Of course, I shan't use their real names." I mused a moment. "For instance, that bizarre couple, the Ritchies— though *she* may be Thackeray's daughter, that is no excuse for her marrying her *godson*, and he actually twenty years younger than she!" I snorted in contempt, and picked up another piece of paper. "Here's how I have described her: 'She is the thin, sentimental, leering, fleshy, idealistic old person who would marry her godson, and who seems quite brimming over at the idea of having babies at an age when she ought to be ashamed of it.' " I let the paper drop from my hand. "And what fun I shall have describing all their abominable clothes! You remember the *soirée* at the Royal Academy? I never saw so many shabby and insane dresses, and so few pretty women in my life."

I glanced at Mary, and imagined from her pursed lips that she thought it the wisest course to let the torrent of my criticism flow without interruption.

"I was quite astounded," I continued, relishing my critique—what a prattling fool I can be— "on coming out, to see so many grand carriages, as the dresses didn't look at all on a par with them! There were some most crazy looking creatures—one with crinkled gauze all tied close about her and visibly no underclothing and a gold laurel wreath of all things, another with ivy leaves tied by each others' stalks on her short red hair—and a dreadful lot of insane slashings and stomachings—" I stopped abruptly upon seeing the most awful expression on Mary's face.

"You think me too harsh," I said.

"Well, although you do describe precisely the facts of the case," Mary said, trying to be diplomatic, "I do believe, Violet, that writing in such a way, unless it be *very well* disguised, will bring great offense to many people."

"And well it should!" I said with spirit. "The pursuit of beauty is not the pursuit of one's own taste in everything!" I rose from my chair and stood before Mary, intent on proving my point—stubborn, irascible fool that I am. "Most people have execrable taste, and they ought not to be allowed to get away with thinking it good."

Mary sighed. "But Violet, to be a self-appointed scourge of society, even though one's observations are just—" she said, breaking off at the look on my face.

"A 'self-appointed scourge'?" I repeated. "Is that what you think I am? Is that what you think of my literary criticism, my work in the arts and music history?" I turned away, unable to say anything more.

"No, Violet dear, that is not my opinion," Mary hastened to say, jumping up and putting her arms around me, though I would not yield to her embrace. "I speak what I believe others—who do not know and love you as I do, my dear girl—what others will think of you, and I want to spare you that."

I was partly mollified at this declaration, and softened to her touch.

"Oh, as to that," I said, "I'm quite able to fend off 'the slings and arrows of outrageous fortune, and the proud man's contumely,' don't you know?" But it was said with a trembling lip, which Mary could not help but notice.

"Perhaps you are, Violet," she said, kindly. "But it may be best not to excite that kind of response in the first place."

"Perhaps you are right," I said, more willing to be on good terms with Mary than to argue further. I dabbed my eyes with my handkerchief, feeling foolish and angry with myself for giving way to tears.

"Why don't we get out of the house for a bit?" Mary suggested. I'm sure she thought a change of subject would be as welcome as a change of scene. "We've been wanting to go look at Old St. Mary's church," she said. "Its crypts go back to the eleventh century." I agreed, though I have no love for churches in general, and went to my room for my cloak, and we set off, in harmony for the time being.

St. Mary's was but a five minutes' walk, and thankfully there were few people about at that time of the day.

"Architecturally, it's known as a 'weeping chancel'," Mary said, pointing up the aisle from the entrance of the church to where the chancel shifted out of the straight line, a little askew. She consulted her guidebook. "It says the angle echoes the head of Christ on the cross, usually depicted drooping to His right."

I closed my eyes, shuddering slightly. Old churches were interesting as buildings, their windows and statues commendable at times as Art, but the religion that built and maintained them was a distasteful puzzle to me. The antique glory of Italian churches far outshone the grey stone and damp, cold interiors of their English sisters, to my mind, although I am always eager to learn about the actual history of any place and people. The original St. Mary's dated from the thirteenth century, with various extensions and reconstructions added in succeeding centuries, with all the wars, fires, revolts, storms and events, natural and man-made, leaving their mark in a variety of styles and decorations.

We stepped up into the Lady Chapel, where there was something more of daylight and a general lightness of masonry and pointed arches, giving it a delicate, lifted feeling.

"What a sweet little chapel," Mary exclaimed, moving toward the altar railing, behind which rose a life-sized statue, in pale stone, of the Madonna with Child. "How delightful it would be to be married in such a place as this," she said, carried away in the moment, and turning to me with a happy smile.

Her words caught me completely by surprise. *Married?* Why was Mary talking about getting married? My astonishment must have shown in my face quite clearly, for she immediately came to me, and

93

stammered, "I mean, if one *were* to be married, not that I was saying… I mean… dear Violet, don't look so!" She spoke entreatingly as I turned away from her, and she caught my arm.

"I thought, you and I—" I broke off my sentence and raised my eyes to Mary's.

"Oh my dear, of course we shall always be friends, the best of friends," Mary began.

My heart was pounding ever more wildly, and I could only gaze at her in growing fear. I forced myself to ask the question that was bursting in my brain.

"You mean, you are saying, that you are, what, engaged to be married?"

"What?" It was Mary's turn to look astonished. "Engaged to be married? What gave you that idea?" She laughed, a silvery, happy sound that restored much of my peace of mind. "I never said anything like that, and it's very far from any reality, my dear girl." Mary threw her arms around me and hugged me close. "I have no thought of marriage at present," she said.

My heart caught at the last two words, but comforted in my friend's arms, I decided not to pursue their meaning.

"Now come," Mary said firmly. "Let's go down to the crypts and see if we can spy any Norman ghosties with a terrible tale to tell of olden times, shall we?"

I complied with a watery smile, but could not ignore the sliver of ice that pierced my heart as we walked arm in arm on the cold stone floor.

Gigia Viani

I sat to him many times that autumn in Venice. I know I was his favorite of all the girls, I could see it in his eyes. The grand palazzo where he stayed at first was now dark and closed, those other rich Americans were gone away, and Signore John moved to the Palazzo Rezzonico. It was dark ways to get there—I'm sorry, my English is not as I wish it to be—many alleys if one did not hire a gondola to come by the water door. The *turisti* were all gone, too, and only those people, like John, who love our *vicoli*—our alleys—will stay when the rains begin and the nights are long and dark.

He was saying he must go back to Paris soon, to paint the little girls he was always talking about. He always talked as he painted, and I could understand most of what he said, though I didn't pay that much attention sometimes. These artists! They see in their heads the painting of all paintings, the—how is it said, *masterpiece*—that will bring them the fortune and the name to the ages. But so they did this, Gigia knows, they would still be hungry—it is life herself they desire.

I helped him to find the shadowy places of Venice, the women who sort the onions and mushrooms, the dark, dark insides of the palazzi—cold and dark to me, but the artist sees the light as it comes through the hole in the roof, or the door, and sees it with different eyes than we who live there. He told me the names of the colors he paints with—ochre and sienna and mauve. I liked that one—Siena—like our city here in Italia, brown and old and rusty—he laughed when

95

I said this to him. He says he is preparing in his head how he will paint the little girls, using the shadows and light of Venice. He told me he could feel the brush in his hand, how he would paint the light on some mirror in the room—soon, soon, he would be there and it would be done. I hope he will make it what he feels it to be, in his head and in his heart.

One day, very soon before he would leave for Paris, I knocked at his door. We had no appointment for me to pose, but I wanted to see him. The servant girl opened it and seeing it was me, gave me an evil look. I did not care for her opinion of me, stupid girl. With a toss of her head, she announced, "*Signorina Viani,*" and stepped aside to allow me to enter. I was wrapped in a long black cloak with a hood that covered my head and most of my face, in all modesty.

"*Ah, ciao bella,*" said John. I had caught him holding the brush to start painting, but he did not look as if he minded my coming. I shook back the hood of my cloak, and looked at him with my dark eyes he had so often painted. I could see he was in love with my looks, as he had been before. There is a wildness in my beauty, I know it—my father was Sicilian—and I have a strong will—my mother is from Florence. I know I am very different from the ladies of John's world—and that makes me hard to resist. Ha! He never knows what I will do next. How easy to be fascinating to such a man.

I walked about the studio, pretending to look at this painting or that. I allowed my cloak to fall away, letting him see my neck and shoulders in my loose gown. A red scarf was around my neck; my hair was tied up but falling down. I knew how I made him feel, and smiled as his eyes stayed on me; I could almost feel his heart beating faster.

"You will take me to dinner, eh?" I said, and turned to look at him. "To Florian's, *sì,* on the Piazza?"

"*Con piacere,*" John said. "I can think of nothing more delightful, my dear, my lovely Gigia."

I smiled at this, then looked down so he would see my eyelashes.

"Gregorio will be there too," I said, glancing at him.

"He will be welcome as well, *ovviamente!*" Gregorio had posed with me for one painting, the soldier in the alley with his lady, *amore.* I'm sure John knew Gregorio and I were lovers in our life as well as in the painting.

Moments later, on the slimy steps at the canal door, he held his arm out to steady me as we got into the gondola. The gondolier, Marco, had also posed for John, and as we stepped past him into the boat, I felt a tremor pass through John's body; I could feel it go through me like a lightning shock. Then he shook himself, and sat down next to me.

"*A la Piazza*," he said, and watched in silence as the gondolier began his dance with the long pole in the dark water, graceful and tilted against the pull of the water and the boat.

"Drink, my friends, drink up!" John always had lots of people around him, he pulled them in with singing and talking and laughing. Someone had a guitar, and he played it. Someone, a German man, I think, yelled out the name of a song, and he sang it, and then made everyone sing it with him. He stood up like a conductor and made them all sing in Italian, and English, and French. Everyone was drinking, and liked it very much.

But it was nearly winter, and the night became cold as shadows came like wolves, dark on the piazza. The ladies shivered, and people went to find their gondolas and go home.

Gregorio and I were sitting a little way off from the main table, against the outside wall of Florian's. John was looking at us, I could see from the side of my eyes. I was leaning my chair back, and my dress was off my shoulders, and I was looking at Gregorio; he was striking a big match to light his cigar. Ah, Gregorio—my handsome soldier, always dressed in black—how the flare of that match lighted up your lovely face! I leaned in to kiss you as you blew out the match—it was like that match lighted a fire inside me, and him—and John. I could feel it, like heat waves coming from him to us. He had been drinking, very much, but he was a big man and it didn't really show, just in his eyes, desiring and sad. He couldn't take his eyes from us.

No one else was left on the piazza, only the waiters moving around, cleaning up.

I came forward on my chair, then stood up, holding out my hand to Gregorio. I lifted my eyebrow slightly—he knew what I was saying. After a moment, with a slight smile, he took my hand. We walked over to John, and I held out my hand to him. It was not possible for him to speak, even if he had wanted it. He grasped my hand, warming it instantly, and rose up to stand by my side, not unsteady at all, but eager and full of life.

Marco was waiting at the gondola, and there were no sounds other than the splash of his oar as he ferried the three of us across the dark waters, under a sky still some hours from the dawn. I kissed Gregorio first, then turned from him to kiss John, searching for his lips in the cold dark as our boat whispered through the canal to his palazzo. The warmth of wine and food had faded from my body, and I had begun to shiver, but John wrapped me up in his arms and held me against him, kissing my face and neck until I was very warm indeed.

The gondola scraped against the stone steps, and John lifted me in his arms to carry me up the stairs. It made me laugh—I felt like ten years old! I held out my hand to Gregorio who had leaped onto the steps, such a sure foot he has, and he grasped my hand as we went into the house. At the door to the bedroom, John turned, like one in a daze, and looked at my Gregorio, my dashing, handsome man. He smiled kindly and leaned forward to kiss John, first on one cheek, then the other, then on the mouth, a kiss that made me hungry for both of them.

A fire was burning brightly in the bedroom—so wonderful! Already warm and waiting for us. We flung ourselves onto the ancient, grand, high bed, drew the curtains around us, and gave ourselves up, the three of us, to the god of love and life.

❧ *November 1882* ☙
Paris

Portraits d'Enfants

Isa Boit

It was the night before John started the portrait of my girls that Florence began showing signs of— what shall I say—the illness that had captured her long ago, and which we thought was gone.

I was awakened in the night by Jane, shaking my shoulder and crying.

"Come to Florrie, *Maman*, you must come now!" I threw on my dressing gown as we stumbled down the hallway in the dark, not waiting to get a candle. The door to Florence's room was open, and she was sitting upright in bed, shaking and holding herself tight. As I drew near, she saw me and shrieked, "I'm going to die, aren't I, *Maman*?"

She fell back on her pillow, her flushed face contorted as she tried not to cry. Her dark hair was wild and loose from its night braid, and her eyes were huge, the pupils oversized and black.

"*Ma chère fille*, no, do not think such a thing." I bent over her as I sat on the bed to attend to her. I made myself speak calmly, to better soothe my distraught girl. "You are not ill, the doctor says there is nothing wrong, please, my dear, calm yourself."

I turned away to accept a cool, damp cloth from Henny, my most trusted servant and companion, who had appeared at my side even before I could think of her, and we exchanged worried looks.

"Perhaps a little lavender water would help," Henny murmured, holding out a cut crystal bottle and a linen cloth. I splashed some drops onto the cloth and gently laid it on Florence's brow. She clutched at me with hands fierce as talons.

"They both died, didn't they, *Maman*, those boys?" she said, her voice a harsh whisper now. "I tried to do what I could, I tried not to be like them!" She wailed softly, and turning, buried her face in the pillow, her thin shoulders shaking with tearless sobs.

I bit my lip hard, keeping back my own sobs. "My darling," I said

101

after a moment, placing soft hands on her back, stroking her tenderly. "Tell me what is wrong, tell your dear mama what troubles you so deeply. Surely you cannot think you are going to—" I found I could not repeat what my daughter said, that dreadful word.

It was very unfortunate, I thought, that Florence was peculiarly late-blooming—at fourteen, she still had not started her monthly flows, although the doctor had assured me that this often occurred with girls of "a nervous disposition" as he had delicately phrased it. That was no cause for fear of her life, but perhaps this was distressing her anew. She needed the proof that she was growing into woman-hood, and I felt dread growing in my heart at this obsession of my daughter's.

I had spoken with Florence on this subject, about two years pre-viously, when it came time to alert her to the coming changes in her body—spoken, to be sure, in somewhat hesitant and careful language, but clear enough so she would know what to expect. Florence had caught at this narrative of the passage from girl to woman with intense interest, and seemed to grow more anxious as the evidence of it elud-ed her, month after month.

As these thoughts rapidly sped through my mind, my hands con-tinued their soothing motions on Florence's back, and I felt that she was growing somewhat calmer.

"Florence, dear," I said, speaking in the tenderest tones. "Are you troubled at all by the fact that you have not—as we have talked in the past, my dear—you remember, about your monthly flow, and all those changes that will bring you into womanhood? Is this what disturbs you, child?"

A sudden check to her weeping made me think I may have found the sore spot. After a moment, Florence nodded her head, and pushed her face into the pillow further.

"Oh, my dear," I murmured, clasping her in my arms and cra-dling her. "Do not worry, pet, do not let this disturb you, it will come, you will see, all shall be well in time, dearest, all shall be well!" Flor-ence turned to rest her head on my bosom, and threw her arms around my neck. We rocked together on the bed, mother and daugh-ter, until her head drooped, and her arms gradually fell away, and I was able to lower her softly back into the bed. With a sigh of relief, and an anguished look at Henny, whose eyes were brimming with tears, I pulled the covers up over Florence's shoulders and quietly stepped away.

"But what is the matter with her?" My husband voiced his frustration, hiding his fears, as he conferred with me in the seclusion of his bedchamber sitting room. A fire now burned brightly against the winter night, and we had drawn chairs close to it, a carafe of wine and glasses on a small table nearby. But I was walking about the room in a restless frenzy, while he twisted in his chair to follow my pacing back and forth. "If the doctor says there is nothing—" He broke off, waiting for my response. When only my silence met him, he spoke again, "Isa, my darling, please sit down," he pleaded. "Talk to me."

I came to a standstill before him, my hands clasped tightly, pressed to my bosom. Ned was looking at me, tears standing in his eyes, and I realized I must speak to him of what was on my mind, cost us what it might. I sank at last into the chair next to his, and gestured for a glass of wine, which he quickly poured and handed to me. He then took one himself, and we both sipped for a few moments in silence.

"On the surface," I began in a steady voice, although my teeth seemed to clamp down on every word before letting it go, "Florence is disturbed—concerned, upset—that she has not yet experienced her monthly flows."

I took another draught of wine. Ned's attention was riveted on my face; he scarcely breathed. "To her, as you know," I continued after a moment, "this would be proof of her womanhood, of the reality she has longed for, that she believes—that she *must* believe in, for her very life."

"However,"—oh, the ghastliness of that word to my heart—"I fear that what that really means—what, all these years—" I faltered, unable to say the words when it came to it.

Ned steeled himself—and said it for me. "What, all these years, we have feared most would arise again, and what we hoped—and oh, with what poor, tattered hope!—had worked its way out of her mind."

I bowed my head as my tears fell, wetting my cheeks, dropping onto my robe, staining the dark silk, only I did not care. "She again dwells on the deaths of her brothers," I said, so softly that Ned might not have heard me, except that he knew. A great sob tore from me, and I flung myself into his arms where he held me close.

"She kept saying she *tried to not be like them, she tried to do what she could*," I wept against my husband's chest. "We have failed her, Ned, we have failed her!"

Our grief was too deep for further words, and we sat silently in the room, Ned rocking back and forth, soothing me much as I had comforted Florence, but our heavy hearts were not soon to be consoled.

Florence Boit

I have very little recollection of what my mother told me about that night, when I was so afraid I was going to die. Maybe because I had often had that feeling as I was growing up—thank God, if there is a God, that I have outlived such adolescent dramatics. What I do recall, most clearly, is what happened the next day.

At breakfast, though somewhat pale, I appeared to my parents to have recovered from my distress of the previous night. Every kind of food that could be considered as at all my favorites had been ordered by my anxious mother, and her fears were somewhat allayed as she saw that I ate reasonably well, which she had not expected after such disorder. But as I say, I had little memory of it, and only felt a little more tired than usual. Both my dear parents watched my every move and look, though they tried not to appear to be doing so. That their efforts were poorly concealed became clear when Mary Louisa, an observant, clear-eyed child, finally spoke into the increasingly fraught silence of the breakfast room.

"*Maman*, why do you keep looking at Florence?" she asked in all innocence. "Is she doing something wrong?"

"No, my dear, you are quite mistaken," my mother said, trying for a nonchalant, joking tone and utterly failing. "Florence is entirely perfect, there is nothing wrong with her."

"As you all are, my dear girls," Papa said hastily. "Every one of you is perfectly wonderful."

"*Merci, Papa,*" my sisters murmured politely, sneaking little glances at each other in childish perplexity; even Julia, the youngest at four, with her large, round eyes and solemn expression, looked as if she knew something was not quite right, but also as if she had the prudence to keep still about it.

"And to show you how wonderful we truly think you are," Papa continued after an inquiring glance at Mama, "today is the day that our dear friend Mr. Sargent is coming to start his painting of all of you!" He looked around the table at us, and was visibly gratified by the positive reception of this news. Even I, who had been avoiding his eyes, looked up from my plate, and found it easy to appear interested. I was. Intensely.

"And what you shall wear is a matter of the greatest importance," my mother said, as if suddenly realizing it. "Come, girls, be quick about your *petit déjeuner*, Henny and I will need to spend some considerable time making up your wardrobe, to be sure."

"But my dear," protested Papa, "I believe that John usually has a good deal to say in those matters. Hadn't you better wait until he's arrived and can be consulted?"

Mama was already rising from the table, and dismissed his query with an impatient movement of her hand. I'm sure my father thought better of importuning her further. He turned to me after she left the room, and said with a wink, "We'll let John sort her out, eh? He's used to dealing with women and their clothes!"

"No, no, no, *mes petites*, this will never do!"

John stood in the center of the Persian rug in the great front hall, surveying the four of us girls lined up before him. Mama and Henny had dressed us in our most formal clothes: each of us wore a different pastel-colored frock—peach, light blue, pale yellow, pink—with an excess of ribbons and lace, plus dainty white gloves.

John shook his head, amused and exasperated. "You look like decorations on a wedding cake," he said. Seeing Mama's stiff smile, he added quickly, "And you would all be most adorable and perfectly attired for a morning's saunter in *les jardins du Luxembourg*, but this is not what I had in mind."

Mama softened slightly, but exchanged weary glances with Henny. "How would you like to see them dressed, my dear John?" she said.

He frowned in concentration for a few moments, studying us, the light, the shadows in the hall and the darkened room beyond.

"No colors," he said at last. "Just blacks and whites, can you do that?" He frowned again. "I recall seeing the girls in those things, what do you call them, pinafores, last Spring, how about those? Over black frocks?" He approached us, still in a line, and smiled kindly. "Black stockings, black shoes," he continued. He contemplated my hair, which had been pulled back and swept up on top of my head. Smiling in encouragement, he reached a hand to the back of my head and began pulling out the hairpins, allowing the soft curls to fall on his hand. "And none of this, let their hair fall naturally." His hand rested for a moment on my shoulder, lightly touching the curls. I looked up at him, my eyes (no doubt) dark and big and intense, though slightly red-rimmed, as I'd been crying. He looked as if he wondered what could have caused my tears.

He looked at Mama. "Can this be done?" he said, though it was not really a question.

"Of course, John, of course," she said briskly. Gesturing to us, she led us out of the hall back to our rooms to change.

"Wait, wait!" called John. "There should be one color." He gazed around the room. "Something—red, yes, dark red, nothing too flashy—one of the girls—yes, Mary Louisa," he strode over to address her directly. "Dear girl, do you have a darkish red dress to wear under your pinafore?"

"Yes, indeed, *m'sieur* John, I have one," my sister answered, then looked up at Mama. "The ox-blood one we bought last winter, *Maman*, remember?"

"*Formidable!*" John cried, not waiting for Mama to answer. "Excellent! We'll see you back here directly!" And he watched us file out with a smile of satisfaction.

John at first posed us as if the elder ones were attendant upon the youngest, with Julia standing stiffly in the center as we were ranged around her in a vague semi-circle. He was pleased with our costumes now—Julia's somewhat more frilly white dress, *sans* pinafore, struck him as appropriate for the youngest, the baby, and he complimented Mama and Henny on their choice. She also clung ferociously to her babydoll, an ugly ragged creature dressed in white and pink, I never liked it, with a chipped ceramic head. Apparently John felt the same, but the look on Julia's face when he bent toward her with a hand poised to remove the doll made him quickly withdraw. I almost laughed aloud, he looked so intimidated by her.

Then he banished Mama and Henny from the room.

"You must, you must indeed leave me alone *avec les enfants*," he insisted. "I want their complete attention, and dearest Isa, if you don't stop fussing with Jane's sleeves I shall—well, I don't know what I shall do, but it won't be very nice!" But as he said all of this with his most charming smile and manner, his hands on the ladies' elbows as he ushered them down the hall, they did not take offence. "Come back in one hour," he said, "and we will give the girls a rest."

Turning back to the room, I'm sure he saw a discernible release of tension among his four subjects, and perhaps felt it as well for his own sake. Jane and I exchanged glances that were explicit enough.

"Now, my dears, we shall have at it, yes?" He smiled and paced back and forth, our heads turning as at a tennis match as he passed before us up and down the length of the hall.

"No, please, if you can, hold still, look forward, not at me," he called to us, his voice firm but encouraging. We held still as statues, poised and mannered.

He didn't like it. We were too close together, there was too much space all around us, he said. He took hold of Mary Louisa's arm and led her gently over to one side, on the left, as he was imagining the canvas. He moved back several steps to view the whole scene. The sun, which had been weak enough in its winter light, was snuffed behind gathering clouds, and the high windows sent but a pale gleam of light into the hallway. The sitting room beyond the arch, which was behind where we were standing, was almost totally in darkness but for a sharp reflection of light in the mirror above the fireplace.

"On the cusp!" John almost shouted it, causing us to start and exchange nervous glances. "I'm sorry, my dears," he said, but continued excitedly. "On the very threshold, are you not? Here, Jane, do stand over here," he said, guiding her gently to stand under the arch between the hall and the sitting room. On either side of the entrance the two enormous Chinese porcelain vases, nearly six feet tall, gleamed with a subtle richness in the wan sunlight. Taking me by the hand, he led me to stand next to one of the vases, facing toward him. He positioned Jane again, on the other side, near the twin vase.

Suddenly Julia, tired of standing still, plopped down on the carpet before the doorway, her doll between her knees. John whirled round at the sound, and exclaimed again. "Well done! Brilliant, my dearest little girl, you are brilliant!"

He ran to the other side of the hall to view his scene. *Better, better*, he said under his breath, but loud enough for us to hear, *and yet, something is not quite right*. All four of us stared straightforward, into the painter's eye, the viewer's eye. He stepped forward to Mary Louisa and gently folded her hands behind her, as a soldier stands "at ease." Julia he prudently left as she was on the floor with her doll. He stepped back again to see the scene from a distance.

He turned his attention to us two older girls, standing half in and out of shadow and light, and noticed there were tears on my cheeks. I was unaware of them myself until he raised a hand, as if to wipe one away. Jane saw my distress at the same moment and, giving a little cry, immediately went to me and took my hand. I turned toward her, facing further into the dark sitting room, and leaned back against the huge porcelain vase that loomed above me. I was so tired, and overcome with emotions I couldn't quite sort out, that I just did what I felt like doing. From John's vantage point, I was entirely in profile, my hand caught listlessly in Jane's. Jane turned to look at John—an accusing look, a demanding look, I thought, which seemed to puzzle him extremely—and then he saw that the scene was perfect.

"Do not move!" he called out. "You are all perfectly where you ought to be, please, please, my dear little ones, please do not move!"

And because we were good children used to obeying our elders, we froze in place and allowed the illustrious painter of portraits to capture us in the empty, echoing hall of shadows and light.

Mon cher ami,

I finally have something exciting and wonderful to tell you! He came to us today, and began painting our portraits, mine and my sisters', as you know. I was not feeling very well, but there is no need to tell you all about that now. Suffice it to say (isn't that a nice phrase, by the way, I just learned it from a visitor of Mama's the other day, a very chatty lady who wore a strange fur stole wrapped around her shoulders—with beady little black eyes staring out! I mean the stole, not the lady!)

As I was saying, suffice it to say that my malaise as Henny calls it caught hold of me and made me quite miserable for a while, but I don't remember much of what went on, only that I felt much better when He was in the house, and I could watch Him and listen to His wonderful voice—He likes to sing and chat a lot while He's painting, did you know that? Some of it was quite nonsensical, and made us giggle quite a bit, except Julia of course who is too young to understand, and I tried to maintain my dignity, as Mama tells me to, only I wanted Him to know that He had made me happy. I actually wept a few tears, I think I feel too much sometimes.

And at the end of the session yesterday, only two hours, there was quite a bit of the painting already done, which makes me sad because I'm afraid He'll finish it too soon and will not come to visit us again for a long time, as when He went away to Italy and we didn't see Him for ever and ever. But before we took our leave, He kissed my hand and put His hand on my hair and told me how I was becoming quite grown up since He had seen me last! Jane looked quite sharply at me when she heard Him say that, but I behaved very well, I think, and merely said Merci, Monsieur, vous êtes très gentil, although I shivered when He touched me. It was a very strange feeling, but kind of nice, too. I am sure He likes me, why would He say those things if He were not thinking about me? I am so glad He is coming again at the same time tomorrow.

What would it be like to be with Him always? Sometimes I dare to think— it's just possible, you know—that if He knew how much I love Him—there, I have finally written it down—I love Him, I love Him, I love Him! And if He knew, surely He would want to love me back! I could help Him in his studio, and prepare paints and clean brushes and serve tea to the people, I could really help. And Mama and Papa already like Him so much, Papa always says He is like a brother to him, a younger brother, so they would surely approve.

But I must be careful and not let anyone, not even Jane, know how I feel, and how much in love I am. If it is possible that such a thing as our being together could happen, it must depend on whether I can tell if He likes me enough or not. And if He does, it will prove beyond a doubt that I am a fine lady, just as I have always hoped. I will pray for that to happen. I hope it is not wrong to pray for that, I think it should be all right as love is such a wonderful thing.

Oh, I hear Jane's voice in the hall! Au revoir—until tomorrow!

As I said before, how glad I am that I am completely grown out of all that adolescent, dramatic nervousness. It was almost the death of me, and quite possibly shortened my mother's life. I cannot say this without feeling so very sorrowful, and yet, I tell myself, I was not responsible, I am not to blame—not for her death, nor John's troubles—only my own.

Only my own.

Carroll Beckwith

"Demons! Demons! Demons!" John lunged toward the canvas, his right arm outstretched as he advanced, his paintbrush ready to strike. The words sounded in the air as a war cry, a captain encouraging his troops to fall upon the enemy. The girls, even the youngest, had become used to his odd cries and quick movements in the last few days of posing, and they scarcely ex-changed glances at his idiosyncrasies anymore. I had been invited to join the sessions and offer my support and perhaps help keep the mama and the nursemaid at bay with my charms. Luckily, John seemed to have them well in hand, and they stayed out of his way.

He laid on the thick paint with rapid strokes, back and forth, back and forth, then suddenly retreated some ten feet, panting slightly. He puffed mightily at a thick cigar, sending clouds of fragrant tobacco encircling his head. It was his usual energetic style.

The painting was almost finished. The *Portraits d'Enfants*, as he planned to call it, was large, as high as *El Jaleo* but not as long; in fact, it was a perfect square, just a touch over seven feet by seven feet.

"Four weeks!" he said to me. "I have surpassed my own record for a painting of this size! This has come as a bolt of lightning, don't you see?" He again dashed forward to the painting then stopped abruptly, turned away for a different brush and dabbed it into stark white paint. Very carefully, he set some highlights of pure white on Mary Louisa's pinafore, on the very edges of the two older girls' black shoes, and a final dash on the left side of the large vase against which Florence leaned. He spoke again, through teeth clamped around the cigar. "Once I had started, there was no stopping me!"

He retreated again, looked carefully from the painting to the sitters and the scene, then heaved a sigh of satisfaction. He set his brush carefully on the table with his paints and equipment.

"There!" he said. He smiled at the girls, nodding his head over and over. I began to clap my approval, the sharp sounds of my palms striking each other echoing in the high, wide hall. The girls remained frozen in place, not sure if they were allowed to move or not.

"*Bon! Allez, allez!*" John waved his arms at them, grinning. "You may move now, *s'il vous plaît. Asseyez-vous,* run about, whatever you please, *mes petites!*"

The littlest girl, Julia, commenced to straightening her doll's dress, and remained on the floor. Mary Louisa spread her arms wide, wincing as she straightened her elbows. Jane stretched her arms above her head, and looked tentatively at Florence—I had learned all their names in a day or two—who then spoke to John.

"*M'sieur* John," she said, "may we see the painting now?"

"Perhaps we should call *Maman* and Papa first," said Jane, glancing at her sister, who nodded.

"I'll go!" cried Mary Louisa, and ran off to fetch her parents, who had not been privileged to see the canvas either.

"Unlike you to hold them in suspense, eh, John?" I murmured to him as we stood side by side before the painting. He glanced sideways at me, and his lip twitched slightly in amusement. "Not getting superstitious in our old age, are we?" I added.

John smiled broadly, shaking his head. "Just a whim, you know," he said. "But once I'd said 'no lookey', why, I felt I had to stick to it. Ah, here they are, then," as Ned and Isa were heard ascending the staircase.

"Are you really finished, John?" Isa asked, puffing slightly from the climb. Ned was but steps behind her, holding Mary Louisa's hand tightly in his own.

"I have executed rapidly what my eyes have seen," John said, with a bow. "With such beauty and innocence before me, I was caught up in a rapture that impelled me forward, ever forward." He laughed heartily. I know how good it feels to finish a painting, and he was confident this one would bring him even greater acclaim at the Salon than *El Jaleo*.

"Line up, line up," he said, herding the girls and their parents to one side of the hall, facing away from the painting. "And close your eyes," he admonished. "No peeking until I say it's all right to turn around and look!"

Ned scooped up Julia, doll and all, from the floor and held her in

his arms as they took their places. Jane and Florence held hands, and Mary Louisa edged closer to her mother.

"All right, then, on the count of three…one…two…three!"

The family whirled around to face the painting. John had placed himself so he could see their faces, but he stayed silent as he allowed them to take in the effect. Ned spoke first.

"John, it's simply magnificent." He took a step or two nearer the painting, carefully keeping it out of reach of his youngest daughter's grasping fingers. "The depth, the reflections, the—the *emptiness* of the space but the *relation* of the children—it's brilliant, unreservedly brilliant." He turned to John, tears in his eyes, and put out his hand. "I'm overwhelmed, my dear John, I—" He could say no more.

John was greatly pleased, and looked back to Isa to see her response. Her carefully composed face indicated she was somewhat less overwhelmed than her husband. But she rose to the occasion, and seconded Ned's approbation.

"Very wonderful indeed," she said, then tried for greater enthusiasm. "It will be an enormous success at the Salon, I'm sure of it." She stepped forward and peered more closely, then stepped back again. "The highlights on the vases are excellently done, and the girls' dresses, just perfect." She studied it a bit longer, and seemed to warm to the portrait.

"You've captured the essence of my darlings exquisitely, John!" She seemed really pleased now. "It took me a moment to—to *encompass*—such a large space, but now I'm used to it, I really quite like it, I do." She turned to him with a bright smile. "It's simply, as Ned would have it, magnificent."

They stood before the painting, nodding and smiling. None of the girls had yet spoken, although Jane and Florence had clasped each other's hands more tightly, and exchanged mute, worried glances.

"Where is Forrence?" lisped Julia.

"Why, Florence is right there, my precious," Isa said, pointing to the girl's tall figure leaning against the vase. Julia looked at the painting, then twisted in her father's arms to peer closely at her eldest sister. "No face," she insisted. "Where is Forrence face?"

"Quite," said Jane in a steely voice. I winced at how much she sounded like Isa in one of her imperious moments. She ignored a motion from her sister to be quiet, and pursued her displeasure. "Why do we not see Florence's face?"

There was an awkward silence, then I spoke.

"Why, that is for the beauty of the composition, you see," I said, trying to sound perfectly matter-of-fact. "If all of the subjects were facing forward, that would be entirely too conventional and perhaps even boring, what? The artist has given us a great deal to ponder, to muse upon, in this highly unusual treatment of four figures in a large space." I turned to Jane, and spoke to her as I would to an adult. "Do you see how that shadowy profile makes for a great mystery? The un-defined, you see, bordering on the symbolic! There is so much more to feel, and think about, in a painting like this, that leaves much to the imagination, don't you think? The artist has captured the mystery of your sister on the borderlands of adulthood, she is *that* close to leaving childhood behind, where the rest of you still reside in various stages."

Somewhat mollified, Jane nodded hesitantly, looking at Florence, who spoke up immediately, lifting her head and gazing at the painting.

"Mr. Beckwith is quite correct," she said, and smiled at me and then, more self-consciously, at John. "That is, I see what he means, and I think the painting is lovely." She put her arm around Jane and held her close, but I could see how much she trembled.

"Delightful!" said their mother. "Well! I think this calls for a cel-ebration, don't you, girls?" She shot a look at her husband, who nodded and handed Julia over. Isa continued to address her daughters as she shepherded them from the room. "We'll go upstairs and get cook to send tea up early, with some special treats for you all, you've been so wonderfully patient all these long weeks."

The three of us men, left to ourselves, experienced a collective easing of tension, and turned back with one mind to the painting.

"Will you show it at the *Société Internationale* next month, before the Salon?" I asked John. "I know you've been asked to show several things already, and the timing is perfect, what?"

He nodded slowly, thinking. "Yes," he said. "Yes, that would be very good." He clapped Ned on the shoulder. "With the permission of the owner, of course, eh? After the Salon, *naturellement* my dear Ned, the painting is yours to keep."

"*Mais oui*," Ned said, inclining his head graciously. "The public must see it and praise it first! And praise it they surely will." He ges-tured to us to precede him out of the room. "Shall we join the ladies for some refreshment?"

❧ *January 1883* ☙
Nice

Emily Sargent

I remember the time we were settled in Nice, how fine and prosperous we felt in our comfortable lodgings near the Place Rossetti in the *ancien quartier*. It was not so far from Paris, so John came to visit us fairly often, for him. Looking back now, if feels to me as if it had been one of the last times we were all together, without troubles, everything seeming to be set on a path to ease and well-being forever—of course, that never lasts. But I never would have predicted that the trouble would be so very dreadful, and all because of that horrible woman John wanted to paint.

John had remarked to me of his satisfaction with our current lodgings—Lord knows we had inhabited many a sad place during the years of his youth and mine, as money and energy alike ebbed and flowed—but now was a time of plenty, of actual, physical prosperity and ease, thanks to his blossoming career. We were ever so grateful to him, but Mama seemed oblivious to what he really needed to do.

"You've been here only three weeks, John, and already you're going away?" My mother's softly fretful voice contended with the louder sounds of clinking silver and glassware, covered dishes being uncovered, and the conversation of the rest of the family as we sat at dinner.

"Mama," I interposed, ever at the ready to protect or defend my brother, "John is a great man now, you know, and we should be grateful that he spends even a little time with his dreary old family." I flashed him a smile, my eyes filling with tears.

"There's nothing dreary about any of you!" he said promptly. "Not in the least, my dears." He turned to Papa who sat next to him; I noticed that Papa, though he seemed tired, also seemed content. "You in particular, Papa, I turn to you for all my opinions of the United States and how it gets on in the world!"

117

Our father beamed expressively at John, and furrowed his brow as if trying to think of something profound to say, but he merely shook his head and continued eating.

"John, you are going to finish my portrait before you go, aren't you?" Violet said, looking worried.

"I wouldn't dream of leaving it unfinished, old girl," he said.

"I thought the one you did of Emily was splendid," Mama offered, looking kindly at me. "She actually looked almost cheerful."

John and I exchanged quick, sympathetic looks.

"What great work will you be sending to the Salon this year, John?" Papa asked. "Another dancing gypsy, eh?"

John smiled and shook his head. "Not at all," he said. "Something entirely different, and I trust, entirely new in the way of portraiture—that is, not since Velasquez at any rate!" He laughed, and dug into his plate of an excellent seafood stew.

We waited for him to say more.

"I call it *Portraits d'Enfants*," he said, "and it's quite large, an almost perfect square, seven by seven feet. The subject is, well, of course you know them, the daughters of Edward and Isa Boit, *les petits anges*! I did it in about four weeks," he summed up, as if that were the most important point.

"I should love to see it!" I cried.

"And you will, my dear," he said. "I have placed well enough at the Salon for three years now that all my paintings can slip in without any judging, I'll have you know!" He laughed, and raised his glass. "To the Salon—this year, and next year, and the year after that!"

"To the Salon!" we all echoed, and clinked glasses and drank to his continued good fortune, and our own.

"And," John added after a moment, "I want you to know that I have taken a lease on a new studio, in a particularly *chic* part of town—not far from the new *Parc Monceau*."

Exclamations of delight and consternation were heard round the table. Amid the clamor, I could discern my mother's voice querying how he could afford it, and I doubled my efforts to join Violet's voice in congratulations and wishing to go to Paris to see it. Papa said nothing, but only smiled and nodded his head in approval; anything his son did was beyond reproach.

"You shall see it, of course, when you're next in town," he said.

"It's at 41, Boulevard Berthier, and I must tell you, is situated very near the *nouveau haut monde* of Paris, all those lovely people with whom I've become acquainted, and whose portraits, *naturellement*, I will be painting ere long."

He turned to Mama and smiled encouragingly.

"You recall Dr. Pozzi, Mama, yes?" he said. "His mansion is a few blocks away, as well as the illustrious Madame Amélie Gautreau, she of the lavender-tinted pale skin and henna hair, I'm sure Emily remembers her, don't you, Emily?"

"I remember her very well indeed," I said. "We saw her at the opera when we were there last year, quite a sensation! Everyone's eyes were upon her, and she looked quite heavenly in her white dress." Privately, I had marvelled at the strange paleness of her skin, and her daring clothes—she looked haughty and aloof, not at all charming, though everyone kept saying she was.

"It is hard to believe she is actually an American," Mama said quietly. "But then, I've always thought that New Orleans should have stayed with the French, it's such a strange, humid sort of city, concerned primarily with drinking and dancing."

John and I smiled at our mother's New England primness, dusted off and brought out to judge a city she had never visited, in a nation upon whose shores she hadn't set foot more than three times in the last thirty years.

"Her French is perfect, Mama," John said. "And she has many relatives in Paris who claim her as practically a native."

"But this new studio of yours," Mama pursued. "Will you live there as well, or keep your separate apartments?"

"It is quite large enough to accommodate me in true gentlemanly style," John said, guessing our mother's concerns. "A small but quite beautiful little house all to myself. The studio will be on the top floor, large, open and full of light, and infinitely more *gentil* in its fitting up for my prosperous *clientèle*, you know, than my old place," he said. "Why, I'll have you know that next month I am expecting the Viscountess of Poilloue de Saint-Perier to come sit for her portrait!" He waited, smiling, as we exclaimed over this bit of news, then continued. "And the first floor is wholly perfect—three large rooms with a lovely formal entranceway to the *première salle*, from which I shall hang some gorgeous tapestries I picked up in Florence last autumn. Kitchen, servants' rooms, *et cetera* all below in back, and a very lovely garden—Guido is even now setting everything up to my instructions."

"'Guido'?" Mama said. She looked at me in perplexity. "Emily, dear, do I know someone named Guido?"

"You remember, Mama," I said, "John told us the other day he had hired a *major domo* to look after his domestic arrangements, and run the house—oh, I forget, you were not in the room at the time." I smiled at John. "You are establishing a very proper household for yourself, dear John, just as you should."

Papa, having finished his meal, stood up slowly and looked at his family. "God bless you all, my dears," he said, folding his napkin and pushing back his chair. "Now I'm going to go into the study to smoke a cigar with my son John." It was a ritual he performed every evening when John was with us.

John also rose, bowed to us, and taking our father's arm, walked with him to the comfortable study down the hall.

Sadly, I don't remember having a single prescient feeling about the disaster to come—how I wish I were more in touch with the spirit world! It would make my dreary little life so much more interesting to get glimpses of the future, and then be able to watch and see if it happens the way I saw it. But perhaps it's for the best—one might not always want to know what will happen, for how would we have the courage or curiosity to act if we knew it wouldn't make any difference?

❧ *February 1883* ☙
Paris

Carroll Beckwith

It was all about to begin, only the beginning may have taken longer than the whole rest of it. You know that's how things go in life, you look back, and see that little things started to happen—but you'd hardly noticed them at the time—and especially if you were waiting for something or desiring something hugely, then of course you're watching every second tick by and it seems an eternity with nothing ever happening. And how disappointing it all is, in the end.

But forgive my cynicism—I have yet to get to the actual, absolute end—for myself that is—and perhaps you will tell me I should wait to pass judgement—but the evidence is mounting for my point of view.

Nonetheless, I was there the day John received the long-hoped-for letter.

"Yes! She has said yes to my proposal! *C'est magnifique!*" He crowed with delight as he strode about the large drawing room in his new house, waving a just-opened letter at me.

"Here, Beckwith, look at this!" He thrust the letter at me. I was lounging on a low sofa, drinking my morning coffee, though it was nearly noon.

"Ah, it's from Ben," I said, looking at the signature first, then commencing to read aloud. "*Greetings, eminent artist, la la la, la di da, my beautiful cousin Amélie would be delighted to allow herself to be immortalized by the most famous and au courant artist of our time*—that would be you, John—*and sends her compliments to you la la la*—*much impressed by Dr. Pozzi's recommendation and sumptuous portrait you did of him two years ago*—*la la la yours truly, Ben del Castillo,* etc." I tossed the letter on a nearby table and smiled at John.

"Well," I said, "looks like your relations with the good *Doctor Love* are paying off rather handsomely, I'd say." I sipped my coffee and watched John through half-closed eyelids.

He glared at me for a moment, then laughed and shrugged his shoulders. "It wasn't like that," he said, then, "Do you really think they are lovers?"

"Not anymore," I said, with a slight shake of my head. "I know—as do you, John—that there was plenty of fire behind all that smoke, when you were busy painting his portrait and she 'dropped by' to see her 'doctor', oh yes, you were their *chaperon*, no doubt, but she always stayed behind, didn't she?" I glanced at my friend, who was busy looking out a window.

"But with that dwarf of a husband, *Señor Pedro*, as he calls himself," I continued, "who could blame her? Theirs is a marriage that is doubly blessed: he's twice her age, and she's twice his height!" I laughed at my own witticism—I am often my most appreciative audience—then said more seriously, "She deserves a far better fate than being nickel-and-dimed to death by his old witch of a mother, who has a firm hold on the purse strings still, though her son is in his forties. Beauty such as Amélie Gautreau's requires lavish expenditures—and it's only right that she should be the *alchimiste* to turn the basest of materials into gold!"

John knew I was referring to the source of the Gautreau family's income: importing bat guano from South America, enough to fertilize all of Europe, or so it seemed, but he didn't respond to my gibe—I believe it didn't matter to him how one made one's money as long as it was honest. So American.

"You know, of course, that their new house is very nearby," he said instead. "Closer to *Parc Monceau*, of course, and it's being entirely furnished according to the lady's own taste—and from an account hidden from her mother-in-law's prying eyes."

I expressed my astonishment. "My dear fellow, this is the first instance I have ever witnessed of your actually knowing any gossip of the town! Pray, where *do* you get your information?"

He grinned broadly. "None of your damned business," he said. "My sources shall remain my own!" He walked over to the sideboard where the remains of the morning repast lay, and proceeded to spread some softening butter on a piece of cold toast.

"But seriously, old man," he said, picking up the letter again and perusing it closely. "This is the portrait I've been waiting for! The famed and fabled Madame Gautreau! I shall have it at the Salon this year if possible—I *could* have it done by the March deadline—or certainly next year, and there will be no end of the commissions I shall get after it shows—especially from the *crème de la crème*."

"I can't imagine why you think you need any more commissions as it is, *crème* or not," I said, and yes, it was said somewhat petulantly. "I've seen your engagement calendar—you've got no less than twenty clients lined up from now til Racing Day—and how you'll manage them all in so short a time is beyond me!" I shifted on the sofa to sit up a little straighter. "And aren't you planning to go to London next month, too?

"Yes, blast and damn it," he said. "Meeting some people that certain *other* people, you know, are awfully determined I should meet and become acquainted with." He mused momentarily as he crunched away at the toast and butter. "Dinner for an American actor, Lawrence Barrett, d'ye know him?" He laughed, and didn't wait for me to answer. "Of course you do! You know everyone!"

I smiled, and nodded acquiescence. "Stunning man," I said after a moment. "Saw him as *Othello* last year in London, added an interesting *frisson* to his relationship with Iago, don't you know?" I cocked an eyebrow at him, but he did not reply. "I believe he's doing *Cardinal Richelieu* this year, you know, a revival of Bulwer-Lytton's play? They say it's his best performance."

"*The pen is mightier than the sword—*" John intoned dramatically, making me laugh. "But you know me," he continued, back on the subject foremost to his mind, "I can work fast and furiously with all those folks"—so he dismissed his clients—"and concentrate on Madame Gautreau as soon as I can—I cannot but think I'll hit on something for her quite soon. This will be the *entrée* into the French aristocracy that will set me up for good!"

"If you can get her to sit still," I said. "She's quite the butterfly, you know, gadding about here and there, as of course she must. The other day, I was walking by the *Place de la Concorde*, and there was a great commotion in front of the Hôtel Crillon, you know, where *Les Ambassadeurs* is—I've taken you to dinner there, haven't I?—and I stopped to take a look and there was your Madame Gautreau, resplendent in white and gold, just stepping down from her chariot with some gentleman unknown to me—yes, even to me! 'There she is!' and

'*La Belle Gautreau!*' could be heard on all sides as the crowd pushed to catch a glimpse." I paused for breath and put on my most scornful sneer. "You'd think it was the Virgin Mary come over from Lourdes for a visit!"

John smiled, then frowned. "I shall have to visit her at once," he said. "While she's still keen on the idea."

"Excellent thought," I said. And shrugged. "Of course, if you need moral support, I'm happy to go with you, you know."

John laughed heartily. "*Moral* support?" He strode over to where I was sitting and cuffed me on the arm. "You're the last person I'd turn to for that commodity!"

We were interrupted by the maid knocking at the door, bringing the day's newspapers. John thanked her, and turned to the front page of *Le Monde*. I roused myself with a sigh, and leafed through the other editions: *Le Soleil, La Republique, Le Pays, La Justice.*

"Good God!" John cried, his attention riveted to the front page. "Wagner is dead!" He read the news aloud, knowing I appreciated Wagner as much as he did himself. We had recently travelled to Bayreuth together for the latest work of the master, *Parsifal*, though not knowing it would be his last.

"*The brief telegram from Venice, dated February 13, announcing that 'Richard Wagner, the celebrated composer, died here at four o'clock this afternoon,' caused a sensation such as we have rarely witnessed; for the mournful news at once suspended even the semblance of antagonism, and those who had been ranged for years on opposite sides in the great Wagner controversy agreed to meet as brothers in the art which they mutually loved, and do homage to one who had so long and steadfastly fought for a faith which he held it a duty to enforce.*"

John took a deep breath and continued reading, "*Richard Wagner was, in the truest sense of the word a hero, for he set himself a task which, in spite of bitter opposition, he bravely worked out; and those who may judge him as he sometimes mercilessly judged others, must remember that in his stern and unyielding nature lay the real secret of his success.*"

John's eyes filled with tears, and he handed me the paper which I continued to read aloud while he paced to and fro across the room. When we had read through all of the accounts in the papers, we sat quietly in his apartment. A warming fire crackled in the fireplace and the shutters were closed against the winter chill. John had indulged himself, when he leased the *maison*, with a small upright piano in his private rooms, for his own pleasure and that of his more intimate guests. Thoughts of the great composer's death filled him with awe and sorrow, and he played several Wagner pieces from memory, softly and delicately, a tribute in his own way to a man of great imagination and vision. It was a shared moment of deep emotion and friendship for us.

We'd had the immense good fortune to be introduced to Richard Wagner while we were in Bayreuth two years before, through the influence and favor of a remarkable woman, Judith Gautier, the natural daughter of Théophile Gautier, the writer. Judith and Wagner were long-time lovers, it was said—and indeed, we saw the truth of it with our own eyes during that visit. But since that time, Frau Wagner had finally put her stern little foot down—on her husband's neck, it was to be presumed—and the affair was terminated. John said he could only imagine what Judith would be feeling today, and he was determined to pay her a visit to express his own grief and affection for the great man.

Thinking of one set of lovers led naturally to thoughts of another, and we talked a little further of Madame Gautreau and Samuel-Jean Pozzi. *Not lovers anymore*, I had said.

"But did you know," John asked me, "that Madame Gautreau and Judith Gautier are friends, *intimates* even, although Judith is nearly fifteen years older?"

"I didn't know that," I admitted, and tried to picture the two women, so completely different, as intimate friends.

Amélie was thin, pale and aloof in her classic angular beauty, while Judith was all softness, dressed in flowing diaphanous robes in the Japanese style, earthy, sensuous and approachable. And Judith was something more—intelligent, witty, well-read, and clever, very different from Amélie, who was more merely ornamental in her presence, in my opinion.

John stood up from the piano and lit a cigarette, then sat down next to me in an old leather chair.

"I hadn't given much credence to the rumors of Amélie's affair with Pozzi," he said, glancing over at me. "She seemed too stiff and proper a lady of society, and only recently married."

I merely laughed at that, but let him go on.

"But later," he said, "I came to understand just how powerful an enticement the good doctor could be." He smoked for a while in silence.

"The first time I met Pozzi," he said, "was more than two years ago—I went to his house with Carolus, to see the famous portrait of Pozzi's little wife Thérèse, you know, the one by Blanchard."

I nodded. It was insipid.

"I don't know what came over me," he said. "I suggested Pozzi should have his own portrait painted—and he turned to me and said—'and are you going to paint it?'" John shook his head with a quiet laugh. "I thought Carolus was going to explode. It was rather nervy of me."

"Nervy? I should say so," I returned. "But you knew very well what you were about, didn't you, dear boy?" I fixed my eye on him until he almost blushed, and nodded.

"I fell completely under his spell," he said at last. "The man was mesmerizing—highly intelligent, good-humored, suave, charming, handsome as the devil—there's no end to the words that could exalt his graces."

"I understand he's a tremendous flirt," I said, lighting another cigarette. "With both men and women, eh?"

"True, true," John said. "But mostly, that is, women were his primary object, physically. But he is not at all the stereotype of the self-absorbed hedonist. He's a brilliant physician and surgeon, you know."

"Yes, I've heard all about how he performs surgery while dressed completely in white, in order to prove to his colleagues that one can meticulously perform surgery without getting a drop of blood on one's clothes." I waved my cigarette at my friend. "A specialist in the new field of women's illnesses, isn't he?" I laughed and leaned my head back on the sofa. "And the women all flock to him, swooning under his careful, masterful touch—in more ways than one, evidently."

"I fell completely under his spell," John said again, thoughtful, and we were silent until the clock struck the hour and I realized I was late for a dinner I had arranged for some fusty bureaucrat, a colleague of my father's. I took my leave, and left John to his reveries in the winter twilight.

Dr. Pozzi

The young painter had been ushered into my boudoir where I was lounging with my wife Thérèse and my devoted friend, Comte Robert de Montesquiou-Fezensac.

"*Soyez le bienvenu, mon cher monsieur Sargent,*" I said, rising from my chair and greeting John Sargent with a friendly handshake and a slight bow, doing my best to combine the American form of greeting with the continental. You can tell much from grasping a man's hand in this way—I think the Americans have made an art of it, is it not so? My hands, which so many have commented upon, are dry and cool, very slender and sensitive, appropriate to my delicate surgical work. As I clasped his in my own, his painter's hand seemed to me large, very strong and sure, and quite warm. There was a sensation of a slight electricity as we touched—I saw it in his eyes, too. I am ten years older than he, but I am not being vain when I say I looked younger. I introduced my wife, and Sargent bowed to her from where he stood.

"And Robert, of course, you know," I said, waving a hand at my extraordinarily dressed friend reclining on a dark leather sofa: head-to-toe in shades of lavender, even his shoes, with a nosegay of violets pinned at his neck instead of a tie or bow. Robert always did everything for dramatic effect, from his swept-back black hair to the superbly cut Van Dyck on his chin, and above his lip, a waxed moustache with twisted, pointed tips, which gave him a barbed demeanour, offset by a mischievous sparkle in his dark eyes.

"I am a great admirer of your poetry, my dear Comte," Sargent said, and bowed slightly. I noticed that he immediately compressed his lips, as if to keep himself from spoiling his greeting by stammering anything further—I had heard that he was not a smooth speaker in company.

"Say no more!" cried the Comte, nodding graciously. "It is enough to be admired, especially by such a large and handsome young man." He peered more closely at the painter, and nodded again. "Of course, you were here with that tiresome man, Carolus what's-his-name—oh, *pardonnez-moi, mon cher, il était votre maître, n'est-ce pas?*" He smiled, his eyes narrow. "You are already a thousand times more talented than he, everyone says so!"

Sargent blushed fiercely, and sought for something to say. I decided to come to his rescue—that blush was utterly charming.

"There now, Robert, enough of this flattery," I said. "You cannot conquer every young man who visits me—and I wish to have all of *monsieur* Sargent's attention to myself just now, you know, for my portrait." I reached out one hand to Robert, and another to Thérèse, encouraging them to stand—and leave. "Yes, my dears, both of you," I insisted, silencing their protests. "I would not be able to keep my countenance if either of you were present, laughing at my vanity and mocking my humble features!" I shooed them out of the room without ceremony, closed the door, and smiled at Sargent with a conspiratorial wink.

"So, what can you make of me?" I said, standing at my ease in the middle of the room. It is true that I am very used to being admired, but I assure you I have no petty conceit in the knowledge that I have striking features and a well-formed body—they are not creations of my own, I simply maintain them. I asked him, "Shall this be a formal portrait? Shall I wear my operating theatre habiliments? Or what do you suggest?"

My informality began to put him at ease, and he gained a little confidence as he contemplated the possibilities for this portrait. He looked around the room, hesitating.

"May I see your wardrobe?" he asked.

How amusing! I led him through the ornate arched doorway into my dressing room; beyond this, I saw his eyes widen as he caught a glimpse of the bedroom—a high, four-poster bed with red and gold hangings, deep carpets and a gilded mirror on either side of the bed.

I flung open the doors of an immense oak wardrobe, and he stepped forward, eagerly feeling the soft velvets, the stiff brocades and smooth gabardines of the jackets and coats hanging there. After a few moments, he stepped back, shaking his head.

"Not the professional man," he said, mostly to himself, but I caught at it.

"Doctor Pozzi at home, then, eh?" I said. I took off the black velvet jacket I was wearing, and undid the tie at my neck, allowing the frilled collar of my shirt to fall away from my neck, and the front of my shirt to drift open slightly.

I saw the color rise to his cheeks again—and glanced in the mirror to see myself as he was seeing me: black hair formed a soft widow's peak above my forehead, hazel eyes fairly glittering with a lively sensuality, alert and smoldering at the same time. Was the painter imagining what it would be like to be touched by these long, delicate fingers, how thrilled my women patients must be to submit to my care?

Sargent put up his hand to hold me where I stood, and looked again around the dressing room. Something caught his eye, lying half hidden among silk pillows across a *chaise-longue*—my crimson dressing gown, my *robe d'intérieur*—such as one might wear for a late afternoon's assignation with a lover, perhaps. He released it from the tangle of pillows, and held it up to me.

Really, so very entertaining. I put on the robe, and tied it loosely about my waist with a thin red cord. Sargent stepped closer to me.

"If I may—" he said, seeming to find it hard to breathe easily. He tugged lightly at the white frilled collar of my shirt until it stood out around my neck, then did the same with the cuffs, allowing them to spill out from the scarlet sleeves. The folds of the gown fell gracefully nearly to the floor. He stepped back to see the effect.

"Yes," he breathed. "Yes, that will do quite nicely."

I turned to look at myself again in the mirror, smiling at what I saw. I turned back to him.

"And how shall I stand?" I said. I put my hands in the pockets, comfortably at ease.

"No, no!" he cried, startling both of us. "Your hands, your hands must be seen, indeed they must!" I removed my hands from the pockets, and lightly fingering the cord on my waist with my left hand, I raised my right hand to my chin.

"Almost," he said, and looked intently at me. "Lower your right hand, as if you were gathering your gown together, like so," and he stepped forward to position my hand where the lapels of the gown began to fold. He was so close I could feel his warm breath on my cheek; we were about the same height. His hand trembled slightly as he touched me, then he stepped back again.

I saw it in his face—it was perfect. *I* was perfect.

This was going to be a magnificent portrait.

ॐ *May 1883* ॐ
Paris

Violet Paget

"'Four corners and a void'? What on earth does *that* mean?" John threw the journal onto the floor impatiently, stood up from the sofa and picked up his cigarette from the ashtray.

"I think it refers to a child's game," I said. I had come to Paris for the Salon opening and an extended visit with friends. I looked up from the review I was reading, musing on the idea. "You know the one, where everyone stands at the edges of the room and the poor child in the center is 'it' or whatever, and has to run from point to point trying to make someone else take her place in the center? Not a bad notion, that," I said, "from a metaphysical perspective." I straightened the paper a little and continued reading. The Salon had been open for a few days and the reviews were pouring in; John's name was prominent in the articles written by the best, most popular critics.

Somewhat mollified, John stood smoking and looking down at me. "What does *Le Journal* say?"

"Well," I said, laughing, "if we make a list of adjectives that all the critics are using to describe you, it's quite gratifying!"

"For instance?" he prompted.

"For instance," I said, "*audacious, singular, revolutionary!*" I laughed again. "Here's my favorite—*weird!*"

John laughed with me this time, and smoked his cigarette thoughtfully.

"You haven't told me what *la famille Boit* thought of the painting," I said after a few moments, laying aside the review. "And have they gone to see it at the Salon?"

"Actually, no," he said. "Or rather, I'm not quite sure. They've seen it, naturally," he continued, moving over to the open window and leaning against the frame. "Both at home and again in December at the exhibition at the *Galerie Georges Petit*. Don't know if they're going to the Salon, I believe they may be leaving town very soon. Ned was rather vague about their plans last time I was there. As for the painting, Ned appreciates the whole, oh, *experiment* of it, you know, as I thought he would."

"And the formidable Mrs. Boit?"

"Oh, Isa came round rather quickly," he said, drawing in a deep breath of tobacco and exhaling slowly. "I don't think she really liked it at first," he said, appearing to think it through. "But, as I say, she came round, and likes it now."

"And the girls?" I gave my friend my whole attention with this question; I felt oddly eager to know the answer.

"Ah, well, how can one know the true opinions of children?" John said lightly. "And these girls are too well-bred to say anything but charming pleasantries."

I made a soft, snorting sound in derision. "You and I certainly had our opinions when we were children!" I said. "And I dare say we're as well-bred as the best of them."

John laughed, and smiled at me. "You, indeed, had *very* decided opinions, then and now," he said, "and no one was ever in any doubt as to what they were, I swear!"

I pursed my lips and tossed my head. But I returned to my question. "I see I have to be more direct," I said. "What did *mademoiselle* Florence think of the portrait?"

John left his post at the window and came back to stand above me as I sat on the sofa. I moved a little to one side and patted the cushion.

"Come, dear friend," I said, "stop towering over me in that intimidating way and speak to me from your heart, I beg you."

He slowly sank onto the cushion next to me, and fetched a deep sigh.

"Truly," he said, "though I do not really understand, I think in some way she was deeply offended, hurt, even." He leaned forward from out of the deep softness of the sofa, and smoked, his face averted from me. "There was *that* in her eyes when she first saw the painting, that looked for all the world like—well, I don't know what." He stubbed the cigarette out almost violently. "And still, whenever I visit, she looks at me with those huge brown eyes, so sorrowfully—I don't know what to do!"

"My dear John," I said after a few moments. "I told you to beware—the poor thing is in love with you!"

He shook his head vehemently. "How can that be? I never encouraged her, I vow—"

I cut him short with a firm hand on his arm. "Simply being there was encouragement enough—oh, not that you did anything, deliberately or otherwise!" I said, catching his wary look. "She's *fifteen*, the time for hopeless love, for infatuation—especially with someone like you, John, who frequents her father's house, a famous, handsome man about town—why, I'd be shocked if she *weren't* in love with you!"

John gave a wry smile, but still shook his head. "Please advise me, Vi," he said. "What can I do to make her feel better, to get over her *infatuation*, as you call it? How can I make her forget me, if indeed she has such feelings?"

I shook my head, frowning. "You probably can't do anything, it will simply be a matter of time. She'll weary of her unrequited love eventually—though the best cure, of course, is for a young, eligible man, perhaps closer to her own age, to come along and fall in love with her himself!"

"Ah," John said, a little grimly. "Perhaps I'd better bring Baby Milbank around to amuse her and take her mind off me!" He glanced at me, as I was looking at him questioningly. "He needs a little distraction himself these days—that mother of his is driving him mad." He told me briefly of Albert's last note to him from Baden-Baden—his mother's cocaine habit was worse, not better, and it was taking a toll on more than his parents' fortune—their marriage was rapidly crumbling as well.

He stood up abruptly. "I'll say no more of that, though," he said, and held out his hand. "Let's go out for a stroll and see what Marcel is serving for lunch."

"Brilliant notion!" I agreed promptly. "I'm starving—but first, I want to see the studio."

We climbed the broad, well-lighted stairway to the second floor. I noted with approval the change from his previous studio with its several flights of steep, dark stairs. Upon gaining the room, I burst out instantly in admiration.

"What a tremendous place!" I cried. "The light, the air—it's fabulous, John, charmingly perfect. And so well appointed," I said, lightly touching several little tables and chairs arranged around the sides of the room, with a large sideboard standing ready to serve claret, sherry or absinthe, crystal glasses winking in the sunlight.

"I'm so glad you approve," he said. "I've tried to anticipate the needs of my clients and their guests—and there have been many these past months, all with their tiresome relatives looking over one's shoulder." He spoke as if deprecating the work, but I could see he was immensely pleased.

"You have indeed been prodigious with your art this Spring!" I said, waving a hand at a cluster of paintings standing on easels. I noticed a set of drawings on a table, and stepped over to look at them more closely.

"Ah, *la belle Gautreau, n'est-ce pas*?" I carefully lifted the sheets, which delineated, in various sketches, Madame Gautreau's head in profile, three-quarters and even from the back, along with several poses of her on a sofa with a book, or just looking into the distance. I was amused. "How do you get on with the great beauty?"

"Monstrously!" John said, picking up some of the sketches and tossing them down again. "She is hopelessly lazy, spoiled, arrogant— and irresistibly charming!"

"Her very vices are her virtues, then?" I teased.

He shrugged and rolled his eyes. "She has need of every bit of charm to keep me at it—but thank God she has immense vanity, too, or she would have dismissed me long ago." He paused, one finger tracing the profile of the woman in the sketch. "She wants this as much as I do," he said, almost as if to himself.

He held his arm out for me to take. "But, devil take her, she has broken more appointments than she keeps—I shall be lucky indeed if this painting is ready for *next* year's Salon! This very day, she sent a note round before noon, cancelling the sitting for later today."

"How very rude!" I said, indignant for my friend.

"True," John said with a smile, "but then, she has freed me to be with you today, so I am grateful for that." We left the studio and descended the staircase.

Just as we reached the street door and opened it, we were startled by a handsomely liveried footman who had just raised his hand to knock. With a smile and a bow, he handed a small, pale blue envelope to John and hurried away. I caught a whiff of lavender as John tore open the missive with a frown.

"It's from Madame G," he said, and as he perused the elegant writing, he began to smile. "She invites me to stay for the summer—after Racing Day—at their estate at St.-Malo, *Les Chênes* it's called—and there she promises faithfully to 'pose for me each and every day, as there will be much less to do in the country than here in town, *cher monsieur Sargent.*'"

"And shall you accept the invitation?" I asked.

"*Bien sûr!*" he said, grinning now. "It's just the thing, don't you know! All that heavenly summer light, country air and country food—we will be so relaxed, *en famille*—just what I could wish! And Judith Gautier lives very nearby, in St. Enogat, and she will be there for the summer months as well—what fun!" He glanced at me; I was watching him closely.

"Of course, her old mama will be there," he said, "and her daughter, and one presumes, *monsieur* Gautreau." He folded the letter and put it in his pocket. "So you needn't look like that, Violet Paget! Madame Gautreau is safe from me!"

"The very idea," I protested, and cuffed his arm lightly. "It's not Madame Gautreau I'm concerned about!" But though I laughed as I said it, and allowed the subject to drop as we went in search of luncheon, I truly believe I felt a strong uneasiness, even a sense of looming disaster, that bode nothing but ill from this venture.

June 1883
Paris

Louise Burckhardt

I hadn't seen John for more than ten months—I fled Paris after that pitiful scene in his studio, literally coerced my mother into racing back to London, then booking the first passage to New York. I thought there I could learn to forget about him, but everyone was mad to talk about "our" famous painter, John Sargent, and of course mother wasn't the least bit shy about telling everyone how intimately we were connected. I don't know how I bore it.

We returned to London in April. I thought I was calm, even rational—I was merely numb. But I came back to enough of myself to realize how utterly selfish I had been, forgetting that I had any friends who might have troubles more sorrowful than my sad fancies. A letter from Isa Boit late in May troubled me greatly—little did I know to what tragedy it would lead.

A Letter to Louise Burckhardt from Isa Boit, dated 24 May 1883

My dear Louise,

Thank you for your last, I'm glad to hear your dear mother is feeling better, though not well enough to come to Paris for the Salon this year. At least Spring in London is comparable in terms of weather. Please give her my regards, and your sister and brother-in-law too when you see them.

You have asked particularly about our dear Florence. I know how attached you are to the child, and she is always asking about you as well. Since you left all those months ago, I have sorely missed our tête-à-têtes, my dear, as you are the only friend I have to whom I have spoken of our sorrow and apprehension about our girl. She moves about the house like a ghost, and weeps and frets so, I fear for her health. She is grown so thin, too, and I can hardly get her to eat anything substantial. The other night, Jane came running to me after we were all asleep, as Florence had risen from bed and was walking about the house—sleep-walking! This was not the first time, she said, but she had not told us before! It was most distressing.

However, I am very hopeful about an idea I have of taking Florence to see the great Doctor Jean-Martin Charcot at the Pitié-Salpêtrière Hospital. Ned is reluctant, of course, as am I, to submit her to further distress, but what can we do? I attended one of the Doctor's public lectures the other day, to get a better sense of his practice and thinking, and was quite astounded (and somewhat heartened, I think) at the progress he claims to make in patients—mainly women—who suffer from what he calls dissociation of consciousness, what used to be called hysteria, I believe. He says it is a nervous disorder and may be due to hereditary causes, which I find difficult to believe, not ever having had such problems myself. But there was a student of his there, an Austrian named Freund or something, who raised a question during the lecture as to whether or not this kind of "dissociation" might be only in the mind, based on traumatic events witnessed or experienced by the patient early in her life.

It was all very interesting but difficult to grasp except one thing: Doctor Charcot uses hypnosis to help bring his patients back to a more normal sense of themselves! He does not call it mesmerism so as to distinguish this new practice, which is scientific and not to be confused with the performances of mediums and spirit visitation. I witnessed his use of this technique myself, that very day, on a young woman he has been treating for this disorder. It was all very strange, very discomfiting I must say, but still, it was nonetheless remarkable in that, while hypnotized, the young woman spoke quite freely of some dreadful incident in her life—I simply cannot repeat the particulars here, suffice it to say it was quite dreadful indeed—and the Doctor insisted that her being able to speak of this incident was having a beneficial effect on her present condition. However, when he "woke" her from her trance, she did not remember a thing she had said! As if her present mind were being protected from the past horror!

Dear, dear Louise, I thank you for your patience with my long complaint. How I wish you were here, my dear, to talk to me and comfort me! Do let me know if you plan to return to Paris anytime soon, as I would dearly love to consult with you about Florence and this idea of going to this Doctor. You know you would be more than welcome to stay here with us. We do not plan to remove to Italy until late in June. With all my love, yours, Isa

I wrote back to her immediately, and was actually adamant with my mother that I go on to Paris alone—at least, without *her*. The

Curtises had come over from America on the same passage with us in April, and I became quite friendly with Ralph's mother. I knew they were planning on a remove to Paris before long, and it was more than easy to get Ariana to invite me to make up part of her entourage, and stay with them at their hotel. How kind and generous she has been—I had the feeling I was taking the place of the daughter she never had.

It was a bold plan, to travel without my mother, but I was nearing my majority, after all, and had begun to think of myself as an experienced woman of the world, who might do as she wished.

"You must come with me to see John's new studio and *maison*, Ralph, please," I said as we sat quite comfortably in the large breakfast room in the Curtis' suite at the Hôtel Crillon on the Champs-Élysées, finishing our *petit déjeuner* of coffee and rolls. I waved a sheet of note paper that I had been reading and then returned it to my pocket. "He has invited me, you know," I said, trying to sound nonchalant. "But I do not wish to go alone."

"I should be delighted, old thing," Ralph said, and smiled kindly. "I haven't seen it yet myself, though he's been there this half-year at least!"

Our brief *tête-à-tête* was interrupted by the entrance of Ralph's mother.

"Ah, dear children, there you are," she said, gliding over to the table and seating herself. She looked complacently from her son to me and back again. "Such a lovely couple you make, my dears," she continued, "quite the picture of domestic felicity. Ralph, I'll take some China tea, if you please."

Ralph immediately rose to fulfill his mother's command, turning to the tea things on a large, wheeled cart nearby, with the barest hint of a wink in my direction. I successfully concealed my smile.

"Dear Mrs. Curtis," I said, "please tell me that you slept well last night, after all the horrors of the crossing and the travel to town that you have endured."

"Oh, well enough," she replied. "That's all forgotten now, we are safe in the lap of luxury here." She looked around the room contentedly. "I have always loved *cette petite pièce*," she said. "Though I do wish

Alfred would think about getting some new fabric for the wall coverings, they are getting so faded, don't you think? *Merci, mon enfant*," she said as Ralph handed her a cup of tea. She addressed her attention to the steaming brew, and talked on, requiring little response from either of us.

After a few minutes we were joined by Ralph's father, an attorney and a man of substance and influence in international business and public affairs—but in society, all gave way before his wife. He was apparently content to figure in the background of the rich tapestries his wife wove of their life, amusing himself with the telling of an occasional "joke" to the assembled company—typically one at which he laughed uproariously and that no one else found amusing.

"Daniel," Mrs. Curtis said, "do come have some tea or coffee, I want you to accompany me this morning on some visits."

"Yes, my dear," he said, though he made no move in the direction of the table, having stopped to pick up the morning papers. He turned quickly to the sporting pages and ran an eye rapidly up and down the long columns of print.

"Hah!" he cried, and poked at the paper with one hand. "Just my luck! Reynard's busted an arm and won't row for Harvard in the regatta this month! Damn! That's going to cost me." He continued to peruse the article, muttering under his breath.

"Please do not swear in the presence of ladies, Mr. Curtis," said his wife, although I could see she didn't expect to be heeded, and didn't really care either. I caught Ralph's eye and exchanged amused glances with him over the table.

"Damn and blast," said Mr. Curtis. Throwing the paper down, he walked over to the table, kissed his wife on her cheek, and nodded cheerily at me and Ralph.

"Well, Miss Burckhardt," he said, "ready to hit the town and empty the shops? Racing Day draws near, eh?"

"It does indeed, sir," I said, smiling brightly. "I am in great need of a new hat, of course, and hope to find just the thing this week."

"But not today," Ralph interposed. "Louise and I have some visits of our own to make," he said, turning to his mother. "We'll walk or take a cab, Mother, so you needn't worry about dropping us anywhere." As he spoke, he rose, folding his napkin decisively, his movements rapid in an effort to escape questions from his mother.

However, as he guessed, she was only too happy to allow the two of us to be off with each other.

I rose also, and kissed my hostess good-bye. "I shall see you later, dear ma'am," I said. I had dressed myself with unusual flair this morning, in a slimmer profile of a gown that had caught my eye in a Paris pattern book very recently, and which my dressmaker had re-created with great accuracy. It was very becoming and a little audacious in its own way.

Mrs. Curtis patted my arm and smiled her approval. "Lovely," she said. "Just lovely."

"What on earth can your mother mean by saying such things?"

Ralph and I strolled arm in arm along the Champs-Élysées, enjoying the sights and sounds of the famous city spread before us. Since coming away from London, I had felt as if a great burden had been lifted from my shoulders, and I couldn't deny that my mother was a large part of that burden. I felt so light-hearted that I found I could laugh at Mrs. Curtis' innuendos, where the very same sort of thing from my mother set my teeth on edge.

"What now," Ralph protested. "Are you saying you don't want to marry me and form an habitation replete with domestic felicity?"

I laughed aloud, and Ralph looked at me approvingly. "I'm glad to hear you laugh again, old girl," he said. "Even if it's at my expense!"

"Oh Ralph, I would of course marry you happily, you know that, except—" here I broke off, my gaiety momentarily checked.

He looked at me most kindly, and patted my arm.

"I daresay we would shuffle along together very well," he said, as if I hadn't spoken. "End up happily ignoring each other, much as my old ones do."

"I have a very different idea of married life," I said seriously, "very different from just about anything I've seen so far." I looked at Ralph, my brows knit. "Am I delusional? Is there such a thing as wedded happiness between equal partners, where a man and a woman can actually talk to each other of things that are important, and make decisions together, and even create something important, something new?"

I spoke with an intensity that stopped Ralph in his tracks.

"You mean, more than just children and family and all that?" he said.

"Yes," I said, then more firmly, "yes, more than just that, something that endures, that is larger than one person, or even two people together."

"Ah," he said, once again moving us forward down the boulevard. "You speak then, of literary or artistic creation." It was not a question. We walked on a moment in silence.

"Dear Louise," he said, pressing my arm against his. "I don't believe you are delusional, but I do think—I wonder—such a path does not necessarily lead to happiness. Indeed," he said with a sigh, "I'm very much afraid that it has little to do with happiness, in a mere, homey, mortal sort of way, don't you know?"

"I don't want *mere, homey, mortal* happiness," I said. "Perhaps I do not even want to be married!" I paused, catching my breath. "I want *life*. I want to be truly *alive*."

And in a soft undertone, barely audible, I added, "I want *him*." I had thought I was over him, but the numbness I felt in America and London was overtaken by being in Paris again, knowing he was here, breathing the same air as I—and then his note, asking me to come to his studio. I took a deep breath, suddenly realizing I had not been breathing.

"Well, well," Ralph said, patting my arm again. He sighed just a little, and looked around for a cab. "The odds are against you on that one, old thing," he said. "But let's go see him anyway, shall we?"

The door was opened to our knock by Guido, John's manservant and *major domo*, who glared at us with reddened eyes.

"*Che cavolo vuoi?*" he said, addressing Ralph and leering at me.

"*Con chi credi di parlare?*" Ralph demanded, highly indignant. "Whom do you think you're talking to? Move aside, you buffoon!" He stepped forward aggressively, causing the man—obviously drunk—to lose his footing and fall onto the floor of the vestibule. Ralph escorted me around the fallen sot who was muttering incoherently and waving his arms as he struggled to stand up.

PORTRAITS OF AN ARTIST

"What did he say to you?" I asked, stifling a giggle.

"Oh, *what the hell do you want*, more or less," Ralph said. He glanced at me, amused. "I'm guessing you don't know a lot of street Italian, eh?"

We stood at the foot of the stairs, uncertain whether to go up to the studio or look in the other rooms for John, when a halloo from above caught our attention.

"I say, what's all the ruckus down there?" It was John's voice, cheerful and loud.

"Just your *porco* of a *major domo*!" Ralph called back.

John appeared at the top of the stairs, then rapidly descended. He started to say something but broke off when he saw I was there as well as Ralph.

"Welcome, both of you, to my humble home," he said, catching up my hand and kissing the back of it. His eyes widened as he took in my *tout ensemble*—I was more than nicely dressed, he couldn't help but notice, in fact, I'm sure he thought me utterly fashionable! The deep blues and greens of my ensemble gave me a more consequential air, much better, I thought, than the faint pastels and ivories I used to favor, along with most young women of my age and class.

"My dear Louise," he said, "how extremely beautiful you look today!"

He was interrupted by a groan at his feet, and he looked down in disgust. He motioned for us to go up the stairs, and turned back to Guido, who was slowly regaining his footing, though unsteadily. In a lowered voice, he reprimanded the man in Italian and half pushed him back down the hall, declaring he would deal with him later.

Moments later, John joined us as we stood in the doorway of his studio, clearly admiring the space, but hesitating to go further, as it appeared a portrait sitting was in progress. With a slightly over-hearty manner, he invited us in, leading us over to his sitter to introduce us to her.

"Madame de Belleroche," he said, bowing to a red-haired woman elegantly dressed in a frilled dark evening gown with a long train, cut low across the bosom and nearly falling off her creamy shoulders. "May I present my friends, Miss Charlotte Louise Burckhardt, and Mr. Ralph Curtis, both of Boston—and the more civilized parts of Europe."

"*Mais oui, madame*," Ralph said, "I hope you know that I am well acquainted with your son Albert, and count myself as one of his good friends and an admirer of his painting."

"Indeed, *monsieur* Curtis," she said, her head inclined graciously, "I have heard your name from my son—he, in turn, admires *your* work." To me, she merely smiled, but I saw there was a brittle, vacant brightness in her eyes that gave them a spark without depth.

"I hope our presence will not interrupt your sitting," I said, addressing John as much as Madame de Belleroche. But I knew that John's sessions were often played out before an audience of admirers, friends, relatives and assorted individuals who endeavoured to charm away the tediousness of a sitting in various ways—singing, playing piano, or gossiping about the latest scandals and affairs. It actually seemed remarkable that Madame de Belleroche was here alone, but John's next remark explained it away.

"In point of fact," he said, "we were about to finish for the day. Baby—that is, Albert," he corrected himself with a smile at his sitter, "has just stepped out to get us some smokes and a bottle or two of something nice to drink. But do make yourselves comfortable while I just finish up here."

He nodded at Madame de Belleroche, who resumed her position, one arm crooked lazily against her waist, the other languid at her side. John turned his attention to his easel while Ralph and I walked about the room, stopping at the large windows to admire the view of the rose garden below.

The slam of the street door and footsteps running upstairs announced the arrival of Albert, juggling two bottles of champagne and a basket of foodstuffs as he came in the door.

"Excellent!" he cried, catching site of Ralph and me. "Curtis, you rotter, where have you been keeping yourself?" He carefully unloaded the goods from his arms onto a side table, and strode over to Ralph, encompassing him in a sound embrace. Ralph had told me a good deal about Albert, and I'd heard something of him from John last year. Albert was younger than both of them by some five or six years, slightly built, but strong, with dark hair and dark eyes, a handsome but often brooding fellow. He seemed in one of his rare happy moods today.

John set down his paintbrush, called out "*C'est tout pour*

aujourd'hui!' and walked over to introduce me to Albert.

"My dear Belleroche," he said, and turning to me, took me by the hand. "Let me introduce you to one of the loveliest and cleverest women of my acquaintance, *mademoiselle* Louise Burckhardt." He smiled as Albert made me a courtly bow, and added, "And she has an extraordinarily beautiful singing voice, as well, especially when accompanied by yours truly."

My heart beat fast as John kept my hand in his, pressing it with seeming ardor and occasionally raising it to his lips as the small group conversed. The tone of his voice, too, made me observe him closely, and I saw glances pass between him and young Albert—teasing, flirting glances, and on Albert's side, possibly a little jealousy? I noticed Ralph watching all of us, including me, and I felt my color rise under the press of John's attention.

What was he thinking? What did he mean by such attentions? I told myself to make nothing of it—he had been perfectly clear all those months ago when I had confronted him. I thought I had made strides within myself, had indeed gained a new, even thrilling sort of independence and distance from my emotions. Our brief affair had awakened something new in me, and our final break had created a resolve to be a different woman. But a wave of desire for him, physically, shook me to the core, and the day it had begun—so long ago it seemed— flamed before my eyes.

We had drunk a little too much wine, and had danced our way out onto the terrace under the warm summer night sky. John's friend Beckwith had obligingly been playing some lovely pieces so we could dance, but it was heaven to get away from him and be alone with John—truly alone. We walked onto the grounds of his friend's country estate, wandering further from the house than we realized. Suddenly there was complete quiet and darkness all around, only the starlight above and a faint glow from the direction where the house lay. I had taken a few steps ahead of him, then turned, and he was right there, towering above me, his eyes bright with wine and desire. I took a step nearer to him. We kissed, and desire shook me. I began to undo the buttons of his shirt.

"Are you sure?" he had whispered. "Louise?" His lips burned my cheeks, my neck—his hands travelled down across my breasts, and I trembled at the thought of my body opening to him. I kissed him fiercely—I wanted him to know that this was my decision, that I knew the choice I was making.

I was not to know how indelible a mark his body would leave, pressing against mine with a weight both physical and emotional.

"Yes," I said. "Yes, please."

And this day, as I stood there in his studio, my hand caught in his own, a tiny flame was sparked again, and I suffered an ecstasy of rising hope that I could not quell.

Albert de Belleroche

The season was over, the Salon closed down, Racing Day at Longchamp was nothing but a dusty memory, and everyone who was anyone was travelling to the coolness of the summer shores, especially to Brittany. John had passed many a summer there, he told me, both with his family and alone, on the beaches at Cancale and St.-Énogat—his very first submission to the Salon, in 1878, was a painting of the oyster gatherers at Cancale, and it had won an honorable mention. He was going to stay at the Gautreau estate, called *Les Chênes* for the great and ancients oaks trees on the property, which was a little inland from the coast, but not beyond a comfortable carriage ride from the sandy beaches with their cooling breezes and welcoming waves.

I was terminally envious, and jealous as well. All I wanted to do was be with him, watch him paint, paint alongside him. And he was going off to that dreadful woman's house in the stupid country.

We spent the last, hot days in the city packing up his paints, brushes, and rolled canvases into boxes and trunks, along with yards of drapery, rugs, costumes, vases and figurines collected from trips to Morocco and Spain, Germany and Italy. Wherever he landed, his "portable studio" as he called it, would provide him with the back-drops and accoutrements he had come to depend upon for inspiration in arranging portraits. With Madame Gautreau, he was hoping, as with Doctor Pozzi, that her own sumptuous wardrobe might ultimately provide the clothing he needed to do justice to her beauty—but he wanted his things with him nonetheless. I'm very much afraid I grumbled a good deal as I was presumably helping him, but I have a rather gloomy temperament and the heat was not helping.

"You could have at least waited two more days to dismiss Guido, don't you think?" I growled as I struggled with a box of canvasses on the stairs. He had dismissed Guido at last—we had all been complaining about him for months—and I know John breathed a sigh of relief as the sullen drunkard left the house—with a generous month's pay he certainly hadn't earned. Clotilde, the cook, thanked John with tears in her eyes, and promised him his favorite dish every day if he wanted it. I always marvelled at how John's servants were so devoted to him, except Guido.

The evenings of those hot days of mid-summer were an entirely different matter, however. He and I, along with other friends, frequented our old haunt from student days, *L'Avenue*, where the owner delighted in the artists who came there to eat, drink and sing. She had a supply of large sketchbooks always at hand for her patrons to fill with drawings in charcoal, ink and pencil—of her, each other, and any person or thing that happened to be in the café, day or night. It was too hot to even think of sleeping, and the people we met in the cafés were full of good spirits and stories, jokes and tales to while away the time into the small hours of the night.

His last evening in town, we sat at an outside table about to drink yet another bottle of the café's quite acceptable *vin blanc*, which I was just bringing out with a plate of cold chicken and bread—I couldn't abide waiting, I went to get it for myself. John was idly paging through one of the sketchbooks that lay on a bench nearby.

"What are you looking for, my dear?" I asked as I put down the wine and food. "You look very intent." I turned to the cover of the sketchbook and saw that it was dated 1881.

John looked up and grinned, his teeth very white against his dark beard.

"I did a sketch of you, two years ago, in this very book," he said. "It was the very night I first saw you. But I can't seem to find it."

"You *won't* find it," I said, seating myself and pouring wine into our glasses, "because it's not there." I smiled at his inquiring look.

"I have it," I said, and felt myself blushing a little. "I took it for my own, about a week later."

We watched each other's eyes, a warm silence growing between us. Our hands were very close on the small table, holding the stems of our glasses. John moved his forefinger to lightly graze the back of my hand, and we continued to gaze at each other steadily.

"*C'est si bon*," he said softly, and lifted the glass to his lips.

"*Vraiment*," said I, also drinking. "*C'est très bon*."

We ate and drank in silence for a time, the night sounds and laughter swirling about us. We seemed enclosed in a golden halo, and no one came over to our table, or called out to John to begin a round song, as had been happening earlier in the evening.

"Tomorrow you go to St.-Malo," I said.

"Yes, to paint *la belle Gautreau*," John said, his mouth twitching slightly.

"I'm jealous," I said.

He looked at me through half-closed eyes, squinting as if to get me in focus.

"You have a look of her at times," he said, and sat up a little straighter. We were sitting very close together in the semi-darkness at the edge of the café patio. He touched my face with lightly, tracing my chin, then the bridge of my nose and my high forehead. "Your nose is not—thank God!—as distinctive as hers, but your chin, your brow, your mouth and neck"—here his hand caressed my throat—"very similar." He laughed softly, and drew back his hand. "I think you two are twins, cosmic twins."

"Then you will think of me when you are with her," I said.

He simply gazed at me, smiling. "Let's go home," he said, and standing up, he tossed some coins upon the table. I rose, very unsteadily. I could never absorb alcohol as John could—no one could—and I leaned against him, an arm around his waist, and he put his arm around my shoulders. We bid *au revoir* to the remaining company, and walked slowly toward the studio on Boulevard Berthier.

The next morning, I lay in his bed, thinking of him—now in the carriage, now at the station, now on the train to St.-Malo. I hoped that he was observing little of the passing countryside, that his thoughts and senses were bound to the taste of me still on his lips and my scent clinging to his flesh. I closed my eyes, feeling the thrill of the night all over again, the surge of desire strong and sweet. I hoped he was feeling the same and that even when he eventually fell asleep, he would awake and want me again.

❧ July 1883 ❧
Paris

Louise Burckhardt

Isa had begged me to accompany her and Florence to Dr. Charcot's office, and I agreed, though with much inward trepidation and not a little skepticism. We were ushered into a small but comfortable room and asked very politely to wait a few moments. I was relieved to see we were the only ones there—I had half expected, I admit, that there would be a variety of strange, mumbling, hysterical women awaiting the good doctor's services.

The renowned neurologist, Dr. Charcot, was a portly gentleman with soft, white whiskers, piercing dark eyes, and a kind, grandfatherly manner. He stood at the doorway to another, larger room, and invited us forward, directing Isa and me to sit on a sofa on the other side of the room, partly obscured by some potted palms, but with a clear view to where he then sat down with Florence. She was exceedingly nervous, though she held herself quite still, her eyes huge, the pupils dilated. *A good subject for hypnosis*, I imagined. We could hear everything he said, in a low, soft tone, as he spoke to Florence.

"Now, my dear, please sit down here with me. Your mama and your friend are just over there, you see, so you are quite safe, and I trust you will find I am not such an ogre as I seem to be, eh?"

His assistants had interviewed Isa prior to this appointment, she had told me, and my imagination told me he would read with interest the account of the family: the early deaths of two sons, the four beloved daughters, their constant travels across continents and oceans, Florence's lack of female development, her nervousness and trouble breathing, the journal that she kept, and the sleep-walking episodes. I tried to think as a doctor of his training might do, considering Florence's artistic father and her mother's restless engagement in society—an intriguing family picture mixing a wealthy bourgeois foundation with bohemian sensibilities. The fact that they were Americans, I speculated, would add an interesting challenge to the doctor's expertise.

"Now, *mademoiselle* Florence, may I ask you some questions?"

Florence nodded hesitantly.

"Do not worry, my dear," said Charcot, smiling. "This is not a school examination, I am only going to ask you about *you*—and will you promise to answer me as truthfully and completely as you can?"

Again Florence nodded. She was breathing a little easier under the influence of the doctor's soothing voice and manner.

Isa and I had to strain to catch Florence's soft responses. We exchanged glances from time to time, and held on to each other's hands, Isa clutching hard whenever she saw a flicker of emotion pass over her daughter's face. Charcot was asking her about her interests, what books she liked to read, what were her favorite songs—topics to calm her down and help build her receptiveness to the treatment to come.

"Do you have any idea why you sometimes have trouble breathing, Florence?" he suddenly asked directly.

"No, *monsieur le docteur*, I'm sure I do not know," she replied, appearing undisturbed by the question.

"And has your mama mentioned to you anything about your sleep-walking?" he asked, though he knew full well that she had been spoken to about it. When she didn't respond right away, he spoke again. "Do you know what I mean by sleep-walking, my dear?"

"*Oui, docteur*, I have heard of it, and read about it in books, but I don't think it is anything I have done. Mama or Jane would certainly have said something to me—it would be very strange indeed to do such a thing." He saw she was growing nervous, and turned the subject to indifferent matters for a few more minutes. Then, glancing quickly at Isa and me, he took both of Florence's hands in his and held them quietly for a few moments.

"Florence," he said, "I'm going to ask you to follow some instructions for a little while, so that I may help you and your dear mama to feel better about *you*, and help you. Will that be all right?"

"*Oui, docteur*," she said in a whisper.

Charcot released her hands and placed them gently on her lap. He moved a bit further from her on the sofa, and took something out of his pocket that gleamed gold in the light from the lamps around the room. The curtains had been drawn before we entered, creating a dim, warm environment.

We watched, scarcely breathing, as Charcot raised his arm slightly above Florence's head, and set in motion a gold watch on a long chain that hung from his hand. Like a pendulum it swung, regular as clock-work, and as we watched the movement back and forth, back and forth, we heard his deep, even voice as he spoke to Florence.

I shook myself to keep from being drawn in by the spell of the words and the doctor's voice. I squeezed Isa's hand, but there was no response.

"See ... it ... swing, see ... it ... swing, back ... and ... forth, back ... and ... forth, breathing in, breathing out ...," the doctor chanted in a low tone. After a few minutes, during which time Flor-ence had scarcely blinked, he raised his other hand and replaced the watch in the line of the girl's vision with his fingers set in a V-sign. His hand drew closer and closer to Florence's face and when he al-most touched her, her eyes closed and she gave a little sigh of release, although she remained sitting upright.

All was silent in the dim room. I glanced anxiously at Isa, and saw that her eyes, like her daughter's, were closed, and she seemed in a state of semi-conscious restfulness. I wanted to shake her and wake her up, but I feared it would do some harm, either to Isa in her pre-sent state, or to Florence, if I caused a commotion during the session. Biting my lips, I sat tensely awaiting what would happen next.

"Florence," said Charcot, speaking in a normal, everyday tone of voice. "If you can hear me, please nod your head."

Florence nodded.

"Good, my dear, that's very good," he said. "Now, I want you to listen to me, and let your thoughts follow along with what I am saying, do you understand? Please say 'yes' if you understand."

"Yes," Florence said.

"Good. One more thing, I am going to touch your hand, like this—" and he tapped the back of her right hand with a firm forefin-ger—"and when you feel that tap on your hand again, you will wake up and be yourself again, do you understand?"

Florence nodded.

"Now, Florence, I want you to picture yourself in your bed at night, all safely tucked in and feeling sleepy. The fire is going out, ticking softly in the background as the embers die away, and you can hear the wind in the trees just a little…can you feel yourself in your bed, Florence?"

"*Oui, monsieur*," she answered, her voice sounding sleepy and small.

"You are falling asleep after a long day, Florence, a happy day with your sisters and your mama and papa, yes, but now, as you lie almost sleeping, some feelings come to you, some thoughts of something not so happy, not so nice…a memory stirs inside you, yes, a memory of something unhappy, something that makes you sad and anxious when you feel this way, late at night and in your bed—"

I could see Florence's face from where I sat, and watched as the girl's countenance clouded and became anxious; tears began to seep from her closed eyes, and her breathing grew labored.

"You are feeling this sadness, this worry, from deep inside you, Florence, and it distresses you so that you want to seek comfort somewhere, yes, someone you can go to for comfort … your sister Jane, or perhaps your mama—" Charcot let his voice trail off and merely observed his patient with keen eyes.

To my astonishment, Florence opened her eyes and rose from the sofa, slowly, and moved as if in a trance across the room. She walked very near to where I sat with the equally entranced Isa, and put her hand out as if she were turning a door handle. She opened the invisible door, and stepping into an invisible room, closed the door behind her and walked a few more steps.

Charcot rose and very quietly drew near Florence. He spoke again in a soft voice.

"But Jane is asleep, yes, you do not want to disturb her rest … so you come back to your own room, yes, you return … but your heart is full … perhaps you will write down in your journal what you are feeling … that will help … yes write it down."

The Doctor followed Florence as she retraced her steps to her "bedroom," and quickly placing a pencil and a book of blank pages into her hands, he encouraged her with quiet words to take up the pencil and write her thoughts in her journal.

For several minutes, Florence wrote. Page after page was turned, and she covered the blank pages with writing until finally she paused, put the pencil down and let the book fall from her lap.

"I'm so tired," she said. "I want to sleep now." She leaned back on the sofa, her eyes closed, her hands at her sides.

"Of course, my dear," Charcot said. "You have done very well, and you need to rest now. In a few moments, I will wake you, and you will feel refreshed and calm."

Charcot picked up the book and pencil and set them aside. After observing Florence for several moments, he leaned forward and tapped the back of her right hand with his forefinger, saying in a loud voice, "Florence, wake up!"

I felt Isa start at my side, waking along with her daughter, and looking around her as if she didn't know quite where she was. Florence sat up, eyes opened, and smiled at the doctor politely.

"Do you have any more questions for me, *monsieur le docteur?*" she asked.

"My dear, we have been going along quite pleasantly and for now, I believe I have asked you enough questions. It is time for you to go home with your mama and your beautiful friend here." He took her by the hand as he spoke, rising from the sofa, and led her back to her mother.

Isa said not a word, but looked at me with mute distress as she tried to come to terms with her own confusion. I took matters in hand.

"*Merci, monsieur le docteur*, this has been an extraordinary session," I said, forming my thoughts as I spoke. "I presume that Madame Boit can expect some kind of report from you about what you have learned and what—" I hesitated, and then nodded toward the journal Florence had written in, assuming the Doctor would prefer that Florence not know about it. "Whatever you can tell us about what you have observed today, we would be most grateful."

"*Bien sûr, mademoiselle*," said Charcot, and bent over my hand with a courtly bow. His keen glance took in Isa's somewhat bewildered state, but he said nothing about it.

"Good day to you, Madame Boit," he said, bowing to her as well. "You shall have my report before long."

He ushered us to the door of his office, where he handed us over to a hovering aide who escorted us to the foyer and the street door.

We stood in the bright afternoon sunlight, blinking a little at the change in atmosphere, and smiling a little uncertainly at each other.

Florence, who seemed the most collected and nonchalant of the three of us, was the first to speak.

"*J'ai faim, Maman,*" she said. "May we go somewhere for an ice, or some cakes?"

Three days later, the report was delivered to the Boits, and Isa immediately sent for me. I found her nervously pacing the drawing room. Ned had taken a short journey with the two eldest girls to visit a family of cousins staying in Aix, and would be gone for a week. Upon their return, the plan was to start, at last, for Italy, for their villa outside Florence. The younger girls were with Henny in the nursery, so we two were assured of as much quiet and isolation as we needed to review Doctor Charcot's report.

"Do read it yourself, my dear Louise, and then tell me what you think. I am half mad from trying, I can hardly understand what it says!"

Isa handed me some sheets of paper, closely written over with a crabbed handwriting, in French.

"Please translate it aloud for me, dear Louise," said Isa, sitting down and leaning her head back against a sofa cushion. "It's hard enough to make out his chicken scratchings without having to read it in French! And I know you will be able to make better sense of his meaning than I."

I complied with her request, and scanning ahead every few lines, began to translate the doctor's report, stumbling only occasionally at a medical term.

My dear Madame Boit,

Your daughter Florence proved to be a most natural subject for hypnosis, as you no doubt perceived, thus indicating to me immediately that she suffers from the neurological condition of dissociated consciousness, in less scientific terms known as hysteria. This can take several forms; in your daughter's case, her symptoms of sleep-walking, difficulty breathing when upset, and extreme passivity accompanied by lack of appetite and energy, all indicate a pre-disposition to this condition. The specific causes of this condition, which occurs almost exclusively in the female population, are at present unknown, but there are theories that it is inherent as a certain inherited predisposition, which may manifest itself upon the occurrence of a "triggering event" — for example, a traumatic experience, physical or emotional, that perhaps even at the time of its occurrence is not considered significant, but later preys upon the patient's unconscious mind to bring forth the physical symptoms as described above.

The exercise which I induced Florence to undertake — of writing as if in her journal — revealed no single, particular past event to which I could ascribe her current condition. There was, as you, Madame, mentioned to me, some indication that the deaths of her brothers holds a deep, morbid fascination for her, but she only touched on this subject once, in relation to her dread of "being like them." I believe that further treatment under hypnosis would reveal more about this particular obsession she has developed.

The majority of her writing, however, appeared to be centered on her strong emotional attachment to a certain gentleman, an artist it would seem, whom she only called "He" (with a capital 'H') and in relation to whom she appears to be experiencing very deep albeit dramatic and apparently unrequited feelings of love. Given her tender age, I presume it is likely that she has become enamored of perhaps a friend of the family, but one who she feels is not likely to return her affections, whether owing to age or other circumstances. It is very common for girls her age to fall violently in love with older gentlemen from time to time; it usually passes with a little time and the application of common sense and often, upon falling in love with a suitable person.

However, in Florence's case, due to her increasing symptoms and her likely neurological condition, it is my recommendation that she be entirely removed from this gentleman's presence (if you can identify such a person?) for some lengthy period of time, and perhaps even from Paris and her familiar environment herein, in order to break her infatuation and provide distance for her from the surroundings that feed it. If you are able, Madame, I entreat you to remove with your family to some other habitation, one that does not have such emotional resonance, for several months to see if Florence improves in a different setting.

Naturally, if her condition does not improve, or worsens, I would very much appreciate your writing promptly to me to let me know, so that we can decide upon a course of treatment at a later date. If upon your return to Paris some months hence, you wish to pursue further hypnosis treatment for Florence, I remain at your service to attend to her.

Yours most sincerely,
Jean-Martin Charcot

I finished reading, and gazed blankly at the pages for a few moments, collecting my thoughts.

"I suppose," I said, "it's rather obvious who the 'gentleman' in question is," and looked up to see Isa looking intently at me. I held the pages out for her to take, which she did automatically.

"Yes," Isa said, looking away. "I read what Florence had written, and it's quite clear it's John." She folded the papers carefully and put them back in the envelope in which they arrived.

There was an awful silence for a few minutes.

"May I ask," I said cautiously, "if you have discussed this with Ned?"

Isa shook her head. "No, not yet," she said, then sighed deeply. "Of course, I will, as soon as he returns with the girls." She looked sharply at me. "Do you advise me to keep this from him?"

"No, my dear Isa, I wouldn't dream of advising such a thing," I said instantly. "I just wondered, perhaps, the effect on him—and his friendship with John—" I left the unspoken question hanging.

"Do you think that he—that *Ned*—would in any way think John is at fault?" Isa asked, with some anxiety. She looked more intently at me. "Do *you* think John is at fault?"

I hesitated, although I knew this would make Isa even more anxious; but I wasn't sure how to express what I was thinking.

"No," I said at last. "I can't imagine John in any way deliberately toying with the affections of any girl so young, and one so much like family to him—indeed, he is not the kind of man to *toy* with anyone's feelings—he may, perhaps, not know the strength or direction of—" I broke off, aware I was saying too much. "It's just that—such a situation might make them feel awkward. Shall you—" I paused a moment, "—shall you tell *John* about it?"

Isa appeared to think it over, then shook her head. "I would not put Florence in such a delicate position," she said.

Another, longer silence ensued, at the end of which Isa rose and looked out the window to the city below her. She straightened her shoulders firmly, as if having come to a difficult decision.

"I believe we shall go home for awhile," she said.

"'Home'?" I echoed.

"Yes," said Isa. "To Boston." She turned back and smiled sadly. "I believe if we had raised our girls in America, this would not be happening," she said. "There, they would have breathed the clear air of the New World, far from this old and degraded culture, and stayed fresh and unspoiled."

"Oh, Isa," I cried. "Do not think so! You cannot think that being on American soil, or Italian soil, or French, could make such a difference, can you?" I thought of my own upbringing in the capitals of Europe, and knew I would not exchange it for all the *clear air* of America. "And do not say your daughters are spoiled—they are angels, they are children of light, dear friend—and it is thanks to you and Ned that they are so!"

I rose and went to her and held her close as she gave way to a sobbing grief in my arms.

"She will be all right," I soothed her. "You'll see, Florence will get over this most trying time, and all shall be well."

But my heart misgave me, even as I comforted my friend. I wondered should I tell John about it myself, without Isa's permission? There was something deeply troubling about all this, but it only hovered at the edges of my thoughts. At length I decided that as long as the Boits were going away anyway, it might be best to let it all blow over, and keep silent.

Amélie Gautreau

Les Chênes, St.-Malo, Brittany

"Je suis fatiguée, tout cela m'ennuie!" I rose abruptly from the sofa where I had been holding a languid pose for what seemed endless hours. "I'm bored, I want something amusing to happen," I said, pouting—as if that would have any effect on my oblivious painter. It was getting very hot, and I was actually sweating, that black gown was so heavy, even though my shoulders and arms were uncovered.

I walked over to where John sat at a small easel, still scratching charcoal onto heavy paper, and came round to look over his shoulder. "Ha!" I cried. "I look like I'm dying, there on that sofa." I laughed, a low tease of a laugh—my mother was very proud of the way she taught me to laugh—as I leaned closer to him, one hand just resting on his shoulder. My hand looked so very small against his tremendous person. "You've caught that brilliantly, *mon ami*," I said, "Madame Gautreau, dying of boredom!"

My fingers caught at the longer hair on the nape of his neck, and I tugged at the locks, seemingly absent-mindedly. I felt a tremor race through his body at my touch, and he sat perfectly still. My hand moved slowly down his back, under his shirt—he was dressed for the summer heat, no tie or jacket, a soft white collarless shirt open at the neck—and my fingers played lightly across his bare shoulders. I pressed my body more firmly into his. It was no more than flirtation, and yet, a wave of dizziness engulfed me, and I wondered, with an

168

amused, detached sense, if I would actually faint.

The deeply plunging neckline of my gown was close to his face; he could inhale my favorite fragrance, lilies suffused with heat. He turned his face toward the scent and the softness and I gripped the back of his head, my fingers clutching his hair, keeping him away, tantalizing him with the closeness of my soft flesh. Then I released him, and he plunged into the depths of my breasts, his lips searching the whiteness of them, the moisture and the warmth. I actually gasped and again grasped his head, this time pushing him to me. His arms went around my waist, I knew he could feel my nakedness under the black gown—I wore no stays, no undergarments—he had dressed me that way, *the better to achieve the clean line of your form,* he had said, that I knew he longed both to portray and to possess. It was the most exotic dress I owned, daring and audacious in the way it used the bourgeois respectability of black to contrast with the outrageously sensual, clinging fabric and deep décolletage.

I placed my hand under his chin and pulled his mouth up to mine. He stood up from the chair, holding me fast against his largeness, lifting my feet off the floor, blind, heady with desire. "Enough," I gasped when finally our lips parted. "Enough. Put me down."

He almost didn't comply—I could sense the desire and the power he felt to brush aside my protests, my teasing, and take me there, on the floor of the small, light-filled studio he'd set up in the south wing of the house, far from the noise and traffic of servants and guests and my ever watchful mother. We had, this morning, been perfectly alone—and this, this *liaison,* had been simmering for days, the promise of it bright in our eyes, from almost the moment he'd arrived two weeks ago. It was very tempting.

He set my feet back on the polished wood floor, his breath quick and shallow. I smiled up at him—though twenty-four and the mother of a five-year-old girl, I was a mere sylph next to his man's body—and from that perspective, I had a sudden thought about some gossip I'd heard from friends in town. I almost laughed.

"Do I look like your precious Albert now?" I said. He looked as if he had been struck, and his grip on my shoulders tightened briefly; he was fighting back some impulse with all his strength. Then he let go of me, and stepped back. I leaned up to bestow a parting peck on his cheek, and smiled as I turned away, without a backward glance.

Albert de Belleroche
Paris

I received several letters from John, sometimes two a day, as he sweated it out in the country. Here's one that sums up what he was going through.

To my darling Albert,

Damn, damn, damn! Dozens of drawings so far of this wretched woman—sitting, standing, in profile, three-quarters face, her back to me, looking straight at me. Pencil, charcoal, pen and ink, watercolors, pastels—nothing suits, nothing stands out! At least I found the perfect black dress! Even she, who adores clothes, had been ready to fling them all out the window after trying on so many. Three weeks and nothing to show for it—it has never taken me this long to hit upon the exact effect I'm looking for!

And the heat is getting to me—to her as well—she's throwing herself at my head! Don't be jealous, little one, although I am amazed that Don Pedro hasn't thrown me out on my ear—though it should be she that's tossed. But then he's probably used to it.

It's like soaking in a warm bath, like being in the womb, enclosed in a woman's world: Amélie, her mother, her daughter, the servants. Like my own family all over again—the matriarchy, the domestic goddesses of the household, the best of it graciousness and comfort—the worst of it confinement, passivity and petulance.

Never mind my complaining, dear Albert. I long to see you, and hope to get this portrait done and meet you somewhere outside the city in August, somewhere cool and cleansing.

Yours ever, JSS.

Despite his attempt at comforting me, I was jealous. I knew him, I knew his desiring soul and body as I knew my own—and the intimacy of portrait painting so easily leads to intimacies of a more carnal nature. I wrote him back immediately.

My dear fellow, you must come back to Paris for the Bastille Day celebrations, indeed you must. I miss you entirely too much, and Beckwith says the same. We simply cannot give you over to that dressed-up mannequin you are endeavoring to paint—one who, by your accounts, is spoiled, lazy, maddening and even unpaintable! I am green with envy and red with jealousy! Do take a break—do come to us, Helleu is here, too, and wild to see you again. The city will simply be uninhabitable after the fête, so maybe we can take a little journey to some cool place for a day or two before you go back to the grind. You must come! We will expect to see you at home on the 13th—or we will send the gendarmes! Love ever, Baby

I smiled as I re-read my note—I knew it would make him laugh, and bring him here to me. It's what he needed! Come back to Paris, be among men again, drink hard and long, get out from under this female world he'd been sinking in—that would do the trick—that would restore him to himself.

Amélie Gautreau
Les Chênes,
St.-Malo, Brittany

The evening after that torrid morning scene, a sudden cooling breeze sprang up after dusk, helping immensely to restore everyone's spirits. John seemed more cordial toward all of us than he had lately been, and there were several more guests at *Les Chênes*, newly arrived that day, which suited all of us perfectly—we had been too long in each other's company and were growing uncivil. And even when John took me aside before dinner and mentioned he would be going back to Paris for several days, it didn't matter to me. My guests were going to keep me too busy to pose anyway—we were already planning excursions and boating trips, picnics and forays into the countryside. It all seemed for the best.

The dinner party was lively and fun. It was someone's birthday,

and everyone insisted on each person preparing a toast for the cele-
brant. John excused himself for a moment, and hurried back with a
sketchbook and crayons. He wanted to capture the moment, he said.
When he returned, Pedro was giving a very creditable toast, and the
company cheered his effort, drinking the lovely cold champagne that
was being poured, and asking for more.

I leaned forward slightly, holding out my glass with my right arm
completely extended, almost uncomfortably elongated. I wore a low-
cut dark dress with a transparent netting across my shoulders and
arms—the appearance of a covering that revealed everything. My hair
was bound in a tight chignon, allowing the lines of my neck to be seen
perfectly.

As I stretched out my arm, all fell silent, waiting for me to speak.
I could see that John was drawing as quickly as he could, capturing the
forward movement of my arm, the slight tilt of my profile away from
him, the softening effect of the cloth and the flowers. He sketched
rapidly, filling in the light colors with crayons, fixing the dark background. I deliberately took my time, enjoying the deferential attention
of my guests. I assumed a slightly melancholy air—how people love it
when I am dramatic! Something told me John's sketch would turn into a beautiful painting—I felt something settle between us—the
beginning of the right thing.

I spoke the words of my toast, holding out my glass at the same
time, and finished up with a lovely compliment to the birthday guest,
which drew applause and acclaim. John didn't stop drawing to join the
toast—he was completely absorbed, as he should be.

The next morning he was up and gone to the train station long
before my eyes opened to another boring day in the country.

Letters

A Letter to John Singer Sargent from Violet Paget, dated 5 July 1883—London

Dear Twin,

Abominably hot here in London, season almost over. Shall be packing my duds soon and returning to Siena—her lofty hills and olive groves may afford some relief, both from the heat and the insufferable, mindless gossip of the so-called Bohemians of Chelsea. With the exception of Mrs. Morris, who is invariably gracious and kind, all the rest of these people are driving me insane with their petty wonderings as to who is sleeping with whom (imagine!), whose creative genius is blocked due to any number of bizarre ideas (wrong diet, drinking too much, drinking too little!, disordered sleep, an *outré* style of cravat—apologies, I get carried away).

Nonetheless, I am gathering absolute mountains of material for my novel, which I shall call "Miss Brown" I think, not only because it is the dullest and commonest of common names, but also because brown appears to be the one color that all these people detest—it is, in my estimation, far too pedestrian and useful a color, unlike mauve or puce or cerulean, to be of interest to such delicate sensibilities.

Speaking of which, I had a very long, satisfying chat with Mr. Henry James—a great admirer of yours, if you did not know this—he agreed with me most emphatically when I said you were the greatest painter of our time—and he nodded quite knowingly when I explained to him the basis for my projected novel, so he is obviously an intelligent creature. I believe I shall dedicate the book to him, what do you think?

Lastly, and I apologize for this hastily written note, as I expect the carriage at the door any moment—yet another evening party!—I met your friends the Boits at an 'evening' two days ago, they are on their way home to Boston, they told me, for a long visit. With what frequency you Americans cross the wide Atlantic! I am quite impressed. They seemed in good spirits, and although I thought they looked a little queer when I mentioned your name, they asked me to send you their love in my next letter. Mr. Boit then said something awkward about not having taken proper leave of you before they left Paris, but his wife gave him such a look that he quite stuttered to a halt! Is it indelicate of me to ask if there is something amiss between you? Perhaps Madame didn't like the *Portraits d'Enfants* as much as she seemed to?

Enough! I shall write you more when I am happy in Siena.

Love ever, Violet

A Letter to Louise Burckhardt from Isa Boit, dated 9 July 1883—London

Dearest Friend,

We are about to set out for home, the ship sails at ten tomorrow morning. What a relief! I never thought I would be so eager to see the homely Boston harbor loom into view, and all the staid, sincere, honest buildings filled with plain-spoken people, my own people. I have become so very tired of "society" in England and on the continent—a little time in my own land will do wonders, I am sure, both for me and Ned, and of course the girls. I believe we may stay there for a year or two, maybe forever. You must come to us, I insist—it's time you saw more of your home land, too, my dear.

As for Florence, I hesitate to write too much, from a superstitious fear of causing an undesirable change—by which you will understand that she is tentatively better. Ever since her 'treatment' by Dr. Charcot, she has seemed to me calmer and less emotional. But she has always liked to travel, and you know we were in Paris for more than two years, with only a few weeks here and there in other places, so maybe the journeying is good for her. All the girls appear to be looking forward to their trip across the ocean. They do not recall any earlier trips, naturally, although Florence has said she remembers the movement of the ship and the great expanse of grey water. I will be so pleased to present my daughters to their aunts and uncles, and cousins, and other relatives. I am quite satisfied within myself that we are doing the best thing possible, and Ned feels just the same.

In deference to your insight, I feel I must tell you that my husband *was* upset to no small degree about having to bar his friend John from the house, and I know he was unhappy that he could not provide a reasonable explanation or make a proper farewell—but that is all behind us now, and for the best. We left town in such a hurry, as I told him, that we saw no one else at all, and practically spirited our girls out of Paris in the dead of night, so if John was offended, it was no more than any other of our friends suffered.

Finally, I must say this, that I have been so full of my own worries, dear Louise, that I fear I have not done well by you, as a friend and confidante. There was *that* in your face which, upon reflection, makes me believe you too were anxious and possibly distressed about something, but in my selfish concerns about my Florence, I am sure I have neglected the duty of a friend by not drawing you out and allowing you the chance to speak your own heart. Again, I urge you to think about coming to us in Boston, where we may be able to spend a good deal of time together.

Please write often, if you can, and I promise also to be a faithful correspondent in the months ahead.

With all my affection, Isa

A Letter to Violet Paget from Ralph Curtis, dated 15 July 1883—Paris

Dear Violet,

La fête nationale yesterday was a bang-up day indeed, though I know you don't have the zest for that sort of thing as I do, but surely, you would have liked it, I think. It's only been a few years since they made it official, and it has grown into an enormous sort of hoop-la, with endless parades and even more endless speeches on every corner. All we lower-caste types, you know, hung around just for the event after the snobs left town—I ran into John and his troupe late last evening, at *L'Avenue*, of course, took me quite by surprise that *he* was there, also Beckwith, Baby Milbank, even Paul Helleu, whom I haven't seen for an age—as I thought he (meaning Scamps) was buried in the country with the Gautreaus. We ate everything in sight, sang lots of *nationaliste* songs and drank the place dry, I swear. Helleu looked quite well, said something of getting married soon—did you know that Scamps, last year, bought a painting from Helleu and paid him a thousand francs for it? Had it from Helleu himself, said it saved his life at the time, turned everything around. What a fine boy our John is, eh?

Scamps and I had a relatively quiet half-hour's talk long after midnight, while the others were dancing and singing with a bunch of *jeunes filles* in from the country, it would seem. I asked him how he was getting on with *la belle Gautreau* and he made the most horrifying face! You would have laughed aloud. Appears she's not only being difficult in and of herself, but he can't quite find what it is he wants to do with her—as you know, an impossible situation for John, who is used to 'ask and have' when it comes to painting. He was in good spirits, however, and seemed bent on relaxing for several days more before returning to *Les Chênes* and attempting the portrait again. As always, he feels confident he'll strike on something.

My father has gone back to Boston, he can never stand being away from business very long, but *Mater* has fortunately commandeered the lives of a few ex-pats who always seem to turn up whenever dear old Dad leaves town, which thank God gives me a little breathing room as she doesn't notice if I'm there or not (so much)—and she has another interest these days, you'll be amused to hear—Louise Burckhardt! Seems they became best pals on the crossing in the Spring, and Louise will be accompanying us the next month or so as we journey across the Alps and over to Florence. I do believe *Mater* really likes her, although personally I think it's the young lady's excellent singing that has occasioned (in part) this invitation—you know how Ariana loves a musical salon.

Do people ever stay in one place anymore? I wonder if, someday, I might have a home of my own—and dare I say, a wife in that home to soothe my lonely heart? But it is all nonsense, of course, I am perfectly fine as I am. Do *not* start, I beg of you, imagining anything between me and Miss Louise—strictly platonic there.

Perhaps we will see you in Venice in September?

Regards to all your people. Ralph C.

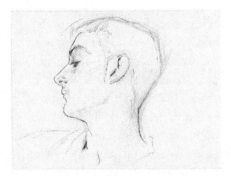

Albert de Belleroche

Haarlem, The Netherlands

I had talked John into joining me and another friend, Paul Helleu, on a little side trip up to Haarlem before he banished himself to St.-Malo again. We were on the night train and, I thought, were all asleep in the stuffy compartment, when we were startled awake by John's voice calling out.

"Inspiration! I need inspiration!"

John spoke loudly and banged his fist against the window of the train compartment, rattling it in the wooden frame and thoroughly waking us, and probably the people in the next two compartments.

"Dash it, man," grumbled Paul. "I need sleep!" He turned to his other side on the leather seat that was serving as a makeshift bed. "Six a.m. train … no sleep … too old for this sort of thing," he muttered, and immediately fell asleep again.

I sat up half-way, stretched out my arms, yawned, and fell back against John, whom I'd been leaning on, asleep, for the past hour. I looked up at him and smiled.

"We're going to see Frans Hals," I said softly. "You have always called him one of your *maîtres*, have you not?"

John returned the smile, and nodded.

"Well, then," I said, closing my eyes again, "look to him for your inspiration. We'll be there soon."

John shifted in his seat so he could put an arm around me, and let my head find a pillow on the greatcoat he had folded in his lap. I felt him looking at me, and after a moment, he rustled out a sketchpad and pencil and began to draw my face. Later, he told me that I had looked uncannily like Amélie from this perspective, much as she had looked on his last night there, when he drew her giving a champagne toast at a birthday party. He had told me all about it, of course, and said that my face, however mysteriously, combined and concentrated his desire with his art at this moment in his life.

"Good day to you, *Heer* Sargent," said the aging keymaster at the Haarlem City Hall. "We were expecting you," he added, motioning all of us through the separate entrance for visitors to the art galleries. John saw the quizzical glance from Paul, and smiled as he heard me say in a low aside, "He telegraphed from Amsterdam when we changed trains." We had availed ourselves of a bath and change of clothes at the small hotel where we had reserved rooms, devoured an excellent meal at a nearby café, and thus refreshed, we had gone straight to the gallery.

There were hundreds of paintings, large and small, from centuries of Dutch masters crowded into the dim halls and rooms of the City Hall annex, recently built to better manage the increasing flow of visitors. Paul and I stopped to admire several paintings along the way, but John headed directly for the large gallery at the back where he knew most of the Frans Hals were displayed.

We caught up with him eventually, and found him standing, hands shoved in his pockets and head tilted slightly, in frowning concentration before a full length portrait of a tall, confident aristocratic man in a cape and a plumed hat, his hand on the hilt of a sword at his side. As Paul and I drew near, John started talking about the painting.

"Hals did few full length portraits," he said. "As you can see"—gesturing with his hand to the other paintings in the room—"most of his people were upper half only, and with nothing much else in the portrait, maybe the back of a chair, or a small table to rest a hand upon." He stepped back from the portrait. "But as you see here," he continued, "in this one, he filled up the background with all sorts of stuff—red draperies, furniture, all sorts of…distractions."

Paul was amused. "Does the student dare criticize the master?" He shook his head. "How the mighty are fallen—"

I looked intently at the painting. "I see what you mean," I said.

"In his other portraits, even some of the large groups, the background is neutral, often dark, with just a shadow thrown against the wall." I walked over to view more closely other paintings nearby that were as he described. "See," I said, "in these, the subject is more intensely...*there*...more alive, somehow, with nothing to distract from the features, the posture, the essence of the human being portrayed."

"And the single chair, or table, he often places in the lower left or right corner, but just in part," John added, pointing to such a one. "It anchors the subject, it throws off the symmetry but yet provides a lovely balance, don't you think?"

"Yes, I see," Paul chimed in. "And the curve or lines of the anchor as you call it, are echoed in the lines of cloth, or the figure of the sitter, yes, very well done indeed."

We continued to walk about the room for some time, each occasionally calling the others over to view a certain effect of light or color, the positioning of a hand, the reflection in a sitter's eyes.

After a thorough examination of the Hals room, we walked in a desultory way through the narrow passages of the gallery and finally out into the light of day, blinking and looking about as if wondering where we had got to. The cobblestone streets, the low roofs of the humble buildings that nestled close to the City Hall, the lowing of a milque cow very close by, perhaps behind a wattle lean-to that was attached to a small house—all contributed to a sense of awaking in a different time.

"What century is it?" I said, laughing.

Paul swept an imaginary hat from his head and made a deep courtier's bow, one foot stretched out before the other. "*Soyez les bienvenus, messieurs!* You are most welcome to the sixteenth century!"

"And what," John said, returning the bow, "does the sixteenth century offer us that is better than the nineteenth?"

Paul thought it over a few moments. "For the life of me," he said at last, "I can't think of a single thing! Our modern world seems replete with everything one could need or want!"

"I'm with you there," John said heartily. They both turned to me—I was busy admiring a dark little window embedded in the wall of a house, multi-paned in diamond shapes with heavy leading between the pieces.

John chuckled. "Baby, on the other hand, would find no better era than the early Renaissance to suit his mournful moods, isn't it so, my dear?"

I smiled and touched the glass of the window with a gentle hand. "There was something so much more *spiritual*—I can find no better word—in the way men went about their work in those times," I said. "Everything invested with a living sense of the eternal, of something larger and higher and better than one's miserable life, wasted as it is in snatching greedily at unsatisfying moments of pleasure to obscure the inevitable truth of one's mortality."

"Lord, Milbank," said Paul. "You are truly a poet as well as a painter to derive all that from one dirty little window stuck in a shabby wall."

"I'll allow that as a compliment, Helleu," I said, taking the ribbing good-naturedly. I glanced at John, who was watching me with a thoughtful, even serious look on his face.

"That is how you see your life?" he asked tentatively. "Lacking the spiritual? Sunk in misery and greedy sensuality?"

My eyes were locked on his face, watching him intensely. We might have been alone in the little alley behind the gallery of great art.

"Not my own life," I said at last. "The world I find myself in, yes, but as for me," I placed a hand on John's arm, "at this moment in my life, I feel riven with the spirit, I feel lifted up as by angels."

John, unable to speak a word, barely nodded, his lips compressed tightly against the cry that both our hearts desired to decant into the air that danced around us.

August 1883

Here and There

The Boits in America

Florence

They didn't know I was nearby, my Aunt and Uncle Cushing, there in the upper hall of their great, airy house in Newport, or I'm sure they would not have said what they did. I slipped behind a convenient pillar with an extra shield of potted palms when I saw them step out of Aunt Olivia's dressing room—I was trying very hard to stay out of everyone's way, it was very wearying to be always answering questions and being polite.

"They do not even sound like Americans," Aunt Olivia was saying to Uncle Robert, my mother's eldest brother, as she stopped momentarily at a mirror in the hall to adjust her necklace, preparatory to going down to dinner.

"Who, Isa and Ned?" he said, patting her shoulders as he stood behind her, smiling.

Olivia regarded her image in the mirror and, satisfied with her looks, turned round to gaze severely at her husband. "No, you goose," she said. "I mean the girls, of course!"

"Why, I thought they were very charming, very well-behaved indeed," he returned, holding out his arm to escort her down the hall.

"Yes, yes, but that is *not* what I mean, and you know it," she said.

Uncle Robert grinned at her, a twinkle in his eye. "Of course, my dear, but still, I thought all the girls, and Florence especially, were so, well, sophisticated, so *knowing*, didn't you think? They quite swept me off my feet."

He walked her down the hallway to the top of the grand staircase.

"That's precisely what I'm talking about," insisted Aunt Olivia, stopping him again. "For girls their age, and especially Florence, as you say, they are entirely *too* sophisticated and worldly." She snapped open her fan with a quick shake of her wrist. "All that whispering in French to each other, and sitting so primly at tea, watching everyone with those huge eyes." She shook her head, and prepared to descend the staircase, gathering the folds of her gown in one hand. "It's not natural," she said. "It's not…American."

"Well," said Uncle Robert, "I for one appreciate little girls who do not run about and giggle and make too much noise with their endless chattering and games and such." The Cushings had three such girls, and two young boys as well, and it was not hard to imagine that the lot of them created more noise altogether than their father—a lawyer and recently a judge—could often tolerate.

"Nonsense," Aunt Olivia said sharply. "Our children are spirited, normal, playful American children, and you know you love and adore them."

Uncle Robert gave a half sigh, and patted her hand. "Yes, my dear, as I love and adore you, and always shall."

She softened a bit at this declaration, and kissed him lightly on the lips.

"Come," she said, "let's go down to your sister and Ned, and see what's what with them. My intuition tells me there's something going on." She arched her eyebrow as her husband tried to hide a smile. He recovered quickly.

"I have the greatest respect for your intuition, my dear," he said, and started down the staircase.

I waited until they were safely down the stairs, then ran off to my own room to share this conversation with Jane—we both laughed heartily at hearing how we were perceived.

Isa

We were ten around the dining table altogether: Ned and I, my three brothers, Robert, John Gardiner, and Thomas—and their wives, Olivia, Susan and Frances. Two ladies who were girlhood friends of mine had also been invited: Anna Sargent and Florence Dumaresq. Newport in the summer was a traditional gathering place for Bostonians as well

as New Yorkers, who travelled north to escape the heat and confinement of the city for the ease and freedom of the country, and both of
these ladies were staying at family homes nearby. I was happy to see
them, and happier still that they provided a little relief from my formidable brothers and their even more formidable wives, especially
Olivia.

The conversation had turned to exclamations of praise and wonder at the paintings, recently exhibited in the United States, by John
Sargent—a person of great interest to everyone, as he was not only
Anna's cousin, but also related in various ways to other members of
the company, by marriage or business or blood.

"We saw his tremendous *El Jaleo* of course," Susan was saying,
"last October in Boston."

"We saw it in New York," Frances said.

There was a brief pause. A butler glided around the table, pouring
more wine.

"I thought it a most unusual and creative painting," continued
Susan.

"It was very large," said Frances.

"Has anyone seen *The Lady with a Rose?*" asked Anna Sargent. "I
saw it in Boston at the Museum of Fine Arts, just a few months ago,
May, I think it was."

"I saw it in New York in March," said Frances.

"You know, of course, who 'The Lady' is, don't you?" Susan said,
looking around archly.

There was a pregnant silence.

"She looked somewhat familiar—" Frances said tentatively.

"The portrait was of my very dear friend, Louise Burckhardt," I
interposed, somewhat impatiently. "She and John are great good
friends, and the painting was a sensation at the Salon last year—as
well as the gypsy dancer." I smiled graciously at Anna. "Your cousin is
so admired in Paris, and is the talk of the town—and one of the most
eligible bachelors!"

"Oh, the Burckhardts, of course, of Brookline, yes?" Olivia said.
"They aren't here very much, are they?" She looked musingly at me.
"At least you two," she said, waving her fork at Ned as she addressed
me, "come back every so often to touch the sacred ground of your
birth."

Florence Dumaresq laughed at this, an agreeable, throaty sound. "Dear Olivia, one would think from your remarks that you are quite the staid provincial, and had never set foot in Europe yourself!"

Olivia bristled slightly. "I have nothing against being cosmopolitan, as you well know, Florence," she said, "but not at the expense of bringing up one's children among strangers and foreigners, far from home and the influence of one's family."

It was my turn to bristle, despite the fact that I had voiced a similar opinion to Louise before we'd left Paris. I opened my mouth to speak, a furious spark in my eye, when Ned intervened.

"Did we not tell you of the magnificent portrait that John painted of our four daughters?" he said. "I wish we had been able to bring it back with us, but John is still entering it in exhibitions, I believe, in London and on the Continent." He turned with a smile to Olivia, at whose left hand he was sitting. "It was greatly admired at the Salon in May, and was said by many critics to be highly original and daring in its presentation."

If Ned had wished to introduce an easier subject, he was woefully deceived in his choice.

"I cannot imagine subjecting my daughters—or my sons—to any such exhibition that could conceivably be called 'daring'!" Olivia said. "What were you thinking, Isa?"

So direct and disconcerting a question caused the whole company to fall silent.

"My dear—" Robert murmured, sending a mild warning glance toward his wife.

I looked at my sister-in-law with eyes of steel, although my voice was mild and engaging. "Ned and I *both* were thinking how charming it would be to have the innocence and childlike grace of our daughters captured by one of the foremost painters of the age," I said. "We are perfectly delighted with the painting, as are the girls"—there I faltered for a second—"and it matters not to us what adjectives the critics choose to describe so ingenious and innovative a portrait." I paused, touched my napkin to my lips, and smiled. "I'm sure you'll think very differently when you see it."

"Of course she will!" Robert interposed heartily. "I'm sure it's a portrait of the highest quality, and such as your very charming daughters deserve. They're delightful children," he added, not to much purpose, but it served to turn the conversation onto safer ground.

"I can't conceive of better behaved children," John Gardiner spoke up quickly. "Why, I sat with the two littlest ones out on the terrace this afternoon and they were so quiet and polite! I was very impressed."

"Your dear Florence, my namesake," said Florence Dumaresq, "is, I am happy to see, a very well-read, intelligent girl. I had a lovely conversation with her just before we were called to dinner, and I assure you, you have a real jewel there."

With such kind of remarks and judicious flattery, my ruffled feathers were smoothed—I know I'm prickly!—and Olivia was reminded of her role as hostess, and admirably restrained her candor for the remainder of the dinner.

But later that night, in the privacy of our own rooms, I gave way to the indignation I was feeling most bitterly against the judgement and innuendos of my eldest brother's wife.

"What right has she to pronounce against how we have raised our daughters?" I said, furiously pulling at the pins in my hair as I sat at the dressing table. "Insufferable woman! I never liked her," I added, applying my hairbrush in rapid strokes to the waves of hair that fell around my shoulders. "It's enough to make me want to leave here instantly…self-righteous Americans…provincial indeed!"

"Here, my dear, let me do that," Ned said, gently taking the hairbrush from my hand, and stroking it in long, soothing passes through my hair. His loving touch calmed me after a few moments.

"How I have always loved to brush your hair, my Isa," he murmured, and I reached a hand up to catch his, holding it tightly, my eyes blinking away tears.

"At least Florence Dumaresq appreciates our girl," I said after a while. "I have always loved that woman, she was the best friend to me, that year my parents died."

Ned murmured agreement, and let me talk myself into a better humor.

"Do you think, Ned," I asked, "that Florence is getting better? Do you think she is recovering at all?"

He frowned, and considered the question. "I hesitate to say 'yes', my dear, but it is early times, as yet. We've only been gone for two months, you know." He continued to brush my hair. "What do you think?"

I sighed. "She still talks of John incessantly, so Jane tells me," I said. "But there has been no more sleep-walking, at least. That seems an improvement, does it not?"

He nodded thoughtfully, and kissed me on the top of my head.

"Let us trust a little more to time and to travel," he said. "Florence cannot help but be diverted by all the new places we are introducing her to."

In the silence and darkness of the night, lying awake next to my sleeping husband, I began to regret our coming to America, and felt a longing to be in Italy again, at Cernitoio, the villa outside Florence where we had frequently been staying. Perhaps there, where we and our daughters had always been happy and carefree, our own dear Florence might find the peace she so sorely needed.

Florence

Mon cher ami,

What a strange place America is! So many tall buildings, so many people and carriages and so much noise of trams and people selling things in the street—at least, in New York and Boston, which we saw on our way here, to Newport. It is very different from other large cities I have seen, like Paris and London and Rome, but it is hard for me to say exactly how. And although our relations are very nice to us, the way they talk hurts my ears, it seems loud and harsh, and they all stare at one so directly!

My cousins ask a lot of questions, some of them quite personal, and they make remarks that are very impolite, like Jeremy telling Jane she didn't look like an American girl, and then asking her if she knew who the President of the United States was—which of course she did—but then, she got him back by asking him if he knew the name of the President of the French Republic, or the Queen of Great Britain, or even the Pope in Rome, and he didn't! But he didn't seem to care that he was ignorant, either—I'm not sure I like Americans, if they are all like Jeremy.

On our way up here, the drive led us through some very pretty towns. I would have liked to have seen where Mama grew up, in the great house at Bellmont, but she says other people own it now, which is sad.

How I loved talking to ma tante Florence, for whom I was named. She is not really my aunt, but she asked me to call her that, and Mama said it was fine. We had a lovely talk about books, and the names of birds and flowers we both liked, and she has been to Florence and seen Cernitoio, though long ago, and of course, Paris and London. Talking with her made me feel very grown up.

And how shall I speak of The One whom I love best? We are so far away from Him now, and Papa said there wasn't any time to see Him again before we left Paris—that was so dreadful, I thought, and it seemed to me that perhaps it was somehow on my account—that perhaps He didn't want to see me anymore, and Papa was trying to spare my feelings! Oh, I pray it is not true. If only I could write Him a letter! But I know that is not at all a proper thing for a young lady to do. Good night for now.

Judith Gautier
Les Chênes, St.-Malo, Brittany

I joined the small party at *Les Chênes* one late summer evening, a day or so after I'd received a note from Amélie, inviting me to stay for a few days. I know she added as an enticement that John Sargent would be there— an enticement, indeed. We sat down to dinner late, we two women, John, and Amélie's mother. Pedro, my old friend, was out canvassing the town for votes, as he intended to run for election to represent the county, but he was expected back before long.

"I cannot believe it has been six months since I've seen you last, John," I said to him, turning to him in a lull of conversation between me and Amélie about some mutual friends. I smiled at him warmly, to help put him at ease. "Your visit to me, at that dreadful time, brought me back from the brink of—I don't know what!" I shook my head. "I was in a very bad way."

"The death of that great man," he said, "was a heavy blow indeed not only to his friends but to all the world, especially that part of it that appreciates the genius of great music." He lifted his glass and looked around the table.

"To Richard Wagner," he said. "We loved him."

We ladies lifted our glasses in turn, and took a sip of wine to commemorate the passing of the great composer.

"And how do you get on with the portrait of my dear friend?" I

192

asked, glancing at Amélie and smiling. "We all expect nothing less than a masterpiece, as of course you know."

Amélie spoke up.

"He makes me stand for hours like some *mannequin* in a shop window, it's *very* uncomfortable," she said in a petulant tone. She waved her hand impatiently and knocked over her wine glass, spilling it on the tablecloth. Her mother cried out in dismay and, seizing a napkin, began to soak up the wine while Amélie simply leaned back, a pouty smile on her face. I contributed my napkin to the cause, and exchanged amused glances with John.

Madame Avegno glared at her daughter, but said nothing to her directly. She rang for a servant to take the wet cloths away, and this accomplished, she addressed me on the subject of the painting.

"Our dear *monsieur* Sargent is making splendid progress," she said, with a reproving look at Amélie, "despite my daughter's lack of appreciation." She smiled benevolently at John, and continued. "He painted the most wonderful vision of my daughter last month, just before he went away to enjoy *la fête nationale*, and has most generously given it to me. I have had it framed already, and it hangs in the sitting room— you shall see it after dinner, or tomorrow perhaps."

"I am gratified that it gives you such pleasure," said John. "It was the beginning of a new idea, one which I am counting on to work for this portrait."

I found this very interesting, and asked him to tell me more.

"Actually," he said, "I was further inspired in Haarlem a few weeks ago, in the presence of the old masters—Van Dyck, Rembrandt, and especially Hals. You are familiar with Frans Hals, perhaps?"

"Yes, definitely," I said. "I have spent hours in the City Hall annex perusing his work—he has a simple palette that is very striking."

"You've hit it quite on the head," he exclaimed. "Those dusky browns and greys, the neutral background, the dramatically framed draperies and figures—this is the foundation of my vision for Madame Gautreau." He raised his glass to Amélie, who nodded graciously.

A slight commotion in the front hall announced the arrival of the master of the house, and a few moments later he entered the room. Amélie, in a gesture of complaisance unusual to her, actually held out her hand for her husband to kiss, and even allowed him a brief embrace—the more easily accomplished as she sat while her husband stood at her side. He greeted me with a kiss on the cheek, but barely nodded in John's direction.

"So, my dear son-in-law," said Madame Avegno courteously, "tell us of your success in gathering the votes of the people, for I have no doubt they are eager for you to represent them."

Pedro remained silent as he motioned for a servant to pour him a glass of wine, then hitched himself up into a chair specially made for him that brought his torso on a level with other diners at the table.

"Not so well but that it could have gone better," he said.

"How enigmatic of you, *mon cher*," said Amélie. "Do tell us more."

"Bah!" said Pedro, and drank deeply of his wine.

"I imagine," I said, knowing I could speak with the freedom of a long-time friend—I was closer in age to Pedro than to Amélie, and had long been a neighbor of his, before he married—"that the people hereabouts are reluctant to trust someone who is so little known to them." I pursed my lips in a comical smile. "After all, your family has only been coming to St.-Malo for some hundred years or so, barely a nodding acquaintance."

John laughed, a soft bark of appreciation, and received a cool glance from Pedro, who sniffed and held his glass up to be refilled. "Peasants," was all he said.

"Well, surely they will consider you more deserving of their trust after the picnic we are providing next week, here at *Les Chênes*, for them all," Amélie said with a sniff. "I shan't have a moment's rest from tomorrow morning until this time next week, and," she added, as if struck by a sudden thought, and turning to John with an insincere smile, "I'm afraid, *cher monsieur*, that I will not be able to sit for you at all during this busy time."

John hid his impatience admirably, and merely smiled as he reached for his glass of wine.

"But then," I said, "as I have no more love of crowds and political events than John can have, perhaps he will honor me with a visit for a few days at *Le Pré des Oiseaux*?"

Amélie opened her mouth to protest, but appeared to think better of it, and closed her lips tightly. Pedro, however, spoke up immediately. "Excellent notion, Judith dear, I'm sure *monsieur* Sargent would be delighted to get away for a bit!"

And you'll be delighted to have your wife to yourself, I thought. John turned to me and accepted my invitation with becoming gratitude. I felt a deep interest in getting to know him better; he would come to see that a few days in my company would more than make up for losing time on Amélie's portrait, and he would come back to it renewed—and finish it.

The next morning brought sunshine and a soft breeze to the terrace where we breakfasted.

"What are you two whispering about?" Madame Avegno called out to her daughter and me as we strolled across the lawn beneath the south terrace. "You look like a couple of schoolgirls," she grumbled, annoyed to be left out of anything interesting. She pulled her shawl around her a little more closely, although the morning dew had long since evaporated into lightly swirling mists above the fields.

John grinned and snatched up his sketchbook. He waved at us as we passed to and fro before him, indicating he was drawing us. We laughed and continued our whispered conference, arms about one another's waist and shoulders. I'm sure we made a charming scene, but John would no doubt have blushed if he knew that Amélie was hinting at numerous indiscretions on his part toward her, professions of love and unquenchable desire which she of course virtuously refused to entertain—and which I, knowing her well, assumed were largely figments of her imagination.

Later in the morning, people began to arrive to begin the preparations for the summer fête, and Amélie and her mother disappeared into the house with them. John and I were left sitting on the terrace, dawdling over coffee and rolls.

"Well," I said, "what do you say we spend the day at the beach near St.-Énogat, and get out of Amélie's way early?"

"Excellent!" he said, and hopped up immediately. "I shall go gather my things, and be ready in a trice."

I laughed. "Not if you're going to bring all your painting gear," she said, "and I know you won't move without it."

"True, very true," he said. "But you'd be surprised how quickly I can move when I'm motivated." He smiled down at me. "Besides, I'm used to packing my gear as you say, so it won't take long." My own calm, natural manner was, I knew very well, imparting to him permission to be the same around me. I rather think I was a new experience for him.

"*Bien!*" I rose also, and we walked into the house, arranging to meet at the carriage door in about an hour.

At Le Pré des Oiseaux, St.-Énogat, Brittany

My manservant, carrying a large basket, preceded us down the steps of the ancient stone staircase that led to the beach. He found a sheltered spot of sand upon which he placed a blanket, setting the basket in the middle, then he bowed and took his leave. The carriage would continue on to my cottage with our clothes and portmanteaux; my house was a very short distance from the stone staircase, with a view of the ocean from the front.

Once the servant was gone, I began to disrobe.

John watched in wonder and amazement as I pulled away the Japanese-inspired robe I wore, tied loosely with a cloth belt, and then, sitting on a low rock, removed my shoes and stockings. Dressed only in a knee-length cotton chemise over short pantaloons, the curves of my breasts and hips were readily outlined and straining against the cloth—I imagined myself a Rubens princess stepping into a pool to bathe.

I saw him watching me, and I smiled broadly.

"Come then," I urged. "Surely you want to jump into the sea as much as I do!"

John began tearing at his necktie and jacket, and within moments was down to his underclothes. Putting out his hand, he helped me up from the rock, and hand in hand, we ran toward the waves together.

The shock of the cold water made us scream, then laugh uproariously. I was a strong swimmer, as was he, and we swam side by side out into the waves, then turned over on our backs and let the motion of the water take us back to shore. Gasping for breath, we staggered back to our blanket and threw ourselves down upon our backs.

"I swear," said John, between deep, cleansing breaths, "I swear I haven't felt so good—so free—in years." He rolled over onto his side, facing me, and grinned. "You're a peach, you are," he said.

I sat up and began to wind a towel around my hair. "Thank you, *monsieur*," I said in mock solemnity. My wet chemise clung to my skin, and Sargent cocked his head at me.

"If only I could paint you like that," he said on an impulse, then blushed and began to stammer. "I—I mean—of course, it would be—impossible—forgive me, I—" he stuttered to a halt.

But I just smiled at him. "I would have no objections," I said, "although my reputation—bad as it is—would suffer, I'm afraid." I reached over and tousled his wet hair. "Come, let's walk along the beach and see if we can find any interesting shells."

We whiled away several hours on the beach, plunging into the ocean when we grew warm, eating the delicious lunch Amélie's cook had packed for us, and growing more fond of each other with every passing moment. I had long ago learned the art of making the person I was with feel like the most important, the cleverest, the most talent-ed person in the world—it was all the more easy to learn, I think, because I grew up surrounded by important, clever and talented peo-ple, beginning with my dear father and his friends. I could see that John was feeling perfectly at ease with me—as if I were already an old friend.

"And where, exactly are all the birds in the field, *le pré des oiseaux*?" John asked as we sat after dinner on the back terrace of my cottage overlooking gardens, meadows and woods near and far. The sun was just at the last gasp of setting, painting the clouds above it in streaks of crimson, tangerine, lemon and ochre as it sank behind the suddenly dark and mysterious forest.

"You know, I've never exactly determined that," I said, smiling. "The birds are spectacularly everywhere, but especially in the forest. I'll have to show you my hidden path into the woods," I said, with a suggestive wink—then I burst out laughing, which made him laugh as well, and feel even more comfortable. I'd lay a wager that he'd never met a woman who could actually deliver suggestive *double-entendres*, or talk about sex at all, to say nothing of making light of it.

"What is that little bit of a building over there, at the edge of the garden?" He nodded in the direction he meant. "It looks like a fairy hut, or something out of the Brothers Grimm."

"Oh, not so grim at all!" I said, wrinkling my nose at the pun. "Montesquiou calls it my 'cigar box', isn't that charming? I shall take you there, later." I glanced sideways at him. "You know the Comte, don't you? A friend of Doctor Pozzi's?"

"Not well," Sargent said, blushing a little. Ah, the telltale blush.

"Ha! No one knows Montesquiou *well*," I said, a little tartly. Then, more thoughtfully, I added, "No one knows anyone *well*, I think, don't you?"

He pondered this, taking time to drink from his wine glass and search the sky for the first star of evening. "I think it rather depends, you know, on how well one knows one's self."

"Ah, now that's very discerning for such a young man," I said. "Do you, then, know yourself? And what is it that you 'know'? Your 'soul'? Your 'mind'? This odd collection of thoughts and urges, loves, hates, desires—what we call a human being—how is one to know such a puzzle?"

He thought an even longer time over these questions, and reached for cigarettes, offering one to me, which I took with thanks.

"You are a close questioner," he said. He leaned his head back and looked up at the darkening sky. He stretched out his arm, pointing with his cigarette to the far horizon, where a star was just visible above the trees. "One's soul is like the sky, filled some days with bright clouds and sunshine, others with gloom and rain, or storms— and at night, in the deepest, darkest recesses, there are stars, and planets, suns and moons—other worlds that swirl around in the abyss and cry out, seeking their lives, their fate, their destiny." He drew deeply on his cigarette, and spoke again. "We are always under the sky, looking up, scanning it for good or ill—but with no way to tame it, or control it—we can only learn to read its signs, and chart our course as best we can."

A long silence shimmered between us in the dusky air.

"You have perhaps missed your calling," I said. "You are a poet, dear John." I reached over and took hold of his hand. Then I laughed lightly. "Or perhaps a philosopher?"

"Artist is enough for me, and more than enough," he said, raising my hand to his lips in salute.

❖

The moon was a waning crescent in the night sky as we made our way through the garden with the help of a single lantern, to the little retreat nestled under the trees. A large wooden door, set on wheels, moved aside noiselessly as I touched it, and the rays of the lantern fell upon a plain mat of bamboo on the floor, with pillows strewn around it, against the sides of the pavilion.

I set down the lamp, and began to light candles in small, flat, glass disks that I set floating in a pool of water along one side of the pavilion. I lighted other candles, tall and slender, around the room, enabling us to see that the interior walls were painted with delicate trees and branches bursting with pink and white blossoms.

"Yamamoto," I said, naming the artist whose silk screens were all the rage in Paris. I bent and blew out the lantern, leaving only the flickering, uneven glow of candlelight in the pavilion. I motioned for John to sit on the pillows, and kneeling on the bamboo mat, I opened the door to a little cabinet-table and took out a long pipe. I lit the substance in the bowl, and pulled at the pipe stem with a slow, even breath. Smoke curled from the bowl of the pipe, and a sweet smell drifted through the room.

I handed the pipe to John, who took it from me without hesitation, and smoked.

After we had passed the pipe two more times, I set it aside, and drew forth a bottle, a little cast-iron pot and a copper pan, and two eggshell-thin porcelain cups from the tiny cabinet.

"*Saki*," I said. "Have you tried it?"

John shook his head in wonderment.

I lighted a fire in the cast-iron pot, blew on the flames until the tiny coals caught and began to glow, and then poured sake from the bottle into the little warming pan which I then placed on the stove. After swirling the liquid around for a few moments, I filled the porcelain cups with the sake, and handed one to John, holding it in both hands and bowing my head as I did so. He bowed his head in return and accepted the cup. The drink was not unlike whiskey, or a strong apéritif, but it had an unusual effect on him.

"It's like swallowing light!" he cried.

I laughed, a sound that rippled from my mouth into the open space between us—I saw it—my laughter—breaking across his face like waves on a shore. We heard each other's voices as a series of echoes. He raised his hands as if to catch the sounds in the air, and looked at me questioningly.

"The effect of the opium," I said to him.

I slowly rose, feeling as graceful and young as a new-born goddess, and held my hand out to him. "Let's walk in the garden," I said.

The next morning, and very late in the morning it was, I knocked at John's door and called his name.

"John, are you decent?" I called. "May I enter?"

Hearing no answer but some abrupt rustling sounds, I opened the door and peeked in. John had thrown back the covers and was sitting up in bed, looking around as if wondering where he was. A typical reaction to such a night as we'd had!

"Come," I said, "rise and shine." I stepped further into the room and pointed to the marble washstand by the window. John began to get out of bed, then he must have realized he was naked, for he drew the covers around him and dragged them along with him to the washstand. He leaned his head over the porcelain bowl, lifted the pitcher of water, and poured the entire contents over his head. Spluttering and gasping, he grabbed a towel and rubbed his hair and face vigorously. There, *now* he was awake.

In the meantime, of course, the blankets had fallen off his body.

I was dressed much as I had been the day before, in a voluminous gown and sandals, my hair done up in a loose bun. I looked him up and down in a friendly manner, and picked up his trousers from the floor to hand to him. He was decidedly handsome, and well endowed. Perhaps I should have taken advantage of him in his altered state last night—but I do have my scruples.

"Come!" I said again, holding out his trousers to him. "It's time for lunch, and we have much to discuss!"

"Do we, Judith?" Sargent said, clearly uneasy about what that might mean, vis-à-vis last night.

"Oh, don't worry," I said, patting him on the shoulder. "I dare say you don't remember much about last night, but I assure you, I'm not the kind of woman to take advantage of a man who is, shall we say, under the influence?" I laughed. "Or several influences!" I grabbed his hand. "I'm starving, and I imagine you are too."

He grinned happily, put on his pants, and followed me down the stairs like a big, hungry puppy dog.

It had begun to rain, lightly at first, then a steady, summer rain, with the hint of thunder in the distance. The chess table was placed between us as we sat before a small fire in the drawing room, surrounded on every side by the trophies and collections that I, a great traveller, had collected, as well as those of my famous father, Théophile Gautier. Although he had never married my mother, he supported us, and loved and cared for me all his life, bringing me up in true egalitarian, bohemian style, a life which produced in me a fierce independence and a deep longing to love and be loved by a man as great, as literary, as artistic—as my father.

John had been playing Wagner on the piano earlier in the day, and the music, the quiet evening, and the melancholy of the rain created an atmosphere perfect for very personal revelations.

"I loved him, you know," I said suddenly after a long pause in which we had both rather absent-mindedly contemplated the chessboard.

John didn't need to ask to whom I was referring.

"He had, more than anyone I've ever known, the 'vital spark' of art," I said.

"'Vital spark'?" he repeated.

"Yes," I said, and leaned back into my chair, musing. "That indefinable bit of the eternal, a particle of creation itself, I would call it, that is *there* in the piece of music, or the painting, or sculpture, that makes you gasp or weep when you see or hear it—that sets it off from every other music or painting that is merely *fine*, or even beautiful."

John bit at his lips and looked down at the chessboard. I knew the question he wanted to ask.

"You are wondering if you have it," I said.

He raised his head. "Yes," he breathed it out slowly. "Yes, I do wonder."

I shrugged, and leaned forward again. "It's not in *every* painting, or *every* line that one writes, or *every* composed piece," I told him. I laid my hand on his, comfortingly. "You will know it when you see it."

"And if I see it often enough," he said, after a little while. "Will it be *in* me, will I at some time *have* the vital spark, as it were, instead of it just showing up in my paintings now and again?"

I had stretched out my hand to move a chess piece, and paused in the act, my brow furrowed. "That," I said at last, "I do not know." I hung fire another moment, then spoke again. "But *you* will. You will know if it is there or not."

I moved the chess piece. "Check, and mate, my very dear John."

Amélie Gautreau

Les Chênes, St.-Malo, Brittany

It was the very last day of posing, thanks be to Almighty God, as I didn't think I could stand one more hour. John Sargent had become perfectly indifferent to me, as I to him, and I only wished him gone so I could turn my attention to others who were beginning to interest me more. And yet, I knew the portrait was going to be a sensation—I had the brain to know that much— and for that, I was grateful.

He and Judith had come back to Les Chênes from her place, and they were whispering together and cozy as two mice in a cheese box. Silly woman, she has no idea how ridiculous she looks, with her blowsy hair and her *japonaise* affectations! I know she is my friend, but I think she sympathizes too much with Pedro against me—they are all against me. How I wish I were back in Paris.

"It's *too* perfect." Judith was talking, but I daren't turn my head.

The *maître* had not told me I could move—for that one thing at least, I had obeyed him during these weeks of sitting. I could, however, see what they were doing in a mirror that faced me.

Judith was looking at my full-length portrait which was, in essence, finished. She was shaking her head slowly, walking back and forth before the painting.

"Remember how we spoke of 'the vital spark'?" Judith said, turning to gaze at John. "That discussion we had some days ago?" He nodded, and frowned. *Pah!* I thought. More artistic pretensions. A painting is a painting.

"No, no, do not frown," Judith said, putting a hand on his arm. "Never fear, you will find it, you will see it, suddenly, and then the portrait will be done."

The two of them stood together, gazing at the portrait, then looking at me where I stood, sweating in the black dress, my right arm turned nearly out of its socket in a backward twist, my neck severely twisted to show my right profile. How on earth he came up with this pose, I'll never know, but I think I will be crippled for life if I am not released soon. The straps of my gown were cutting into my shoulders, the edges of the diamonds glinted in the light—a pretty sight, but really not at all comfortable.

"Too perfect, you say," John repeated. He laid down his brush for a moment, and walked over to me. He was muttering under his breath—*what will be less perfect? Something to throw off the balance—something unexpected.* He lifted a hand toward my hair, my chin, let his hand hover over my shoulders. I could feel the sweat running in rivulets down my back. He lifted the diamond-studded strap on my right shoulder.

And let it fall.

I heard a gasp from Judith. *"Mon Dieu!"* she said softly. *"C'est ça!* That's it!"

John stepped back, scarcely daring to draw a breath, and apparently agreeing with Judith.

"So simple a thing," he said softly, "it says everything about the moment, the woman, the pose—it is the vital spark!" He nearly ran back to the painting.

"My dear Amélie," he said, picking up a tool. "Just a few more moments, dear lady, and you shall be free of me and all this wretchedness of posing."

I sincerely hoped so! He continued to talk rapidly as he scraped away the painted strap from the shoulder. "You have been so patient, all these long weeks, in the midst of all your busy engagements, but you shall see, oh how you shall see, that it has all been worth it—a thousand times worth it! I cannot but think that you will be happy and astounded and delighted, and all manner of good things." It seemed he hardly knew what he was saying, but I too caught his enthusiasm, my mind running quickly across the whole range of conse-quences this painting would create—for himself, for me, for his career, his future, my reputation.

Judith stood back a little, watching him paint, smiling at me, smiling at him, nod-ding her head in agreement with everything he said. I take back what I said about her, she is a good friend, and a reasonably attractive woman.

The fallen strap was in place on the painting. When John at last released me from my frozen pose, I stretched and then slowly walked over to look at it—this portrait of me. It made me catch my breath. It was more than good, more than right—it was magnificent, and we all knew it.

❧ *Autumn 1883* ☙
Florence, Italy

Four Friends in Florence
Ralph

"I have just met the woman I am going to marry."

John smiled broadly as I pulled him into a corner of the elegant drawing room of the mansion my parents had leased in Florence for the season.

"*Marry!* This is good news indeed, my dear Ralph," he said. "Do I know her? And more importantly," he added with a grin, clapping me on the shoulder, "does your mother approve?"

"Hang my mother!" I said merrily. "I don't give a fig, but nonetheless," I added after a moment, "I'm sure even the dreaded Ariana would approve of her."

"But wait," John said, "you said you 'just met her'?" He looked skeptically at me, and paused to light a cigarette from the one I was puffing away at. "Aren't you being a little precipitous?"

"The heart knows what it wants," I said.

"True enough," he said. "But is it sure it can have what it wants?"

I shook my head, and waved my cigarette in the air to dismiss such pessimistic thoughts.

"Her name is Lisa," I said. "Lisa de Wolfe. She's from Cleveland."

"Cleveland! Of all places," John said, highly amused.

"Well, her family's from Boston, of course," I amended. "They have a big spread in Ohio, apparently."

"And how did you meet her? Where? When?" he asked, taking my arm and leading me out onto the terrace.

"Just now," I said. "A few minutes—or hours—ago—it *seems* like hours have passed since then!"

"My word," John said. "You *have* been hit hard, haven't you, cousin?" But he smiled sympathetically, and I did not take offense.

"She is the most beautiful creature I have ever beheld," I said. I took a deep drag of my cigarette and tossed it over the stone balustrade into the gravel of the enclosed patio below. "And her conversation is delightful! She is quite well versed in art, particularly sculpture, and we had a long, wonderful discussion about the French versus the Italians." I sighed deeply. "I never thought I would meet such a woman, and yet, there she is!"

"Is she still here?" John asked. "May I meet this vision?"

"Dash it all, no," I said. "Her horrid *chaperone* swooped down upon us and took her away. I didn't even have time to find out where she's staying, or for how long." I had a sudden thought. "*Mater* will know, however, as she knows everything that happens here—or anywhere, for all that. But how to ask her without arousing her suspicions—I couldn't bear any interrogation just now—not yet!" I looked at John with an inquiring eye. Seeing what was coming, he laughed good-naturedly.

"I shall get it out of her, dear cousin, never fear!" he said. "We shall find where the lady is hid!"

Violet

I was visiting Florence at the same time as John as well as Ralph Curtis. I remember I was sitting at a writing table, working through a final draft of my novel *Miss Brown*, which I would soon be sending to my publisher. I hoped, and intended, that it would be in the mail by the middle of November, which would allow for publication sometime late in the Spring—that is, if everything went perfectly, which of course it would not. It was difficult enough to finish and edit a work of this size—it was running to three volumes of more than three hundred pages per volume so far—but added to that daunting task was the fact of my family's constant moving about, so that I had no fixed place for more than a few weeks at a time. Here I am in Florence, I mused, for perhaps two months—before that, in London, where I got precious little done other than several rounds of frustrating meetings with publishers—and soon, after Florence, back to Siena—or maybe Paris! It was impossible to predict where my mother would determine would be our next abode. How I longed for a place of my own, a home to be settled in, a little cottage to always come back to after wandering about the capitals of Europe.

I put down my pen and sighed.

I'd had such hopes for a life with Mary Robinson, but that seemed further away than ever now—not that Mary had actually become engaged to some man, as I had long feared—but I'd heard rumors of a strange, philosophical Frenchman with whom Mary had been spending a good deal of time recently. I'd heard none of this from Mary herself—just well-intentioned, insufferable *friends* making sure I knew.

I turned my attention back to my book. I *must* work on it while I had the silence and emptiness of the afternoon at my disposal. I picked up my pen and read the next paragraph.

*And the older people, and the women of the aesthetic world—the spinsters with dishevelled locks and overflowing hearts, who kept little garlanded lamps before the photographs of pale—*I crossed out 'pale' and wrote 'puny' instead— *puny English painters and booted and red-shirted American poets—all agreed with her. But the younger men merely laughed, and neglected the solemn, smut-engrained parlours of Bloomsbury, the chilly, ascetic studios of Hampstead, for Madame Elaguine's curious, disorderly, charming house in Kensington—*

A knock at the door broke my concentration, and I called out impatiently, assuming it was my mother, "*Che vuoi?* What do you want?" But it was only the maid, come to bring a telegram. It was from John Sargent.

You must come to us tonight. Ralph needs his friends. Will send a cab at eight. Ciao! JSS

Louise

Ralph was very drunk.

John was doing his best to keep up with him, and a lesser man would have been felled with the effort. The Curtises' *major domo*, showing the finest Italian understanding of the situation, had sent up platters of chicken and pasta, bread and cheese, along with the wine and whiskey that flowed in quantity in his patron's son's chambers.

A gentle tap at the door was followed by a footman ushering in Violet Paget, who entered with a worried look, stopping just a few feet over the threshold to view the scene.

"What on earth is going on?" Speaking low, Violet addressed John rather than Ralph or me. Ralph's eyes were closed; he was leaning back against the sofa he had laid upon, and I was applying some lavender water to his forehead. I could see Violet's anxiety increase as she took in the scene. "Is someone dead?"

John grimaced and shook his head. "No, not quite," he said, and rose a trifle unsteadily to offer Violet a seat at the round table that held the nearly untouched food and many empty bottles. When they were both seated, he spoke to Violet in a soft voice.

"If only there were something we could give him for a broken heart."

Violet glanced again at Ralph, who showed no signs of waking under my ministrations. I carefully rose from the sofa, and joined them at the table. John poured us both a glass of wine which I gratefully accepted, and after a moment's hesitation, so did Violet.

"Pardon my lack of manners, Miss Burckhardt," Violet said to me. "I didn't see you at first." I nodded graciously. "But what has happened?" she said.

John leaned over and whispered, so Ralph wouldn't hear. "He met someone a couple of days ago, a young lady"—he sighed again— "it was love at first sight, at least on my poor cousin's part," he said. "He swore to me he would marry her, or no one, and, well, it turns out the lady is already engaged to be married." He looked over at his cousin with great affection. "Poor Ralph. He is devastated."

I felt a moment's tension—unrequited love was so very delicate a subject between me and John—but as he didn't look at me, I wasn't required to look nonchalant. I took a great gulp of wine, and reached for a piece of bread.

Violet sipped her wine, then frowned. "But he just met her, you say? Do you not think—I mean, don't you suppose he will, well, get over her before long?"

John shrugged. "One would think so, but frankly, I've never seen Ralph like this. He truly is broken-hearted. It *does* happen, you know," he said, sounding a little defensive.

Violet considered this, and nodded in agreement.

I realized suddenly that Ralph was attempting to rise from the sofa, and I alerted John. He sprang up immediately to help, and putting one of Ralph's arms around his shoulders, began to walk him slowly up and down the room, then over to the window for a breath of fresh air. After watching the two men for a moment, I turned back to Violet, reaching for the wine bottle to pour another glass for myself. I offered it to her, but she declined.

"How nice to see you again, Miss Paget," I said. "Though the circumstances are not the happiest—"

"We must hope for the best," Violet said. "Ralph generally takes things pretty lightly, so maybe a little time will help restore him to himself."

"I certainly hope so," I said. "But I have never seen him like this."

After a little time at the window, Ralph was more alert and awake. John brought him back to the table, and we four friends sat in the room lighted only by a few candles, drinking and attempting to eat. Ralph protested at first against trying anything I was urging on him, but soon gave in and had some bread and butter.

Everyone was beginning to feel the effect of too much wine. For Violet, it took the form of volubility combined with a sense of freedom in the company of these two men, intimate and old friends of hers, and what appeared to be a sudden feeling of camaraderie for me.

"I know all of you," she said, her speech slurred slightly. "I know your stories—I know what you desire—and what you have *not* got that you have"—she hiccupped ever so mildly—"that you *have* desired."

John looked at her, benignly amused. I pursed my lips, then laughed softly. Ralph merely stared, his brow furrowed, as if he did not speak her language.

"My dear Miss Paget," I said. "How wonderful you are! Do tell us, please, who we are and what we desire." I glanced at John and attempted to sound light-hearted. "It's like being at a fortune teller!"

Violet shook her head. "I am no fortune teller," she said. She gazed fondly at John. "Cigarette, please?"

He obliged by holding out his cigarette case, from which she took one. After a moment, he held it up to me. I hesitated, then took one. Ralph took one as well. The air above our heads was swirling with tobacco smoke moments later.

"There is one sentence, I believe," Violet spoke again, "one statement that would serve for each one of us, for all of us."

"And what, dear Vi," Ralph spoke up for the first time. "What statement would that be?"

Violet's lower lip trembled slightly, and there was a shine of tears in her eyes as she looked at each of us in turn.

"I cannot have the one I love," she said.

There was a long, swelling silence in the room as we watched each other's faces, unafraid, unflinching, acknowledging the truth of it.

"Nonetheless," I said, lifting my glass, "we drink to Love!"

"To Love!" "To Love!" "To Love!"

The Boits at Villa Cernitoio

Ned

The sun rose and blessed the hills at Cernitoio, where we had come after fleeing America once again, and to spend the winter.

"My sister-in-law would have broken me," Isa had said on several occasions to me, as we retreated from our native shores back across the wide Atlantic. "I shall not breathe easily until we are in Italy. There, we will have peace."

The villa was ready for us, the servants notified, the rooms aired and dusted, provisions acquired, and the chariot waiting at the train station. The humble farm wagon was pulled up behind, ready to bear the burden of our worldly goods, at least those we brought with us.

"The girls are tired," I murmured to Isa during the luxuriously slow ride to the villa.

"Of course they are, poor dears," she murmured back, smoothing Jane's rumpled dress as she lay against her, drowsing in the mid-day autumn warmth. Julia was fast in Henny's arms, sound asleep, and Mary Louisa's head drooped against my arm. Only Florence was alert and wide-eyed, intensely drinking in the passing countryside. She turned excitedly to us.

"I remember this way!" she cried, although her voice was low, so as not to disturb her sleeping sisters. "At the top of the next hill, we will see Cernitoio, will we not?"

I smiled and patted her shoulder. "How well you remember, my dear!" I said. "It must be full eight years since we were here last."

"Yes," Florence said. "I was only seven years old the last time we were here. Imagine that!" She laughed—a merry sound grateful to our ears. "How different I am now, going on sixteen!" She turned back to looking out the window, eagerly waving and smiling at a young boy walking through a nearby field, leading a small herd of goats to a stream.

"How on earth did they discover we were here—so soon!" Isa angrily threw down a note card that the servant had just brought in. It was from Ariana Curtis, inviting us to dinner in two days' time. She rose from her chair and began pacing the morning room of the villa, which gave out onto a splendid view of rolling hills and sun-dappled olive groves. It was the morning after our arrival. "I knew we would be found out sooner or later, but heavens, how word travels in these remote places!"

I remained seated, silently allowing my wife to express herself, and sipped my coffee, feeling generally content and happy. Cernitoio always soothed me, and more—it made me feel like painting again. It had been many months since I'd picked up a brush, and the scene outside the window was inspiring. Maybe after breakfast—

Isa looked impatiently at me, and stooped to pick up the note that had fallen to the floor. "She says here that John Sargent is staying with them, as well as Louise."

"Ariana does love an entourage," I said mildly. "I expect there's a few more."

"That's not the point," Isa said. "I will not have Florence unsettled by a visit from John, or even to hear people talking about him," she said. She looked severely at me, as if I had offered resistance. "He cannot come here, you know."

I sighed deeply, and put down my empty coffee cup. "Yes, my dear, I know." I gazed at her sorrowfully. "But how can it be avoided? You won't let me tell him the reason," I argued, "and I cannot countenance simply, well, *insulting* him by refusing to invite him to visit, which we would be obliged to do were we to meet at the Curtises. Nay," I added, "he would feel no doubt that he could come to see us even without any invitation."

Isa pursed her lips, thinking hard. "Then there's nothing for it but to tell them we are in quarantine," she said. "I shall give it out that the girls are ill with, what? Scarlet fever, perhaps? Something that will keep people away but won't alert the authorities and call down the wrath of the insufferable Italian bureaucracy upon us." She laughed, a grim sound.

"Better to make it the German measles, or something only children have," I said. I watched her face. "That might make it possible for you and I, at least, to go into Florence and see our friends," I said tentatively, "and provide an excuse at the same time for them not to come visit us."

"Why, Ned, you are positively Machiavellian," Isa said. "That's an excellent idea!" She gazed at me through narrowed eyes. "I wouldn't have thought it of you."

I shrugged, ill at ease with the whole situation, but wishing more than anything for peace and quiet. I rose slowly from my seat, walked over to where Isa stood and kissed her on the cheek.

"I'm going to collect my things," I said, "and wander out into the olive grove." I didn't need to be more explicit—she knew I was wanting to paint.

"Lovely, my dear," she said, kissing me back. "It will do you good."

I saw her watching me, minutes later, as I walked with slow steps toward the grove, carrying my wooden box of paints and brushes. A young lad followed me with a small table, a chair and an easel in a little green wheelbarrow. I sighed, and fought back an urge to weep. Florence *was* getting better, I was sure of it, but I knew that Isa was determined to do everything she could to protect her daughter, even if it meant making me unhappy.

Florence

I remember that day at Cernitoio as if it were yesterday—and it has been a very long time since any of us have been there. So much has happened in between—war and death and change we could never have imagined or foreseen. It was happier days then.

"This is where we used to play when you were just a baby," I said to Jane, pointing at the freshly scrubbed tile floor of the villa's enormous kitchen. A scullery maid was serenely washing vegetables at a large sink in the corner, readying them for the luncheon soup. The shutters were open to the cool morning air and sunshine, and the sound of goats bleating in the nearby meadow mixed with the fragrances wafting from the herb garden just outside the door.

I knew Jane was remembering my strange, frightened behavior a year ago in Paris, in response to her question about playing with a boy on this very floor. She glanced at my face, but I was determined to show only composure and peace.

There was a bustle at the door from the garden. The villa's cook, a woman named Maria Caterina, of no young age but of an active, spry and good-humored temperament, came sweeping in and caught sight of us.

"*Signorinas!*" she cried. "*Florentina, mia cara bambina!*" She hastily shed her cloak and parcels on the large wooden table and embraced first me, then Jane. She stepped back and smiled at us happily, talking non-stop in as much English as she could muster.

"*Bellissima!* So pretty," she said, smoothing our hair and patting our cheeks. She regarded me with special satisfaction. "You, *signorina*, so grown, a fine lady, eh? I remember, you, there *sul pavimento*"— pointing to the tiled floor—"*come un maschieto*, like a little boy, no wear the dress—" she explained to Jane —"*come sempre in la sporcizia,* always dirty—and now, *sembra graziosa che mai,* prettier than ever!"

Jane looked anxiously at me to see if this reference would disturb me as it had done before, but I continued calm and happy, smiling at Maria Caterina.

"I am a grown-up lady now," I said. "It doesn't matter what I was when I was a child."

The cook continued her effusions until we were interrupted by Henny coming in with my little sisters, whom she had never seen, and who immediately claimed her tender affections as well as the little pastries she extracted from a cupboard and handed out.

Jane and I stepped away from the revelry in the kitchen to the relative quiet of the herb garden, where we walked hand in hand for a time, stopping to pinch various leaves in our fingers and, sniffing at them, attempting to identify them.

Jane couldn't repress her curiosity any longer. "Florence," she said, trying to sound indifferent, "what a funny thing the cook said about you." She looked cautiously at me. "Were you really such a—a tomboy?" She almost held her breath as she waited for the answer.

"Oh, yes, indeed," I gave a light laugh. "I expect I was a little terror! I never wanted to wear pretty clothes, and I was always running away to be with the goat-boy." I smiled at her, but I could see Jane felt uneasy—maybe there was something odd about the way I smiled—I admit I didn't feel quite right inside. But I wanted to reassure her. "But I am a young lady now, and as you know, I love beautiful clothes and having my hair brushed, and soon, Mama says, I can wear long gowns and go to balls—next year, when I am sixteen, and we are back in Paris."

"But you are happy here in Cernitoio, aren't you?" Jane said anxiously. "It is so beautiful here, I love it already, and I never want to leave." She seemed surprised at the strength of her own feelings. She looked to me for my response.

"It *is* lovely here," I said, giving her a hug. "Don't worry, we'll be here for a while, and we'll always come back, never fear. Mama and Papa love this place too much," I said. "And I heard them talking, last night, about how they think they're going to buy it some day, so it will always be here when they want it."

"Oh, that would be wonderful!" Jane said, looking happier.

I did not know until much later the enormous effort my parents made at that time to keep me away from John Sargent. But a meeting was inevitable, if not in Florence, then back in Paris when we returned in the following Spring.

๑ *February 1884* ๛
Paris

Carroll Beckwith

Sometimes, when something is finished, that's it. Done. *Fini. Fait accompli.*

And sometimes, it's not.

"You need to stop fussing with it," I said from my place on the sofa in John's studio. He turned round and glared at me, which only made me laugh.

"I shall make a copy," he said, "and that will fix it."

We both stared at the finished portrait of Madame Gautreau, and John scowled. He touched a finger lightly to the tortuously twisted right arm, and noted with dismay the layers of paint and evidence of cracking. He'd scraped and redone so many sections it was beginning to look like patchwork.

"Go on, then," I said, waving a hand. "Make a copy, by all means, if it will satisfy you." I turned back to the newspaper, and muttered, audibly. "It won't be as good, though."

"I shall do it all the same," John said, "only I don't think I have what I need here."

He stood looking at his tubes of paint and brushes.

"Beckwith," he said, "let us go forth into the day, and visit old *Père Tanguy* to buy some supplies. Do go with me, old fellow," he said on hearing my sigh of protest. "I'm too nervous to be alone, and I'll tell you what, I'll spring for lunch, *Aux Deux Magots*, eh?"

I gazed at him with mock long-suffering eyes. "If I must," I said.

"Good man!" he said. "We haven't been there in an age, and I hear the sausages are getting quite tasty!"

Too nervous to be alone. I reflected on what he'd said about himself that morning, and thought ruefully that it was a rare experience for

John. After lunch, we returned to his studio, once again facing the formidable portrait of Amélie. He had prepared a new canvas with a prime coat of light grey, made by mixing lead white and ivory black in linseed oil—he wanted the overall effect to be cool, he said, in subtle support of the distant and unattainable affections of his subject.

He *was* nervous—I could see it. No other painting had created this effect in him, as far as I knew—on no other painting had he placed such a burden of ambition, of hopes and dreams, of longing and a kind of fevered striving for place, fortune, fame. He had said again and again, this was to be his *entrée* into French high society—to those Parisians of impeccable lineage who closed ranks against foreigners and others whom they disdained for any number of reasons, none of them having to do with true talent, worth or merit.

"Stop worrying," I told him. "You will tame them—after Amélie's portrait shows at the Salon to resounding acclaim, every high-born lady will want to be the subject of the next famous painting by the celebrated young artist, John Singer Sargent." I puffed away at a cigar and wagged my finger at him in my best imitation of a know-it-all old codger. "You'll see."

"The *American* artist," he said, half to himself as he dabbed generous portions of vermilion, rose madder, viridian green and bone black on his palette. "What am I really, Beckwith? When I talk, or even think, Italian and French come as naturally to my mind as English. I have spent less than a year, at most, of my nearly thirty years in my own "native" country—and yet, I feel in my heart that I am an American. And yet—"

"And yet—?" I prompted.

He shook his head, put down the palette, and turned to me. "You've read those stories by Henry James, haven't you? Sometimes I feel that he's writing about me—the young American in Europe—but I'm already compromised, you see, I feel it, here," he put his hand on his heart. "Am I not living a decadent life, in the way James has depicted it—a son of the New World, battered and bewildered, seduced and stained by the corruption and deceit of the crumbling Old World of Europe?"

"My dear boy," I said, feeling a little shaken by his earnest, heartfelt confession. I shook my head, and tried to counteract his depression. I sprang up from the sofa and poured myself a whiskey, and one for him, too.

"You're letting anxiety about this blasted portrait suck away your strength, your confidence." I said, handing him the glass. "None of what you're saying is true—in fact, didn't Mr. James say to you, the other night, 'You are the embodiment of America facing down the Old World—with your high, clear vision and your strong portrayals of the 'real thing'—you are the 'real thing'—you are the hero of the stories I have yet to write!'" I gulped down the whiskey, and hit him lightly on the shoulder. "Or some such thing as that."

He smiled a bit then, and nodded a reluctant yes.

"In fact," I said, "the old guy seemed rather pointedly attentive, didn't you think?" We had been introduced to the renowned writer at an evening party the other night at Madame Roger-Jourdain's salon, just down the avenue from John's house, at No. 45. Mr. James had taken a great fancy to John, so it appeared to me, staying at his side most of the evening, and engaging him intensely in conversation.

"And," I pursued, "if I heard him correctly—of course, I was trying not to listen—he actually was trying to persuade you to move to London and make a name for yourself by painting the portraits of the English aristocracy! Damn good notion, too, I thought."

John looked as if he were thinking about it, then shrugged and said, "First, I must conquer the French." He turned back to the painting, the copy he was making, and became lost in his art.

I returned to the sofa, and picked up the newspaper again, but my thoughts were focused on John's remarkable outburst—him, corrupted? Compromised? Despite his youthful peccadilloes, I think all of us, all his friends, regarded him as honest and pure, single-hearted and generous, a shining light that helped us all to see the beauty in the world a little more clearly.

After a while, a gentle tap on the door brought his manservant into the room with the mail on a tray. John took a break from painting, and sorted through various bills and letters of business, setting them aside for the moment, and concentrated on a large, elegant ivory envelope, addressed to him in a man's small neat hand.

"It's from Henry James," he said, and opened the envelope eagerly. He scanned the note, then read it aloud to me.

My dear Mr. Sargent, as I find myself having to stay over in Paris for a few more days before I return to London, I am hoping you will not take it amiss if I invite you, with so little notice, to dine with me at Ledoyen at 8:30 this evening? I realize that it is not very near your studio, therefore I will gladly call for you at 7:45 in a cab I have hired for the occasion. And, if possible, might I seize the opportunity of viewing your studio when I arrive? Awaiting the pleasure of your reply, I remain sincerely yours, H. James

"What a delightful invitation," I said. "Now you'll be able to bask in the glow of his adoration all evening long."

"For God's sake, Beckwith," he said, though he didn't seem angry. "I think it will be all right—he is actually a quiet sort of man, I felt rather comfortable with him."

"And Baby's out of town, right?" I said, pushing up from the sofa once more. "So you have nothing and no one to keep you home." I glanced at the barely begun copy of Madame Gautreau, and added, "You certainly can use a break from her, don't you think?"

"Yes," John nodded. "Yes, I should get out for a change of air and subject."

I hoped for more as a result of Mr. James's interest in John—the writer had influence among the *ton* of London, and seemed eager to take on the young painter as a protégé. Oh, I had heard the tattle about him, along with Oscar Wilde and all that crowd, but I believe James was thoroughly a gentleman—he had certainly come across as decidedly Bostonian, with a strong Puritan streak. John would be safe in his hands.

Henry James

I rang the doorbell to John Sargent's studio promptly at a quarter to eight o'clock that evening, and stood a few steps back. I remember I was dressed for the cool rainy night in a suit of dark grey and a soft hat, and I carried an umbrella. John quickly descended the stairs to greet me personally, as I had imagined he would. I bent my head in a brief salutation as he opened wide the heavy door.

"Good evening, my dear Mr. James," he said, and held out his hand, American style. Although my grip was firm enough, John, I could see, recalled at the last instant that I had complained to him of "the crushing handshakes of our fellow Americans," and he lightened his own grasp accordingly.

We climbed the steps slowly to accommodate my somewhat elderly pace—though I was not yet forty at that time, I know I appeared to John's eyes to hover closer to his father's generation than his own. He maintained a convivial silence, turning to smile encouragingly at the landing, courteously allowing me to catch my breath until we reached the second floor.

The lamps were lighted to chase away the winter shadows, and a fire was burning briskly on the hearth. He had foreseen the need for a *remontant*, and led me to sit at a small table near the windows overlooking the street below. He poured some sherry into glasses and after a few sips, I was able to look about me as I regained my breath.

"What a lovely space you have here, Mr. Sargent," I said, gazing around keenly. "How happy you must be in your creations, here, above the fray and bustle of the streets below."

"Thank you," he said. He topped off our glasses, and sat down, facing the window. We gazed out at the twinkling lights of the city. Our silence was not awkward, but not yet quite easy.

"You, too, must have such a retreat," he said after a few moments. "A writer's study, all brown and dim and crammed with books, yes?"

I inclined my head and smiled. "Do you see that in your painter's eye?" He turned and looked at me, critically, as if sizing me up as a subject.

"Someday, I shall paint you, shall I, Mr. James?" he said.

An odd thought crossed my mind, but I took care not to let it cross my face. I smiled again. "Our Puritan forebears would no doubt consider it frivolous idolatry," I said, and sipped more sherry.

John laughed, a short bark of jollity that acknowledged in a moment our common Boston background and all the weight of its heritage on our expatriate shoulders. Yes, he was as I had thought—pure American youth, and yet there was the uncanny *savoir faire* of Europe in his face, almost a frightened weariness, at times.

We sat for several moments more, growing more comfortable with each other. I roused myself, now recovered from the labor of mounting the stairs, and began to stroll about the room, looking at the portraits arranged carefully as for exhibition. John continued in his chair, watching with amusement as I leaned into, and stepped back from, the various works on display.

"I saw, last year in London," I said, my voice echoing slightly in the high-ceilinged room, "your splendid 'Doctor Pozzi' at the Academy. Did you know that he had been placed in the same room as the two Cardinals?" I turned an inquisitive eye to him, and he shook his head. "Ah, you should have seen it," I said. "Millais' 'Cardinal Newman', a very holy man and a very superior model," I continued, peering closely at a portrait of Albert de Belleroche, whom I knew but slightly, "though unfortunately dressed in a garment of a very furious red, painted with a crudity which caused it to obliterate the face, but without justifying itself. It is violent, monotonous, superficial, uninteresting; it is nothing but a cape, and yet it is not even a cape."

I could see he was amused at my studied manner in relaying my criticism of the exhibition—I presume he knew I wrote critiques for the London journals—and he let me comment without interruption.

"The Cardinals have had poor luck this past year," I continued, "Cardinal Manning having been sacrificed simultaneously to Mr. Watts, whose effort is less violent than that of Mr. Millais, but not more successful." I sighed, and turned to the portrait of Madame Gautreau. I had heard much about it from John's friends in the past days. I looked it up and down, but moved on after a moment, and continued where I left off.

"The best that can be said of Mr. Watt's portrait of Cardinal Manning is that it is not so bad as his portrait, at the Grosvenor, of the Prince of Wales, of which I shall say no more, as I fear it would expose the artist to the penalties attached to that misdemeanor known to English law as 'threatening the Royal Family.'"

John laughed aloud at this sally, poured himself another sherry, and rose, bringing another full glass to me.

"But your flamboyant physician," I said, taking the glass and lifting it in salute, "out-Richelieus the English Cardinals, and is simply magnificent."

He bowed his thanks, and smiled mischievously. "Do you know what he is called, here in Paris, by his patients?"

I shook my head, raising an eyebrow.

"*Le Docteur Amour*," he said, laughing.

"Indeed," I said, and took another sip of sherry. "Doctor Love. Well."

"Did you see my Venetian studies, at the Grosvenor?" he asked, obviously feeling more comfortable.

"Yes, most wonderful," I said. "I thought the figures of the women, sitting in gossip over some humble, domestic task in the big, dim hall of a shabby old palazzo, were extraordinarily natural and vividly portrayed."

I pondered those paintings in my mind; they made me feel wistful. "You have seen and captured that part of Venice," I said, "which the tourist does not know, and which only such as you and I, wandering the narrow walks in the shadows, have the heart and the sensibility to observe, and to love, observing."

"Yes," John said, softly. "Thank you for saying it so well, I never—have the words—" His voice trailed off, and he walked away to restore the glasses to the little table by the window. I remained standing before the portrait of a gondolier, gazing down at the sharp and feral face, and with what I trusted was an impenetrable look on my own.

"Shall we go to dinner then?" John said, returning and glancing at his watch. He added in a kindly, though jocular tone, "Going down the staircase will be much easier than coming up!"

I smiled faintly, and bowed my head. "Seeing you, in your studio, is worth any number of stairs, my dear Mr. Sargent."

Albert de Belleroche

I came back to John about a week after he'd had that dinner with Henry James, and heard all about it. That is, I heard about the one thing that mattered, to John.

"He barely looked at it, Albert!"

John was distraught. The great writer had disregarded the portrait of Amélie—had, in fact, looked at it and passed it by without comment. This eventful non-event hummed in John's brain long after the dinner with the famous writer had dimmed in his memory.

"He ignored it—he must have thought it bad, very bad, and simply refrained from commenting to avoid embarrassing me. I can think of no other explanation."

I could, and I told him so. "He was simply being catty," I said.

"Everyone knows he's not interested in women, anyway, and she's *such* a woman, my dear, as cannot fail to disgust a certain sort of man."

He looked at me curiously, and seemed about to say something but didn't.

He was still fretting and fuming over the copy he was working on, which was now more than half-finished. We both squinted at it in the flickering light from the oil lamps and candles he had lit to dispel the gloom of the winter evening. Beckwith was right, I thought, it wasn't as good. But what was he to do? The original portrait fairly glittered in the candlelight from a hundred tiny surfaces of paint that was cracked and crazed, like a badly glazed ceramic. And yet, I rather liked it that way.

"Look here, John, don't you see how the layers of paint give it depth, make it glow?" I tried hard to persuade him to leave off making the copy. "You're really getting a bit tiresome, you know—you must trust your hand, you must trust what you created in such a passion."

231

He looked at me again, in that curious way, and I could see what he was thinking—that I wasn't *there* with him, that I was a little removed, preoccupied. It was true—I had my own work I was preparing for the Salon this Spring, and, well, there were other distractions, but I didn't want to think of that now. I was restless. I needed a change.

John sighed deeply, trying to shake off his gloomy thoughts. I thought of something he might consider.

"Perhaps you ought to invite some other friends to view the painting, and get their advice?" I suggested. "Ralph's family is here, aren't they, and your Louise"—I'm sorry, I couldn't help myself, it always made me go mad with jealousy every time I thought of her and John—"and dear Violet, right?" I hastened to add. John's own family were rather dispersed for the time, with Emily in Ireland for a long visit with some relatives there, his father and little Violet back in Nice for the winter, and his mother at Baden-Baden for a few weeks. I keep track of these things; I like to know where people are.

"And Carolus-Duran! Of course!" I said before he could reply. But my idea seemed to cheer him up.

"Well," he said, "that might not be so bad—we could have an evening party, and everyone could view the original and the copy—and help me decide which I should send to the Salon." It passed through my mind that he had never asked this particular question of any friend or colleague before, but I put it away swiftly, arguing to myself that after all, it was the public who would be judging the portrait, so why not canvass some portion of the public ahead of time?

He said he would send the notes of invitation out the next morning, determined to release himself from this agonizing limbo of indecision.

An abundance of candles lighted the second-floor studio on the evening of John's little gathering of friends and colleagues. Beckwith came early, to help with the arrangements, thank God. John's cook was fond of Beckwith, and he managed the other servants deftly, unlike John's reluctant attempts to give orders and instructions, or my bullying them all. Thus, all was as it should be when the guests began to arrive—a butler (the cook's well-looking brother, hired for the evening) stood at the top landing with a tray of glasses filled with chilled champagne, and the maid, prim in black and white, stood at the ready to help serve the guests from the substantial feast spread out on the sideboard. I was very pleased to see it all turn out so well.

The Allouard-Jouans were there, as were the Roger Jourdains, John's neighbors. Edouard Pailleron, the actor, and his wife came as well, bringing Louise Burckhardt with them, an arrangement which I could see surprised John as he greeted them at the door; I was at his side, and we exchanged quick glances, but of course we had no leisure to explore it further. Judith Gautier arrived accompanied by a striking, black-haired young poet named Alain; she winked slyly at John as he bent to kiss her hand, and lightly tapped the young man with her fan to keep his attention riveted to herself. But I saw him sneaking glances at me all evening, I can tell you.

The room quickly filled with people walking among the different paintings, strategically placed around the studio. Against the farthest wall, covered by curtains strung from the ceiling, John had concealed the two portraits of Amélie, the original and the copy. I had persuaded him to uncover them dramatically as the highlight of the evening once everyone had assembled.

Carolus-Duran and his wife were the last to arrive. John met them at the door of the house, and led them upstairs. He saw to it they had champagne, a place to sit, and something to eat. He was very nervous, as was I, in sympathy with him. I felt every glance, every nuance of conversation, every look at his paintings, as tiny arrows in all my senses—even the texture of the food, the bubbles in the champagne seemed to me a new sensation, prickly and exquisite. How I wanted to be alone with him, and all these chatty people gone in an instant! And yet, in another way, I felt it was good to be in other company. I am a strange and moody person.

When the moment came to unveil the portrait, John took a very deep breath, steadied himself, and stepped in front of the curtains. He tapped on a champagne glass with a silver spoon, calling the party to attention. Everyone turned to him, heady with wine and expectation.

Although he stood before friends and colleagues, and therefore, should have been comfortable, John suddenly experienced a complete loss of composure. He could not speak. Rising emotion nearly closed his throat, and he looked around at the dear and friendly faces with brimming eyes—there, Louise watching him anxiously as she whispered something to Violet, whose plain face brightened with an amused response; Beckwith, trying with all his might to make John laugh by contorting his face and wiggling his eyebrows at him; Ralph, his face unusually somber and sad—John had told me about his tragic love—but forcing a cheerful façade all the same. John turned his eyes to me, and I smiled at him—I saw his face glow, and he caught his breath. I had that effect on him still, I remember thinking. He swallowed hard, abruptly drank the champagne remaining in his glass, and attempted to speak.

"It's a damn shame!" he said at last, and with a sharp yank of a silken cord, pulled aside the curtains to reveal his portrait of Virginie Amélie Avegno Gautreau.

Even for those who had already seen it, the effect was stunning. The painting perched mere inches from the floor, making it seem as if Amélie herself had just entered the room and had paused, looking to the side for a moment, before she walked in further.

"*Mon Dieu!*" Madame Duran was heard to say. "Is she about to speak?" She cast a furtive glance at her husband whose face was like a mask.

"Good God, John," Ralph said, drawn out of his haunted reticence by the magnificent painting. "I shall withdraw my own entries for this year this very minute! They don't stand a chance!"

"Indeed, it is most wonderful." Pailleron breathed the words softly. "She is alive."

Others of the company began walking closer to the painting to see it more intimately.

"I want to reach out and put that strap back on her shoulder," said Violet impudently, and stretched out a hand as if to do so.

"By no means, *mademoiselle*," Carolus-Duran said. "That strap, that fallen strap—" he broke off, as if unable to find the words he sought. His wife clung to his arm, and looked again at his face. He turned to John, pointing at the copy that had also been uncovered, although it stood slightly to the side and behind the original portrait.

"Do you think to remedy the imperfections of the original by making a copy of her?" he asked. John looked at him steadily, not surprised to see that his *maître* understood exactly what he had in mind. He waited for more, as Carolus-Duran returned to gazing at the painting. The assembled party were silent, waiting also for the *maître* to speak again. Everyone knew that Carolus-Duran was a member of the Salon's inner circle and would be able to judge more accurately than anyone how the portrait would be received. His opinion would be decisive.

"Should the artist conceal his art?" the older painter demanded, of no one in particular. "Will you take this living being and turn her into a shadow, a shade of Hades, bereft of the passion and tumult that accompanied her birth?" His black eyes glittered with a strange, fine light as he once again looked at John directly. "This painting will be a sensation at the Salon, and you must send the original—more alive, indeed, than the very woman herself, in my opinion!"

"Hear, hear!" cried Beckwith, applauding the *maître's* remarks. The rest of the group joined in the applause, and the butler appeared with a fresh bottle of champagne, whereupon all of us lifted our glasses in a toast to the painting's successful exhibition at the Salon.

Later, as guests began to depart, Sargent pulled Carolus-Duran aside for a quiet word alone, but I was near enough to hear. I could tell that our *maître's* pronouncement earlier had restored his confidence, and John was visibly feeling only affection and gratitude for the teacher who had guided his early years.

"I'm damned grateful to you," he said, his eyes misty with emotion and champagne. He kissed Carolus on both cheeks, and then turned away as someone called to him from across the room.

"Bah," said the elder painter, and turned to take his wife's arm. They were standing near the portrait, but he didn't notice that I was nearby. He turned to look at it again, and said in a grave undertone to his wife, "That fallen strap—it may break him. I know *les Parisiennes*, it will throw them into fits." I saw a shiver of a strange exultation cross his face, and then he shrugged. "Or not."

He started as I stepped out from behind the painting; he showed a carefully bland face to me. "Good night," he said simply, and turning, signalled to his wife that he was ready to leave.

"*Bonne chance!*" he called out as they reached the door, and I saw him smile to himself to see John's ruddy face glowing with cheerful assurance.

∞ *March 1884* ∾
London

Henry James

I had persuaded John Sargent to visit London that Spring, which at first he was reluctant to do, but he was won over, I believe, by my representation of what, to put it in gross business terms, I could "do" for him.

"He has a high talent," I was saying to my friend Edmund Gosse, as I awaited John's appearance at the Reform Club. "And a charming nature, artistic and personal, and is civilized to his finger-tips. He is perhaps spoilable," I said thoughtfully, "although I don't think he is spoiled—yet. But there *is* a certain incompleteness in his art, and in his extremely attaching, interesting nature, a certain want of seriousness." I leaned back in the large leather chair, situated in a shadowed corner of the Club, and sipped at a small glass of sherry. "Nonetheless," I continued, "I like him so much that—a rare thing for me—I don't attempt too much to judge him."

Gosse laughed. "Not *too* much," he said. "Right. I know you, Henry, and that means only about twice as much as anyone else."

I smiled thinly, and attempted no riposte.

"But you do seem rather taken with him," Gosse mused, his eyes glinting at me over the rim of his glass.

"I merely want to give him a push," I said after a moment's consideration.

Gosse smiled, and said nothing more on the subject.

A few moments later, John was ushered into the sitting room, informed by the stiff butler as to my whereabouts, and strode toward us with an uncertain smile on his handsome face. We rose to greet him, and I introduced him to Gosse as "the only Franco-American product of any importance in all of Europe," an epithet to which John roundly protested.

"Nonsense," said Gosse amiably, "if Henry deigns to compliment you, you must understand it is a rare and fortunate occurrence! You must get him to put it in writing, and sign it, and your fortune shall be made forever." He smiled broadly at me; I stifled a sigh. Taking John's arm, as if I needed the support, I bid good night to Gosse, saying, "This young man and I will be dining here tonight, Edmund. I hope to see you later, though, after the theatre? We will be at The Lamb, I believe."

Graciously taking the hint, Gosse immediately bowed good night to us, a smile curling his lip under his thick moustache, and retreated to another seat to finish his whiskey.

Over a simple dinner of roast beef, potatoes and onions, we discussed what I discerned very early was the topic of paramount importance to his mind: his submittal of the portrait of Madame Gautreau to this year's Salon. It was easy to get him to talk about it—a mere touch opened the floodgates.

"The framing took forever," he lamented. "But it cannot be ignored—it is a detail that many of the Salon judges often pay as much attention to as the painting itself! But I was satisfied at last, and the painting is now safe in the holding rooms at the *Palais de l'Industrie*, and I don't have to see it again until Varnishing Day."

"And what title have you determined for it?" I asked.

"Simply 'Madame X'," he said, shrugging a little. "Out of deference to the lady."

"Surely," I said, helping myself to a bit more of the roast, "everyone will know who she is?"

"Of course," John said. "It's just a bow to convention, in a way." He looked worried, and leaned forward to speak in a lower tone, more confidentially. "I don't mind telling you that the prospect of its appearance before all Paris in the Spring makes me tremble with some inexplicable dread—I can't explain it."

I remembered that I had not liked the painting, though I had refrained from saying so. I decided that a little white lie would not be amiss here. "It is a truly prodigious portrait," I said, and was gratified to see him light up at my praise. "I think it will be a sensation." And of course, there are more ways than one to create a sensation, as we were to learn in May.

We were served the cheese and some port, and I relayed to John the ambitious schedule that I had planned for him during the coming week. Today was Saturday, and from tonight until Friday next there was scarcely a waking moment when we would not be in company together. There were many prominent artists and art dealers among my acquaintance, and everyone wanted to meet him. He looked rather taken aback, and received my information in silence.

"My dear Mr. James," he said at last, "I am overwhelmed at your generosity, but really, I say—" He broke off, shaking his head. I could tell that the prospect of meeting so many new people was more than daunting to him.

"You need do nothing more than murmur a few pleasantries, admire their work, and accept their adoration," I said. "Everyone has seen your paintings here, at Grosvenor's of course, and in Paris as well, and everyone is dying to meet you." I reached over and patted his arm lightly. "You have got all, and more than all, that Paris can give you, my friend—you are wanted here, in London, where there is such a field!"

"I've already got several commissions in England," he blurted out. He took a long draught of port to cover his bluntness. I lifted an inquiring brow, encouraging him to continue.

"The Vickerses," he said, "in Sheffield, out in the country. Three young women, daughters, not very pretty girls." He set down his empty glass, and a waiter appeared to refill it from the bottle on a side table. "Shall probably be there for two months from the middle of July. Want me to do the whole family, it seems."

"Excellent," I said. Inwardly, I shrugged. I knew the name, Vickers, a munitions manufacturer, solid merchant class. "Well," I said aloud, "you will be here more and more then, and that will be good."

The club butler appeared at my side and said something in a low voice.

"Our carriage is here," I said, touching my napkin to my lips. "It's off to the theatre."

Emily Sargent

It was my first journey entirely on my own—at the age of twenty—and I had managed to make it to Ireland to visit some relatives there, and was now safely situated in a set of lovely rooms at John's hotel in Kensington—how delightful that he was in London at the same time as I, for to tell the truth, I was lonely for all my dear family, but mostly for John.

"Emily, dear old girl!" John embraced me heartily as soon as I opened the door.

"John, good Lord, you've grown thin!" I blurted out, before I could think twice about it. "Are you well?" I looked at him anxiously, leading him by the hand to sit on an overstuffed sofa in my sitting room.

"Oh, Mr. James has been running me ragged, I swear," he said, laughing. "But I positively have broken through his powerful grip on me in order to be here on your arrival—and actually to dine with you!" He made a funny face. "There's this horrid stuff the English call food, *quelle horreur, n'est-ce pas*? I don't know when I've eaten so much bad beef and potatoes! But the people are so damned pleasant and flattering! It's giving me quite a swelled head, I assure you."

"You are very much admired here, John," I said, nodding my head knowingly.

"Ah, tell me, what do your spies in London say about me?" He leaned forward, kissed me on my cheek, and spoke again before I could answer. "Dashed if I'm not more than pleased to see you, old thing! How are Mama and Papa, and Violet?"

"I'm sure you receive letters from them as regularly as I do, don't you, John?" I looked closely at my dear brother.

"Yes, yes, of course," he said, "but I'm afraid the substance of them goes out of my head very quickly—I've been distracted of late."

"Well, they are all as well as can be, putting aside Mama's *primavera* ailments, of course," I said. "What has been troubling you?" I settled back comfortably on the sofa, ready to hear him out at length.

John smiled at me, and sighed gently. "What a luxury to have such a sister," he said. "One who will listen and not judge, or advise, or remonstrate with me—just listen and sympathize."

I could see that the thought alone was enough to make him relax and breathe freely again. He waved away my question altogether.

"Nothing worth thinking about anymore, now that you're here, dear Emily," he said. He took a cigarette out of the case in his pocket and lit it. Leaning back, he smiled cheerfully.

"Shall I tell you of all the unusual creatures I have met on this trip so far?" he said. "Mr. James has been taking me round to quite a zooful!"

I smiled, and took a letter from my pocket. "Oh, I know all about it already, John," I said, waving the letter. "Violet Paget has written me faithfully about all your doings amongst the Bohemians of London." I consulted the letter. "Let me see—on Sunday you went to the studio of the eminent Edward Burne-Jones, who, Violet says, has 'the silliest, dreamiest ideas of art that ever were created, a poor copy of Dante Gabriel Rossetti'—remember, this is Violet's opinion, not mine—and then you went to Edwin Austin Abbey's studio on Monday, and enjoyed yourself very much."

"Abbey's a capital fellow, indeed," said John. "Both he and his wife were so friendly and cordial to me as to make me feel quite at home." He puffed at his cigarette. "Very different from Burne-Jones, a bit of a stiff, though a wonderful painter."

"And then," I continued, "on Tuesday you went to the Grosvenor and the Royal Academy, and dined with Mr. James and his friends at the Reform Club, and well, there the letter ends, and I fear I shall have to wait until the mail comes today to find out what you did on Wednesday and Thursday!"

He shook his head, half laughing, half chagrined. "I know Violet is an intrepid gossip," he said. "I can say that only to you, of course, but I had no idea she was tracking me so closely. And I only saw her once, at Burne-Jones's, but I don't believe she was even at Austin Abbey's studio, at least, not while I was there!"

"These new friends can be of great service to you, John," I said, putting away the letter, and rising with some difficulty from the sofa. He watched me as I crossed the room, crabwise and halting as usual. "It is very good of Mr. Henry James to take you about so." I paused with my hand on the door to my bed chamber. "We all expect so much of you, poor dear," I said, looking at him with a loving smile. "But you do know that I will love you, we *all* will love you, even if you never paint another picture in your life." And as I slipped into my bedroom to get my wrap for dinner, I glimpsed John's eyes brimming with tears.

Louise Burckhardt
Paris

It was the first day of a new life for me.

I was spinning from the velocity of the change, leaning against the open French doors of my apartment—my own apartment, all mine—looking out into the Spring morning, but seeing nothing of the tender green leaves, nor hearing the sounds of birds or passersby in the street below.

A few months earlier, I had gained my majority, and with it, an unexpected inheritance from my godmother, recently deceased, enough to enable me to strike out quite handsomely on my own, as I had so long been desiring. The apartment, situated on the third floor of a respectable old building on the *Rue du Bac* just off the *Boulevard Saint-Germain*, was the immediate result of the settlement, and I had acted quickly and decisively in all the matters of leases, furniture and domestic services.

From start to finish, this monumental change had taken exactly one month, and I had told no one of my plans until the day I was able to move myself, my books, my music and my clothes into the apartment. My mother is still stunned, and my sister has written me off as "simply mad." But I have gained what I needed most—independence.

I felt as if I had stepped onto firm clouds—light and airy, ever-shifting, but holding my weight.

And now, the next step.

In my hand was a letter from Madame Edouard Pailleron, wife of the eminent French actor. The socially prominent couple, whom I had met a few years earlier through John Sargent—he had painted their portraits, and that of their children—had been impressed by my singing, displayed on various occasions at John's studio and other soirées we had attended. They had long been urging me to exercise that talent

245

on the stage, a notion that so baffled and confused me that I had never given anything but discouraging replies to such a wild idea. But now—

I read the letter over again.

Dear Mlle. Burckhardt, It would give my dear husband so much pleasure if you would seriously consider taking on the role of Floriana in the musicale he is producing for next season. As he has told you, there is little acting in the part and a great deal of singing—perfect for you, a novice in the theatre! Floriana is a genteel young lady who sings in private performances at country houses, just as you do, and I assure you, having reviewed the role specifically with you in mind, I find nothing at all improper for a lady such as yourself to represent her.

Nothing, I thought, except the act itself of being on the stage! What would my sister think of me now? What would my poor mother—? But I stopped myself there—I had done all *this*, I thought as I gazed around my apartment—to get away from anyone ruling my life, present or absent. I bent my head to the letter again.

I write you myself to add my encouragement to my husband's, and to let you know how entirely you will have my support. I quite know how difficult a decision this will be for you—vraiment, it will change your life as you know it. But is that such a bad thing?

Clever Madame Pailleron, I thought, she is quite sharp, and knows where the tender spots are.

I let the letter fall onto a little table by the door, and stepped out onto the tiny balcony. A fresh breeze caught my skirts and ruffled them around me, playful and intimate. I began to hum one of the songs that "Floriana" would sing in the musicale—I had procured the music after Monsieur Pailleron had named the songs to me. The melody swelled in my head, and I felt at that moment I could pour forth the song with luscious, rolling notes and a captivating style. Only the sight of the passersby on the street below kept me silent—but if it were an audience, would I be intimidated? No more, perhaps, than I ever had been in the drawing rooms of my friends, when I sang to the gathered company after dinner.

But—the final obstacle, in a way—was I cutting off, with a single stroke, all chance of marriage, were I to take this incredible step? Marriage, at least, to a *respectable* man? My heart told me that the only man

I wanted was John Sargent, and I had all but given up entirely any hope of a marriage with him. Why indeed, I demanded of myself, did I have *any* hope at all? What did I need as a final proof that he didn't want me, would never want me?

I shall give it one more chance, I decided, turning back into the room, and picking up the letter again. *And if he denies me one last time, I will take it as the extinction of all my dreams in that regard, and*—I glanced at the letter—*and I shall take up monsieur Pailleron's proposal.*

Thus determined, I shook myself free of any thought that would bind me to gloom and insecurity, and decided I would speak to the cook about preparing a light luncheon for some friends I was dying to invite to my new apartment.

A Few More Letters

A Letter to Louise Burckhardt from Isa Boit, dated 27 March 1884—Cernitoio

Dear Louise,

We are all in a flutter here, and are proceeding to pack our trunks and make for Paris in the next few days. You won't have heard, of course, but Ned has had a painting accepted for the Salon! Not that *that* should be any surprise, as it's happened before, but it's been some time, and frankly, I did not have my hopes up. We have told no one of his entry, so I beg you to keep this to yourself for the time being. I hope to persuade him to let me arrange a dinner in his honor, to celebrate the occasion, but you know his modest nature—nonetheless, I want all our friends around us to cheer him on.

And I do mean *all* our friends, dear girl, which will include John—poor Ned was so insistent, I could not refuse, nor did I feel it was necessary. Florence has been so content, and generally cheerful, all this time we've been at Cernitoio, that I am quite sure in my mind that she has gotten over her sad infatuation with our dear friend. She will be sixteen in May, and I do beg of you to help me think through her *coming out*, so that all will be perfect and *comme il faut* for her. We will have to go to the shops on our return, of course—your news of the latest fashions this Spring is quite intriguing, and I look forward to your assistance for some new ways to spruce up my own wardrobe which, after several months to ourselves in the country, I do not mind telling you is rather sad-looking.

I shall send you a note as soon as we're in town—you're with your mother now, is that not so? And therefore, at the hotel on the Rue Hauptmann where you usually abide?

All my love, Isa

A Note to Albert de Belleroche from John Sargent, dated 29 March 1884—
London

Dear Baby,

I shall be at home on 3 April, please do your best to be there waiting for me—it's an age at least since I've seen you and paid attention as well! That damned and damnable portrait no longer holds me in thrall, and now that I've grown weary of dashing about in the interminable English rain, eating Bohemians and talking to sides of beef—or is that the other way round?—anyway, I shall soon be home and all shall be well, most well.

Yours ever, JSS

A Note to Henry James from John Sargent, dated 30 March 1884—London

My very dear Mr. James,

How can I express my gratitude? I am overwhelmed with your courtesy, your attention, your dinners and your friends! You have introduced me to a new world of art and design. I am quite taken with the pre-Raphaelite style, and have fallen in love with all the dear ladies, the artists' wives and models. Such a lively scene you have there in Bloomsbury—how do you manage to get any writing done yourself? Which leads me to think that you have made great sacrifices to entertain humble me, for which again, thanks. While Paris is my home, you will always be welcome at my fireside, indeed anywhere at all, but I believe I must say, in all truth and with great respect, that I shall not be calling London "home" in the foreseeable future.

With all my thanks, J.S. Sargent

A Letter to John Sargent from Ralph Curtis, dated 31 March 1884—Paris

Dear Scamps,

When did you say you were coming back to Paris? I've heard from the Salon board, and two of my paintings are 'in' for this year, but I know they don't stand a chance of being noticed next to your Madame 'X'. I can only hope mine will be placed on the other side of the hall. Also, did you know? Ned Boit has entered a painting, too, and has had it accepted! I heard it from Carolus-Duran myself, ran into him on the boulevard this morning. I'm happy for him, it's time he turned to his art again. They're planning to be back in Paris within the week, I understand from a letter Louise got from Isa.

Speaking of whom, Louise has done a bunk from her *mater* and set herself up in her own apartment! Knock me over with a feather, you could. Huzzah for her, I say, wish I had her spunk. Haven't said a word to my own *mater* as yet, as she's likely to kill the messenger, don't you know? She'll find out soon enough, and I'm not sure I want to hear what she'll say about it.

Send me a telegram when you're back (we're at the Crillon, per usual) I'll take you to dinner, am in need of your good cheer and *L'Avenue's* best spirits.

Ever, Ralph C.

A Note to Isa Boit from Louise Burckhardt, dated 31 March 1884—Paris

Dear Isa,

What wonderful news about Ned, although I must warn you, don't expect it to be a secret for very long—not in this town! I am only too happy to help you with dear Florence, although it's so hard to believe she is all grown up now. Also, I have some surprising news of my own, but I wish to tell you in person. I shall keep watch for you, and will send a note when I know you're in town and ready for visitors.

Yours, Louise

❧ *April 1884* ☙
Paris

The Party at Herr Spitzer's House

Amélie Gautreau

It was the beginning of the Spring season in the city, and invitations to private parties were piling up on my silver tray, delivered twice a day. Al-though I discarded many with no intention of even replying, I considered each one thoroughly, as did my mother.

"Ah, here's one there is no need to think about," I said, handing an elegant pale blue envelope to my mother. We were lounging in my boudoir—that is, I was lounging, recovering from an unusually late night at the opera—and my mother was sitting at a table, quite completely dressed and alert, as always.

"The Spitzers?" My mother pronounced the name with an undercurrent of distaste. "Isn't he the man whose father was a cemetery caretaker?"

I laughed. "Oh, Mama, don't be so old-fashioned! No one thinks about that sort of thing these days. Besides," I added, taking back the invitation, "he's been incredibly wealthy ever since he found that Rembrandt in some barn or something, and his collection of Renaissance *objets* is said to be breathtaking." I read over the invitation and set it aside to be answered at the appropriate time. "This is the first invitation we've had from them since they moved into the *Musée Spitzer*, as he calls it, and I intend to go. All the columnists will be there, too, you can be sure."

My mother responded by wondering what I would wear, and the ensuing discussion lasted some time.

Carroll Beckwith

"Why is Herr Spitzer inviting me to his soirée?" John stared at the invitation in his hand, and spoke aloud to me. I had recently returned to Paris from jaunts to more exotic realms—Constantinople, Athens, and Jerusalem—and I was visiting John for the day.

"Spitzer! Lord, I hope it says you may bring a guest," I said, and immediately snatched the card from his hands and read it over with greedy eyes. "I hear he has a violently swell collection of swords and axes and armor from the Middle Ages, you know, love to see all that."

"'Violently swell'," John repeated, shaking his head. "Where do you get your expressions? I'm not sure whomever you're hanging out with these days is doing your diction any good."

"Diction be damned," I returned calmly. "And when did 'hanging out' become part of the Queen's English, my lad?" I flipped the card onto the desk in front of John, and putting my arm around his shoulders, gave him a quick kiss on the cheek. "Pretty please, with treacle on top, may I go with you to the Spitzers?"

He laughed and pushed me away, cuffing me on the arm. "Well, if you put it that way, how can I resist?" He regarded me from a little distance. "But I dare say you've got an invitation of your own waiting for you at your digs, don't you think? If he's invited a beggar like me, surely you're on the list as well?"

"Oh! Well, quite possibly," I said. "I *did* dine with them when I was here last autumn, but then, I'm not the *sensation* you are this term, my boy—I hear that positively everyone's after you, from here to London and back again."

"Rubbish," said he, and turned back to the mail on his desk.

The evening of the Spitzer's soirée arrived, and as it turned out, I had indeed received my own invitation. John had promptly asked Albert to attend with him, and told me he was especially gratified that Albert had accepted, as his young friend had been more absent than present of late, and when in company, seemed to him more moody and preoccupied than usual. Although I did not see Albert very often in company with John, I privately agreed with John's assessment—and moreover, when I *had* seen Albert *not* in company with John, well, let me just say I was able to discern the reason for his absences and his preoccupation. But I said nothing to John, not my place you know. Just an observer. He would know, soon enough. I met up with them at the door of the Spitzer manse, all of us dressed in our finest evening attire, alighting from our carriages at the appropriately late hour of ten o'clock.

The *grande maison* was alight with candles in chandeliers and gas lights throughout the many gorgeous rooms. The entire first floor was given over as a showplace for Herr Spitzer's fabled collection of medieval armaments. On the second floor, half the rooms displayed examples of Renaissance domestic arts—ceramics, vases, dinnerware, tapestries and furniture—collected from throughout Europe, while the other half was dedicated, for this evening, to the guests for dining, drinking and dancing.

"I say," I muttered to John. "Spitzer's rich as Croesus, what?" I already had a glass of champagne in one hand and a cigar in the other. "Would you look at that armor? Magnificent! Only, I wouldn't want to have to wield one of those swords!"

We strolled around together, admiring the armor and other *objets d'art*, and availing ourselves of champagne, cigars and *petits hors d'oeuvres* from silver trays borne deftly through the crowds by servants dressed in Renaissance livery.

In one of the smaller rooms, displaying religious objects and vestments from the fifteenth century, John, whose attention was wandering while Albert's was fixed, noticed a short but robust man with thinning hair hovering at the edge of a small circle of elegantly dressed men and women.

"Look there," Sargent whispered to me and Albert, pointing discreetly. "Isn't that Perdican, the columnist for *L'Illustration*? Yes, see, he's actually taking notes!"

Albert made a face. "Gossip, that's what he trades in," he said, and turned back to gaze appreciatively at an intricately bejeweled crucifix.

But John was more interested in watching the human scene, as was I—it was amusing to see the efforts of the men and women near the columnist to address him with smiles and bows, courting his notice with witty observations they hoped would appear in his weekly column. The ladies, of course, were intent on appearing highly fashionable and beautiful—it was known that Perdican directed the efforts of several illustrators in the wake of such an event in society as this—and therefore, they might be called upon in the next day or two to pose for an illustration.

A sudden hush swept like a wave into the room from the doorway, and everyone turned to see what had caused it.

Amélie Gautreau stood under the arch of the doorway and paused, to great effect. An immaculately dressed gentleman, *not* her husband, stood a step or two behind her, serving, I noted with appreciation, as a dark backdrop against which her white gown gleamed like a new moon rising against a black sky.

Having made her entrance, Amélie nodded to a few acquaintances and continued into the room. I noticed lifted brows and thinned lips among the ladies as they ran their eyes over Amélie's plunging décolletage and sparkling diamonds. I was standing near enough to one pair of ladies to hear a whispered, contemptuous *"arriviste!"* but thought no more of it than that the ladies in question, older and not very attractive, were simply envious.

Amélie caught sight of John and moved in his direction, one hand lightly touching the arm of her escort. Now, this might be very interesting. I had heard enough from John of their relations in the country as to make me quite curious to see how they would meet. It took a few minutes for her to cross the short space, as she was stopped numerous times by acquaintances and friends to laugh and talk. I noted that Perdican was hovering near her, and stopped whenever she did, listening to the conversations and remarks.

"Monsieur Sargent," she said as she came near, her hand outstretched, and her low voice so smooth and inviting it caused even Albert to turn from his crucifix. He started, and looked with astonishment at the face and figure before him. To me, a bystander, it was a marvelous sight, but to poor Albert, I can only imagine it was like looking into a mirror, only the mirror image wore a dress! Amélie, too, looked startled, but instantly covered her surprise, literally, by opening her fan and holding it to her lips. I saw a gleam in Perdican's eye as

the columnist leaned forward.

"It has been too long, *Madame*," John said, taking her gloved hand and bowing low over it. He seemed oblivious to Albert's reaction upon seeing Amélie in person for the first time.

"I shall never forget those happy days in the summer," Amélie murmured suggestively. "How lovely that we shall have a permanent memorial of that time, soon, to grace our *maison*."

"A great tribute to the greatest of Paris's beauties, *Madame*," John said. Her words must have delighted him—I knew he had hopes that the Gautreaus would buy the painting from him after its success at the Salon. It hadn't been a commission, as with other paintings, and if it were as successful as he presumed it would be, they would be willing to pay a great deal for it.

Perdican took out his notebook and scratched a few words in it, looking speculatively from John to Amélie and back again. I could almost hear his mind ticking—he only needed to check his sources at the Salon to verify what his sharp mind told him they were discussing—what a prize for his next column!

Amélie inclined her head graciously, and giving one slight, uncertain glance at Albert, moved away, the immaculate gentleman and the persistent columnist in her wake.

Albert turned to John and pulled at his sleeve, drawing him out of the room and into a sheltered nook away from the crowd. I followed at a discreet distance. They sat down on a little sofa, somewhat secluded by two large palm trees in colorful pots.

"You *told me* I looked like her," Albert said, "but I didn't think it would be so very, well, so *very* like!" He shook his head. "Extraordinary!"

"Even though you've seen the portrait?" John asked. "Didn't you see the resemblance there?"

"Well, yes," Albert said, blushing slightly. "But I thought, well, I thought that perhaps you were taking some liberties, because of…you and me…" He let his voice trail off.

John lifted a hand to Albert's face, and touched his cheek softly.

"I thought only of you even as I painted her, my dear," he said, and swiftly, not caring whether anyone could see or not, he kissed Albert firmly on the lips. I couldn't take my eyes off them, shame on me, and after a moment, when John drew back, I saw only a restrained, closed look in the younger man's eyes which sent an icy chill even to my heart. Albert looked down, his thick eyelashes like black shadows upon his cheeks. I moved away, not wanting them to know there was a witness to this sad little scene.

But I had not been the only witness. As I crept stealthily away, I saw they had been observed by one other person—Louise Burckhardt. Having noiselessly descended a side staircase that gave a direct view of the sofa in the secluded nook, she clearly had seen it all—the soft touch on the cheek, the tender kiss.

And the look on her face told me that she knew she had lost him, finally and forever.

Three days later, an ostensibly discreet but patently obvious paragraph appeared in *L'Illustration*, in Perdican's column, accompanied by, among others, an excellent drawing of Madame Gautreau in her bewitching white gown. Well, it was good publicity—but Perdican got the *liaison* part of it all wrong.

> And *finalement*, also at the astonishingly lavish *fête* at the *Musée Spitzer*, a wise little bird discovered a *liaison* between two of the town's favorite *Americains*, or *peut-être* one should say, *Franco-Americains*—one a tall, handsome and bearded artist whose exhibitions at the Salon have been more than well-received for several years now—and the other, a truly magnificent vision of a woman, a professional beauty, one might say—and how the tale will end will be seen on Varnishing Day! *N'oubliez pas*, you heard it first from Perdican!

Morning Visits
Isa Boit

I was waiting anxiously for Louise to arrive. We had been in Paris for several days, and I had expected a note from her, which had finally come this morning, stating she would visit at one o'clock unless it were inconvenient. I had noted the address for the answer—240, Rue du Bac, No. 3—and mused deeply on what that meant. *Come, come,* I had written in reply, *for I long to see you!*

I heard the clang of the door bell, and after a few moments, steps ascending to the drawing room. Louise appeared as the door was opened for her, and I felt a little clutch of relief that it was indeed she and not some other friend come to visit. I rose to greet her—so unusually dressed, I noted with a strange wonder—and kissing our greetings, we sat down side by side on the small yellow sofa.

"Oh, Louise," I started in straightaway, "I have heard such things about you! And I have wondered even more." I leaned back and eyed her *tout ensemble*, not hiding my astonishment. "Where on earth did you learn to dress like that?"

Louise laughed gaily, and smiling at me, she jumped up and twirled around, the better to show off her new clothes.

"Why, don't you like the way I look?" She was almost saucy.

"My dear, you look stunning," I said, though with a shake of my head. "But you are so changed since I saw you last, in October wasn't it, in Florence?" I looked keenly at her, and motioned to her to sit down again. "What can have brought about such a change? And this the least of it, so I understand," I said. "What's all this about your own establishment?"

"Ah, so you have already heard," Louise said, pretending to pout, "or perhaps, have figured it out from my enigmatic note!"

"The strange address on your note this morning, yes," I said. "You must tell me all that has happened."

Louise's face clouded over slightly but she rallied quickly. She related all the particulars of her removal from under her mother's wing, as she put it—her godmother's bequest, her own determination to be independent, the secrecy and excitement of leasing her own apartment—all the delicious, heady details.

"And your mother, how is she taking this revolution?" I asked in amazement.

"Oh, she'll come round," Louise said airily. "It's been three weeks now, and I've had a note from her every day, beseeching me to come to my senses and return to her." She smiled, a little sadly. "I can't say I'm proud of the trouble I've caused her, but then, you know how my mother likes to dramatize! I think she's rather enjoying herself." Again a clouded look passed over her face. She shook herself, and patted Isa's hand. "I fully expect her to appear at my apartment any day now, and then she'll be fine."

"Well!" said I. "This is something which I must ponder for some time, to grasp it all. But I must say, my dear," I said, "all this freedom has you looking exceptionally well! I've never seen you so—" I faltered, not finding the right word.

"Alive?" Louise said. "Do say that I've never looked so 'alive' because that's how I feel! Devastatingly, shockingly alive."

I merely looked at her in wonder.

The door opened, and tea was brought in by the maid, followed immediately by Florence, who flew into Louise's outstretched arms.

"*Ma petite! Je suis si heureuse de te voir!*" Louise kissed Florence on both cheeks, and made room for her on the little sofa. Florence had grown in the nine months since Louise had last seen her, and with her hair pulled back and arranged on top of her head, she looked older than her nearly sixteen years. However, my dear girl had not filled out in a womanly way as yet, but still had a lean and angular look about her, not entirely unattractive.

I rose to make the tea while Florence and Louise exchanged rapid sentences in French.

"What did you think of your visit to America?" Louise asked.

Florence shrugged, and glanced sideways at me. "It was all right, but I thought my cousins were ignorant, and *Maman* was not very happy with her relations."

"Florence!" I said, reprovingly. "How did you get such a notion?"

Florence gazed at me with serious, steady eyes. "I am not deaf or blind, *Maman*—and you are easy to read."

"Am I indeed, child?" I said, feeling uncomfortable under the scrutiny of this precocious girl.

Florence turned back to Louise. "And have you seen much of our friend, *monsieur* Sargent?" Her voice revealed nothing in particular, as if she were asking politely after a mutual acquaintance. Louise, however, was on her guard—I knew I could count on her.

"I have seen him now and then," Louise said evenly. "He is much engaged, and has spent a good deal of time away from Paris—in London, and other places."

"Is he here now?" Florence asked, and a note of urgency crept into her voice. "Surely he has some magnificent painting planned for the Salon this year?" She turned to me as I drew near and offered a cup of tea to her and to Louise. "We shall go to the Salon to see it, shall we not, *Maman*?"

"Of course, my dear," I said neutrally, then smiled. "And to see your father's painting as well, yes?"

"Oh, yes, I nearly forgot," Florence exclaimed, turning excitedly to Louise. "Papa painted the most beautiful landscape at Cernitoio, and has had it accepted by the Salon board this year, isn't it wonderful?"

"It is indeed," Louise said, taking the cup of tea from me. "I cannot wait to congratulate him personally."

"I am planning a dinner," I said, sitting in a chair next to Louise, "as I believe I mentioned to you when I wrote you from Italy. I want all of Ned's friends around him to celebrate his painting—*before* the judges make their decisions."

"May I attend this dinner, too, *Maman*?" Florence asked, looking from me to Louise. "Surely I am old enough now, with my sixteenth birthday just weeks away." She put her hand on Louise's arm. "Don't you think I am old enough, dear Louise? It would be my first grown-up dinner, and as you will be there, I don't think I would be frightened by the company."

"Frightened! No, indeed, my dear girl," Louise said. "You have nothing to be frightened about—all friends of the family, all celebrating a wonderful event." She looked at me—her look urged me to acquiesce in her daughter's wish.

"Well," I said, "I suppose your Papa would be pleased."

"*Merci, Maman!*" Florence cried, and running to me, threw her arms around me, kissing me several times.

"There, there, child," I said, "it is not worth half this display." But I was pleased that it made her so happy.

Florence seated herself again next to Louise. "I will need a new dress, I think," she said, and touched Louise's gown tentatively, with a furtive glance at me. "I want to be just like you, dear Louise."

Louise laughed at this, but a quick exchange of glances with me led me to think she would not wish that fate on Florence.

Before Louise left us that day, I found a moment with her quite alone, as we were descending the stairs to the front door. I stopped her on the landing.

"I have a favor to ask," I said, taking Louise's hand in my own.

"Of course, dear Isa," Louise said, though she looked slightly uneasy, anticipating the request.

"Before this dinner of mine takes place," I said, "I beg of you to go see John, and ask him to be very, very circumspect in his address and attentions to Florence, when he sees her here." I know I must have looked exceedingly anxious, though I tried to appear calm. "He must not pay her any unusual attention—in fact, it might be best if he appeared almost indifferent to her, and not spend any time talking with her."

"My dear Isa," Louise said, looking pained. "What on earth shall I tell John is the reason for this strange request, as he will, you know, find it *very* strange?"

I considered for a moment. "Tell him only that it is a favor to me, and that he must trust me," I said, then added, "And tell him that I will reveal all to him in time. He must trust me," I repeated. "Will you tell him all this?"

Louise sighed, and I gripped her hand even more fiercely.

"Yes," she said. "It doesn't feel right to me, but as you wish it so much, I will tell him."

I let go of Louise's hand, and kissed her.

"Thank you, dear," I murmured, and turned away.

Violet Paget

I was beside myself, and I didn't know to whom to turn, here in Paris. There was John, of course, but lately he had seemed more remote than usual, more preoccupied. I needed a truly sympathetic ear into which I could pour my troubles—a female ear, if the truth were to be told.

My feet took me almost by their own accord to an address I had learned but the day before, from Isa Boit: 240, Rue du Bac. A smart-looking maid asked me in and took my card up, then returned almost immediately. I expected a denial, but she asked me to follow her upstairs, where Louise Burckhardt met me at the door to the drawing room.

"My dear Miss Paget, this is an honor," she said when I appeared.

"Oh! Miss Burckhardt, I hope you don't mind my coming in this spontaneous and unannounced way," I said immediately. "I realize how very early in the day it is, but only hoped that you would consider me in the light of a friend, and not mind the inconvenience." I spoke rapidly, and I'm sure Louise saw that I appeared somewhat flustered.

"You are a friend indeed," she said warmly. "And do call me Louise," she added, smiling and indicating a chair for me near the window. "I believe, after what we have, ah, experienced together, we may put aside the usual formalities." She turned to ring the bell. "I'm sure you would like some tea, yes?"

I sat down rather abruptly, and nodded my acceptance of the offer of tea. Louise gave the order when the maid appeared, and then turned back to me and sat down. I spoke quickly in a vain attempt to cover my flustered feelings.

"You refer of course, to last autumn, at the Curtises' palazzo in Florence," I said. "Yes, I have since thought of that evening a great many times, and wondered often if you thought me mad, or simply impertinent?" I smiled faintly, and hastened to add, "Oh, and do, please, call me Violet, I should like it of all things."

"Well, then, Violet," she said, "I'm happy to tell you that I thought you neither mad nor impertinent, but—how shall I say it?— refreshingly candid. You spoke so clearly to the one thing that was sore in all our hearts at the time, and in a way that I believe helped us—the four of us there—to see each other as friends and comrades, fellows in the battle of life, as it were."

I stared at her for a long moment, then nodded. "Thank you," I said at last. "That is exactly my own feeling, only you have said it better than I could have expressed."

Tea arrived, and we were silent for some moments while we helped ourselves from the sturdy tea-cart that the maid had trundled into the room.

I sat back into the chair, a little calmer now but still agitated. I looked brightly around the room.

"You have a very pleasant space here," I said. "I must say, I am quite shamefully envious of your situation—it is just what I so dearly want for myself, and what I know is, at least at present, beyond my reach."

Louise merely smiled and sipped her tea. She's a sharp one, I thought to myself, and obviously can see that I'm buying time, avoiding saying what I came to say.

"Have you spoken with John at all lately?" I asked abruptly, and continued when she shook her head.

"When I was in London last month," I said, putting down my teacup, "I was running round the same circles that John was visiting for a week or so—you know, the Chelsea and Bloomsbury folks, the pre-Raphaelites and such—" I paused to see if Louise knew what I was talking about, and continued when she nodded. "Well, you may or may not know that John was being squired about by Mr. Henry James, and his whole crowd—Gosse, Wilde, all those sorts—and I fear—" here I stopped outright. Again I looked directly at Louise, gauging her character.

"May I speak candidly, Louise?" I said, having made up my mind on the issue of character.

"Of course," Louise said. "I wouldn't want it any other way."

"John is in danger of being cast into the same cauldron as those decadents in London, and I fear what it will do to his reputation."

Louise considered this statement, struggling to hide her surprise.

"Do you call Mr. Henry James a 'decadent'?" she said.

I waved a hand in dismissal. "No, no, not *him*, but then again, some of the company he keeps—" I didn't finish my sentence.

"What is it that you contemplate doing?" Louise asked. When I didn't answer, she pressed on. "Do you want to warn John, perhaps, against becoming corrupted, or lecture him on the consequences to himself of the questionable behavior of his acquaintances—or perhaps, his own behavior?"

I looked as I felt, discomfited. "Well," I said, "when you put it that way, I sound like an interfering old busybody, don't I?"

Louise smiled. "John is after all, an adult, and we must assume, aware enough of his reputation to safeguard it better than you or I could do."

I nodded, remembering past conversations with him. "Yes," I admitted. "He is much too aware of the trajectory of his career, as he sees it, to allow himself to be caught out in something that would ruin his respectability."

Louise observed me closely. I could see that she felt there was something more at work here than met her eye. She rose and poured more tea, and then sat down in a chair nearer to me this time. She waited a moment, and then spoke softly.

"What is it, Violet? There is something more, isn't there?"

I turned to her with wide eyes, then lowered my gaze. "Yes," I said. "Yes, there's more." I placed my cup on the table, and folded my hands in my lap.

"You may or may not know," I began, "that I have recently had a book published—a novel, really—called *Miss Brown*. It's about the life of the bohemians and aesthetes in London, a satire, it was meant to be, in fact, a lesson about the true nature of beauty and principle, but how so much of what they say and think is completely hypocritical if one looks at their behavior."

Louise remained silent, waiting for more.

"I have lately had a letter, from a friend," I said. I took a deep breath, seeing in my mind's eye the words that Mary Robinson had written. "She tells me that over there, in London, everyone is highly incensed, indignant—and being very, very nasty about my book, my views—even about me personally." I raised my eyes to Louise; I was near tears. "They are being horrid! Even Mr. James, to whom I dedicated the book, has refused to write to me with a single word of comment!" The tears began to fall freely now. "Apparently they all think I am being deliberately cruel in representing them as decadent, and foul, and immoral—but that's not what I meant to do at all! I never meant any particular person, either, and they are all exclaiming over my betrayal of their confidence!"

Louise laid a sympathetic hand on my arm, and handed me a handkerchief which I used to dab at my eyes.

"And you think that your own experience could serve as a warning to John—?" Louise said, tentatively.

"Perhaps, in some way, I'm not sure how, but I know he thinks well of that crowd, and I don't want him to be pulled in as I was, and deceived, so dreadfully deceived." I gave a big, final sniff, and took a great gulp of tea, which seemed to restore me somewhat.

Louise sighed, with furrowed brow.

"My friend," she said firmly, "this fearfulness does not suit you." She smiled as I stared at her. "Do you believe that what you wrote was untrue? Will you let a few whining, self-defending critics force you to abandon your principles, or repudiate what you have written?"

I smiled faintly.

"This is not to say," Louise continued, "that one cannot learn greater caution or perhaps a more accommodating tone, perhaps, but we needn't be frightened away by conventional persons' bourgeois indignation and moralities."

"Of course not," I said.

I wondered at Louise's including herself in her comment, but as I looked around again at the elegant apartment, I had an increased sense of my friend's new independence, and what it might be costing her.

"Perhaps all you need to do," Louise continued, "is to relate to John what you have just told me, and he will be able to draw his own conclusions in reference to his own life."

I thought this over, and nodded my acquiescence. I blew my nose vigorously, and attempted a watery smile.

"You are perfectly correct, and I am being a goose. I think that is an excellent idea. But," I hesitated a moment, "would you be so good as to come with me to John's studio today? I shall feel so much better if you are there to support me in the telling of my sad tale, but I don't want to impose."

There appeared a strange look on Louise's face—I couldn't read it, but it was very brief.

"Yes, of course I will accompany you," she said. "I was planning to visit him today anyway, so we can go together. Everything works out for the best."

She rose and smoothed her gown. "I'll just be a few moments getting ready, do help yourself to more tea. I'll send for a carriage to come round in fifteen minutes."

Ralph Curtis

I opened the street door to John's house when we heard the bell ring, thinking it was, well, anyone I suppose, other than whom I so delightfully greeted.

"*Buon giorno!*" I cried. "What a blessed sight the two of you are! And just what I need today for a little pick-me-up, eh?" I kissed both Louise and Violet quite happily, and led them up the stairs. John appeared at the door of his studio, and ushered them in.

The first order of the day from me and John was a barrage of questions to Louise about her new status as an independent woman.

"I am completely amazed," I said, "but damn me if I don't think you the bravest sort of old thing I've ever come across! I kiss your hand, my dear, in sheer admiration and awe."

John was equally impressed. "To think that you would so far defy not only your mother's objections—and violent they must have been—but your sister's as well!" He rolled his eyes in astonishment. "You are striking out on behalf of all womankind, you know."

"I have no idea of that sort of gesture," Louise protested. "What I do, I do for my own quite selfish reasons, I fear."

"You have done what so many others of us, poor confined women, only dream of, and are afraid to take the step," Violet said solemnly.

"You! 'Confined!'" John said, laughing at her. "You are one of the most free, most well-travelled women of my acquaintance—you are positively everywhere, as you well know—and now, with the publication of *Miss Brown*, your fame will reach the ends of the earth. Oh yes," he said, seeing a bit of surprise in her face, "I know all about it, Emily keeps me up to the mark on all your literary ventures."

"Has she then," Violet said, a little tremulously, and glancing at Louise, "told you of the latest gossip from London?"

Both John and I shook our heads, and sat down to listen.

Violet's sad tale was soon told.

"Nonsense, utter nonsense!" John was roundly dismissive of *Miss Brown*'s critics, and robust in his support of Violet's talent. "You must do as Louise says, Violet, and pay them no mind whatsoever—they are not worth a second thought!"

"Beggars all, is what I say," I chimed in. "You have far too fine a talent, old girl, to be cowed by a bunch of smarmy Brits, eh—begging your pardon, of course." I always forgot that Violet wasn't American.

Soon after this conversation, while Violet and I were talking of other matters, Louise wandered away to view some of the portraits John was working on, and that eventually drew his attention away from us, who remained on the sofa near the windows. It was too far for me to hear anything that was said, but it looked rather serious.

Louise Burckhardt

I had been gratified, momentarily, that John followed me to where I stood looking at his paintings.

"You are looking remarkably well, Louise," he said, his eyes clearly showing his admiration.

"Thank you," I said calmly, but my heart was beating fast. *No time like the present*, I thought, and turned a little further away from Ralph and Violet, so as not to be overheard.

"You have received your invitation to the Boit's dinner, have you not?" I said.

John nodded, and frowned slightly. "Yes, and I own that I have been puzzled for some time regarding them—they seemed so aloof, so distant when I saw them in Italy—did you notice? I could only assume they were under some worry over the girls' health."

"Yes, yes, I believe that was it," I said hastily. "As to that, I, ah, spoke with Isa yesterday, and she has asked me to relay a message to you, one which I'm sure you'll find peculiar, that is—" I faltered to a stop, looking down. This was a good deal more difficult than I had imagined. I raised my eyes to his puzzled face, and launched into it.

"Florence will be present at the dinner, as she is almost grown-up now, you see, and Isa wishes that you would be particularly careful *not* to be too attentive to her." I stopped as a pained look crossed his face along with increased bewilderment. "Oh, I know how very strange this sounds," I said in a rush, "and you must not ask me any questions, but only trust her, trust Isa—she will explain all to you at some future time—but for now, please do not be overly pleasant or charming to poor Florence when you see her."

John was silent a moment, taking this in, and then nodded his acquiescence. Taking my hand, he kissed it, and said, "Then I shall transfer all that attention to you, my dear."

I didn't smile. "As you wish," I said, and turned away.

Ralph and Violet were deep in conversation as I approached them on the sofa, but they broke off when they saw me draw near.

"My dear Violet," I said, "if it is not inconvenient for you, I would prefer to leave now, as I have many errands in the town."

"Oh, I can stay here with Ralph and Scamps, can't I?" Violet said, turning to the two men, who promptly agreed.

"Are you sure you need to go right now, Louise?" John said. "Cannot you come out with us to lunch, or a walk in the *Parc Monceau* gardens? It's so beautiful this time of year."

I shook my head, and repeated that I must take leave of them now, but would see them all at the Boits' dinner in a few days.

John went with me to the street door, and watched silently as I walked away down the sidewalk to the cab stand on the corner—I had refused his escort, and I could see that he felt it. But what was I to do otherwise? Even in my heart, at last, I had accepted it was all over between us, and must act accordingly.

At the Moulin Rouge

Albert de Belleroche

"Only two days now until Varnishing Day," John said to me as he paced back and forth across his drawing room. "Tonight is the dinner at the Boits, for Ned, and then one more night—and I shall know my fate!" He grasped the hair on his head and pulled at it. "I shall go mad!"

"John, do sit down, you're wearing a trench in the floor," I said mildly, "and you're making me nervous, too!" I smiled affectionately at my friend. "What is there to worry about? It's a magnificent painting, and in three days' time you will laugh at how anxious you have been."

"If only I could believe it," he said. He stopped his pacing long enough to look at me and smile. Then he lit another cigarette and began walking about again.

"That does it," I declared, jumping up from my chair and taking him by the arm. "We're going out and put your nervous energy to good purpose! Let's go catch the afternoon show at *Le Moulin Rouge*— Lautrec and I have been there often—there's quite a rousing show on Thursday afternoons, even a bit of a circus."

He grumbled, starting to protest, but allowed himself to be pulled along. Toulouse-Lautrec and I were fast friends—similar family backgrounds, and a similar interest in the bohemian undercurrents of Paris—although Lautrec's art was so much more garish than my own—he saw people through the caustic light of his own wretchedness, where I just dreamed of better souls in lovely bodies. I'd been spending a lot of time with him lately, and with others at *Le Moulin Rouge*. It was time to let John know.

Once in the carriage, I was the nervous one, fidgety and finding it hard to sustain a conversation. I could feel John watching me narrow-

270

ly, and my heart sank.

The antique but newly restored windmill loomed into view, looking as gaudy in the late afternoon sunlight as a tawdry circus at a country fair. We paid the fee and entered past the somewhat tattered red velvet curtain that hung in the doorway, lifted on a long pole by a dwarf dressed in motley, who bowed to us, grinning his typically evil smile, but then he recognized me, and bowed again, truly polite and affable this time. He motioned to me to bend down that he might whisper in my ear, and I couldn't help the telltale blush that spread over my face. I'm sure John noticed.

We were led to a small table in the first circle, next to the stage, just as a juggling act was ending. The audience mostly cheered, some booed, and all called for more drink.

"I believe we are just in time," I said. I winced at John's clouded look, and was relieved when the diminutive waitress came to take our order.

"Champagne," I said, "you know the one I like, Bertholde."

"Whiskey," said John. "Something Irish, if you've got it. The whole bottle."

The ringmaster came to the center of the sawdust stage—a portly, red-faced man in a shiny black tuxedo with ridiculously long tails, and a top hat with a gauze bow. He swept his hat off his head, revealing a pink and sweaty scalp with a scraping of hairs dragged across the top. He was a crowd favorite—carnations and roses were thrown at his feet when he bowed before the audience.

"*Mesdames et messieurs*," he said, his voice surprisingly deep and loud, "the act you have been waiting for so patiently this afternoon—and which you can see again this evening at eight o'clock, right after the dancing bear—without further ado, I give you Lili, our singing angel come down from heaven to touch this corrupt old earth and redeem us all!"

"Now you will see something truly remarkable," I whispered to John, and then I forgot anything or anyone existed except Lili.

The crowd was hushed as the slight form of a lovely young girl danced in from the side of the stage. She was, despite poorly applied makeup and tattered feathered wings attached to her back, a vision of innocence and grace. She pirouetted a few times around the stage, then stood still in the center, her arms folded in front of her. She lifted her head, and began to sing.

Her voice was pure music, although the song she sang was little more than a music hall ballad popular in the town this Spring. She wasn't more than fourteen, although the sad eyes in her smooth face made her look already worldly-wise.

The crowd went wild when she finished her first song, and stomped and called for another. The canny ringmaster protested it could not be done, but pretending to be persuaded by the audience, brought her back out for a second song.

She sang an operatic version of the *Ave Maria*, and one could almost hear the fall of tears in the cavernous room. I felt the tears streaming down my cheeks, and awoke from my dream long enough to see the same on John's face.

A standing ovation that lasted several minutes greeted the final *Amen*, and Lili was whisked away, out of sight, until her performance later in the evening. I turned to John; now was the time. "I've asked her to model for me," I said.

"Really," he said. He poured himself another glass of whiskey. "She's rather young, don't you think?"

I shook my head. "She's already had a harder life than most people three times her age," I said. "But that hasn't taken the spirit from her, or her angelic innocence. She will make a fantastic model, sublime and beautiful—" I broke off, and looked straight at John, willing him to acknowledge, finally, what was happening between us.

"Would you like to meet her?" I asked. "I am allowed backstage, they think of me as a kind of *bienfaiteur*, I believe." We exchanged a long, sweet look, and after a moment, John smiled.

"Go, then, on your own," he said. He took out his watch and pretended to be concerned at the lateness of the time. "I'll just finish my whiskey, and then I've got to get back if I'm to dress in time for the Boit's dinner."

"You're sure?" I said.

"No question, old thing," he said, trying to sound hearty. "Off you go."

I bent toward him and gave him a swift kiss on his cheek. "*Au revoir, mon ami.*"

"*Adieu,*" he whispered. I felt his eyes on me as I walked away.

The Dinner at the Boits

Ned Boit

The drawing room was bright with candles, flowers and conversation when John arrived at our home. It had been more than a year since he'd been to the house, and that in itself felt strange to me, even though we had not been there for a considerable period ourselves. Isa had told me of her request to Louise regarding John's behavior to Florence—I did not approve, and told her so; I was sure it would make him uncomfortable, and furthermore, was quite unnecessary. I was the first person he saw upon entering the room, and though I greeted him with true welcoming affection, there seemed to be a shadow across his features which I had not seen before—what, I wondered, had he been through all these long months when we had not seen him?

Isa moved toward us, smiling like her usual self, and John made an effort to cast off his gloominess and greet her with sincere joy. I clung to his hand after shaking it thoroughly, as if I didn't want to part, and indeed, he held me by the arm for some minutes as we stood in the doorway.

"Good Lord, John," I said. "I can't believe how long it's been, and dash it all, I've missed our talks, don't you know?" I looked at him with tears in my eyes, and was quite overcome.

"My dear Ned," he said, and tried to help me recover by striking a lighter note. "And here you are, quite the hero of the evening, surprising us all with your Salon entry this year, and no one knowing a thing about it! I can't wait to see it myself," he said. "I'm genuinely delighted that you have at last found your way back to your art."

"Well, well, come in then," I said, "here are many of your good friends here as well."

273

"Ah," he said, nodding his greeting across the room to Ralph, Violet and Louise, whose mother stood near her. "Louise's mother has apparently reconciled herself to her independent daughter?"

"Yes," I murmured, but added, "however, it takes but a hint to get her started on her grievances about it all, so be warned!"

Together we greeted the Allouard-Jouans, and then we stood talking with Edouard Pailleron and his wife for a few moments. I admit that Florence and her troubles were the furthest thing from my mind, but suddenly Isa was by my side, nudging me fiercely. "Ned," she whispered in my ear. "Remember your promise!"

Florence had standing by the fireplace, dressed in a long, slim gown of palest green. Her hair was swept up off her neck and away from her face, giving her a completely grown-up air. Her mother and I had commented upon it earlier, and she was very pleased. And now, we all watched as she approached our little group by the window—her graceful curtsey and soft smile completed the charming picture she made, and her French was perfect, as always, as she exchanged pleasantries with the Paillerons.

I could see John was amazed at the change a year had made, and he turned to me to say something when Isa caught his arm. She'd seen where his eyes had been directed, and the warning look she gave him was enough to chill even my blood; I can only imagine how he felt. He took her gaze straight on, then lowered his eyes and turned away from her, and away from Florence without having greeted her at all.

Louise Burckhardt

 It would have been a moment of high comedy, all of us so carefully watching John and Florence, except that it was shot through with such a sense of almost Greek tragedy. I saw the tense exchange between John and Isa, and fretted about Isa's insistence on secrecy—surely it would be better if John knew the real truth about Florence? It was always best to have things out in the open, I felt that more and more.

"Why the troubled face, *mademoiselle* Burckhardt?" Edouard Pailleron spoke from slightly behind me—he had turned from his wife's conversation with Florence to see me standing alone. He smiled, and stopping the servant passing by with a tray of champagne, took a glass for himself and offered one to me. I accepted it gladly.

"It's nothing," I said, and smiled at my *patron*. "Do you still think we should make our little announcement tonight?" I asked. "After all, this is a celebration for Ned, and I wouldn't want to take anything away from his moment."

"I have already consulted with the formidable *madame* Boit," he said, "who, as you must know, would have no scruples about putting me in my place if she felt it right to do so." He smiled in a thoroughly charming, self-deprecating way. "Although she is as yet unaware of the nature of my 'announcement', she is perfectly happy to provide the venue for it."

I could not but smile at his teasing manner, but inside, my anxiety mounted. I began to have second thoughts—not about my decision that I was about to make public—but about how my friends, and especially my mother, would take the news.

"Do not fear," Pailleron whispered to me, bending down slightly, "*Madame* Pailleron and I are here to support you, and you are doing nothing more than what some of our most respected ladies have condescended to do, I assure you. And you will be a great success!"

I felt heartened by his confidence, and tried to quell my fears.

Florence Boit

Every moment of that dinner party is etched in my mind. It was my first "coming out" occasion, and my mother had made a huge fuss about my clothes and hair. I remember thinking, if He likes how I am dressed, then it is worth it. *Such* an obsession.

I had of course noticed John from the moment he walked into the room, and my heart beat faster at the sight of him. *Now that I am a young woman*, I thought to myself, *surely he will take notice of me. If only I could have Jane nearby, I would be perfectly happy!* I waited in a fever of impatience for him to move my way, all the while trying to appear calm and converse with the other guests.

"My dear Miss Florence," said that odd and interesting Violet Paget, drawing near and addressing me politely, "how well you look tonight! And how delightful that you are joining us to help celebrate your papa's happiness."

"It is very good of Papa and *Maman* to allow me to join the party," I said. "And *mademoiselle* Burckhardt was very helpful to me in the arrangement of my hair, and choosing my dress for the evening."

"No one I know is so well suited to giving such assistance as Miss Burckhardt," said Violet, and we glanced over at Louise, catching her eye so that she turned and walked over to us.

"Florence was just saying how much of a help you have been to her," said Violet.

"Oh, it's easy to dress someone well when she starts out with Florence's beauty," Louise said, kissing me on the cheek. She was always so very kind to me.

The dinner bell was rung, and the guests began to turn toward the dining room doors. Monsieur Pailleron was heading over to escort Louise, but John, not noticing, cut him off. I had at first thought he was coming toward me, but he offered his arm to Louise instead. He nodded briefly at Violet, and bowed to me with an indistinguishable mutter. Violet couldn't help but notice that I was distressed, and just then that affable man Ralph Curtis sauntered up to take her into dinner. I'm not sure how the direction was given, but Ralph immediately bowed low before me.

"My dear, lovely Miss Boit, may I have the honor of escorting you into dinner?" he said, his handsome features the very picture of courtly admiration.

I blushed slightly, and took his arm.

As I looked back, I could see that Monsieur Pailleron, with a very good grace, presented himself before Violet, and led her into the dining room.

The dinner passed pleasantly with conversation both intimate and general, depending upon who was sitting next to whom. My mother always did that sort of thing very well. The dinner was exquisitely prepared and served—elegant cold artichoke and lemon soup, delicious roasted vegetables, a spring salad, roast fowl, spring lamb—dish after dish appeared, greeted by exclamations of delight, and all accompanied by excellent wines and iced water. When the last course had been cleared, and before the ices were brought in, John rose and tapped his glass for attention.

"We are all aware of why we are here—to celebrate the good fortune of a wonderful artist, Edward Darley Boit!" A round of applause followed this statement, then he shushed us all again. Lifting his glass in my father's direction, he smiled and proposed a toast. "To Ned, our very dear Ned, may the Salon always make such good decisions as it has done in your case, may the critics fall over one another in their haste to praise your work, and may you continue to paint for a great many years to come!"

"Hear, hear!" "Bravo!" were the cries around the table as glasses were raised and champagne was drunk. I took a tiny sip of champagne, just a sip, as I did not really like the taste, but thought it only proper to do so for a toast. Over the rim of my glass, I gazed at John, who sat across the table from me but one down—Louise was directly across, with Edouard Pailleron on her left. I thought Louise looked ineffably beautiful, her color high but not too much so, and her butter-yellow gown ravishing with her dark hair and eyes. That *monsieur* Pailleron thought so as well was obvious even to me, but most of my attention was on John and his interaction with Louise.

He admires her greatly, I thought to myself, with a little sigh. *He will probably marry her. There never was a chance for me.* My heart sank, and all at once I felt tired, *so very tired*. I wondered if it were proper for me to be allowed to leave the table for a short time. I thought my mother had said something about that, earlier in the day, but she had been giving me so many instructions about how to behave at dinner that I couldn't remember exactly what I could and could not do.

As if reading my thoughts, my mother caught my eye and motioned with her napkin, pressing it to her lips and looking down. Ah, yes, now I remembered. I merely had to rise, place my napkin on the chair, excuse myself with a soft murmur to my right-hand partner—which was Ralph Curtis—and walk quietly away. Perhaps if I spent a little time by myself, I would be collected enough to return and no one will have noticed. I was about to take an early opportunity to do this when Edouard Pailleron rose from his seat at Louise's side, and addressed the table.

"I have a little announcement of interest to this particular company," he began, smiling graciously at the assembled party. "Nowhere else would there be as delightful a time and place, in such an intimate gathering, surrounded by friends and family, to break this happy news." He noticed the ladies giving sly glances at his wife, who sat on John's right hand, and he laughed delicately. "No, no, it is nothing to do with any blessed events from heaven on the way!" he said, causing his wife to purse her lips and pretend to be embarrassed, but her eyes were merry.

"What I have to say pertains to the lovely creature sitting next to me," he said, and turned to look at Louise. "I ask you to join with me, and *madame* Pailleron, in wishing every happiness and success—" he paused for effect. I held my breath, expecting him to announce the engagement of Louise to John, irrational as I immediately told myself that had to be.

"—to *mademoiselle* Louise Burckhardt, as she claims the role of Floriana in my musicale to be produced at the Opera House next Fall!"

Monsieur Pailleron achieved the stunning effect he desired—the group was, at first, quite speechless with astonishment. Louise's mother, in fact, turned white as the tablecloth, and looked as if she were about to faint.

"I say!" Ralph Curtis was the first to speak. "*Brava*, old thing! Just the sort of dash only you could take a run at and be completely successful! I lift my glass to you, dear Louise!" He turned to the actor. "Edouard, put me down for two boxes right this very minute, for the whole run of the show!"

Ralph's enthusiasm triggered a more vocal response from the rest of the company, with cheers and applause rising in volume.

John had taken Louise's hand and was holding it between his own, pressing it with a great show of affection. "Dear Louise," he was saying, "dear Louise, this is just splendid, I can't tell you how very pleased I am." *Madame* Allouard-Jouan and my mother both rose from their places to bestow kisses and embraces upon Louise, who was overcome with the emotion of it all.

The servants appeared with the lemon ices, restoring a bit of order to the dinner, and everyone sat down again, happily conversing and exclaiming over the news. Mrs. Burckhardt, who had not yet said a word, but looked more red than white now, was seen to drink two glasses of champagne, one after the other, before she could bring herself to speak.

"Well, my dear," her slightly querulous voice etching its way through the tumult around her, "I shall have to think about this for a very long time before I know how I feel about it."

"You should feel only joy and happiness, dear Mrs. Burckhardt," said my mother. "We have all enjoyed your daughter's lovely singing, and now she will have a true audience, the audience she deserves."

"A very long time," Mrs. Burckhardt repeated, and signalled to the servant to pour her another glass of champagne.

The ices were finished, the ladies rose when my mother did—at last, it seemed to my weary mind—and the gentlemen remained to drink their port and talk about the things men talk about when ladies leave the room.

I stealthily made my way up to my own room, where I thought I might rest a while in peace, but then I remembered that Jane would be there, waiting for me, though most likely asleep at this late hour. I wasn't ready to talk to Jane just yet, and I had every intention of returning to the drawing room, especially as it had become clear that Louise would sing several songs for the general pleasure, accompanied by John on the grand piano. I dreaded seeing them together again, and yet I felt impelled to witness what gave me such pain.

I remembered that my mother had told me that a small sitting room on the third floor, complete with a *petite salle de bain,* had been fitted up for the evening for all the ladies to rest in and restore themselves, should the occasion require it. I went inside but there was no one there at the moment. I took up a soft cloth from the marble stand and, soaking it in cool water, wrung it out and patted my face. A glance in the mirror showed me that my hair was still perfectly in place, and I was surprised to see how calm I looked, given the turbulence I felt inside.

There was a little alcove off to one side, partly hidden by a curtain, inside of which I knew there was a pretty little sofa, what was called a fainting couch—perhaps I might just rest there for a few moments before going back downstairs. I sat down very carefully, so as not to wrinkle my dress, and laid back slowly on the slanted back of the sofa, against the soft satin pillows. *I shall close my eyes just for a moment*, I thought, *just for a moment.*

I was awakened by the sound of voices nearby, in urgent conversation. Their tones were low, but I could hear every word perfectly. I must have been asleep only a few minutes. I soon discerned the voices as Louise and my mother.

"Everyone can see how much he admires you, Louise," my mother was saying. "And, I must say, it's about time that John settle down and choose a wife."

"Isa, please," Louise said. I thought she sounded weary, and irritated.

"What could be better?" my mother chattered on, heedless of Louise's response. "He an artist, you an actress, or at least, a singer! You are made for each other!"

"John will never marry me," said Louise. "And frankly, I do not want to marry him."

I could easily imagine the look on my mother's face at this statement.

"Why, Louise! What do you mean? When he is so admiring, and so successful? I assure you, a little bit of effort on your part will fix him, do you not see that?" My mother was insistent.

"Isa, please!" Louise said again, and there was the sound of something hitting the table with a sharp *thwack*—a hairbrush, perhaps.

"John will not marry me, or anyone, for that matter," Louise said firmly. "He is not the marrying kind."

"I think I may know a little more about men and their ways, my dear—" my mother was beginning, but Louise interrupted her, as if pushed beyond her limit.

"For heaven's sake, Isa, are you blind?" There was a pause, endless to my waiting ears. "He prefers the company of *men*." There was a longer pause. "*Il aime les garçons, est-ce que tu comprends maintenant?*"

There was a very long pause. My mother murmured something indistinguishable, and a few moments later, the two ladies left the room.

I sat in the darkness of the alcove, hardly crediting what I had heard. And it is at this point that my mind has played a trick on me, for I do not recall exactly what happened after that, or what I really thought then. I remember a feeling of deep elation, and discovery, and something very close to joy and fear. I sat there for a little time, I think, and then went back down to the drawing room to listen to Louise sing, and especially, watch and listen to *Him* play. I remember having a most delicious sense that everything was all going to work out beautifully.

The Day Before the Salon Opens

Ralph Curtis

"Do come and dine with me tonight, Ralph," John implored me. We had met at *L'Avenue*, fortuitously, late in the afternoon, and I could tell he was all at loose ends. "I simply cannot bear to be alone al evening."

"Of course, cousin," I said. "We will, together, stare down the bogeyman under the bed, and make him run away."

"Thank you," he said, getting up from the café table. He was clearly too restless to sit still. "Eight o'clock?"

"Til then," I agreed, holding out my hand. We shook hands warmly, and he walked briskly away.

I remained at the café for some time, chatting with various acquaintances, then slowly wandered this way and that until I reached the Hotel Crillon, feeling in my own way as nervous and anxious about the next day's outcome as John was.

"Tomorrow is a significant day in more ways than one," I said as we sat over dinner that evening. I had been trying with all my might to infuse some optimism into John's thinking about the Salon, but had given up the fight after a while, and we had been silent for a time when I spoke my thoughts abruptly.

"Yes?" He looked closely at me. "What is it, Ralph?"

I sighed heavily, and tried to laugh it away. "Oh, it's just," I said, "just that tomorrow is Lisa de Wolfe's wedding day." I picked up the bottle of wine and poured myself another glass.

"My dear Ralph," John said. "I did not know—and here I've been carrying on about my own stupid nonsense—I'm sorry, *mon ami.*"

"No, no," I said, feeling foolish. "Shouldn't have brought it up. No account to anyone but myself." I drank, and set the glass down carefully. "It's only," I said, "well, I never imagined that I would be slugged so hard, don't you know? Cupid's arrow and all that." I managed a faint smile. "All for nought. End of story." I put a shaky hand to my forehead, and took a deep breath.

The clock on the mantle chimed twelve. We counted out the hours silently, then raised our glasses for a final toast.

"*À demain,*" I said.

"*À demain,*" John said.

I rose unsteadily, and looked around for my coat, which he helped me find.

"If you'll be so good as to procure me a carriage," I said, in a mock formal manner, "I believe I shall retire for the night."

"To be sure, dear cousin," John said, nodding to his manservant, Emile, who had just entered the room. "You have done me an immense favor, spending all this time with poor me."

I laughed and shook my head. "I dare say you won't be 'poor me' after tomorrow, what? I'll see you at the Salon by mid-morning, and buy you a bottle of champagne at *Ledoyen* to celebrate."

He clapped me on the back, then embraced me fiercely. We walked to the front door.

"I'll see to the locking up," I heard him say to Emile, who was waiting on the curb in front of the house, having hailed a passing cab. A few drops of rain were beginning to fall. John saw me safely inside the carriage, and I saw him light up a cigarette as the cab started down the dark street.

30 April 1884 – Varnishing Day

I arrived at the *Palais de l'Industrie* some two hours after the doors opened. I had checked the day before on the two watercolors I had submitted, and was content with their place in the exhibition. I looked around for John, but didn't see him in the front rooms.

Thirty-one *salles* were given over to oil paintings of every description, the last five or six rooms for portraits—a *genre* popular with the crowds, as they hoped to recognize people they knew, but not held in very high esteem by the Salon board. Several more *salles* were filled to overflowing with other media—watercolors, charcoal, pen and ink, and sculptures. John's portrait of Amélie, I knew, was in *salle* thirty-one, and it took some ingenuity to find one's way to the room.

The air was thick with the smell of turpentine—many artists were applying a last-minute coat of varnish, and members of the public had to keep a sharp eye out as they made their way through a forest of ladders, pails and brushes set on boards, and harried Salon clerks rushing about, looking imperious and disdainful.

I strolled through the rooms, feeling unimpressed in general by the scores of paintings, stopping only occasionally to view something that really caught my eye, such as Pierre Puvis de Chavannes' huge mural-like painting, *The Sacred Grove, Beloved of the Arts and Muses*. It was in the style most acceptable to the conservative Salon board as well as the public—an allegory of classical serenity, a pastoral setting in which the nine Muses, many of them nude, were posed sitting or standing among classical columns near a peaceful lake, with two winged angels descending from the heavens.

"Don't go in for the allegorical much, myself," said a voice near my elbow, as I stood contemplating the painting. I looked down, and saw Toulouse-Lautrec, whom I knew through John's friend Albert, standing at my side, sneering up at Puvis's work.

"Hello, Lautrec," I said, bowing to him. "I agree, especially as there seems to be a bit of a mash-up there what with the angels among the pagans, don't you know."

Toulouse-Lautrec laughed, a queer bark of sound.

"However," I continued, "I do admire the flat sort of way he's laid on the paint, very thin, very fresco-like, don't you think? There's something a bit new in that."

The little man hummed to himself, and grimaced. "*Alors*," he said, "it may be. His technique is passable." He bowed to me, and said, "Going to see *la Gautreau*? I hear from Albert that she's quite sexy, eh?"

I smiled. "See for yourself," I said. "*Salle trente-et-un*. John is half-crazy with worry over how it will be received."

"Bah!" said Toulouse-Lautrec. "Who cares what these fools think!" He cast a contemptuous look at the well-dressed people milling about the room. "If they like it, to me that says it's no good! Tell John that from me, *monsieur* Ralph!"

I bowed to him, and the gruff artist disappeared into the crowd.

As I continued through the exhibition, I heard growing murmurs from the people passing to and fro about "*la Gautreau*". I was not surprised to hear it so named—Amélie was well-known throughout the *haut monde* of Paris, and to the general public through the society columns in the papers, whereas John's name was relatively obscure outside the art world.

"Have you seen it?

"Where is it? *Où est la Gautreau?*"

"*Oh, quelle horreur! Elle est decomposée!*"

"*Non, quelle audace! C'est magnifique!*"

My curiosity piqued, I was hurrying to *salle* thirty-one when I heard my name called softly. I turned, and saw John nearly hidden behind a door in the hallway.

"Scamps!" I said, as he took my arm and pulled me out of the train of passers-by. "What on earth—?" I looked in amazement at my cousin—his eyes were bloodshot, as from a sleepless night, dark circles under them drew the color from his face, and he had a frightened, beat-down look about him. "Are you—have you heard discouraging remarks about the portrait?"

John waved his hand. "*Non, non,*" he said, and shook his head. "Nothing to do with that. But come," he said, starting to walk toward the portrait rooms, "let's go hear the worst, shall we?"

It was well-known that the first few hours of Varnishing Day would fix the general opinion about which paintings were the best, and the worst, both in the eyes of the public as well as the critics, who could be counted on to debate, ridicule, praise and discuss the exhibition for the next several weeks.

As we drew near *la Gautreau*, both of us sensed a vortex of excitement in *salle* thirty-one. The crowd was denser, and it was almost impossible to get into the room.

The ladies were the most vocal. We edged into the small room, and could clearly hear the volley of remarks thrown at John's painting.

"Shameless, really!"

"Why, she isn't even wearing a petticoat!"

"And that red ear! Next to that dead skin—she, a beauty? *C'est une horreur!*"

"She's indecent, look at that strap, as if she just—you know—!"

"Or is just *about* to—you know—!"

On the other hand, there were artists among the assembly who spoke up about the painting itself, not the subject.

"*Superbe de style!*"

"*Quel dessin!*"

"*Magnifique!*"

One man, obviously an American by his dress, stared at the painting for some minutes, then said aloud to no one in particular, "Don't like it," and turned away.

I looked anxiously at John. "Don't worry," I whispered. "I'm sure the tide will turn by this afternoon." I repeated to him what Toulouse-Lautrec had said, but John just shook his head. He had gone very pale, and looked near to collapse.

"I must leave," he said. "I will see you later, Ralph." He looked away as he spoke. "Will you come to my studio this afternoon? I must go to the Boit's now, I must go."

I assured him I would come to Boulevard Berthier later in the day, and spoke again my optimism that all would be well, but he merely shook his head, and quickly disappeared into the crush of people trying to come through the door.

I arrived at John's studio late in the afternoon, and learned he was not at home. I told Emile I would wait there, and asked for a bottle of wine and a glass.

The day had not gone well for the portrait of Amélie—in fact, the critics were already starting to say that the entire exhibition was dull, pedestrian, replete with worked-over ideas from previous years—but *Madame X* was, apparently, the worst of a bad lot. It had become an irresistible flashpoint for mean-spirited gossip and reams of newspaper columns in an otherwise arid desert of boring paintings.

The tide, as I called it, had indeed turned in the afternoon, in favor of the painting, but only a little, and only from artists and friends of John's who tried staunchly to stem the flood of disapprobation, of absolute repugnance for *la belle Gautreau's* deathly skin color, her scandalous décolletage and slipped shoulder strap, the aura of unapproachable, unrepentant sexuality in her stance and her figure.

I had discussed it again and again with friends, over the annual Salon luncheon at *Ledoyen*, in the *salles*, out in the street—*yes, yes, it was almost all a reaction to Amélie herself, not precisely to the painting—but how could you separate the two?* Amélie's fate was John's fate, and it looked as if both their reputations would be ruined. What lady of society would want a portrait by him now, given this one that was being openly mocked and derided for its representation of a woman—supposedly a beautiful woman—in such a hideous way? His over-reaching ambition—her insolent narcissism—they would go down together, deservedly, people were saying.

I paced back and forth across the studio, smoking and drinking glass after glass of wine. I heard the door bell sometime around five o'clock, and hoped it was John. Emile soon came to the door of the studio, looking flustered.

"*Monsieur*, it's Madame Gautreau and her mother," he almost whispered, looking over his shoulder with a frightened air. "They want to see *monsieur* Sargent. What shall I tell them?"

I considered my options—it wasn't my place to offer explanations to them—but then, having had a bit too much to drink, I thought, *what the hell*—it might be saving John a bit of the confrontation.

"Show them up, please, Emile," I said. "And bring up another bottle of wine and—and some tea as well."

A few moments later, Amélie and Madame Avegno appeared at the door, wan as ghosts, and trembling from head to foot. With Amélie, I could see it was from exhaustion and shame, but as for her mother, her tremblings were all from anger and righteous indignation.

"Where is *monsieur* Sargent?" Madame Avegno demanded, looking around the room as if expecting to catch him hiding behind a curtain. "I must speak with him immediately."

"He is, alas, dear *madame*, not here at present, and I do not know when to expect him." All of which was true, I thought, as I had expected him long before now. I gestured to a set of chairs on the side of the room. "Will you not be seated, please? Do rest yourselves."

Amélie sank into a chair, tears streaming down her face, which she dabbed ineffectively with a lace handkerchief.

Her mother took up the battle anew. "The painting *must* be taken down," she said. "There is no other recourse. My daughter is the mockery of the town!"

Amélie's tears increased at hearing this, and her mother turned to her, pointing at her as if to prove a point.

"She will die of shame! We will not be able to hold up our heads in the street!" The proud little woman actually stamped her foot as I continued silent. "I demand that *monsieur* Sargent appear, and that he take down the painting from the Salon!"

"My dear *madame*," I said. "What you ask is impossible. The rules of the Salon forbid it. And *monsieur* Sargent is not here, I assure you, so he cannot appear, no matter how much you stamp your foot."

Madame Avegno was not amused. Amélie made a small, coughing noise, like a hiccup, and spoke to her mother in a low, wretched voice. "Mama, let us go. I told you this was a bad idea," said the poor woman, whose usual pale make-up was streaked with tears, revealing a pink and blotchy face. "I just want to go home—I just want to lie on my bed and die!"

"You see! You see!" exclaimed Madame Avegno. "She will die, and it will all be the fault of that horrid, horrid painting." She cast a glance upward, as to the heavens, and spoke as if delivering a curse. "My people will see this as a reason to require satisfaction! They will fight!" She swiftly gathered up her daughter and hustled her down the stairs to their waiting carriage just as Emile was coming up with more wine, followed by Clotilde with a tea tray. They looked fearfully at the departing ladies, then turned to me with questioning eyes.

"Is *monsieur* Sargent in trouble?" Clotilde asked, her voice quavering.

"Oh, I expect not," I said, trying to sound reassuring. "He'll be along soon, and this will all blow over, you'll see." But although the servants were a little comforted, I was not so sanguine. Madame Avegno's threat of a duel I dismissed as preposterous. But as for the painting itself, the coming days and weeks would bring the proof—success or scandal?

I sighed, poured a glass of wine, lit a cigarette, and sat down to wait for John.

John Sargent

It was the morning after the Boits' dinner, the last day before the opening of the Salon. I must retrace these steps in order to explain—perhaps mostly to myself—what occurred in those twenty-four hours.

The city seemed to be holding its breath. It was very early in the morning, just after dawn, as I rose, dressed, and slipped outside to walk the grey and silent streets. I stopped at a corner to light a cigarette.

Twenty-four hours, I thought. The day has finally come. I knew I didn't need to see—again—on which wall, in which room, at what height, the portrait had been hung. But I would go to the *Palais de l'Industrie* anyway, some time this afternoon, to view it again. It was well-placed, though in the very last *salle*, number thirty-one, where the portraits done in oil were exhibited. There was good light, and the other portraits in the room, I had noted with satisfaction, were much smaller, and not nearly as dramatic as my *Madame X*.

I finished my cigarette and flipped it into the street. The sun was coming up over the edges of the trees of Parc Monceau in the far distance, and the grey light was melting into pearl tones of pink and tangerine.

I wished I had something more to do—a portrait that needed to be done today, this very day, so I could throw myself into work, absorb my mind and senses, relieve the tension that had been building so long.

And then there was Albert. Well, he was gone—in truth, I had seen it coming for some time, but I wouldn't, couldn't bear to acknowledge it. He was a very young man, and was for a time—I was sure of it—in love with me, but now there was someone else. Lili. I'm sure she was quite a fine person, but not deserving of my Albert.

I lit another cigarette, and walked through the western gates of Parc Monceau. I had to think of something else or I would go mad—the ache in my heart was so pressing. I steered my thoughts to the previous evening—the dinner party at the Boits, and Louise's astounding announcement. She had shone with a new, fresh light, and I was very happy for her. I had offered to paint another portrait of her—as Floriana—to memorialize her first role, but she had laughed and demurred, saying she preferred to wait—for luck—to see if she were any good in the part first.

My thoughts moved on then to Florence, and her first "appearance" in company as a young woman. Her behavior had been exemplary, but then, Florence had always seemed mature for her years. I had noted something odd, however, after dinner, when the gentlemen and the ladies were all re-assembled in the drawing room. Florence had been a little excited, more voluble, perhaps even feverish, as she chatted to the guests. She was among the most urgent in persuading Louise to sing—and scarcely seemed to notice that I was to perform as well. But once, I caught a look from her—a deep, intense, piercing look that almost made me fumble at the keys, but then she had looked away.

I shook myself as I paced the smooth gravel of the walks. I had kept my promise to Louise, and Isa, and had avoided Florence all evening. I suddenly felt impatient with women—their secrets, their promises, their need for drama, their need for love. Love! I had loved Albert and lost him. I loved him still and yet...

"Damn, damn, damn!" I muttered. "I shall have done with the lot of them."

I turned from the path I was walking on, and headed back home, where coffee and breakfast, and the day's newspapers, would be awaiting me.

Later in the day, I met up with Ralph at *L'Avenue*, and secured his promise to dine with me, as I didn't want to be alone. The evening was silent and melancholy—and I was deeply concerned to see him still so affected by his encounter with the woman he believed he was meant to love. I was not in a mood to think very favorably of women and their loves—the loss of Albert seared my heart, and I felt reckless, almost desperate. But I kept it to myself.

After seeing Ralph off in his cab, I paused outside the house to light a cigarette, and stood for a moment enjoying the cool Spring night. A light rain was falling. As I turned back toward the door, taking the keys from my pocket in order to lock up, I was startled by a slight figure, dressed in dark clothing, who stepped out from behind the bushes planted on either side of the steps.

"*Qui va là?*" I said. "Who is there?"

"*Pardon, monsieur*," said a soft, low voice, and the person stepped out further into the light cast from the street lamp nearby.

It was a young man—a boy, really—dressed in common clothing, a cloth cap on his head. He spoke in French.

"My name is Jean-Marc," he said. "You are *monsieur* Sargent, the famous artist, yes?"

"Artist, yes," I said. "Famous? That remains to be seen." I looked narrowly at the boy. "What can I do for you, Jean-Marc?"

"*Je voudrais*—I would so much like to learn to be an artist, *monsieur*, and I have come to ask you to take me on as an apprentice," Jean-Marc, his voice barely above a whisper, spoken in a rush through chattering teeth.

I smiled. "Now? In the middle of the night? Strange time to apply for a position, don't you think?"

The rain began to fall faster, and I saw that the boy was shivering. Deciding that there was no harm in him, I motioned with a hand toward the door.

"Let us get in out of the rain, shall we?" I said. The boy ducked his head in passing, and preceded me up the steps. I locked the doors carefully, and turned to him, giving him a mildly inquiring look. The only light in the hallway spilled in from the dining room, where the servants were cleaning up.

"You've run away from home, haven't you, Jean-Marc, if that is your true name?" I spoke softly. The boy looked at the floor, then spoke up.

"Oh, it is my true name, sir, and I"—a pause—"I have no real home. Not anymore."

I frowned. "How old are you?" I said, more sternly. "Fifteen? Sixteen?"

The boy's head came up at the challenge—clear brown eyes with thick lashes met my own in a look unafraid but not bold.

"I'm going on seventeen, *monsieur*, and I know how to mix paints, and prepare canvas, and I can be very helpful in a studio, arranging props and costumes, and—" Jean-Marc ran out of breath, and shrank back a little.

"Yes, well, we shall see, perhaps—in the morning," I said. I led the way into the dining room.

"Are you hungry?" I asked.

"*Un peu, monsieur*," the boy said, eyeing the platter of beef in the cook's hands; she was taking it back to the kitchen.

"Prepare a plate for my guest, please, Clotilde, and bring it to my study."

"*Oui, monsieur*," she said. She lowered her eyes after a keen look at the boy.

A fire had been laid in the study, and I knelt down to light it, motioning to the boy to sit in a large chair drawn up close. After a while I'd gotten a good blaze going. Clotilde arrived with a tray full of good things, and a small glass of well-watered wine, which she placed on a table next to where the boy was sitting. Then she curtsied to me.

"*Merci*, Clotilde, that will be all," I said. "You and Emile may retire for the night."

"*Oui, monsieur*," she said, and glancing once more at the boy, she left the room.

The room was lighted only by the fire now, which sent flickering shadows into the far corners. Jean-Marc ate hungrily, but his manners were impeccable. He was pale, and his delicate, angular features struck

a chord that resonated in my nerves as I sat across from him, smoking. But the boy was very young, surely younger than he had admitted,
and obviously a runaway. I stifled the rising desire that flicked at me,
and smoked another cigarette. There would be time in the morning
for more questions, I decided, especially as Jean-Marc had already
smothered several yawns even as he ate, and now his head drooped
over the tray.

"Come, Jean-Marc," I said. "Let's get you to bed, eh?"

"Oh, *monsieur*, I do not want to trouble you," the boy started to
say.

"What? So you'll go back outside and sleep in the rain?" I strode
over to a large cedar chest and removed some blankets which I then
spread on the sofa.

"Here," I said. "Sleep well, little runaway, and we will talk in the
morning." I suddenly remembered what the morning would bring,
and laughed aloud.

"You're a very good diversion, did you know?" I said, smiling
down at him as he was gratefully getting in under the blankets. He had
finally removed the soft cap, releasing a badly cut tumble of short
brown locks.

"*M'sieur?*" he said sleepily.

"Good night, little diversion," I said, and gently stroked the boy's
hair; my hand was trembling as I did so, and a flame of desire shot
through me like lightning. But I drew back as if burned, and made
myself turn away. Checking that the screen was properly placed in
front of the dying fire, I pulled back the thick curtain that hung across
the door to my bedchamber. "Sleep well, *mon petit.*"

Only softly breathing silence answered me.

The dawn was just breaking as I woke abruptly, startled by some
movement in my bed. I lay on my side, and with growing consciousness felt the unmistakable warmth and weight of a sleeping body
pressed against my back.

With great caution I moved closer to the edge of the bed, away
from the sleeping form, and turned to look—Jean-Marc lay peacefully
asleep, the tousled brown locks falling across his face. He was dressed

as he had been when I left him on the sofa, in his badly fitting trousers and white collarless shirt. I could see the fragile blue veins in his neck where the shirt fell away, and a sudden tenderness welled up in me at the sight.

I dragged my mind back to the night before—had I?—had we?—but no, it was impossible! Jean-Marc clearly must have crept into my bed long after I was sound asleep.

I gazed at the sleeping face, and in the growing light of morning, began to realize it was a familiar face, a face I knew. Just then, Jean-Marc stirred, still asleep, and spoke—in English.

"*Maman*? Where is Jane? I want to be with Jane."

With a muffled cry of horror, I leaped out of bed. Florence! It was Florence Boit! But how? Why? What did this mean?

My sudden movements had awakened the girl, who sat up, looking around her in a dazed way. I could see now, clearly, that her hair—her beautiful long locks—had been crudely cut away, leaving it short and uneven all around her head. Her clothing was obviously borrowed—or taken—from a house servant.

I grabbed my dressing gown from a chair and, wrapping it around myself, forced myself to appear calm in order not to frighten her—she was staring at me, sleepy-eyed, from the bed.

"My dear Florence," I said, "Dear child, whatever on earth are you doing here?"

"'Florence'?" she said, looking puzzled. "*Je m'appelle Jean-Marc, monsieur.*" She looked up at me, and smiled shyly. "I woke up, and was cold, and a little frightened, and I hoped you would not mind—"

"You are Florence Boit," I said, my voice thick with shock. I felt frozen in place.

"*Non, monsieur.*" She shook her head. "I do not know anyone of that name, and it certainly is not me."

I felt a chill through to my very heart. The child was sincere—she was not acting. But what did it mean?

I willed myself to move. Ned and Isa might very well be, at this moment, frantic with terror upon discovering that Florence was missing. I must send them a message instantly.

"My dear—Jean-Marc," I said, trying to sound calm. "Rest yourself here a little longer, it is very early still, while I go rouse the cook to make us some breakfast—would you like that?"

"*Oui, monsieur,*" Florence said, leaning back against the pillows.

I left the room slowly, then ran to the back of the house where Clotilde and Emile slept. I knocked quietly but rapidly on Emile's door, whispering his name urgently.

"Emile, Emile, wake up! It's of the utmost importance! Emile!"

The sleepy man opened his door, his clothes already half on. I stepped into the room with him, urging him to dress quickly.

"Find a cab," I said, "and go, like the devil is after you, to the Boit's house on Avenue de Friedland—number 32—tell them that they must come here, immediately—tell them their daughter is here, safe, with me. Now go, man!"

Emile ran to the door and was gone.

I shall pass over the travesty that was Varnishing Day—it is still painful to remember. Even more painful, however, was my visit to the Boits that afternoon.

"I weep for my poor child."

Ned hid his face in his hands, as I sat across from him in the study where, as I thought now, it had all begun.

After rushing to my house in the early hours of the morning—this very morning, though now it seemed an age had passed—the Boits, with my help, had been able to persuade Florence to go with them, "these lovely people" as I had told her, and I promised I would come by later to see her—*him*, that is, Jean-Marc. She was reluctant, but she went.

Now Ned told me that on her arrival home, Florence had begun to tremble, and breathe with difficulty. She was led to her bedroom, where she had gazed, increasingly agitated, at what should have been familiar objects.

"The break came," Ned told me, "when dear Jane entered the room and ran to her sister, to embrace her." He passed a trembling hand over his eyes, as if wishing to erase the memory.

"Florence gave a great start, and perceiving her image in the mirror, she put her hands up to her hair, like so—" Ned mimicked the touch of wondering hands tentatively feeling the ravaged curls of hair.

"She gave a piercing shriek, horrible to my ears even now—it echoes!—and fell down upon the floor in a fit."

Ned covered his face once more, and sobbed into his hands.

I was distraught beyond any ability to speak. I rose and then knelt next to my friend, embracing him. After a few moments, Ned regained somewhat of his composure, and resumed his tale.

"Doctor Charcot arrived. We had sent for him already, and he took charge. We were all to leave the room." He sighed heavily. "Isa was close to hysteria herself, but is calmer now, and refuses to leave Florence for an instant."

"And Florence?" I asked.

"The doctor gave her something to make her sleep—laudanum, I think—after her shock—and what she has gone through—" Ned could not finish.

They sat for some moments in silence. Ned roused himself slightly.

"I haven't asked you about the Salon," he said.

"Don't even speak of it," I said. "It is utterly unimportant to me now."

I felt a sickening dread in my heart about Florence—she had come to *me*, dressed as a boy. I feared what it could mean, although the most obvious explanation must be—*had* to be—impossible.

"Do you have any understanding," I said finally, forcing myself to speak, "of what she was thinking—to lead her to act in this way?"

For answer, Ned took from his pocket a small, dark-red, leather-bound book and with a deep sigh, handed it to me.

"My very dear John," he said, rising slowly, an old man bowed by Fortune. "I cannot bear to tell you in words what we have learned, so I beg you to read it for yourself."

He acknowledged my puzzled look, and said, "It is Florence's journal, our daughter's own words. I have marked the pages you must read." He averted his eyes then, and said, awkwardly patting my shoulder as he slowly moved past, "Be assured, dear friend, that Isa and I neither blame nor judge you. You are, and always will be, our dear friend."

And he left the room, closing the door silently.

I sat stunned and scared, the diary unopened in my hand. I feared I knew not what, and was scarcely cheered by Ned's assurances of loyalty and love.

I opened the book, and began to read.

I read enough of the first set of marked pages to understand that Florence was infatuated with me, considered herself deeply in love, and desired more than anything a return of her feelings. I remembered Violet's warning to me, so long ago, and swore at myself for my arrogance and insensitivity.

The most recent journal entries were, for me, of an entirely different order of pain, and my soul writhed in shame and anguish as I read the words.

... I understand it all now, because of what I overheard Louise tell Maman—il aime les garcons! She said he would never marry her, as mama insisted he would, nor would she marry him. And for this to be the reason! No wonder he has never returned my love!

But the best part of all, which he does not yet know, which no one knows, I have been so clever in hiding it all these years—is that I am, in truth, a boy! Jane almost guessed it once, but she was easy to persuade—and then, that day in Cernitoio, when Maria Caterina reminded me what a "tomboy" I had been, I turned off her remark so well with my calm, ladylike behavior! But I see now what my destiny was to be—I fooled the Fates when I was young, in deciding to become a little girl instead of a little boy, so I would not be caught in their traps—like the myths say—and forced to die like my brothers, before I was ten years old! I tricked them! Oh, how I tricked them, and now, here is my reward, for waiting all these years, pretending and trying to be a girl, as nice as that was some of the time—but now, I can be His! I can be what He prefers, as Louise said, 'he prefers the company of men'!

So now I know what I must do—turn back into a boy, and start a new life with Him. I shall do it soon, very soon, while my courage is high. Remember? He said that to me, the day of my fourteenth birthday, at the Salon, "someday you too will be tried, and will find your courage"—what prophetic words. Tomorrow shall be that day!

This was the last entry in the book, and was dated the day before, 29 April.

The book fell from my hands, and in the dim, silent study, I wept until I had no more tears to give.

৩০ June 1884 ৪৩
Paris

Leaving Paris

The Salon was closed, finally, but the scandal continued.

I carted off the portrait of Amélie, and put it away in my studio—but not before I had scraped away the offending fallen strap, and painted it firmly back on her shoulder, even though the Gautreaus were quite obviously not going to purchase it from me now, or ever. I turned it to face the wall.

There were outrageous cartoons—Amélie, one breast exposed, with the caption depicting her insisting that people "leave her alone"; another, exaggerating the heart-shaped bodice and transforming Amélie into a Queen of Hearts playing card, with lewd overtones. One wag wrote a poem as from "The Beautiful Madame Gautreau to Mr. Sargent"—the first stanza read,

> Oh my dear painter, I swear to you
> That I love you with all my heart,
> But what a strange expression!
> But what a strange color!

The critics dissected, discussed, and argued over the portrait's—and Amélie's—merits and demerits in every column, every paper, every journal for weeks.

Puvis's fresco-like *Sacred Grove* was given first place, and Toulouse-Lautrec had immediately parodied it in a large, exquisitely rendered copy, but with the addition of several ridiculous anachronisms—a clock embedded in one of the pillars, for one, and a parade of gentlemen dressed in the latest fashion coming through the trees to leer at the nude Muses in the Grove. There was one figure in the crowd of men, a small, unmistakably dwarfish man in a top hat with his back to the viewer, quite obviously relieving himself at the edge of the woods! I smiled when I saw it, but sighed also, realizing the mockery would do Puvis no harm, unlike the torrents of disdain that were falling upon *my* head.

Amélie had retreated into the country before the end of the season—and no indignant relatives of hers had come forth demanding satisfaction, as Ralph had foreseen. I was almost sorry I didn't have the opportunity to defend my own honor, as I told Ralph, but there was little humor in my statement.

The Boits were gone, too, back to Cernitoio for a time, and then perhaps, Ned had told me, they might try again for an extensive stay in America—but he promised to write, and begged me to write him frequently. He was certain that in a few years, Florence would be well again, and we might be able to meet without any harm to her. I was not hopeful, but we parted as brothers and the best of friends.

"I am not slinking off like a whipped dog," I declared to my friends one day late in June. "I have work—I have commissions to see to in London—the Vickerses," I said, showing Ralph and Violet, who were both in attendance, my appointment book, as if to prove it.

"No one's saying you're slinking off, old thing," Ralph said.

I was silent for a long moment, then I threw the book down on the table. Lighting a cigarette, I walked over to the large south windows of my studio, and contemplated the gardens below.

"Maybe I should chuck it all," I said in a low voice. I looked back at Ralph, who had opened his mouth to protest. "No, seriously, I could be a good businessman, don't you think? Like *Señor Pedro*? Import bat guano or some other commercial thing—no critics to get in the way there!" I took a deep breath. "Or maybe I could, even at this late date, become a professional musician—perhaps Pailleron could give me a part in his next musicale!" I laughed, a short, derisive sound. "I could accompany Louise in her debut role."

"John, you're talking utter nonsense," Violet said. "Do you not recall what you said to me when I was here in April, yammering on, full of self-pity about how I and *Miss Brown* were being treated? Buck up, man, their criticisms have no relation to your brilliant talent—yet maybe you should, as Henry James has long been saying, try your hand in London now where there are people who can appreciate you without all this insufferable, mindless gossiping."

She sniffed indignantly, then smiled fondly at me. "I will say, though, that you seem to me to have lost a bit of your, how shall I say it, youthful obliviousness? Shallow nonchalance?" She laughed as she saw my look of surprise. "Oh, yes, my twin, I say it as I see it—but be assured, it is no more than what I have been forced to experience my own self—I'm just ahead of you by a couple of months in the sad path of *growing up*!"

This made me smile at last, more genuinely, and I strode over to bestow a kiss on Violet's cheek. "Silly old thing," I said. "You are very good to me, you know."

But later, when my friends had departed, I grew melancholy again—they didn't know about Florence, and what had happened there—the private grief that I shared with Ned and Isa, the shame that I alone felt like a knife in my heart. I thought again, as I had frequently, of Louise, and what Florence had overheard her saying to Isa. I knew I couldn't face her, not knowing what she knew.

I would leave Paris, tomorrow—I had given her my all, and she had taken everything from me.

One Year Later—September 1885

Village of Broadway, The Cotswolds

"Quick! Quickly, now, down to the gardens!" I roused the others from their game of tennis, or sitting in chairs under the trees, to help me bring my paints, brushes and the over-sized canvas—along with the children—to the riotously blooming garden to catch the half-hour or so of perfect light.

I was staying in the village inn near the Millet's house, a warm, inviting domestic world presided over by the utterly maternal, delightful Lily Millet. I had become one of an intimate clan of artists, illustrators, writers and simply very interesting people—Edwin Austin Abbey, the Frederick Barnards, Edmund Gosse and his wife, the Alma-Tademas, and Henry James among them. Broadway had become the charmed center of a circle of light, and I was growing content by degrees.

It had been a difficult year. To the French, I was an American interloper, an outsider who had been served his just desserts. To the English—and the Royal Academy in particular, which was several years behind even the French Salon in its conservative view of art—my paintings were too French, my style too flamboyant. Despite Henry James's tireless efforts on my behalf, my commissioned portraits had diminished after that first summer, when I had stayed with the Vickerses in Sheffield. I had difficulty meeting the expenses of Boulevard Berthier, and was reduced to painting portraits of my landlord's wife and daughters as payment; I did not renew the lease when it came due. I still needed to support my family, and the fees from any portraits I painted went to them. For now, my own household was in storage, awaiting a new home—somewhere, sometime.

"Dorothy, child, come along now! John needs you in place!" Lily

Millet urged her daughter to the garden, and I gave her an answering smile as she hurried by me, holding her daughter's hand. I felt a twinge at the top of my head as my foot slipped on a stone, giving me a slight jolt. The wound I'd received, just weeks ago, was healing very slowly. I put a tentative hand to the spot where the bandage had recently been removed, and felt the crustiness of the scabbed-over place.

"Are you all right, John?" Frank Millet asked me anxiously. He'd been in the boat with me and Edwin—we were floating down the Thames not far away—and I had recklessly dived into the river, not heeding my friends' warning about hidden dangers. An embedded spike, from some long-demolished dock perhaps, had deeply cut my head, and I had needed a doctor's attention immediately. Then, two days later, rising from my bed and somewhat dizzy, I had hit the same spot again on a window shutter, hanging carelessly open above my bed, re-opening the wound and causing it to bleed afresh. Indeed, I wondered not a little at the time whether I hadn't done it on purpose—it would be soothing to be unconscious, even for a little while.

"I am well, Frank," I said. "Just a little twinge." I smiled shakily, and patted my friend on the shoulder. "Does me good to be reminded to go a little more cautiously, eh?" I paused to take a deep breath, looking around at the people who had become my friends, even, it seemed, my family. They were amiable, courteous, warm-hearted—everything my tattered heart longed for—and they had taken me in as one of their own. I felt like an old piece of silver plate redeemed from a pawn shop, the tarnish rubbed away by kind, attentive hands to make it shine again.

"Come, John!" Lily called to me from the garden. "We are ready for you!"

❖

I had conceived a painting made of light and flowers, with two little girls in the midst of the garden, lighting paper Chinese lanterns. The divine late-summer light, the overblown flowers, the children's intent, innocent faces, presented a magical twilight time that spoke to my longing for peace and tranquillity, far from any taint of age or corruption.

I called it *Carnation, Lily, Lily, Rose* after a popular music-hall tune everyone had been singing all summer. The making of the painting had become part of the family life of Broadway, everyone trooping down with my gear at twilight, then gathering it all up again half an hour later and back into the house for supper.

I didn't want it to end, and I would spend the rest of the long, lovely summer days slowly pulling the sunset colors from the sky and making the faces of the children bloom with the light, and the grace, and the peace I felt all around me.

I could not know, as I stood considering the scene, that this painting would win accolades for me in London, would make my fortune once again—*the young American artist*—and I would soon happily transfer my life, as I had transferred my affections, to the welcoming green and pleasant land of England.

❧ Afterword ❧

A Note to Readers from the Author

Historical fiction strives to be a fascinating and artful blend of imagination and fact, and we authors do our best to create a world for our readers that is as realistic and accurate as is needed to transport them into that different world for a time. A lot of research lies behind this story of John Singer Sargent, as well as a great deal of imagination. Every major character in the book is real; the only exceptions are minor characters such as housekeepers and waiters. For the most part, the characters are in places they really visited and lived, at the points in time they really were there. The letters and correspondence are all fictional; nonetheless, after reading a great deal of the major characters' correspondence, I was able to infuse certain realistic touches—such as pet names, salutations, style of writing and abbreviations—that would give the flavor of the real person.

The speculation about the relationship between Sargent and Louise Burckhardt was very real indeed; even Henry James made a note of it in one of his letters. As for "Madame X", Sargent complained in many letters that she was driving him mad—and the negative reactions and media coverage of the portrait are absolutely true—verbatim as they appear in the novel. In truth, every "event" that occurs to the characters really happened—it's the conversations and in some cases, the motivations, that are imagined.

The one notable exception is the background story about Florence Boit: it is completely fictional, and her diary in my novel is fictional as well. There is no evidence of any mental illness of the sort that is revealed in the story, although frankly, she was a strange person. The following paragraphs will help you see how very real my depiction of the major characters in this novel is.

Most of all, I hope you enjoyed the story and felt the characters to be real and sympathetic—I miss them now that they're out of my head and onto the page!

Sincerely,
Mary F. Burns

Notes on the Characters

John Singer Sargent – January 12, 1856 – April 14, 1925. During his career, Sargent created roughly 900 oil paintings and more than 2,000 watercolors, as well as countless sketches and charcoal drawings. After the scandal of *Madame X*, Sargent leased a studio on Tite Street in London late in 1884, and it became his permanent studio for the rest of his life. He bought a house next door for his sister Emily, and she helped maintain his household for many years. Though somewhat soured on painting portraits, Sargent experienced many years of great renown in England and the United States, where he eventually painted portraits of two presidents (Theodore Roosevelt and Woodrow Wilson) and many eminent men and women. He reserved his non-commissioned paintings, mostly watercolors, for his "own" art—the landscapes and the people he loved most. When World War I broke out, he served as an official war artist for the Allied Forces. His youngest sister Violet married and had three children, of whom Sargent was very fond. He never married.

The Boit Family – Hard times lay ahead for the Boits, at least emotionally. Isa died in 1894, and the four girls, with their father, continued their travels throughout Europe, Great Britain and the U.S. But none of the girls liked America very much, and Ned, too, preferred the ease and openness of Europe to his native land. He was married again in 1897 to a very young woman, a friend of his daughter Mary Louisa, confusingly enough named Florence, and together they had two boys. Unfortunately, his second wife died a few weeks after giving birth to her second son, in 1902. After recovering from this untimely death, Ned renewed his interest in his painting, and mounted several exhibitions of his work (one with Sargent in Boston). Ned died in 1915, in Florence. As for the Boit daughters, Florence was a rather odd duck, never evincing the slightest interest in marrying or attending the usual social events. She was an avid player of the relatively new sport of golf—which she introduced to the Boston area, inspiring the local rich folks to build a course at a country club in Newport. She and a cousin, Jane Boit Patten, nicknamed "Pat" to distinguish her from the innumerable Jane's and Jeanie's in the family, became fast friends and in later years, lived in what was called a "Boston marriage", two spinster ladies living together. Florence's sister Jane, very

PORTRAITS OF AN ARTIST

unfortunately, both before Isa died and afterward, was ill a great deal, both physically and emotionally, and spent several periods of time in and out of "retreats" and institutions where she underwent various cures to allay her apparently rather violent fits of anger and depression. Not much is known about Mary Louisa except that she and Julia were always together, and Julia became fairly well known for her paintings and illustrations in water colors. Florence died at age fifty-one, on December 8, 1919, in Paris. With the outbreak of WWII in 1939, the three remaining sisters moved back to the United States. Julia and Mary Louisa (also known as "Isa" like her mother) lived in Newport, where Isa died on June 27, 1945, at age seventy-one. Jane (or "Jeanie" as she was known) died at the age of eighty-five on November 8, 1955, in Greenwich, Connecticut. Julia passed away in February 1969, at the age of ninety-one.

Violet Paget – Violet had a nervous breakdown when the news of her dear friend Mary Robinson's engagement came to her, but she recovered and went on to write a prodigious number of short stories, essays and literary and art criticism, all published under her *nom de plume*, Vernon Lee. Throughout her adult life, she found and lost three or four female companions, often with devastating effects (to her general health), but was finally able to have a home of her own. She resided in the Palmerino Villa, on a hillside just outside of Florence, from 1889 until her death in 1935, with a brief interruption during the war. Her library was left to the British Institute of Florence and can still be inspected by visitors, and a considerable number of her personal papers was given to Colby College in Waterville, Maine.

Ralph Curtis – Ralph ultimately did marry Lisa de Wolfe, after she became a widow in the early 1890s. They were married in 1897 and by all accounts were very happy together. Sargent painted a very lovely portrait of her which, quite amazingly, hung in the Palazzo Barbaro in Venice until 1998, at which time it was "re-discovered" and purchased by the Cleveland Art Museum. Ralph died in 1922, at the age of sixty-eight.

Louise Burckhardt – In 1889, Louise married an Englishman, Roger Ackerley, who was a fruit merchant, known as the "Banana King" of London. Evidence of her career (that I was able to find) is limited to a brief mention of her by her husband's son (by his second wife) who wrote a biography of his father and referred to Louise as "an actress" who died young and childless, probably of tuberculosis. Louise died lamentably early in 1892.

Amélie Gautreau – Madame Gautreau never fully reclaimed her place in Paris society after the debacle of the portrait. In a move redolent of irony and desperation, Amélie commissioned another portrait of herself in 1891 by Gustave Courtois, in a soft, white, gauzy, fluffy sort of gown, showing a three-quarters left profile, half-length—and with the left shoulder strap fallen down on her arm! No one even noticed. Nine years later, the irascible and heartless Comte Robert de Montesquiou wrote a poem about her, one line of which tells all: "She still walks around, a fine-looking wreck." She died in July 1915 at the age of fifty-six. After her death, Sargent finally agreed to sell the portrait, to the New York Metropolitan Museum of Art, for a mere $5,000, but insisted its title remain *Madame X* , saying that "on account of the row I had with the lady years ago…the picture should not be called by her name" and admitting, in a note to the museum board, that it was "probably the best thing I've ever done."

Albert de Belleroche – As the son of an aristocratic family, Albert didn't have to paint for a living, and early on decided that he would not be a "slave" to patrons or sitters for commissions. He did fall in love with "Lili", a young woman associated with the Moulin Rouge, and painted frequently by Toulouse-Lautrec, but she became Albert's exclusive model and mistress for upwards of ten years, from the early 1890's on. Albert became entranced with lithography in 1900, and dedicated himself to working in this medium, in which he was soon considered the consummate expert, with his lithographs in high demand. In 1910, at the age of forty-five, he married the beautiful Julie Emilie Visseaux, who was twenty-eight years of age and the daughter of his friend, the sculptor Jules Edouard Visseaux. Lili was insanely jealous and tried to break them up, contributing to their decision to leave France and settle in England. He and Sargent remained lifelong friends. He died in 1944 at the age of eighty in Southwell, after a long illness.

❧ Primary Source Material ❧

Evan Charteris, *John Sargent* (New York: Charles Scribner's Sons, 1927).

Vineta Colby, *Vernon Lee: A Literary Biography* (Charlottesville, VA: University of Virginia Press, 2003).

Deborah Davis, *Strapless: John Singer Sargent and the Fall of Madame X* (New York: Jeremy Tarcher/Penguin Books, 2003).

Barbara Dayer Gallati, Richard Ormond and Erica E. Hirshler, *Great Expectations: John Singer Sargent Painting Children* (New York: Bullfinch Press, Brooklyn Museum, 2004).

Peter Gunn, *Vernon Lee: Violet Paget, 1856-1935* (London: Oxford University Press, 1964).

Erica E. Hirshler, *Sargent's Daughters, The Biography of a Painting* (Boston: MFA Publications, 2009).

Henry James, *The Painter's Eye*, ed. John L. Sweeney (Madison, WI: University of Wisconsin Press, 1989).

Charles Merrill Mount, *John Singer Sargent: A Biography* (New York: WW Norton & Co., 1955).

Stanley Olson, *John Singer Sargent: His Portrait* (London: MacMillan London Limited, 1986).

Richard Ormond and Elaine Kilmurray, *John Singer Sargent: Venetian Figures and Landscapes, 1874-1882, Complete Paintings: Volume IV* (London: Paul Mellon Center for Studies in British Art, 2006).

Elizabeth Prettejohn, *Interpreting Sargent* (New York: Stewart, Tabori & Chang, 1998).

Marc Simpson, Richard Ormond and H. Barbara Weinberg, *Uncanny Spectacle: The Public Career of the Young John Singer Sargent* (Williamstown, MA: Sterling and Francine Clark Art Institute, 1997).

Primary Internet Source for information: www.jssgallery.org

❧ List of Portraits ❧
(in order of appearance)

Drawing of Madame Gautreau, John Singer Sargent, Madame Gautreau (Madame X), c. 1883, Graphite on off-white wove paper; 24.6 x 26.6 cm (9 11/16 x 10 1/2 in.) Harvard Art Museums/Fogg Museum, Bequest of Grenville L. Winthrop, 1943.319. Photo: Imaging Department © President and Fellows of Harvard College, p. 172

Madame Gautreau Drinking a Toast, 1883 © Isabella Stewart Gardner Museum, Boston, p. 176

Head in Profile of a Young Man, 1883 © Yale University Art Gallery, New Haven, CT, p. 182

Judith Gautier, 1885 © Detroit Institute of Arts, p. 196

Photograph of original painting of *Madame X,* 1884 © New York Metropolitan Museum of Art, unknown photographer, p. 209

Henry James, 1913 © National Portrait Gallery, London, p. 233; detail: p. 245

Carnation, Lily, Lily, Rose, 1885-86 © Tate Gallery, London, p. 311

❧ Acknowledgements ❧

This second edition of my book, published by my own independent press, is in nearly every respect the same edition as the first one in 2013. I am, however, still very grateful to name and acknowledge my friends and colleagues who contributed to making this novel a reality: Harald and Jenny Hille who corrected my French and Italian and gave of their considerable literary erudition to help with the tone of the conversations and char- acters; my constant reader and writing critic, Robert Densmore; my stalwart cheerleader and spouse, Stu; friends Jan Basu, Nancy Siegel and Lily Thang who read the book and furnished interesting feedback and commentary; Marc Simpson, curator of American Art at The Clark Institute in Williamstown, Massachusetts, for reading drafts and setting the story on a better path; the very helpful folks at the various museums who helped with the image rights and licensing (Jennifer Belt of Art Resource, Thomas Haggerty of Bridgeman Art Library, Clive Coward at the Tate, Elizabeth Oustinoff of Adelson Galleries, Emma Butterfield at the National Portrait Gallery, Laurie Kind at the High Museum, Corrina Peipon at the Armand Hammer Museum, Wendy Hurlock Baker at the Smithsonian Archives of American Art, Marta Fodor at the Boston Fine Arts); fellow authors Paula Marantz Cohen, Laurel Corona, Stephanie Cowell and Lev Raphael for their reviews and accolades; and Elise Frances Miller, fellow author, for her encouragement and introduction of my work to our publisher Tory Hartmann of The Sand Hill Review Press.

Other books by Mary F. Burns

The Love for Three Oranges – Book Two
of the Sargent/Paget Mysteries

The Spoils of Avalon – Book One
of the Sargent/Paget Mysteries

Isaac and Ishmael: A Novel of Genesis

J-The Woman Who Wrote the Bible

Ember Days

To see book trailers, contact the author, and order these books,
please visit the author's website at
www.maryfburns.com.